Maria's Awakening

Sept 17, 2016

To Martha,

May you always have
love in your life.

Blessings,

Ella Rea Murphy

Maria's Awakening

Fall 1948

Ella Rea Murphy

Windstar
Books

Editing by Tania Seymour
Cover design by Jane Hagaman
Cover photo: www.comstock.com
Interior design by Jane Hagaman

Book production by:
Quartet Books
www.quartetbooks.com

If you are unable to order this book from your local bookseller, please visit www.ellareamurphy.com to order directly from the author.

Library of Congress Control Number: 2012931128

ISBN-13: 978-1505425239
ISBN-10: 1505425239
10 9 8 7 6 5 4 3

Dedication

*To Bill, my longtime friend; my daughter, Terri; my son, Greg;
and my three granddaughters, Carol, Sharon, and Stephanie*

Contents

Acknowledgments

A lifetime of friends and family have helped me write *Maria's Awakening* and the four subsequent books that continue to follow Maria's life, although, at the time, neither I nor they were aware of their impact. Many of their names escape me but not their stories. To my past friends, my family, and current supporters, I would like to thank all of you for your encouragement, including:

Bill, a friend from long ago, who provided divine inspiration; P. M. H. Atwater, who, in the beginning, showed me the way; Terri Ellison, my daughter, for her continued support, encouragement, and computing expertise; Gregory Murphy, my son, for his interest and concern; my granddaughters, Sharon and Carol Ellison and Stephanie Murphy; and my friends, Debbie Willing, Shirley Booker, Shirley Dukes, and Sarah Magerfield, for their encouragement; Barbara Connelly for her enthusiasm; all of my other interested friends; and the Quartet Books staff, Jane Hagaman, Tania Seymour, Sara Sgarlat, and Cynthia Mitchell, for their invaluable service and advice.

1. Meeting Bill

A very small degree of hope is sufficient
to cause the birth of love.
—Stendhal

Pow! A pillow hit Maria's head as she lay on her bed, wondering if Susie was awake. Well, she got her answer. Another pillow sailed past Maria's head as she looked over at her college roommate of six weeks. Maria had been pleased to meet Susie, a high school acquaintance, last summer to decide if they wanted to be room-mates at Iowa State University. Susie was standing up on her bed, her red hair sticking up at all angles, poised and ready to throw another missile.

"That's it, this is war! I'll take no prisoners," Maria shouted, leaping up for a better vantage and launching a fast one at Susie's midsection. Yelling and singing a bit of her old La Grange High School fight song at the top of her lungs, Maria aimed another pillow at Susie's head.

With that invitation, Susie ducked and threw one back at Maria. Then she hopped off her bed, ran across the room, and started batting Maria with another pillow, yelling, "I've gotcha now!"

Surprised that Susie, the intellectual one, had started the fight in the first place, Maria jumped from her bed to retrieve a pillow from the floor and escape Susie's pummeling, "No fair, no fair."

Their door opened cautiously and their dorm mates from across the hall peeked in to see what all the shouting was about.

Susie stopped her attack and Maria stood up, looked at Susie for a moment, and they both threw their pillows at their dorm mates. Donna and Jeannie laughed, then asked if they wanted to go to breakfast with them.

"Sure," they said in unison.

"We sound like twins," Maria said.

"Our poor mother," Susie said, looking at Maria with mock horror on her face. "When do you want to go, gals?"

"Right away, before all the food is gone," Jeannie said.

"Okay, I can be ready in five minutes; I'll shower later. How about you, Maria?" Susie queried.

"I never miss a meal, willingly; I'll get ready, too."

They trooped over to the dining hall, which was in another building. The weather was warm. Maria was glad it was Saturday, and she didn't have any classes like some poor slobs. She poked Susie on the way over. "You throw a mean pillow."

Standing in line with her friends, Maria asked, "Everything looks good to me; what's everyone going to have?"

"Who knows, let's just start at this end and work our way to the finish line, and see what we come up with," Donna said smiling, acting as if she hadn't eaten for a week.

With their trays piled high, they made their way to the only open table near a group of girls who immediately started giggling and pointing at the trays of food that Maria's group was putting down on their table. One gal said, "My, you girls look like you can really eat."

Although surprised that they were under such surveillance, Maria's group chose to ignore them. Maria heard one of them say to Miss Obnoxious, obviously the leader, "Come on, Maude, let's leave the chubbies alone to stuff themselves."

Giving each other puzzled looks, Donna asked, "What was that all about?"

Susie and Maria shrugged and dove into their food.

"Yum, yum," Jeannie said. She was as big as a mouse and looked like cheerleader material.

"Yah, Jeannie, you'd better watch it, or you're going to top out at 105 pounds soon," Donna said with a wry smile.

Walking back to their dormitory, Maria wondered about Maude. She had known that kind of girl all her life, especially in junior high and high school. There were one or two in every class. All it took to raise a girl like that was to treat them as if they were entitled from the day they were born.

"I imagine Maude came from a small high school where she reigned as princess. I'll bet she and her ladies in waiting all came to school together and were used to running the social agenda in their little corner of the world," Maria said.

"So who cares," Jeannie said. "Let's change the subject to meeting men. Are either of you going to the Farm House open house and dance tonight?" Her eyes were dancing with anticipation.

"Are there a bunch of farmers there? Is it a frat house or what?" Maria asked.

"We're going, aren't we?" Jeannie asked, ignoring Maria's farmer comment and looking at Donna for support. "We're dying to see what the guys look like. I've heard that they are real cute, big with lots of muscles because most of them are Ag majors and come from farms."

"What's an Ag major?" Maria asked. "I don't have a clue."

"They study agriculture; their parents want them to learn the latest ways to farm, and Iowa State is the best place to learn it," Donna replied, sounding very sure of herself.

"So they are all farmers or going to be farmers," Susie said with a grin. "I'm glad I'm busy. Chuck and I have a date." Susie's boyfriend was a football player and, being a boy from La Grange High, had no interest in farming. He was on a football scholarship.

"You're lucky you already have a boyfriend, Susie. I hope I can find someone," Donna said wistfully.

"You will probably meet him tonight and end up on a farm," Susie said with a malicious grin.

3

"You're bad, Susie," Maria said, laughing at her. "All right girls, let's walk over together around seven thirty. What have I got to lose? I'll knock on your door when I'm ready."

They split up at the dorm, each with their own agenda for the day.

"Do you need anything at Dog Town, Susie? I need some shower supplies." Maria had checked her little bank account that morning and was pleased to find that it had twenty dollars in it. She wished that her dad would give her more than five dollars a week, but ever since her parents had divorced and he had married Betty, she held tightly to the purse strings.

"I'm game; let's see if Dog Town has any more stores than it did last weekend. What a dog of a town."

"Just as I thought, it's still the same as last week," Susie said, laughing at her comment as they strolled into town. There were three businesses: a drugstore, a Spud Nut Shop, and a gas station.

"Well here goes nothing," Maria said, ducking into the drugstore with Susie right behind her. Their low expectations were well-founded.

Susie said, "You're psychic; they don't even have a good candy bar. In the future, let's take the bus to the big city of Ames to do our shopping. This place is really in the boonies. I never dreamed it would be so far away from everything."

"Me either, what a change from La Grange. I guess we've got to tough it out. I hope the best is yet to come, or I'm going to wish I never came," Maria said, looking dejected. She was glad that Susie was from the same high school as she was. Their background was the same as far as school was concerned. Although she hardly had known Susie in their two-thousand-plus student population, Maria had been in a couple of Susie's classes. Maria had watched Susie arrive and leave with either Chuck or some girls from the in-crowd many times. Susie was always at the top of their class with outstanding grades and seemed to have it all. Maria, on the other hand, was on the fringe, struggling with some of her courses, living with her alcoholic mother, and trying desperately not to let her friends know what kind of life she had.

"Why are you going to the Farm House, tonight? It doesn't seem like your kind of fraternity," Susie asked, looking perplexed.

"I don't know," Maria answered. She had a feeling that it might be fun but was skeptical. She comforted herself with the idea that she could always walk home. It was only about ten minutes away from her dorm.

Fluttering around in her mind was a warm premonition that she couldn't explain. She didn't want to expose it to Susie's sharp scrutiny and analysis, but she knew she was feeling a gentle push to go to the Farm House. Just because Susie was Phi Beta Kappa material didn't mean that she had all the answers, Maria thought, a little ruffled by Susie's question.

With the weather enticing her to be outside and enjoy the sun and softly blowing breezes, Maria forced herself to walk into the stale atmosphere of the library, needing the reference material there to create a paper for English. Her work was starting to pile up, and she had just started the term. She sat there, yawning, wishing she were outside. After lamely looking up some material in the card catalog, she finally said out loud, "To heck with it," catching a couple of smiles from fellow students in the library who obviously felt the same way.

The dance kept stealing into her mind and the prospect of going became more exciting as she strolled back to the dorm. Rationalizing that she would work on the paper tomorrow, she began wondering about what she should wear for the party. Just before she reached the dorm, the Campanile began its hourly assignment of keeping everyone informed of the time, whether they wanted to be or not.

Opening their dorm room door, Maria found Susie reading on her bed with her hair in a turban towel, her exposed body saturated with cosmetic cream. She looked like an ice-cream cone.

"I see you are getting ready for your date. How about dinner with me before we both go out?" Maria asked, chuckling to herself at her comparison of Susie to a cone.

"Just give me a minute while I wipe this stuff off. Chuck likes my skin soft and my hair clean. He likes to put his face in my hair, especially if it smells good."

"How romantic. What else does he like?" Maria asked, rolling her eyes.

"It's time for dinner, roommate," Susie said, quickly changing the subject.

After dinner, they went back to the dorm so that Maria could shower before the dance. Susie again asked Maria why she was going to the party. It irritated Maria that Susie was being so pushy. She wasn't going to admit anything about her premonition to Susie. It was too personal. Maria said, "What do you care? You're going out. I'd like a night out, too. I've been at Iowa State for three weeks and haven't gone out yet. It's time I do something fun." She gave Susie an irritated look, standing up for herself for the first time since they had met.

After Maria's outburst, Susie backed off. "I'm sorry. My mother has told me that my intelligence gets me into trouble and lets me think I can be obnoxious at times. I hope you have a nice time, tonight," Susie said, giving Maria a genuine smile.

Maria was still steamed, but said quietly, "Thanks, I will," and turned to give her semidry hair one last brush before it was time to go.

At seven thirty, Maria, Jeannie, and Donna embarked on their adventure—three freshmen girls going to a frat party. It was a short walk, just enough time in the warm fall weather for Maria's thick hair to dry completely.

Surveying the big frat living room as they walked in, Maria's first impression was a thumbs up. It seemed clean enough, and the sofas and chairs looked comfortable. As the girls streamed in, she watched the guys standing around, looking over the prospects. She felt a little like meat on the hoof.

"Hi, thanks for coming. My name is Jason," a tall, good-looking guy said with a welcoming smile. He asked for their drink orders. Maria knew it would be a soft drink because Iowa State University was a "dry" school. "We have root beer, Coke, and ginger ale." Maria thought it was a nice touch having him offer them drinks.

"We don't care, surprise us," Jeannie said.

The three girls plopped down on a comfortable couch, enjoying the idea of being seated and not on parade. Maria began studying the guys. They appeared reserved but friendly, not rushing the girls, giving them a chance to feel more relaxed; she, for one, appreciated that. It seemed like a typical early fall party, with both the guys and gals feeling their way along. She could hear dance music playing in the background.

Jason came back, balancing lots of drinks on a tray and looking a little harried. She appreciated the drink service; it meant she didn't have to move and face the guys watching her wandering around looking for a drink. Some nice-looking frat brothers came to Jason's rescue and helped to hand out drinks. Maria noticed that all of them were clean shaven and wondered if that was a frat rule. She wondered if all the other fraternity men were as good looking as these men and if the level of testosterone was as high at other parties as it seemed to be here.

A big area had been cleared for dancing and, as Maria sat there sipping her Coke, she started to relax. No one was dancing yet. It was too early; the party was just getting started. Some of the guys were beginning to drift over, attempting to mingle with groups of girls both standing and sitting. *Clumping up,* Maria thought. *That's not the way to meet guys. The girls need to break up a little and give the men a chance.* But it seemed the guys' hormones were pushing them to be brave, and they began to work their way into the groups, talking to the girls, looking them over and trying to see who might be interesting enough to ask to dance. That was a tall order.

As Maria sat observing all the maneuverings between the men and women, it felt good to be just looking on from the sofa. She wasn't exactly hiding out but liked being a watcher, because she still was questioning why she was there. After fooling herself into thinking that she'd leave after a little while if she stopped having fun and go back to the dorm to study, she laughed out loud at her ridiculous daydream. She didn't want to go back to a boring evening alone.

Something made her look up at a fellow across the room who was watching her. Maria's breath literally caught in her throat as their eyes met. Her premonition had brought her here, and now it was playing itself out as she felt his eyes on her. Maria had never believed people who said that they fell in love with each other at the first glance, but there was definitely something going on between her and that man.

One of her friends asked her, "Are you okay," because a strange little sound had escaped Maria's throat.

"I'm fine," Maria said, as she took a sip of her drink and peeked over at the man. He wasn't staring, exactly, but he was watching her. Was she glad or scared? He didn't move. They kept eye contact and just when she thought he was bordering on being a pervert, he got up and walked slowly across the room, holding her gaze all the way.

Maria stood up and smiled; he gave her a wonderful smile in return and reached for her hand. She was tongue-tied, but he wasn't. He knew exactly what he wanted, and he quietly asked her to dance. Maria thought, *Who is this tall, good-looking god?* Besides a muscular physique, he had the most electrifying blue eyes that she had ever seen.

Following him to the dance floor, she couldn't shake the feeling that they knew each other somehow. If he knew how excited she was feeling, he would have laughed. She felt as if she were fourteen and going to dance with Clark Gable.

It dawned on her, causing her to freeze for a moment, that she was actually going to have to dance with this man, and she wasn't sure she could. She stumbled slightly from nervousness. Even though he was a little ahead of her, he was still holding her hand and must have felt her misstep, but he ignored it. Giggling a little, she couldn't help but notice what a strong, well-proportioned guy he was from the rear. *Maria,* she said to herself, *what are you thinking about?*

He stopped at the edge of the dance floor, turned, and looked at her with a beautiful smile; he slipped his arm around her waist, took her hand in his, and started to dance, moving slowly around the room. He was smooth and Maria was absolutely besotted by him. As they were beginning to feel their bodies moving in rhythm to the music, she realized why dancing was so intimate. Here she was with a complete stranger's arms around her, being mesmerized by a love song, following him around the dance floor so closely that she could hear him breathe.

She loved the songs that were being played and was glad they all seemed to be slow dances. The Farm House men had been very clever with their record selections.

As they were dancing, Maria was delirious at having him hold her in his arms, but began to instantly worry that after the dance, he might just thank her and walk her back to her seat. What if that happened?

Their bodies bonded more and more as they danced. It couldn't be just her feeling this current of energy running between them, could it? Should she try to talk or should she be quiet? Maria was concentrating on being light on her feet and didn't know what to say, so she decided not to say anything. Worried that he would think she was boring, she thought about talking, but she didn't want to sound stupid.

He was very quick on his feet, very rhythmical, and very gentle in the way he held her. As she relaxed, she found it easier to follow him. He was sexy, quiet, and in control of himself. Maria wondered if he were an upperclassman, because he seemed older than some of the other guys. Her mind was racing a mile a minute.

She felt like putty in his hands and was amazed at herself; she had never felt like that so quickly before and realized that she had an instant crush on him. Even though she had only met him a little while ago, it felt as if she had known him forever. She was floating on air, and her feelings were overwhelming her with an intensity she had never experienced before.

The dance sequence ended, and she held her breath. *Please don't say thank you and take me back to my friends,* she prayed. He didn't move and used the pause between dances to introduce himself. "I'm Bill Morgan," he said simply, mesmerizing her with those blue eyes of his and keeping his arm around her waist.

"I'm Maria Banks," she squeezed out as calmly as she could. She wanted to impress him with her whole heart. She smiled up at him while her legs turned to jelly.

"That's a pretty name," he said.

Maria's heart was pounding, and she hoped that he couldn't hear it. The music had started again, and he took a firm hold on her and swung her into the next dance. Their feelings pulled them together, closer and closer. Bill closed the distance between them by pulling her into to him until her face was on his shoulder, and he put his chin lightly on top of her head.

All of a sudden, someone yelled that the next dance was the last one because the girls had to get back to the dorm before curfew. Maria couldn't believe that the evening had disappeared.

Bill looked at her with that beautiful smile. "May I walk you back to the dorm?"

"I would like that," Maria casually said, but she was screaming inside that she might die from the excitement of being with him.

He was rather quiet, walking along beside her back to the dorm, not physically touching her; but she thought she could feel intense vibes between them. At the steps to the dorm, he smiled down at her. "May I call you for a date sometime?"

Maria was in orbit, she was so happy, but she tried to appear calm. She gave him a little grin. "Yes, if you like." She ran up the stairs and something made her turn to see if he was still there. He was, and he was watching her. She gave him an embarrassed little wave and went inside.

When Maria walked into her room, she was exhausted with emotion and physically tired from dancing all evening. Susie was right behind her, looking happy and in love. Maria started to say something at the same time that Susie did, and they both laughed. Maria got the giggles, as a release from the emotions she had felt all evening.

Susie looked at her. "It wasn't that funny."

"I know. I've just had the most incredible evening I have ever had and met the love of my life."

"That's a little strong for one evening together, isn't it? Besides, aren't you the girl who said you weren't interested in farmers?"

"I know: but Susie, I don't care if he's an Eskimo. I'd go live with him in an igloo."

"Well, thank God he isn't; I'd never get to see you again. You absolutely amaze me. I never thought of you as an impetuous kind of gal. You come off as quite self-contained and older than your years. That's a compliment, in case you're wondering."

Maria knew Susie was trying to make up for her comments after dinner. "I know, Susie, and I can't explain the feelings that were flowing between us tonight." Maria sat down on her bed, lay down, put her pillow over her face, and groaned.

"That's the third time you've said, 'I know.' Maybe you'll feel more normal tomorrow and be able to look at this evening with a different attitude. Why are you groaning? Are you sick?"

"Maybe," Maria said from under her pillow. "Right now, I don't want to talk anymore. I'm going to take a shower for about an hour. When I get back, I'll find out why you looked so happy when you walked in tonight."

With that, Maria took her towel and basket of toilet articles and floated down the hall to the bathroom. The water beating on her calmed her down and slightly restored her good sense. Of course, she wondered and worried, would Bill decide not to call her in the light of a new day?

If he doesn't call, what will I do? she asked herself. *But he's going to call.* She kept going back and forth in her head with that scenario.

Stop letting those worries run around in your head, she told herself, *just breathe deeply.*

When she got back to the room, Susie was in her bed and almost asleep. Maria crawled into her bed and shut her eyes. She promised herself that she'd ask Susie tomorrow how her date with Chuck went. When she shut her eyes, she began to see Bill's beautiful eyes in her head. She turned over and stuck her head under the pillow. She prayed, *Dear God, please help me sleep.*

Her prayer worked, because Maria woke up and it was Sunday morning. It seemed late; the sun was streaming through the window and filling the room with dazzling light. It made her feel so alive. She wondered how Bill was this morning. Was the sun brightening up his room? Would he call, or was last night a mirage? All those questions were swirling around in her head again.

"Ugh," Maria groaned as she felt a pillow hit her and looked over at Susie's bed.

Susie was sitting up in her pajamas, saying, "Wake up and let's go eat breakfast. It's eleven thirty."

"It's really that late? Are they still serving breakfast?" Maria asked.

"Yes and yes; let's get going before they close the doors." Susie jumped up, grabbed her towel and clothes, and ran for the bathroom. "I'll be back as soon as I wash my face."

Maria threw on her jeans and tee shirt, brushed her tangled hair, and was ready as Susie pounded back into the room. They ran over to the dining hall and made it before the doors closed.

"Whew, that was close." Maria took a tray and put a little food on it.

"What's with your appetite?" Susie piled her tray with a little of everything.

"I'm in love, and I can't eat."

"You're kidding. I thought after a night's sleep, you'd be more rational," Susie said. "How can you be in love after one night of knowing this guy?"

Maria shrugged helplessly.

Susie shook her head. "I thought that you would be the last person I know who would be acting like this."

Maria shrugged again and shook her head. "When I figure it out, I'll let you know."

Susie didn't push Maria this time. "Come on, girl, let's eat up and get out of here."

Maria went through the motions of studying, doing her laundry, talking to the dorm mates who had gone to the dance with her last night, and listening to their stories about what happened with them. They said that they hadn't danced much but had had a lot of laughs with a couple of guys who said they would call them—soon. They liked the Farm House men.

Jeannie said, "I noticed you dancing all evening with a really good-looking guy." She was obviously fishing for information, but, except for Susie, Maria couldn't tell anyone yet how she felt about Bill. It was too personal and close to her heart. She was almost embarrassed by her intense feelings for him.

As the day wore on, Maria couldn't study anymore. She snapped her history book shut. "Hey, Susie, do you want to go for a walk? I need to clear my head."

Susie had just finished an article for the newspaper. "Sure, and we can take this to the newspaper office."

Heading out into the gorgeous weather to deliver the article and enjoy the outside for a while was just what they needed.

The campus was laid out as a quadrangle, with buildings all around the perimeter. It was a long way to walk from one end to the other. Maria thought she knew why there were no fat students at Iowa State. Students were not allowed to have cars on campus, and there was no bus service. It seemed as if they walked miles—every day. One couldn't gain a pound *and* go to classes there.

As they were walking, Maria noticed a group of guys playing ball on the Quad. "Those fellows seem older, don't they, Susie?"

"Yeah, they're war veterans," Susie said.

It was 1948, three years after World War II; there were lots of older veterans returning to colleges all over the country, and Iowa State was no exception.

"They must be going to school under the GI Bill of Rights," Susie said. "There are several in some of my classes. They seem very serious about being in college and are setting a high standard for the rest of us."

Once they'd dropped off the article, Susie seemed to have another specific destination in mind. They were headed toward a group of trees; over the hill, nestled near the trees, was a lake.

"Boy, this is one busy place," Maria said, as they approached it. "So this is the famous Lake Laverne, known for its amorous setting." There were people canoeing in the lake, walking around it, or sitting on the bank. Some of them looked very much in love, some were throwing balls to each other, others were reading, some were lying in the sun on blankets, and a few were kissing.

Maria took one look at all the romance and wanted to get out of there. Her feelings for Bill were too raw, and she felt uncomfortable. Maybe she was afraid that her feelings were going to be trampled; Bill might not call. "Let's go get a Coke at the Union, Susie. I'm thirsty."

"Okay, that sounds good." Susie gave Maria a deep look. "He'll call."

Susie's becoming a good friend, Maria thought, *even if she needs to be reminded that she sometimes gets too pushy.* Susie understood a lot of things without having to be told much. Maria knew that Susie's parents had been divorced, too; perhaps that was why Susie seemed so aware of Maria's feelings, having also suffered with a break-up. Susie had told her that she lived with her mother, who was a bigwig in Chicago.

"When we get back to the dorm, let's study for a while and then go for dinner, such as it is," Susie said. They both disliked the food on Sunday evening, the buffet was a cold one with pretty pallid sandwich makings. Maria wanted a hot juicy hamburger made with prime Iowa beef from the Union but would have felt guilty for not eating the "free" food in the dining hall.

After their unappetizing supper, which consisted of an apple for Maria, she spent some time sitting outside on the front steps looking at the stars. She wished that curfew would hurry up and come, because the guys never called until after curfew, when they knew the girls had to be in the dorm. For a second, she thought she saw Bill standing in the shadows with some gal, but she knew it couldn't be him. Finally, couples were gathering down on the bottom steps, saying their goodbyes. She got up and went inside. She couldn't watch them kiss each other.

The dorm phone began ringing: girls making future dates, planning meetings, getting homework assignments, or just chatting.

Maria tried to keep her mind on her studies. She found herself reading and rereading the same paragraph. That couldn't go on, or she would flunk out of school after her first semester. But she was worried that Bill would give up trying to reach her on their one first-floor phone. She wanted everyone to go to bed, study, shower, or do anything but talk on that phone. After about a half hour had passed and four different calls came in for girls on the floor, it was getting late; then the phone rang again, and someone called, "Maria, it's for you."

As she ran down the hall, she silently thanked the heavens that he had finally called her. Bill hadn't forgotten or decided that he didn't want to talk to her; he was actually on the other end of the line. She was so excited, her mouth was dry. She picked that phone up and held it like a life preserver, because she was drowning in emotion. "Hi," she breathed into the phone.

"Is this Maria?" The poor guy wasn't sure he had reached her, because she couldn't say her own name.

All that came out was, "Yes." She was tongue-tied, again.

"I thought about you today and wanted to come over and see you this afternoon, but I decided that you might think that I was too pushy, so I waited like I said I would."

She tried to be calm and not come on too strong. "It would have been nice to see you, but it's just as well. I've been busy studying."

In his incredibly sexy voice, he asked, "Would you like to take a walk around the campus with me tomorrow evening after dinner?"

She wanted to jump through the phone and into his arms, remembering how they felt when they were around her while dancing. But instead, she said as casually as she could, "Yes, I would like that a lot."

"Great, I can't wait to see you again. I'll pick you up around seven thirty."

"I'll be ready. Thanks for calling. Good night."

"Sleep well, Maria," Bill said in a very sweet way and hung up.

Monday was a busy day for Maria; she had lecture hall classes in the morning and chemistry lab in the afternoon until six in the evening. By the middle of the afternoon, she was feeling cooked. She couldn't concentrate on her experiment. She had to repeat part of it; the assistant wouldn't let her go on until she had better results. But the assistant was nice and must have felt sorry for her because he came over and helped her with her technique using the test tubes. With his help, she stumbled through the experiment.

As she was running down the sidewalk to get back for dinner and a shower before Bill came over, the old "what if" game was playing in her head again. What if Bill didn't like her and they only had one date? Would she be able to be witty and make their date fun? Why she was so obsessed with making Bill like her?

By the time she reached the dorm and ran up the stairs, Susie was waiting for her and off they went to dinner. The cafeteria food made her sick to look at it.

"If I didn't know better, I'd say you're pregnant. Smells always make expectant women feel awful, not to mention looking at the food," Susie said, with a know-it-all smirk.

Maria gave her a look that said *shut up,* and she ran from the dining hall. When she got to her room, she grabbed her towel and shower basket, went to bathroom, and hurried into the shower. As the water began to work its magic on her skin, she closed her eyes and felt she could stay in there for an hour, but she only had ten minutes.

When Maria returned to her room, Susie was back from dinner and getting ready to go out with Chuck.

"It looks like you and Chuck are really good these days," Maria said, apologizing with her tone for being so touchy at dinner.

"Chuck is in a great mood because he has been playing a lot of football," Susie said.

"Well, wish me luck, tonight. It's almost time for me to go out with the man of my dreams."

"I do, and I'll want a full report when you get back," Susie said, giving Maria a big grin. "Now get going so I can get going, and wipe that silly look off your face before you see Bill."

Maria said, "I'll try not to embarrass myself around him."

"Just remember, he's lucky to be dating you, not the other way around. Be nice, but don't be goofy."

2. Dating Bill

How delicious is the winning of a kiss at love's beginning.
—Thomas Campbell

Maria smiled at Susie's slightly irritating comments as she ran out the door, but nothing Susie said could dampen the thrill Maria felt as she raced down the hall and went flying into the front room where the guys waited for their dates. Bill was facing the double doors, waiting for her with those big, blue eyes, grinning at her athletic entrance. She put on the brakes and tried to compose herself, but she had blown it. Her cheeks felt hot and red from the excitement of seeing him.

Maria thought that it was amazing how many little details crossed one's mind when one was trying to be smooth and appealing. What should she do if he took her hand and held it? Her palms were hot and sweaty with anxiety. All she could think of was ways to casually dry her hands while they were walking. It turned out that he made no move to get too close. They walked slowly, talking about the weather and other boring subjects that she brought up because she couldn't stand the silence. What a motor mouth. At the same time that she was speed talking, she was casually waving her hands around, trying to dry her palms. He probably thought he was out with a nonstop talker with a nervous disorder.

Gradually, she calmed down, talked less, and relaxed; her palms dried quickly then. Meanwhile, Bill had steered them over to Lake Laverne. She wondered what he had in mind.

"Would you like to go canoeing sometime on Lake Laverne?" he asked.

That was an interesting idea, and she said, "Yes." She had underestimated him, thinking all he wanted to do was have an evening exploring her body.

Bill was smooth and taking his time; his comments made sense and were unpretentious. Her attitude about farmers was wrong; they were pretty nice and intelligent, too. He sounded very well educated.

They walked around the lake, then headed towards the Campanile. Ah, ha, he was headed for the campus initiation spot. It was a big thing for the freshman girls, to be kissed under the Campanile. She wondered if he was going to give her an initiation that night.

He took her hand, smiled, and they kept strolling along. She felt the energy start to flow when their hands touched, and she wondered if Bill felt the same thing. Not wanting to spoil the moment, she kept quiet. She had the sensation of floating along beside him.

Suddenly, Maria knew that there would be no initiation tonight; instead, he had taken her to a quiet place to talk. She couldn't believe it. He actually wanted to talk.

"I'm an Ag major," Bill told her, "and my home is a farm about a half hour south of Des Moines. I thought about commuting, but I wanted to put some distance between myself and my parents. They're good people, but my dad wants to control me. Now that I'm a junior, my interests are changing. I will be graduating in two years and have ideas about my future other than farming. But enough about me. Why did you choose Iowa State? There are so many good schools in Illinois."

Maria wanted to say so that she could meet him, but simply said, "I followed my sister and brother-in-law out here." He appeared as if he had a question about her comment but didn't say anything. She had been delighted to hear that he was thinking about future options other than farming.

Letting him know a little about her was probably a good idea. She didn't want to hide anything from him, but she didn't want to scare him away either, so she kept it light. "I'm from La Grange, Illinois, a suburb of Chicago." To try to impress him, she told him some of her farm stories. "Do you know St. Charles, Illinois? My dad had a dry farm in St. Charles that he loved."

"Yes, I'm familiar with that whole area. Did you know that St. Charles is famous for some of their race horses? I've always loved horses; there's something very graceful and powerful about them," Bill said.

"My horse, Jetty, lived in St. Charles. She was part thorough-bred. I used to ride her over to the farm, sometimes, from the stable where she was boarded."

"So you are a horseback rider? That surprises me. I didn't take you for an outdoor girl. Did you ever work on your dad's farm?"

"Yes, many times, and I learned to drive dad's little Ford tractor. I even got it stuck in the mud, even after my dad cautioned me not to go in a certain area that was boggy. It didn't look boggy to me, but it was."

Bill became more interested with their conversation. "What did he do? Call a farmer to pull you out?"

"You're right about that. The tractor that the farmer drove looked about six times as big as our little one. He pulled ours out easily."

"Your dad sounds like a patient guy. I hope I can meet him someday."

What did she hear? Bill wanted to extend their dating to include meeting her dad someday? Wow, that was encouraging.

Bill looked at his watch and asked her if she would like a drink at the Union. Maria was starving because she had skipped dinner—her nerves doing a number on her stomach—but she pretended that a cool drink would be fine with her.

As they stood up, he took her hand in his and started back, walking easily. In the Union, with their drinks before them, he told her about a few mistakes he and his brothers had made on their farm that cost his father some money and added a few gray hairs to his dad's head. He started laughing when he was telling her his stories and got very animated. As she sipped her Coke with one hand; Bill reached over and took her free hand in his in a move to connect them more fully. She wouldn't have pulled her hand free for anything.

"You know," he said, "I've had more fun talking to you tonight than I thought I would. You're talented in the listening department. Some girls never shut up. When we started this date, I thought, Bill, you've made a mistake, but I was wrong. You are a good listener and funny, did you know that?"

She was flattered and didn't know quite what to say in return that wouldn't sound silly, so she changed the subject. "Well," she said, pausing to think what to say, "I think we'd better run for the dorm because it is almost curfew time." *Our date has wings of love carrying it away so fast,* she thought.

He jumped up, grabbed her hand, and they ran out of there—at top speed for her and only medium speed for Bill with his long legs. Through sheer joy, Maria started to laugh as they ran along and Bill began laughing, too. Maybe they were laughing because their first date had turned out so well; she didn't know, but they were high. When Bill laughed, he looked so inviting. *What a darling man,* she thought.

Little Miss "What If" was at work again as they ran for the dorm. She wondered if he were going to kiss her. She wanted him to, but what if he didn't? He was taking his time for a reason, and maybe he didn't want to raise any false hopes in either of them. Maybe he was shy; she wasn't sure, but shy somehow didn't fit his profile.

When they got to the steps to the dorm, they stopped. He looked at her, and she knew he was going to kiss her. She could see it in his eyes. *Yes,* she thought. He slowly wrapped his arms around her, looked at her, then at her lips. He closed his eyes and so did she. Maria had waited for that kiss all of her nineteen years, and the electricity that flowed through them was almost unbearable. The wait was worth it. He didn't stop kissing her until the Campanile had stopped its nine o'clock bonging. He was drinking her in with his lips.

Releasing her slowly, his hands on her shoulders, he looked into her eyes and seemed to be memorizing her face. An odd flicker crossed his face that was so serious it worried her. That fleeting look passed, and he grinned that slow, beautiful smile of his. He seemed slightly at a loss for words, but he finally said that he would call her tomorrow to make plans. He looked at her with a question in his eyes.

Maria thought, *He wants me to say something so that he knows I'm as interested as he is in another date.* "I'll be in class for most of the day, but you can reach me either early in the morning or later in the day. I would like to see you again." Her eyes said she loved him while her lips said, "Good night."

She ran up the stairs, turned to look at him once more, standing there, and ran in the door with the housemother warden locking the door behind her and giving her disapproving looks. That whole idea of curfew was ridiculous anyway, she thought, as she went to her room, but she really didn't care because she was madly in love for the first time in her life.

As she opened her door, she wondered how she had been so lucky to find Bill. Her new life was so exciting now. It was a huge change from her life of the past few years, which had been very dreary, taking care of her mother. She was away from that whole problem; it was her mom's new husband's problem. Maria was on top of the world.

It was late afternoon, and Maria had just walked into the dorm when she heard their hall phone ring. She picked it up, "Stevens Hall," she said.

Bill laughed. "Do you have a new job being telephone operator?"

"Yes," recognizing his voice and being in a playful mood, she said, "I screen all the calls and only accept the ones who have nice voices."

Bill was now into the game. "Do I qualify? I'm anxious to talk to a certain young lady about some date plans."

"I guess I'll let you talk to her; your voice quality is okay," Maria said, hesitating as if she were weighing whether to let him speak or not.

"So, phone operator Maria, thanks for being so understanding. I need to explain my schedule so we can make our plans. Farm House is having a Chapter meeting tonight, and tomorrow night, I have an evening class to make up for one the professor had to cancel."

Maria definitely felt disappointed, but thought maybe it was good that they let things cool down a little between them. She had some reservations about where things were going with them, and after their emotion-packed kissing scene, she wanted to be sure that they had more in common than that. Also, she knew she didn't want to be a farmer's wife.

"Well, with my new job, I'll be busy in the evening for a couple of nights making sure only the sexy voices are connected to their girlfriends. It's quite a responsibility," she said. Perhaps he was trying to put some distance between them. Maybe he had another girlfriend and was trying to decide which girl he wanted to date.

"I'm glad I have an in with the phone operator. Let's see each other Friday night. How does that sound to you?" he asked.

"I think I can arrange to have someone take over the phone service for me. What time?"

"I'll be there around seven thirty. I want to show you where I spend a lot of my time at the Ag Building and a few other little places."

"So where are those other little places? I'm not so sure I want to see them," she teased.

"You'll love 'em, trust me," he said with a laugh.

"When one hears 'trust me,' that's the time to run the other way."

"Don't worry, little girl, I won't have any candy with me."

"All right my trustworthy friend, I'll see you on Friday. Now I have to get back screening calls."

"Goodbye and sweet dreams tonight, Maria."

Since meeting Bill, Maria found that her happiness was spilling out into her everyday activities. Her classes became more interesting, her dorm mates weren't as irritating when asking her questions about Bill, her roommate seemed more accepting of her, and her life had moved up a notch. With energy to burn, she now found that she could spend hours studying without getting edgy. Since arriving at Iowa State a month ago, she was learning how to make better use of her time, instead of daydreaming and not concentrating. She was actually learning how to be a good student—except when thoughts of Bill intruded.

It was Wednesday afternoon, and Maria was returning from a stint at the library. The dorm was quiet when she walked in; Susie was getting ready for a date. "Hi, what's up?" Maria asked. "You're going to see Chuck for dinner, right?"

"No, I'm being rushed by the Chi Omegas and going to their house for dinner. I wish you were going out for 'rush week.'"

"I'm on top of the world and can't think of another thing right now besides Bill. I haven't felt any need to join a sorority."

"You're making a big mistake. I'm going to put your name in for rushing next semester with the Chi Os. They are a great bunch of girls."

"Susie, I appreciate your feelings about this, and maybe I'll feel differently next semester, but for now, I've got all I can handle. Have fun and tell me all about it when you get in tonight." Maria was a little irked that Susie was acting high-handed with her, but decided not to make an issue of it. Maria wasn't sure whether she would like to be "controlled" by some gals just a year or two older than she was.

"Aren't you going to see Bill again tonight, my little lovebird?"

"He's got a Chapter meeting tonight, tomorrow night he has a make-up class, and probably a big project due Thursday or Friday, so we aren't going out until Friday night." Maria felt slightly irritated by her teasing. Susie had hit a sore spot, but didn't know it. She was just in a good mood and wanted to bring Maria along with her.

"You may get caught up in your classes then, if life is keeping you two apart. Go to dinner; I have to run to the Chi O's House. See you later."

Maria knocked on Jeannie and Donna's door to see if they were in and going to dinner. She heard someone say, "Come in." She opened the door carefully, in case they were waiting to throw pillows, but they were calmly sitting down. "Are you going to dinner?" she asked.

"Yes, let's go."

Off they went to the dining hall. It was fun to have such nice dorm mates across the hall. They told her about their double dates with the Farm House guys that they had met at the dance. The guys were funny. They took two canoes out on Lake Laverne. While out on the lake, they all got to laughing so hard at their paddling techniques that they almost capsized their canoes. They ended up at the Union for coffee, still laughing about their lake adventure.

"What fun. Are you going out with them again?" Maria asked.

"Friday night we're going to the Union to dance," Jeannie said. "How are you and that good-looking guy doing?"

"His name is Bill Morgan, and I'm going to see him again Friday night. Maybe we'll stop in and dance, too. I'm not sure about our plans yet."

"That would be great if you came to the Union," Donna said.

Walking back from dinner with them, Maria thought how nice it was to have friends already. They could have been obnoxious, but instead, they bordered on being too nice, which was a "defect" she could stand.

That night and the next, Bill called her, sometimes quite late, but no one cared if the phone rang. The students were all a bunch of night owls, studying until the wee hours sometimes. Maria could tell that Bill was looking forward to seeing her as much as she was to seeing him, even with her mild concerns. She wondered what he was feeling. Maybe he'd start to open up. He sounded so sexy on the phone. Their hormones were doing double time, these days.

When Friday came, Maria felt a little tingle working its way through her body every time she thought about seeing Bill, even though she kept telling herself to take it easy. She decided that they must start talking about the things that were important to her.

By afternoon, the tingle had built to a delicious urge. She felt comfortable with her courses and was caught up with her assignments for the week. When she hit the dorm Friday afternoon, she was wild with happiness. No matter how much she tried to talk sense to herself, she couldn't get over that incredible feeling when she thought about Bill.

No one was in the showers; she could tell by the silence. She smiled; being first in the shower meant that she got hot water, her hair had time to dry, and she wouldn't be rushed. She was pleased at her timing.

Susie walked in just as Maria was brushing out her tangles and announced, "I'm starved."

They flew over to the dining hall and filled their trays with serious portions of food. "I see my roommate has her appetite back. The magic must be slowing down a little," Susie said.

Maria ignored her comment and asked her about her night with the Chi Os.

Susie said that it went well and she was going to pledge Chi O this weekend. Maria knew Susie was right for the sorority, and the sorority was lucky to get her.

Back in the dorm, Maria was feeling devilish. "So, how's old Chucky?"

"Don't let him hear you call him Chucky. I'll find out soon enough how our evening will go by how much football Chuck has played."

Maria thought that she should say something encouraging to her roommate, who seemed to be suffering quietly with a guy who thought he was pretty special and sounded a little self-absorbed. She wished that Susie, who was so cute and funny, would think about branching out and dating other fellows. As sharp as Susie was, she was locked in to their relationship and didn't realize what was out there for her.

"Have you ever thought about looking around a little, Susie? You are a very eligible gal. You deserve a nice guy."

Susie gave Maria a look that said "off limits," and Maria felt it. The temperature in the room seemed to go down a few degrees. *Boy, did I touch a nerve,* Maria thought, as she checked herself in the mirror before leaving. "Bye, Susie, have fun," she said weakly, as she shut the door after herself.

Maria talked to herself all the way down the hall about being cool and careful, but when she burst through those double doors and saw Bill in the front room, she forgot all her plans, ran over to him, and hugged him. It seemed like they hadn't seen each other for weeks instead of a couple of days. Happily surprised by her actions, he laughed and took her hand. As they started down the steps, she caught her toe on a step. Bill grabbed her so fast, she squeaked.

"Are you okay?" he asked. "I didn't hurt you, did I? I don't want to lose you just as we're getting to know each other." As he said that, Maria saw that little flicker of sadness pass across his face, then disappear.

As they walked along to the Ag Building, Bill put his arm around her shoulder and moved in close to her. Keeping step with him, she put her arm around his waist. He looked at her, quite pleased. "Another surprise from you tonight, Maria; you are my little dickens." He gave her a smile that made her legs weak. They continued on without saying much of anything, but the feelings were flowing fast and furious between them.

She could feel the muscles in his back and waist moving. He was *all* muscle, and she couldn't resist telling him so.

He laughed. "My muscles are part of being a farm boy."

To Maria, who had known a lot of guys who were not in such good shape, he looked and felt fantastic.

They approached the enormous Ag Building and sat down on the steps in front of it. Bill praised the professors. They had taught him how to farm in far better ways than were traditionally used. He felt that his teachers were very dedicated, and he respected them very much.

"After I graduate, I'll probably farm; but what I'm really interested in is passing on the knowledge about better techniques that I've gained here to the farmers of Iowa and beyond." He sounded so earnest and full of aspirations.

As she listened to his future plans, Maria felt very special that he had opened up to her and shared some part of himself that she imagined not too many people knew about. She found herself wanting to know more about him the more he talked. He was so innocent in a way and yet so grown up. He was a such a natural speaker that she loved listening to him.

All of a sudden, he said, "That's enough about me. Let's talk about you." He stood up, pulled her up, and started down a side path. "Do you like flowers?"

"I love flowers. My dad and I grew all kinds of flowers. Why?"

"Right behind this building is a group of flower nurseries, and there are dozens of flowers back there. I'll bring you here during the day sometime to see them all in the light." He looked so pleased that he had found a nice surprise that she liked, and he took her around back.

"They would be so much fun to see in full sun, but I can still see them quite well. Dusk is a beautiful time. Do you suppose I could pick one or two?"

He put his arms around her, drew her very close to him, leaned over, put his lips up to her hair, and whispered that she could pick as many as she wanted. She looked up at him; he found her lips and kissed her. What a beautiful backdrop for making love. The asters and zinnias were nodding their rainbow-colored heads, moved by the wafting of a slight breeze, saying hello young lovers.

Neither of them spoke for a moment. Then Bill took her hand, and they walked back to the main sidewalk. He moved his arm to around her waist. She put her arm around his waist, too, and they slowly retraced their steps. The intensity of their feelings had shaken both of them.

A little way down the sidewalk was a small bench, nestled back into the trees. Bill sat down and opened up his arms to her. Maria's stomach did a back flip, and she sat down next to him, unable to process all her emotions. To try to gain control of herself, she looked up into the sky. "There must be a mighty giant, filling the sky with twinkling stars from a huge bucket. Look at the sky, those stars were put there for us."

After a moment or two, he said, "I can't ever remember looking at the stars like this."

She could feel the heat of his body next to hers as they sat back, looking up at the sky. After a few minutes of silence, basking in the awe that they felt with the magic of the evening, Bill turned and kissed her again. She didn't want to stop the kiss and lost contact with her surroundings for a while. Reality set in, however, when she felt Bill trembling.

She gently pulled back. "Let's go to the Union for a Coke or something."

He nodded, shook his head, ran his fingers through his hair, and stood up. He smiled at her, and she knew that he was trying to get himself under control. Maria stood up, and they walked silently, arm in arm, back to the Union, still astonished by the passion between them.

Maria felt as if she had been kissed into oblivion. She felt all tussled and wanted to repair the damage when they walked into the Union. "Could I borrow a comb?" she asked. He fumbled around in his back pockets and produced a small one. She headed for the ladies' room.

He was staring at the wall menu when she found him. He asked, "What would you like?"

She had an urge to say, you for the rest of my life, but instead she said, "A Coke."

Finding a booth, they scooted in facing each other and smiled, but they were at a loss for words. He took her hands and held them.

Bill took a deep breath. He said, "You are a darling girl."

Out popped, "You are the handsome prince, the one who comes and enchants the princess."

Bill grinned at her. Out of the corner of her eye, Maria saw her dorm mates dancing in the side room with their dates. They were having a wonderful time. Bill turned to see what she was looking at and saw them jitterbugging like mad.

"Would you like to dance with me again, sometime?" Maria asked. "We had a lot of fun at your party. You're a good dancer."

"Maybe, but first I want to get to know you better," he said.

His comment was a little sobering, and she asked, "Do you want to know what I think about my course of studies here?" She thought, *If he wants to be serious, I'll tell him about school.* "I'm having a hard time adjusting to the heavy science curriculum at Iowa State. I thought there would be more emphasis on all the arts, but it's mostly science."

"Didn't you read the catalog before deciding to come here?" he asked.

"I thought I had, but evidently not well enough. I needed to ask more questions about the school. I hope I didn't make a mistake." She couldn't explain to him her need to escape her home and her mother or her grasping-at-straws technique in choosing a college.

"If it was by accident that you came, I'm glad. Maybe I can help." He tapped his watch and nodded that it was almost time for curfew. They headed back to the dorm.

Maria still had so much to say to Bill, but she didn't want to spoil the last few minutes of their date in deep discussion. Tomorrow night, maybe they'd be able to sort out some of their feelings and talk more about their relationship.

When they got to the steps of the dorm, they stopped. Bill put his arms around her and his face in her hair. They hugged for a long time, it seemed, then Bill whispered in her ear, "I'll call you tomorrow afternoon to make plans for the evening. I've never felt like this before, and I want to talk about our future."

"Okay, my handsome prince, I'll be waiting," Maria said, trying to keep a light tone. The Campanile started to gong. She ran up the stairs, turned, blew him a kiss, and went in the door. She looked out and saw him standing there, looking up at where she had been. Then he turned and walked away. She stumbled down the hall, exhausted by their incredible evening. She thought about his parting comment about wanting to talk about their future. She didn't know what to make of it.

Bill called on Saturday morning. Everyone on Maria's floor was dead to the world, sleeping, when the phone rang. Maria was in bed, only half awake. She heard the phone, popped up, threw herself out of bed, and ran down the hall. She thought that it was probably not for her; there were twenty other girls on their floor. She picked up the phone, hoping whoever it was hadn't hung up, and almost yelled "Hello!" She surprised herself. No soft dulcet tones were flowing from her vocal chords that morning.

It was Bill. He very quietly and pleasantly said that he wanted to talk to Maria and would she call him. She was caught. She asked herself, *What do I do now? Say that it's me and sound like a freak, or pretend to go get her?* She decided to own up and said meekly, "It's me."

He laughed, which just delighted her. "You have a really good farm voice, one that the cows could hear wherever they are."

She wasn't so sure that she liked his description, but she laughed too and let it pass because she was so happy that he was on the phone.

"I'm sorry for calling so early," Bill apologized, "but I wanted to get hold of you before you went to breakfast or to class."

Actually, Maria wouldn't have cared if he had called her in the middle of the night.

"My frat is having an impromptu get together tonight. Would you like to come? I didn't know about the party last night, because we just decided this morning to have it. I know I said I would call in the afternoon, but I couldn't wait to ask you." He lowered his voice and said very quietly, "Our date last night decided some things in my mind, and I want to talk to you about where we're going."

Maria wanted to jump through the phone, but said in as calm a manner as she could that she would love to come to the party.

He chuckled when he heard her answer. "There's a lot more to you than I'd realized, including a strong, come-to-dinner voice." He laughed again. He had no idea how much more she had stored up in her, waiting in the wings to surprise him.

What a day Maria had: doing her laundry, running to Dog Town for notions she needed, going to chemistry lab for three hours. She was trying to concentrate on running her life, although all she wanted to do was think about Bill. She wondered how she could be so crazy in love with him. She hardly knew him. That thought kept surfacing and was a little unsettling. She was afraid, in the back of her mind, that their relationship was going to dissolve and disappear as quickly as it had appeared. The idea gave her the shivers.

She hoped that no one else would call her for a date, because she didn't want to turn them down, but she didn't want to get sidetracked from this relationship, either. Unfortunately, she had a note on her door when she trudged home from chem lab that Bobby and Ed had called and asked if she would call them back.

Normally, she would have been pleased with the attention, and she was sort of interested in why Ed had called. She didn't think it would be for a date, but maybe to offer her a ride to her sister's home in Rock Falls for Thanksgiving—but why so early? It was only

October, plenty of time to plan for Thanksgiving. Nonetheless, she felt a little thrill when she thought about his phone call. Ed was in his fifth year, studying veterinary medicine. She had met him when he worked for several summers as an intern for her brother-in-law, Dr. Don Dawson. She had still been in high school and was very intrigued by him; she thought him cute and very sexy. He had a dimple in his chin and a slight overbite, which just fascinated her but eluded rational explanation.

During the summers when he worked for Don, Ed usually had lunch at Maria's house. Don liked to talk over the morning calls they had made and make plans with him for the afternoon rounds. Maria loved sitting there, listening to them, but she was so shy, she could hardly eat.

Ed kept his distance during her high school years, but before she went to Iowa State, he had become more and more friendly. His casual interest made him all the more interesting to Maria, but he was illusive. She had been dating some local boys from Don's little farming town in Illinois, so she was busy socially, but Ed was mysterious and fascinating. By the time she was a senior bound for college, she had relaxed a little; she wasn't quite so tongue-tied and could actually talk to him.

He hadn't offered her any advice or help on being a freshman, probably because he didn't give her much thought. That was okay with her, she pretended, because he was too old for her anyway. Plus, Maria had a feeling that he had plenty of testosterone flowing through those beautiful veins of his and with all that charm, she suspected that he was a "bad boy"—almost dangerous—and her instincts said to take it easy.

She called Bobby back. He invited her to go dancing. She thanked him and said that she had a party to go to, but would love to go dancing sometime soon. She had met him through a couple of friends when she had been in school for just a week, and they had gone dancing in the Union. She liked Bobby, so she hoped that they could keep their friendship going.

He said that the jukebox wasn't going away and would be waiting for their next dance session. "Maybe you would be up for some dancing during an afternoon when we both aren't too busy?" he asked.

"That's a great idea! Call me." Maria was relieved that he was easily put off.

Anyway, she had to focus on one relationship at a time; if she really wanted to dance, she knew whom to call.

After getting through that conversation, she needed a big drink of water. She was nervous about talking to Ed. His title was enough to shake her a little. He was going to be a DVM, Doctor of Veterinary Medicine, in the spring. She had never had a chance to talk to him without the whole Dawson family present. Maybe she'd get to know that illusive guy a little better on their 250-mile trip home.

She called the number that he left, but there was no answer. She wished there were a way she could leave a message. Message machines were just becoming available in the new technological age that was beginning to sweep the nation. Unfortunately, the average person didn't have one.

As Maria began focusing on her evening, she thought about what she would wear. How casual should she be? She was afraid if she went there in jeans, all the other girls would have on skirts. If she went in a skirt, they'd all be in jeans. She knocked on her dorm mate's door for advice.

"It's Maria, and I need to talk to you about what you are wearing to the Farm House party tonight."

Jeannie opened her door. It looked to Maria as if she had just awakened from a nap. Suddenly, someone Maria didn't recognize walked up behind her and said, "You should wear what you wore to parties in the suburbs."

Maria did a double take. The girl seemed upset with Maria, and as Maria looked at her, it dawned on her that this girl had been the one in the dining hall that they had labeled Miss Obnoxious. Her friends had called her Maude. Maria asked, with a lot of irritation in her voice, "Do you live here?"

Maude looked mad. "Of course, I live here."

Maria gave her a strange look. "Why do you care what I wear? I wasn't asking you. And what was that comment about the suburbs all about?"

Jeannie was standing listening to their exchange with her mouth open. Susie was just coming down the hall and said, "Hi," to Maude as she walked into her room.

Maria left Maude standing in the hall, followed Susie into their room, and shut the door. She asked, "So what do you know about her?"

"Besides the fact that we ran into her in the dining hall, she's in one of my classes. She told me the other day that she lived a little south of Des Moines on a farm."

Maria repeated what Maude had said to her.

Susie just shook her head. "What was she doing on our floor?"

"I think she was sniffing around, looking for trouble," Maria said.

"No, she was probably visiting someone," Susie said. Maria felt that there was more to it than that, but she couldn't put her finger on it. Susie obviously didn't want to discuss the subject, and this was her way of saying enough was enough.

Somehow, while making phone calls and encountering Maude, time had slipped by Maria again. Where was that calm, confidant person she was trying to cultivate? She seemed to be getting wilder and more confused by the moment. No dinner for her; they would have plenty of food at the party. She had to take a shower, cool down, collect her wits, and try to look as pretty as possible for her date.

The dorm was quiet. Everyone else was checking out the buffet at the dining hall. Maria was enjoying the little warm drops of water pelting her skin. She felt better and better as the water soothed her and washed away the incident with Maude.

3. The Frat Party

Life has taught us that love does not consist of gazing at each other, but in looking outward together in the same direction.
—Antoine de Saint-Exupéry

Going to the party with Bill was so satisfying. Maria couldn't explain that feeling of happiness she had when she was with him. It filled up so many little empty places in her. They didn't say much, but she knew he was thinking about their relationship. They ambled along, hand-in-hand, enjoying touching each other. His gait was longer than hers, and as hard as she tried, she couldn't avoid taking an extra step now and then just to keep pace with him.

He had been lost in his own world, but when he realized that he had been moving faster than usual, he gave her an apologetic grin and put his arm around her waist. "Now we are a matched team," he said, as he slowed down. She loved the farm references that he used.

Maria had decided to wear jeans, and she had guessed right. The frat fellows had thought up all kinds of games involving running, hiding, twisting, and turning to win. Bill's fraternity was so much fun. They made up crazy games to play indoors and out, which was a welcome change and set them apart from the Greek fraternities.

Since Maria was paired with Bill for every game, she guessed that Bill had let his wishes be known to his frat brothers that she was to be his only partner for the evening. When they were hiding together, he grabbed her tightly and put his lips up to her ear, saying, "I just love playing these games with you."

She looked at him and was surprised to see such feeling coming from those big blue eyes. All of a sudden, he grabbed her hand, pulled her up, and they ran for the finish line, winning the game. He was so quick on his feet, it just amazed her.

She heard the guys kidding him about how fast his girl could run, and he would have to run fast to catch her. He looked at them and said, "I will catch her when the time comes."

Someone said, "Oh, Bill, you'd better watch it."

Skipping dinner had made Maria thirsty and hungry, and the smell the burgers sizzling on the grill wafted into her nostrils. She wanted one. Bill had gone inside for a minute, so she went over to the grill. She was helping herself when someone said, "Maude, I'll get you one." She froze when she heard that name. Did someone think she was Maude? Was that awful Maude Bill's last girlfriend? She couldn't believe it. Someone as nice as Bill hooked up with Miss Obnoxious. So that was why Maude was down on Maria's floor. She was checking out her competition. How did she know that they were dating? She must have seen them together at the dorm.

Bill was just coming out the back door and must have heard his frat brother trying to be a gentleman by helping out Bill's date. Bill looked like a truck had hit him. When Maria turned toward his friend and said, "Wrong name, mine's Maria," his friend winced, and Bill gave her a weak, apologetic smile.

As Bill walked up to her, he had that strange, serious look that came over him sometimes when they were together. That gal must have been around here more than once to make Bill and his frat brother look so squeamish. Several other people had stopped talking and were watching what was going on.

Maria wanted to say, show's over, let's get on with the party, but instead she made a foolish mistake and tried to stuff the hamburger in her mouth to stop the nervous giggles that she felt coming. She thought what a nervous nitwit she was. All at once, she was sneezing and coughing at the same time. She needed something to drink and squeaked out, "Please get me a drink of water." She took a big drink and cleared her throat, calming the coughing fit. She settled down further once Bill brought her a root beer and they both sat down to eat.

Slow, seductive tunes began to play in the rec room, and the evening mood was getting a little softer and quieter. Maria's hormones were beginning to race through her veins, and she was looking forward to dancing with Bill.

Bill took their plates to the kitchen and came back for her with his arms wide open. She thought what a sexy turn-on it was to see him standing there like that. She got up slowly, walked across the room with an inviting smile on her face, and slipped into his arms with her heart pounding.

They were dancing to a slow tune when Bill whispered, "You got your wish to dance."

They fit together so well that they already anticipated each other's movements. Maria thought that being in his arms seemed so normal and yet so exciting at the same time. Sometimes, she felt as if she had known him for a thousand years. Thinking that, a shiver went through her. It came from a place deep inside her.

Bill immediately checked to see if she was all right. "Are you cold?"

She just shook her head no, buried her face in his shoulder, felt his strength, and danced.

After a few more dances, Maria could sense from his body language that Bill either wanted to talk or kiss her. "Let's go," he said. He took her hand and slowly led her into the study. As they left the group on the dance floor, it almost felt like they were going into his bedroom.

They were quite alone in the study. To have a guy want to have a serious talk with her was a delicious, new feeling. This was a much more adult approach to dating than in high school. Bill had said that he wanted to get to know her better, so that's what she supposed this conversation would be about.

Maria found out very quickly that she had guessed wrong. He turned the light off and gathered her into his arms for a wonderful kiss that lasted way too long and was saying things to her that she wasn't yet prepared to deal with, but she didn't want to stop him. However, the kiss made him so passionate, that she had to gently push him away. She didn't want to give the impression that she didn't love it, but from the intensity of it, she knew they had to stop. It was more than just a kiss. It represented a much more sexual adventure. One thing she knew for sure, Bill was a very ardent young man; fortunately, he also had a lot of control and respect for her. There was no frantic groping in the dark. He was trying to keep calm, but his young nature kept bursting out and pushing them into uncharted territory.

Maria turned the light on and looked at him. "Let's sit down and talk about our future, if we dare. We need to try to understand what's going on here," she said. She hoped her mention of the word future would give him the courage to talk to her.

They sat very close, like Siamese twins.

Bill said, very quietly, "I've never felt like this before with anyone. I'm really confused about what to do."

Maria sensed that part of this talk was referring to a third person. She knew it had to do somehow with Maude and had a sinking feeling that was choking her. She couldn't bear to have him tell her that he was committed to Maude. She felt frozen and shivered, waiting to hear if she was going to lose him sometime in the future, after his passion had cooled down.

He pulled his fingers through his hair and looked at her. She looked back at him, sort of smiling. He wasn't smiling; he was staring carefully into her eyes. He asked, "How are you doing?"

Maria didn't know what to say, so she asked a question in return. "Do you mean right now or in the future?" She felt that he was stalling, perhaps groping for words.

He said, "Before we talked last night in the Union, I had wondered if you are you happy or disappointed with your course of studies. You made it plain that you might be in the wrong school. I got to thinking about us, and it worried me that you might leave and go to a different school soon."

"Well, after I talked to you, oddly enough, I thought about my life more and realized that I'm taking a general science program for freshmen; it isn't so bad, and I don't have to declare my major until next year. I'm sort of interested in dietetics and/or business as possible majors, and even if I decide to transfer, most of my courses here will probably be counted." She looked at him. "I'm leaving my options open." Then added, "My dad suggested that I look into dietetics as an interesting alternative to medicine, if I didn't want to pursue a medical career. Iowa State has a good dietetics program."

"So you did get some help as to what to do career wise from your dad. You said that no one had helped you when you were trying to decide where to go to school."

Maria was struck by the fact that he remembered her comment. He had really listened to her. His perspective was good for her. Maybe she enjoyed feeling sorry for herself.

Maria assumed he was wondering how she would fit into his life, just as she was wondering how he would fit into hers. He came from a farming family that was successful and had raised him to love the land. She was a suburban girl who loved horses and sports. Were they suited well enough to think about the future? Maria also guessed that Maude was more of a threat to their relationship than she had known. As Bill started to tell her about himself, she realized that her fears may have been well-founded.

"Maude and I grew up together. She lived on a farm not far from mine. We were at a church picnic one time, and I kissed her. It was really just puppy love, but I got all serious and said we were going steady.

"I couldn't go to college right after high school; I needed to work for a year to help pay my tuition. Working for Mr. Gunderson in town, repairing trucks and tractors, was a decent way to make money. I didn't mind the work, but it was a bit boring. I dated other girls, of course, but Maude was still around."

The Second World War had been over for a year when Bill started school at Iowa State in 1946.

"Even after I started school, whenever I'd go home for a visit, I'd see Maude. I was kind of surprised when she showed up here this year; I didn't think college was her thing. Anyway, I'm twenty-one now and a junior; it's really time to start thinking like a grown-up." Bill ginned. "It's weird, though; I still feel young when I see the campus and classes full of World War II veterans, coming back to school on the GI Bill. You know, I really respect them, and I'm pleased that the country hasn't forgotten them after they've served so bravely."

Maria pondered this and thought about how the war had begun to change women's roles from homemakers to breadwinners. They had left home and gone into the war factories to make the things necessary to win the war. There were songs about them, such as "Rosie the Riveter." There were movies and plays made about them serving in the women's branches of the armed forces: the WAVEs, WACs, and military nurses. As a result of all this national publicity, women were beginning to come into their own and develop careers by the millions. Doors were opening for them, and they were never going back to simply being wives and mothers who stayed at home.

Maria was part of this new generation. Her dad had instilled in her a desire to make something of herself. She thought of her sister, who had no way to take care of herself financially, married with five children. Her sister was stuck, and Maria didn't want that for herself.

"Would you like to know more about my background other than my dad's farm?" Maria asked.

"I would love to know who you are and where you came from," Bill said.

"Well," she paused to think how she was going to introduce herself to Bill in a calm, logical manner. "I came from the dual background of living in a posh suburb in the winter—La Grange, Illinois, home of the Brookfield Zoo—and summers in Wyoming. When I was a teenager, I went to a huge high school, La Grange High, and was part of an academic crowd of women who were all going to college and beginning to think about careers, rather than getting married and having children."

"Do you want a career rather than a marriage?"

"I want it all: a career, a wonderful husband, and children some-day," Maria said and looked at him with an air of determination.

She continued with her story. "During my summers in Wyoming, I spent a lot of time in an area called the Salt River Valley, riding my range pony, exploring the mountains, and generally being wild and free. Before my dad built his ranch on the side of the mountain, I stayed with my grandparents in the valley. My grandfather was a real mountain man who had settled the valley in the 1880s as the marshal of the territory and kept peace with the Rosebud Sioux. That was where I learned a lot about life on a ranch and developed my love for horses."

"Now I know why you seem so free to me and why I find your personality quite exciting. You were treated like a boy in some ways, being allowed to go where you wanted. I can almost see you riding your pony like the wind. Your dad was quite a guy to give you that chance to be so free," Bill said, looking at her with admiration of her childhood lifestyle and the influence it had on her now.

"My dad taught me to seize the day, so to speak. He taught me to play, laugh, and enjoy life. He was a wonderful teacher because he took me places where I could have fun but also learn and be a student of human nature.

"From these two worlds," Maria said, "I became who I am today. I had a brilliant, loving father who practiced medicine in Oak Park and imparted his wisdom to me throughout my childhood. My mother was a western gal from the Salt River Valley. My dad met her there. She was seventeen, and he was thirty-five. He decided to stay and practice medicine in the valley after going out there on a

43

hunting trip. After a while, he realized that he wanted to go back to Illinois and brought my mom and my sister to La Grange. I was born and raised there.

"My mother was not cut out for the suburban life of La Grange and got lost along the way. She was never able to make the adjustment and fell into a lonely pattern of drugs and alcohol with periods of sobriety, and, during those years, she was a distant mother. At various periods during my life, my mother would escape the social demands of La Grange society and being a doctor's wife by running back to Wyoming to be with her gentle farming family.

"I would come home after school to a cook and a housekeeper and know that Mom was gone. She never took me aside to explain that she was leaving or anything. Maybe she didn't know how; I don't know, but it hurt me a great deal emotionally. Like most kids, however, I had stamina, intelligence, and hope that things would get better. My dad was a big contributor to my faith in myself. He saved me."

Maria looked at Bill. After giving him the story of her life, she felt drained. She hoped that what she'd told him about herself wouldn't scare him away, but if it did, so be it. Better for him to find out all of her skeletons before they went any further. She closed her eyes and just cuddled up to him. She was done talking for the evening.

Bill said, "Now I really know why I am so drawn to you. You look at life so differently from all the other girls that I have dated because of your interesting and unusual background. I don't want to lose you. I want to explore our options together so we can be a team." He gathered her in his arms and kissed her so tenderly that she felt tears forming.

Bill saw that her eyes were brimming, and he whispered, "Why the tears?" He took his handkerchief out of his back pocket and carefully wiped them away, then kissed her eyelids.

"I guess it was harder to talk about my background than I thought," Maria said. "When you kissed me with such sweetness, it just did me in."

"Your mom had a hard time, and I imagine it made you so sad when you were growing up. You must have missed having her in your life."

"I always thought that I had done something that caused her not to like me. As a kid, I didn't know that her problems didn't have anything to do with me."

Bill pulled Maria in as close as he could, putting both of his arms around her, and whispered, "Thanks for being so honest with me. It makes me want you all the more. I'm going to be your prince and keep you safe." He gave her that wonderful smile and kissed her again.

Maria couldn't believe her ears; he was committing to her for the future, even after everything she had told him. She was thrilled beyond measure. When she opened her eyes, his face had taken on a serious look.

"I'll bet you are wondering about Maude," he said.

"Well, yes." She waited, watching his face. What was he willing to say about her?

"I have to make some tough decisions in the near future. It's driving me a little crazy," Bill said.

"Can you tell me about it? Can I help?"

Bill just shook his head no. "But I promise to explain more after I talk to my folks."

It seemed that Bill was through talking about his problems. He wrapped Maria in his arms, burying his face in her hair. She could feel him fighting—and losing—an emotional battle. He took his face out of her hair, turned his head, found her lips, and kissed her until she couldn't stand it. She felt such passion, tenderness, and sadness in him.

"I'm amazed at your strength, Maria."

"What do you mean by strength?"

"I thought you might get mad or give me the silent treatment when I didn't tell you what was bothering me about the Maude problem. Instead you just let me move in close and kiss you."

"It's not strength, it's knowing when to shut up and just enjoy being loved."

Bill said, "I go around some days wondering where it is all going to end."

Maria felt a chill go through her, but she just smiled at him and said that it would work out the way it was supposed to, although she nearly choked while saying it. Maria was playing for high stakes, Bill's and her future, and didn't want to lose it all by saying something stupid.

Someone yelled from the other room that they had to get the girls home before curfew.

Staring at each other in utter amazement, Bill and Maria wondered where the evening had gone. It seemed like just minutes, not hours, that they had been dancing, kissing, and talking. Bill stood up slowly and pulled her to him. He put his hands around her face, which she loved, grinned, and slowly kissed her good night. She went weak in the knees.

They left by the side door to avoid Bill's frat brothers and their comments. Bill slipped his arm around her. There were no more words to say. They walked quietly and silently. Reaching the dorm, he kissed her lightly and said that he would call, soon. That sad look flitted across his face, and she felt sick to her stomach. Maria smiled her best smile and said that she would be waiting. Up the stairs she went, turned around, threw him a kiss, and waited to see what he would do. He threw one back to her, grinned, and walked away.

4. The Commitment

Come live in my heart and pay no rent.
—Samuel Lover

On Sunday, as Maria stretched to wake up, she watched from her front window in the dorm all the good little church goers heading to church. She had no inclination to go to church, having been raised by a father who felt that most of the churches preached hellfire and damnation, which he said was a terrible way for the mind to start the day.

She felt at loose ends and so did Susie; Maria couldn't settle down to study. Instead, they bundled up, as it was getting cool in the mornings, and went outside to get a fresh perspective.

As they strolled along, Susie said, "You would be perfect for Chi Omega."

Maria turned that around. "I hope Chi Omega would be perfect for me."

Susie laughed, gave her a shove, and ran. Maria pushed her athletic legs into gear and, grabbing a handful of leaves, caught up to Susie and dropped the leaves in Susie's hair.

As Susie picked leaves out of her hair, Maria said, "I really hadn't thought about joining a sorority, but the idea is making more sense to me as the winter approaches. Somehow, the cold weather makes me want to hole up in a warm burrow until spring." Belonging to a group who liked each other, for the most part, might be nice, she thought. Maybe she would go out for rush next semester.

Maria scooped up another handful of leaves, dropped them in Susie's hair, ran for the dorm, and watched Susie attempt to catch her. Susie was the brains of their dorm, but Maria was the athlete. In their room, as Maria's breathing returned to normal, she thought that Susie was a lot of fun most of the time, so she could put up with Susie's attitude about Chi Omega. They also talked about a lot of things, which was nice. About the only thing they hadn't discussed were the elephants in their room. Susie's elephant was Chuck, but she couldn't see it. Maria's was always there, morning, noon, and night. Its presence loomed large in the corner. It was Maria's concern regarding Bill's problem with Maude.

Maria found it was harder to settle down and make an organized plan for herself, including thinking about her current curriculum, since meeting Bill. Just when she thought that things were going to be smoother for her than they had been in years because of the problems living with her mother, she met Bill. Falling in love had turned her life upside-down or maybe right-side-up for the first time in her life.

When he called Sunday night and asked if he could see her right away, all her resolve to be strong and not say yes the second he asked her to be with him went out the window. She turned to jelly as soon as she heard his voice. All Maria could think of was being with him. She didn't care what else she had to do for her classes; she just asked when he would be coming.

Bill said in that wonderful voice of his, "As soon as I can," with so much urgency that she was thrilled but concerned.

With no make-up, just a freshly scrubbed face and a dab of Evening in Paris cologne behind her ears, she ran down the corridor to wait for him, but he was already there, so handsome, standing waiting for her. She felt excited, as if they were running away. They ran down the stairs hand in hand, and Bill stopped at the bottom of the stairs and kissed her, not able to contain himself. There they were, out in front of God and everyone. Maria thought to herself that he evidently didn't care who saw them. All she could think of was Maude looking out her window at that moment and casting an evil spell upon her.

"Come on," Bill said, grabbing her hand again and striding up the sidewalk to the Campanile. She ran along beside him, thinking what he must have had in mind. Under the Campanile, while it was playing its most beautiful songs, he took her in his arms and kissed her with so much love and passion that she knew he was there on a mission. He held her at arm's length and keeping her gaze, he said. "I love you, Maria." His voice quavered when he spoke.

When he uttered those magic words, Maria could sense that he had thought long and hard about it. This was not an idle comment. It was a big step. He had hinted at it when they were talking last night. But this was a firm statement that he was making to her while the carillon chimed. The emotion of the event shook her so much, she felt the tears coming.

Bill kissed the tears from her eyes and cheeks, took out his handkerchief, and carefully wiped her tears away—all the while looking into her eyes and smiling a smile that made her feel like soaring out to the edge of time and back. "How do you tell a girl who has captured your heart how much she means to you? I spent the day going over our conversation of last night, replaying all the things we talked about, and I felt that I had finally found a woman who speaks to me at a level that touches me in a way I have never experienced before. Studying was out of the question. I couldn't get you out of my mind. Calling you was the only way I had to keep from popping. I'm going home to see my folks next weekend to do some serious planning, and I want to see you as much as possible this week before I leave. I'll only be gone Saturday and be back on Sunday."

Maria listened to the most important man in her life pour out his love to her, and she was jubilant. Now it was her turn to answer her darling man and to show him how she felt about him. She began by saying, "All day, I was worried that I had said some things last night that didn't sit well with you, even though I knew I had to come clean about my past. I couldn't lie to you, because I love you so much. Taking the chance of losing you when you heard how mixed up my world has been, I waited today, afraid you'd call and say something like, 'I enjoy your company, Maria, but feel that we are not enough alike to take this any further.'"

As she uttered those dreaded words, even though she knew he didn't feel that way, she started tearing up again because the feelings of losing him were so close to the surface.

Another couple was walking up to the Campanile. Maria coughed a little, trying to finish her thought, but she was losing it, with her emotions welling up so fast.

Bill took her hand and held her close. "Don't try to talk; I get the picture of what's been going on in your head today. You've said all that I will ever need to know. You are my woman from now on, make no mistake about that."

They were sitting on a bench at the entrance to the Union. Bill's arm was around her, and they watched couples, singles, and groups of people walk into the Union for the better part of an hour. As Maria began to recover, she thought how absolutely wonderful Bill was to just sit and let her regain her control, without putting any demands on her to shape up. She loved his kindness.

"Well, I guess I'd better get back to dorm before the doors are locked," Maria said, sadly. "I hate to leave you. I feel so good when we are together. But I have plenty to satisfy the elephant."

He laughed. "Satisfy the elephant? What does that mean?"

Maria said, "That's an expression about living with an enormous problem that is with you all the time and only goes away when the problem is solved. The elephant represents the problem. He may be gone for a while when I get back."

As they walked back to Maria's dorm, Bill said that he wanted to explore a new relationship with her that included a sexual component and wanted to talk with her about how she felt about it. "Don't say anything now; just think about what I have said. I'm committed to you and told you so tonight." He put his arm around her waist and looked at her to gauge her feelings on the subject.

In the culture of the late 1940s, women were put into two categories: the good marriageable ones who were virgins and the fast, wild, naughty ones who had intimate relations with men without much thought. It was all so black and white. Maria had put herself into the "good girl" category, with the cultural attitude that women didn't go all the way unless they were engaged and almost ready to be married. The famous cliché of that period was: "Why buy the cow when you can get the milk for free?" Young women from her background never even talked to each other about getting and using contraceptives. They were led to believe that those items were only for married women, and she had never questioned the logic of that until now. She had planned, until Bill, to be in the "good girl" category for the foreseeable future.

Maria had to say something about such an explosive subject, even though Bill didn't expect an answer tonight. She said, "I don't know how we were going to continue to survive being together without changing the rules, but I'm afraid."

Bill said that they were already together and laughed. "Just think about what I have said, but don't feel I'm going anywhere if it is too much for you right now. I just wanted to be honest with you about my feelings."

As they ran to the dorm, Maria knew that another elephant would be waiting for her regarding this new problem she had to solve.

"Call me," she said, as she was hurrying up the stairs, and blew him a kiss.

As she flew up those stairs, she was the happiest girl in the world. The most darling man of her dreams loved her and had told her so. How could she be so lucky? Nothing could stop them now, except her fear of getting pregnant or Bill leaving her because she was a risqué woman.

Maria told Susie what had happened under the Campanile.

Susie seemed pleased but wary. "You've only known this man for a week. You need to take it slow."

"But we're so compatible with each other."

"Maybe, but it's too soon to be sure about anything."

Maria felt a little shiver while she was talking to Susie, wondering if things were going too fast for them. Bill had added a new element to their relationship tonight: sex. She needed to talk to Susie about that, too, but Susie would probably be upset that Bill was talking about sex so early in their relationship.

Susie said, "How do you think Bill's family will take to you as a girl who doesn't have a farming background? And the bigger question is, how would you like to live on a farm for the rest of your life?"

The thrill was definitely fading by the time they finished talking. Everything Susie said left Maria wondering what she was doing, dating a man who was so different from her. Maria knew that Bill was going home to see his folks on the weekend to discuss things, and she knew that she'd be one of the things at the center of their discussions. She was getting a case of cold feet.

Maria heard the phone ring as she was getting ready for bed. She knew it might be Bill. Her heart started thumping as she ran for the phone. It was about eleven. His deep, calm voice asked for Maria, and she said quietly, "I'm here."

"How are you? What are you thinking? I love you." He said it so quietly.

With goose bumps moving up and down her arms and legs, Maria said, "I'm fine and in love with a handsome man whom I wish I could see to talk about what he mentioned tonight. I'm afraid that I can't be strong enough to keep things calm between us, and I'm afraid to make the next move. You're right to bring up a change in our relationship, but it's hard to talk about it on this very public phone."

"I know, that's why I called. I'm dying over here now, not being able to hold you and talk to you about what happened with us tonight. I know I jumped the gun. I don't know what got into me. But I also know that we have to figure out what we are going to do. We have to do this right. I can't stand to hurt you in any way."

"I feel like we're trying to tame a tornado, sometimes, when we are together," Maria said.

"I know what you mean. I hate being away from you and when I'm with you, I go a little crazy. When I'm kissing you, all the resolutions that I have made melt away. After our incredible conversation and everything else that happened tonight, I didn't want to leave you. Oh, Maria, I need to be with you," he whispered hoarsely.

With that last comment, she heard a slight coughing or choking sound coming through the phone and then silence. "Bill, honey, are you okay? Say something."

There was a clearing of his throat, and he said, "God, Maria, we've got to talk about everything before I go home to see my folks next weekend."

"I'm ready, willing, and able to jump out my dorm window in my pajamas if you say the word."

"Don't tease me, please, Maria. I need you so badly."

"I wasn't teasing you; I really would do that if you could promise me that you could push me back up into my room. Can't you just see us, you trying to shove me up to the window sill so I could grab on and pull myself back in? You're strong but not that strong. I'd have to get Susie to pull at the other end," Maria said, laughing.

She felt she had to lighten their conversation, somehow. Bill seemed so emotionally torn up.

"Okay, okay, I give up." He was laughing when he said, "Let's meet sometime tomorrow to talk. What classes do you have?"

"I'm free after lunch for the afternoon," she said.

Bill said that he would meet her at the Union around one fifteen and they could go over to the golf course away from everyone. She thought for a moment and asked how the weather would be tomorrow. She didn't want to freeze.

"As far as I know, the forecast is for sunny and cool weather in the sixties. Wear a sweater."

"I'll be at the Union at one fifteen with bells on."

"With what on?" he asked.

"It's just a silly expression meaning the person is all excited about the meeting and will be all dressed up wearing bells to announce her arrival."

"You are full of little sayings; it makes you so interesting."

"I'll see you tomorrow, handsome. I love you. Sleep well."

"I'm going to try to study for a while; I've got a big project that is due in a couple of days and haven't done much about it because of a certain little gal who is driving me crazy."

"Who is she? She isn't very nice to be making you crazy. I'll have to talk to her tonight. I'll tell her that she is ruining my boyfriend's studies and his health, so stop it." She could hear Bill laughing at her.

"I feel much better now that we have talked. I'm so glad I called you. I love you, in case you've forgotten," he said.

"Me too, handsome; see you tomorrow."

"Goodnight, honey." There was a small pause and then she heard, "I love you so much, you little dickens."

As the phone went dead, Maria was physically tired, but life seemed better. Bill had a way of easing her worries. He shared his concerns with her, too, which gave them a bond. She knew it wasn't easy for him to juggle everything in his life, either.

All Maria could think of, sitting in class the next morning, was her date with Bill in the afternoon. When the time finally crept to the appointed hour, she ran down the sidewalk as fast as she could to lessen the tension. She loved to run; sometimes, just for the joy of it. She slowed down before she reached him to collect herself, and she practiced being calm and serene. Bill's face lit up when he saw her, making her feel like a million dollars. He had a light blanket slung over his shoulder. He slipped in next to her on the sidewalk, grinned, took her hand, and picked up the pace.

The college golf course was well kept by the Ag department. It was used as a learning tool in good land management but also benefited the college golf team. It was open to the public, but very few outsiders seemed to take advantage of it.

"This golf course is our own private country club," Maria said, as they walked along the footpaths.

"I suppose you've spent a lot of time at country clubs in La Grange."

"A few." What was he getting at? She had a little ping of anxiety.

Bill stopped on the path and said, "You are one of the most interesting girls I've ever met, but I don't know what you think about me or my background. I've never been to a county club in my life."

"I haven't really thought about your background because I like—no scratch that—I love to be with you," she said, pretending that she hadn't spent hours wondering about his background. "Tell me all about you. I told you about me at the party, but you only gave me the bare bones. No holding back, give me both barrels." Maria said, laughing from the pure joy of being out in the fall air with her handsome prince.

They found a shady spot under a big tree far off of the fairway, hidden from golfers and stray balls. Bill spread the blanket on the ground and said that he was an expert in blanket spreading because of all the church picnics that his family had taken him to over the years.

"You are my wonderful blanket spreader. My goodness, another talent that I didn't know about. You are just full of surprises."

"That's exactly why I love you, you make everything so funny. I never quite know how you are going to react." He grabbed her and gave her a quick kiss on her nose.

It was one of those beautiful fall days, a little chilly, but the sun was out and perfect at that moment. Bill moved away a few inches, ran his hands through his thick hair, and looked at her with love written all over his face.

"Well, I don't know about both barrels, but here's a little more. I've been a farm boy all of my life, but I happened to be fairly intelligent and had parents who could send me to an in-state college. I've lived my whole life in Iowa. Our family never took vacations, as such, because we had to keep the farm going.

"Spring, summer, and fall are the big months for farmers. Families depend on their farms to produce enough food to get them through the winter. My mom knew growing up what it was like to be hungry, so did my dad, and they never forgot it." He looked so intense and caring when he talked about them. "They love the land, and they are great folks."

"So far so good," Maria said. "I'm thrilled that you have nice parents, and they didn't beat you much." Listening to him open up to her and make himself as vulnerable to her as she had done made her feel closer to him. "I'm jealous of your family's closeness and values. I'm also jealous of the way you were raised, but I'm thrilled that you are making me part of your life."

Bill grinned at her and hugged her close to him, but Maria could sense that he was waiting for something. To keep from blowing this, Maria was trying to keep a little levity in their discussion. She felt nervous. She knew that what she said next would be very important to him. She was laying all of her secrets out there for him to see and thought, *I've got to trust him.*

Maria sucked in a little air. "Now it's time for truth and consequences from me. First, I want to level with you about my family background. It isn't like yours. My parents are divorced. My dad left my mother and me when I was fourteen and married his secretary, Betty. She is thirty years younger than he is. We were heartbroken, but I saw the handwriting on the wall when he asked me once, when I was very young, if I would like Betty as a new mommy.

"He had stayed in the marriage, raising me and my sister, for twenty-eight years, but he was intrigued and flattered that yet another woman young enough to be his daughter would be interested in him. My sister was married, and I was going into high school when he left." Maria looked at Bill, so close to her that she could hear him breathing. He gave her a smile that was so tender that it made her choke up.

Maria had developed a veneer to protect herself when anyone asked her about her parent's divorce, but watching Bill, listening so intently, she knew that the sweetness and kindness he was showing her would crack the shell. There was so much feeling buried inside her that she had never shared with anyone before about the divorce that when Bill put his arms around her and hugged her, she just fell apart.

"I'm so sorry that you had to go through that," he said. "How did you manage after the divorce?"

Maria wanted to stop talking about herself, but she couldn't ignore his question.

"No one has ever been interested in knowing how I felt about the whole thing until you, Bill." As she was telling her story, she realized, with a lot of pain, how little thought the members of her family had given her over the last four years.

"I had a terrible time, at first, when my dad left. I didn't blame him, because my mother was so hard to live with as she got older. I was faced with going to a big high school and living alone with my mother in our large home in La Grange. My mother was depressed by the whole thing and spent a great deal of time in her room. I kept my grades up, because I knew I needed to go to college and have a life of my own."

By now, Maria was feeling a little frantic. What would Bill think about all this? Perhaps if she made light of some of it, she could lessen the desperation. She didn't really want talk anymore, but she said, "It wasn't all bad. I had lots of friends to be with and one or two very *special* friends."

Bill took the bait and asked, "Were your *special* friends boys or girls?"

Maria laughed and said that they were both. "You wouldn't want to love a wallflower, would you? However," she added, "the boys in my life up until now were just that—boys."

They hugged again. Her story, good or bad, was out there for him to know, and she was concerned that she'd shocked the heck out of him. The culture in 1948 did not encourage divorce in any way. It was looked upon as a terrible thing.

Bill kissed her, gently at first, to comfort her, because he knew words would not help. Gradually, their hormones began calling, and his kisses turned into passionate, urgent messages. Without saying anything, he was trying to show her that he understood, she would be fine, and he loved her.

Finally, they pulled apart. He looked at her with those big blue eyes of his. "You know what's really important to me, and something you express so well?"

Maria shook her head.

"Your ability to love. I can't believe your response to me when I kiss and hug you. You are a very passionate person. I've dated a few gals with backgrounds like mine who seemed to take my attempts to love them very casually. You are so special to me because you appreciate every little thing that I do. Most of all, you allow me to love you. For a man, that is one of the most important things there is in a relationship. Maybe the way you were raised made you a very strong and loving person. Whatever the reason, I am so glad that you're my girl."

With that last statement, the tears started to flow again. What was wrong with her? Until Bill came along, she thought she was handling things pretty well. He was the first man to ask to see beneath her surface personality, and he had accepted her, even with all her warts, because he loved who she really was. She was not a misfit to him. Since the divorce, she'd felt like she didn't belong anywhere or to anyone. Maria flung herself into his arms for one more kiss to stop her tears. It was the most emotion-filled, achingly delightful kiss that they'd had because of what they had discovered about each other.

Before they got back to her dorm, Bill stopped, leaned over, and whispered that he would call her. His voice was hoarse with emotion. He didn't say another word, just walked with his arm around her. When they got to the dorm steps, he hugged her, and she whispered that she would wait for his call. They were drained.

5. Bill's Invitation

And think not you can direct the course of love,
for love, if it finds you worthy, directs your course.
—Kahlil Gibran

It was late in the afternoon when she returned to the dorm. Susie was sitting on her bed going over her notes for a class. Maria was amazed, because she rarely saw Susie studying. Her roommate had an I.Q. in the genius range. Maria was sure she was going to make Phi Beta Kappa before she left college.

"Where have you been?" Susie asked. "Judging by your general appearance, you've had quite an afternoon."

"I've been walking on the golf course with Bill, and we did a lot of talking."

Susie raised her eyebrows and asked, "Was that all you did?"

"I don't ask you what you do on your dates, and you can't ask me."

Susie laughed. "I'm hungry. I'll beat you to the dinner table." They ran at breakneck speed down the hall and out to the dining hall, laughing all the way.

Maria was starving. All the walking she and Bill had done in the afternoon, plus the emotional talk that they engaged in, not to mention all the cuddling, had used up a lot of energy. Judging by how she felt, Bill was probably eating everything in sight, too.

As they strolled back from dinner, Maria felt that she was ready to study with a lighter heart. Susie would be out; she had a date with Chuck.

Maria was writing up a chem lab report when the phone rang down the hall. She jumped out of her chair to run for the phone; it might be Bill. Someone had picked it up and was yelling loudly for Maria. She thought the person at the other end of the phone would have punctured eardrums from the pitch of that yell.

Thinking it was Bill, she answered with a lot of love in her voice. Ed said, "My, you sound sexy over the phone."

She was embarrassed when she realized who it was. She changed tones and said that she thought it was someone else calling her. She didn't want him to think that she answered the phone like that for everyone. "I tried to return your call, but I couldn't. I have sort of forgotten to try again because I've been fairly busy," she said, shading the truth a little. "So what's up?" Maria tried to be as sharp and businesslike as she could.

"Well, I was wondering if you would like a ride home to Rock Falls at Thanksgiving."

"Wow, that would be great. I didn't know how I was going to get to Don and May's house. Rock Falls is probably out of the way for you. Where do you live? Nearby, I hope."

"My folks live in Lanark, just a few miles from Rock Falls, so it's no trouble to take you with me."

"Are you going to have other riders, too?"

"Why, are you worried about being alone with me?"

Maria heard him chuckling as she ignored his comment. "I just thought we could all help with the gas. What's your fee?" Something possessed her to say, "It had better be money."

"Well, I'll have to see what would be appropriate for the occasion," Ed said, sounding sexier by the minute.

Maria's teasing had turned Ed's response into a different conversation between them.

"Are you still there, Maria? You seem quiet all of a sudden."

"I'm here, and I have to go study, so let me know what time you're coming by for me."

"I'll get you last after I pick up the other gals, probably around one in the afternoon on Wednesday. If that changes, I'll let you know. See you next month."

"Thanks so much, Ed. See you then."

Maria had just walked back to her room when the phone rang again, and she turned and ran for it. She answered it a little more crisply than before, in case it wasn't Bill. But it was.

"So who has been hogging the phone? I have been trying to call you for quite a while."

Maria didn't want to tell him that she had been talking to a guy all that time, so she said, "I don't know, probably someone who is in love," shading the truth again.

Bill laughed. "You are always quick with the answers." Bill paused before continuing. "I've been thinking about all the things we talked about today. How did you turn out so well with what happened to you?"

"Most of the credit goes to my daddy; he was my buddy and took me everywhere with him. When I was little, he read to me at night. He gave me love and encouragement. I love my daddy," Maria said in a southern accent.

"Are you sure you didn't come from Virginia?" he said with a chuckle. "Let's talk about our plans."

"What kind of plans shall we talk about? Ah, love plans." Maria teased.

"I want to take you out to dinner Friday night before I go home Saturday."

Now, she was thinking, where could they go for dinner around here? Dog Town boasted of a Spud Nut Shop and that was it for food. Ames was five miles away and the buses didn't run very late. She didn't even know where her bus schedule was.

"So where can we go? I guess we can make a meal of spud nuts," she said, laughing.

"Are you laughing? I happen to be able to borrow a real car, and I am going to take you to Des Moines for dinner at a place I've eaten at with my family. So, smarty, what do you think of that?"

Maria was flabbergasted and delighted. Because they were Depression babies, every meal counted, and not eating in the dorm or fraternity house when it had already been paid for by their parents was not done. The Depression had made big impressions on them about being frugal.

"You are being very daring; I hope you realize that," Maria said, laughing again. "I would love to go!" She was almost yelling into the phone.

Bill must have been pleased with her response because he said, "I love a girl who is so enthusiastic that she almost jumps through the phone."

"Hold your arms out, here I come," she squealed.

"Let's get together Thursday for some more talks. What do you say?"

"Yes, yes, a thousand times yes," Maria sang into the phone.

"So you sing, too."

"Not so you'd want to notice."

"How do you make me feel so alive?" Bill breathed into the phone.

"Pure talent," she said in her southern drawl.

"I wish I could kiss the dickens out of you right this minute. I'll meet you at the Union around one fifteen; again, if that is okay with you. Will you have time for lunch?"

"I never miss a meal, and I will have plenty of time. I wish you could kiss the dickens out of me, too. Let's try on Thursday. And now I have to go and hit the books." She made kissing sounds over the phone which made Bill laugh some more, then he hung up.

Maria was just sitting down at her desk, getting ready to put the finishing touches on her lab report, when the phone rang again. She hoped it wasn't for her. She had spent way too much time on the phone, and her worries had vanished after Bill's call.

It was Bobby, for Maria, someone screamed down the hall. She hurried to answer it as quickly as she could. It never rains, but it pours. She knew he wanted to go dancing with her. When should she tell him? Saturday night while Bill was away? Sure enough, Bobby wanted to go to a dance Saturday night, and she said, "Yes," reluctantly. She argued with herself that she wasn't doing anything bad, just dancing with a friend, but in the back of her mind, she was afraid that one of Bill's fraternity brothers might see her in the Union dancing with Bobby. She had loved dancing with him, but she might be sorry. Did she want to take a chance for an evening of fun? They made plans to meet at the Union around eight. She was tired of all the things she had to think about. She hadn't wanted to hurt Bobby's feelings and spoke too soon, just to end the call. She told herself, *If someone rats on me, I'll just say that it was innocent fun.* That was the truth, after all.

Maria studied until Susie came home all starry eyed. Susie wanted to talk about Chuck. Maria closed her books to listen. She decided to rest in bed while she talked to Susie and tried to make some intelligent comments, but she slowly faded away. She had had enough of any kind of emotion, good or bad, for one night.

Thursday seemed like such a long way off. She had to remind herself why she was in college. She told herself that she was there to get a degree, even if she was in love. She reluctantly listened to herself, went to every class, turned in papers, and took tests. On Thursday morning, she congratulated herself for all the work she had done for the week. She was going to see Bill after lunch as a reward. She flew out of bed, took a shower while it was still dark out, dressed, and ran to breakfast. Getting up was the hard part; going to her class was easy.

Things were going well so far academically. She had a 3.0, which meant she had a "B" average, and that was good for freshmen. Susie probably had a 4.0, but she never talked about it.

Maria decided that she would skip lunch so that she wouldn't have to hurry. She saw Bill waiting in front of the Union, looking very handsome eating a hot dog. She ambled up to him and asked for a bite. She opened her mouth, and he put the hot dog into it for her bite. He offered to get her one, too, but she shook her head. "Yours tastes better, but I'm not really hungry." She was too excited about being with him to be hungry. "Didn't you have time to eat lunch?" she asked, wondering why he was eating a hot dog.

"No, but I had a big breakfast. Our food is great and the cook makes big breakfasts for all of us farm boys." With that he grinned his wonderful grin, hoping she would laugh at his inference about the belief that farm boys were automatically big, strong, and hungry. He had their blanket over his shoulder, and he was dressed in a nice-looking long-sleeved flannel shirt.

"Who dresses you in the morning?" Maria asked. Bill looked stunned for a moment, then a big grin spread over his face.

"Who do you think?"

"Who picks out your clothes?"

"My valet, why?"

Maria was surprised by his quick answers "Well, he's got pretty good taste for a farm valet. I didn't know that they worked on farms, too." Feeling his shirt, she put her arm around his waist and said, "I like the feel of your goods," knowing she was being a little flirt.

Bill looked down at her. "That's enough from you." He looped his arm over her shoulder, feeling her sweater with his fingers. "That's soft, too," he said quietly. "It's just like you."

She felt the heat rising between them. Everything they said to each other seemed to ignite their fire for each other. Neither one of them could stop it.

"Come on," he said, "we'll never get there if we don't speed up." Maria knew what he wanted to talk about and was trying to keep things calm until they were alone on the golf course.

Another beautiful day for their walk, she thought. The leaves on the big trees were beginning to drop. Winter was on its way all too soon. When they found their tree, Bill bowed with a flourish and spread his blanket on the grass. "You bring out the kid in me," he said.

She felt he was a little embarrassed by being playful, but she loved to encourage it in him. He sat down and pulled her down next to him. He put his arms around her. "Who wants to go first in the contest to bare our souls to each other?" Maria started to giggle, and he said, "I've figured out why you laugh at the oddest times—to break the tension, right?" He was beginning to read her.

Maria couldn't resist making a smart remark. "You sound like my sixth-grade teacher. She always knew that when I was nervous, I giggled."

Bill pushed her down and, holding her firmly in place, said, "No more comments out of you." He kissed her, then pulled her up to face him again.

Maria wanted to be honest with him, because she knew it would come back to haunt her if she tried to hide and not say what she really felt. At the risk of repeating herself, she told him again about her life growing up in dual living conditions in La Grange and the Salt River Valley. She wasn't even sure what she had said to him before, because her emotions clouded her memory sometimes.

"It helped me cope with change, I think. I liked both places, but I am more of a city girl, and I want to have a career and work for a while, even if I am married. I guess I want to know I can do it." She quoted her dear old dad by saying, "He always told me to become self-sufficient because my husband could die or leave, and I must be able to care for myself." She took a big breath and waited for Bill's reaction to what she had just said. Maria had watched him listening very carefully to every word she said.

He paused for the longest time and then said very slowly, "I don't want to lose you. I realize that you are a different sort of woman from what I have been brought up with. I guess I shouldn't be surprised by your feelings about being independent and wanting a career. You have been out there for a long time making your way, and I admire you.

"I'm going home this weekend to talk to my folks about you. They don't have any idea what has happened to me since I met you. They think that I'm probably dating Maude and maybe a few other girls, but not just one."

Bill looked at her. Was he trying to read her feelings about what he had just said? He had finally mentioned Maude's name. She was out of the shadows again, hovering around them like an unwanted guest. Maria waited for him to continue. Her stomach was doing flip-flops, but she was trying to remain calm.

"My folks know Maude's folks, and they have been friends for a long time. I have known Maude since I was little. We went together in junior high and high school. Most of that time, I also had other interests, but I thought I loved her. I started to change as to what kind of woman I was interested in after being in college for a couple of years. When I saw you at our party, I felt I knew you. It was so strange. I had to come over and talk to you, and when I did, I had to walk you home. And you know the rest of the story. Now, I'm in love with someone who doesn't fit the mold that my farm family expects. She is exciting, funny, very loving, very pretty, and intelligent."

"Who is this 'she'?" Maria asked, teasing him because she needed to say something after Bill had poured out his heart to her.

"You are something else," he said, laughing and pulling her up close to him. He put his face in her hair and said that he loved the way it always smelled so nice. Then he became quiet. Maria could feel his breath in her hair. Finally, he whispered, "You make me feel like a guy. I want to move mountains for you, and I want to really make love to you."

Sex had come up several times now. Maria knew it was pushing forward more and more, but she didn't know what to do about it. She was at a loss for the right words, ones she knew that he wanted to hear. Thoughts of trying to get birth-control material seemed so remote for her. She had an almost paranoid fear of getting pregnant, and she couldn't begin to explain this to him. She had visions of being pregnant, all alone, and with nowhere to turn.

Maria thought she would do anything he wanted her to do, but having a sexual relationship was something else again. She felt a mixture of fear and fire when she thought about sex. To give herself a chance to think and regain her composure, Maria lay down on her stomach on the blanket, put her head down, and closed her eyes.

Something was tickling her arm. It was a tiny leafy branch in Bill's hand. She turned over, looked at him, and smiled. He put his hands in her hair and stroked it. They didn't say anything for a while. Finally she said, "No matter what happens to us, I will never forget you." She closed her eyes and the tears started to run down her cheeks again. "I wish I could stop crying around you. It's just that you touch my heart with the things you say and do for me, and it makes me cry for some reason."

He said, "I wish I didn't make you cry. That isn't what I intend to do when I tell you how I feel, but I take it as a compliment that you care for me so much that you cry."

"I must be a mess, with my red eyes." Maria wiped her eyes and tried to put a smile on her face.

"Yes, you are, but you are an adorable mess." Bill jumped up, then reached down and pulled her up, too. Maria knew he couldn't take anymore tears today and neither could she. He put his arms around her and twirled her around in the grass. They went faster and faster. It felt good and got their blood moving. It was getting really cold out, with a breeze coming in across the course. "Let's run to the Union and get something to eat," Bill said. "I'm starving."

It felt so good to have fun with him. He took her hand and they began to run. Trying as hard as she could, she couldn't get even with him when he was running. "You run pretty well for a girl," he said and laughed.

"Where did you learn to run so fast?" she asked, breathing hard with the effort of trying to keep up with him.

"I had plenty of practice running away from my brothers." He slowed down so that she could catch her breath. Bill wasn't breathing hard; he was in such good shape.

6. Maude's Threat

You cannot separate the just from the unjust
and the good from the wicked,
for they stand together.
—Kahlil Gibran

They flew down the stairs to the cafeteria with pink cheeks and love in their eyes. Maria looked over the board and told Bill what she wanted to eat and drink. Bill had just placed the order when Maria felt someone come up behind her. She turned, and there was Ed, smiling and looking at her in a very intimate way.

"It's nice to see you," he said.

She couldn't have fitted a piece of paper between them. He seemed to be getting a kick out of making her feel a little uneasy. She moved away and looked at Bill.

Bill stuck out his hand. "Hi, I'm Bill Morgan, glad to meet you," but she didn't think he was, judging by his body posture.

Ed looked at Maria with a grin, then looked at Bill and slowly put his hand out to shake Bill's hand, but it seemed with great reservation. "I'm Ed, an old-time friend of Maria's."

What was he doing? He seemed like he was toying with Bill. Was he upset that she was there with Bill? Didn't he think that she had a life of her own? It was the first time she had run into him since she'd started school. She had only seen him from afar, driving to the vet building in his new car, or talked to him on the phone.

"I'm looking forward to our trip to Rock Falls in a few weeks," Ed said, with a big grin on his face.

Maria squeezed out, "Yes, I appreciate your offer of a ride to my family for Thanksgiving."

"We'll have a lot of fun," he said, winking at her.

"I think our food is ready," Bill said, with irritation; she hadn't heard that tone before.

"See you," she said and moved over to help Bill with their trays of food and drinks.

When they found a couple of empty seats in the crowded room, Bill whipped the food onto the table in short order. She knew he was upset, but she waited to see what he would say.

After a few bites of his sandwich, he asked, "Who was that?" He had an edge to his voice.

"Ed is a senior in vet medicine, and my brother-in-law has hired him for the past few summers to work for him. I've known him for a long time because I spent many a week at my sister's home helping her with my five nieces and nephews."

"Well, it seems there's a lot more about you that I don't know," Bill said, with a more relaxed look on his face. "You must be good with kids if you took care of five of them," he said, grinning.

Maria ignored the comment about her babysitting qualities. She thought he was relieved that she hadn't dated Ed, but that he was more of a friend of the family. She reached across the table, took his hands, and said that she loved the fact that he was so protective. She blew him a little kiss across the table. "I'm hungry," she said, picking up her sandwich and taking a big bite.

Bill smiled at her gesture of sending him a kiss, but he asked, "What was the wink all about?"

"I haven't the slightest idea." Maria didn't know what game Ed was playing. "You don't miss a trick, do you?" She laughed as she said it.

"I may be a farm boy, but I am quick when it comes to protecting my territory."

"Let's eat and enjoy," she said, savoring her food and his wonderful company.

"You are a little dickens, you know. I can tell you are the baby of the family."

"So are you; the baby, that is. That's why we understand each other so well. They say the youngest children in a family are the most spoiled, happiest, funniest, and smartest."

"Who are 'they' and what do 'they' know? But on second thought, I like your description of us."

She laughed and finished her food. She thought that she had better watch it, or her clothes wouldn't fit, and Bill would think she was piggy.

Maria began to think about all the things they had said to each other under their tree that afternoon. She wondered if she had made a fool of herself, crying so much. She kept asking herself why she had shed so many tears this fall. It seemed like they came up out of nowhere. She looked at Bill, sitting there eating his hamburger, and sent him a silent thanks for all the love he had shown her today.

They walked back to the dorm, and it dawned on her that Maude had probably seen them together many times, and it must have hurt a lot. Maria suddenly felt guilty about that. She wanted to ask Bill if he had talked to Maude recently, but she didn't have the courage.

Bill said that he was going home to think about them and what to do about a lot of things. "I'll call you tonight. You are my good luck charm; after I talk to you, I can study like mad. I'm going to call you from home on Saturday night and make love to you over the phone."

"That will be some feat. They'll have to write it up in Ripley."

He laughed hard at her comment; she knew he loved her attempts at humor.

Oh dear, she thought, *if Bill calls me up on Saturday night, I'll have to miss his call because I'll be dancing. I will have to call Bobby and change that to Saturday afternoon, unless Bobby is going to the football game—what a mess.* As Shakespeare said, "Oh what a tangled web we weave, when first we practice to deceive." She decided to tell Bobby the truth.

Bill asked her why she was so quiet, and she said, "I was thinking about all the things we talked about this afternoon—some good, some not so good."

When they got to the dorm steps, she hopped up one step so she could be the same height as him and could reach his nose, then she rubbed noses with him. He shook his head and laughed at her. "What was that for? You are full of surprises, but don't stop." He hugged her and whispered that he loved her.

"I'm practicing for winter weather when we won't be able to kiss because our lips will freeze together."

On her way up the stairs, she turned and mouthed, I love you, then continued to the top and waved. He grinned and walked away.

Susie was getting ready for an early date with Chuck at his fraternity house. Maria asked Susie why dinner on Thursday night, and she said that the active members were going out en masse to a big party being held in Des Moines at a brother chapter at Drake University. This meant that the dining hall was freed up for the pledges, and it was a great chance to eat at the frat house without the actives around.

"Did you have another getting to know each other date on the golf course?" Susie asked. "Did you find out lots of good things about your farm boy?"

"I had a great time, and I have a lot to think about tonight. I hope I can study. It's so hard trying to juggle everything."

Susie said, "I talked to the Chi Os about you. They're very interested in rushing you next semester, especially since you'll probably have a 3.0 average."

Rushing was the furthest from Maria's mind at that moment. "Well, I'm happy that they were interested in me. They *are* one of the nicest sororities on campus."

After Susie left, Maria said to herself, *Time to bite the bullet and call Bobby.* She didn't look forward to breaking their date for Saturday night. *This is going to be hard to do,* she thought. She got the campus phone book out to find out what the number was for Friley Hall, an independent men's dorm. It was a huge place with several levels, and she didn't know what floor he was on. She had never called a guy at school. In the current culture, women didn't call the men unless it was an emergency. The idea was that the men did the hunting and chased their women, not the other way around.

Someone answered, and she asked him how she could reach Bobby Myer. The guy said to call the second floor and gave her the number. She thought, *This is a pain.* She called the new number and the phone rang and rang; nobody picked up. *Great,* she thought, *how am I going to reach Bobby?* She gave up; she would try again after dinner.

Running over to the dining hall for dinner, she decided that she had better exercise some restraint at the buffet tonight. All her life, she'd had to watch her weight very carefully. She was not one of those girls who could eat anything. Her appetite was like a barometer of her emotions. When she was happy, her appetite increased with her delight; it was the first thing to disappear with trouble.

After dinner, the phone was constantly busy; the calls never let up. Guys were calling gals for dates for the weekend. Maria thought, *I'll wait until tomorrow and try to reach him during the day on Friday.*

Maude's face kept popping up in Maria's mind as she tried to read an assignment. She looked over to the corner, and the elephant was still there, waiting. She had so many problems, she didn't know which one he was waiting for anymore. What kind of a relationship did Maude and Bill have in high school? Maria had never had such an enduring love with her little boyfriends in junior high and high school. But she had never lived in a small farming town where all the activities centered on the church, either; where families were always together at all the church socials and Sunday-school classes.

Maria began the wondering game with herself, which was always dangerous to play. She began to list all the things that she and Bill hadn't had time to even touch on during their incredible love affair. She ticked off things like religion, where to live, careers. *Maria, you are getting ahead of yourself. Haven't you heard of patience and trusting that you and Bill can work out a lot of things slowly?*

She heard some voices close to her door, listened carefully, and thought, *My gosh, someone is talking to Maude outside my room.* What was Maude doing at her door? She froze for a moment and then said to herself, *Stop being such a baby, get up and open the door.* She did just that and found Maude standing a couple feet from her, and she was mad.

Maude was taller and outweighed Maria by twenty-five pounds. She had a flat face, wide with heavy cheek bones, straight brown hair cut close to her head in an athletic style. She wouldn't win a beauty pageant, Maria thought.

Maude said, "I've come to have it out with you."

Maria was so surprised at Maude's aggressive behavior that she didn't think, she reacted with anger. No one was going to go after her like that. "What do you mean, have it out with me?" Maria yelled at her. She was ready for a fight because she knew it had to do with Bill.

"Bill's been my boyfriend for a long time," said Maude, "and you think you can come between us? Well you can't. My parents have promised that they will give us over two hundred acres of prime Iowa farm land when we get married, and Bill's parents have said that they would match the acreage. It means that Bill and I will have a wonderful place to raise our children. I was born and bred on a farm. I know how to be a good farm wife." She was acting so sanctimonious that Maria thought of a chicken fluffing her feathers at another chicken and strutting around the barnyard.

While Maude was talking, Maria couldn't help smiling at the funny image in her mind. This seemed to infuriate Maude. Maria thought to herself, *How can I make this meeting less confrontational?*

She also wanted to end the scene, because quite a few people were gathering around them, listening. Maude was so mad, she was unaware of her audience. And Maria was expecting a call from Bill any minute now.

"Are you sure that Bill wants to stay on the farm? He seems slated for bigger, ah, I mean different, things."

"How would you know? You haven't known him all his life, like I have." Maude continued to fluff her imaginary feathers in Maria's mind.

"People change when they grow up. They go away to school and suddenly they see a whole new world open up to them."

"And I suppose you are the one who is going to show him this new way," Maude said, with a clipped little tone in her voice.

More people were gathering now, having seen the crowd at the end of the hall. Maria thought their argument would probably end up in the college newspaper if there was reporter in that bunch of onlookers.

Maude was hurting, and Maria didn't blame her. If it had been the other way around, Maria would be dying of pain. *Losing Bill would be too hard to bear,* she thought. "I don't know, but I hope so," Maria responded carefully.

Maude looked as if she was either going to try to hit Maria or cry; Maria wasn't sure which. "I'm going home this weekend because Bill will be there seeing his folks" Maude said. "My folks told me that he was coming home. They saw his folks in church last Sunday. My folks said that the Morgans were excited to see him and told my folks to make sure that I came over to their house this weekend. They like me. They say that I am like a daughter to them already," she bragged.

Hearing those last words made Maria feel incredibly empty, but she tried not to show it. Her hands got cold, which was a sure sign that her emotions were going wild. Her mind started racing from one thought to another. What in the world was she going to do? Both sets of parents love Maude and can't wait to shower her and Bill with their precious Iowa soil for their wedding. How will Bill be able to stand up against the tide? What did she have to offer in exchange for his love? Daughter of divorced parents, city girl, no religion to speak of, and certainly no big dowry to help them get started.

Maria felt sick to her stomach. "I've got to study," she said, "so please go." Maria was finished, exhausted, discouraged beyond measure, but she didn't want Maude to have the satisfaction of knowing it.

Maude said as she started down the hall, either sure of herself or giving the performance of her life, "Don't forget what I said. Bill and I are going to get married. It's a given."

Maria remembered something a friend had told her after they'd had a little fight. She called after Maude, "Be careful to keep your words soft and sweet, Maude, in case you have to eat them."

Maria lay down on her bed and put her pillow over her face. What was she going to do? At least it was out in the open, now. Maude had confirmed everything that Maria basically had surmised, but now it was real. She couldn't dismiss it; she got it straight from the horse's ass, so to speak. Though laughing at her little joke, she still didn't feel good. She wished that Susie were there to talk with her. It amazed Maria that Maude chose the evening that Susie was away to come down to see her. She guessed it was meant to be.

Maria lay on her bed for a long time, trying to compose herself enough to study for tomorrow. What was she going to say to Bill when he called? She had to be honest, but how honest? Anything that she could say might come back to bite her in the butt.

The phone had finally stopped ringing; quiet hours were on and everyone, including Maria, was trying to study, but Maria was too preoccupied. Her mind was playing tricks on her because so many things had happened to her today. When the day had started, she had felt so good; now she was in the depths of despair. She had never thought that her freshman year would be an emotional roller coaster.

She was still lying in her bed, looking at the ceiling and clutching her pillow to her stomach for comfort, when she heard the phone and knew it was Bill. She just knew it. She hurried down the hall to answer it. "Hello."

Bill said, "How did you know it was me?"

"Sometimes, I can tell whose calling me, especially if I like them a lot."

"What's wrong? You aren't happy. What's happened since I left you?"

From the very start of their relationship, Maria had decided that she would be as honest with Bill as possible in all circumstances. There was something about him that demanded it. The only fib she had told him was when he asked who had been on the phone, and she hadn't wanted to say it was Ed, for some reason.

"Maude came to my room after dinner and told me that you and she were planning to get married," she said softly.

There was a long pause while Bill cleared his throat a lot. Finally, he said, "There is only one thing for you to remember, and that is I love you."

Choking back the tears, listening to him, knowing that their lives were going to fall apart when he went home on the weekend, Maria felt defeated. He couldn't withstand the families' pressure on him.

He said, "Did you hear me? Did you hear what I just said? Say something, please, Maria."

She cleared her throat and tried to speak, but the tears were coming fast and furious, and she was croaking instead of talking.

"I'm so sorry that I haven't been able to get Maude to understand that we are finished," Bill said. "I've been talking to her about it until I am blue in the face ever since I met you. I've tried to let her down gradually, but she won't take no for an answer. It's been weighing on my mind for weeks. She just called and threatened me."

"She did what? What kind of a threat did she make?"

"She said that our love affair was just a passing fancy, and once I got over it, I would be back with her. She is going to tell her folks that we have been intimate all fall and that I owed her an engagement ring to make a decent girl out of her."

"She is really playing hardball, isn't she?" Maria said, having found her voice again.

"My only defense is my word against hers as far as the intimacy goes."

"I can't imagine making someone marry me by threatening them. What kind of a marriage would that be in this day and age?"

"Let's just make our dinner plans," Bill said, switching topics rather abruptly.

Maria knew that he was at the end of his rope right now, and they needed to change the subject. She was relieved to not have to think about Maude for one minute longer, or forever, for that matter.

"All right, my love, give me your plan."

"Do you want my dinner plan or my other plan?"

"I'd like to hear the dinner plan first, and then the other plan, because I work better on a full stomach." She was trying to pull them out of their funk; she heard him laugh.

"I'll pick you up at five thirty in my limo and whisk you away to our secret castle, where I will raise the drawbridge over the moat and keep everyone out."

"Am I going with King Arthur or Bill Morgan?"

"That's one of the reasons I love you, you get my attempts to joke. By the way, I am Sir Bill from the land of great possibilities, not King Arthur," he said, laughing.

"All right, Sir Bill, what's your other plan, oh magical knight of great possibilities?"

"I want you to come home with me this weekend and meet my parents."

Maria was so surprised, she squeaked when she spoke. "That will be something."

"I know, I've really put you in the hot seat, but I can't think of any other way to change things for us. When Maude told me she was coming home and what she planned to say about me, I thought that your wonderful presence would help us. Seeing you in person is a lot different from me trying to explain you to my folks and how I feel about you."

"Fine, Sir Bill, oh knight of great possibilities; perhaps this is our only chance or possibility to win over your parents, the king and queen." She gave Bill a lot of credit for doing this, and she wanted to go down fighting, win or lose.

"You're my girl, Maria. Let's have dinner like we planned and then drive home after dinner and surprise them. I know I'm asking a lot, but I think it is the only way. You will delight them like you have me."

"I will do anything to help us, but I think you should let your mother know that you are bringing home a surprise guest, so she can clean up the guest room. If I were her, I would be upset that another person arrived with you without any warning. I love you, and I hope I can show them how much this weekend."

"We are a matched pair, and no one is going to change that. Do you feel better now?"

"You have an amazing way about you, Sir Bill; it's like magic to me. I can't wait to see you tomorrow afternoon."

"I wish I could show you how much I love you. Someday, I plan to. Sleep well and think about us being together," he said quietly.

"I am in your arms right now." Maria hung up the phone.

Susie was coming down the hall from the shower, all wrapped up in her big fuzzy towel and looking very refreshed. "So, how's Sir Bill?"

"I didn't know my roommate had such sharp hearing. How long were you listening to my conversation?"

"I just slowed down a little to walk back to the room with you," Susie said with a laugh.

"Oh, I'm so touched by your thoughtfulness of waiting for me. Did you think that I couldn't find my way back by myself?"

"You are so gone over Bill, I don't think you could find your way to the Union right now." Susie ran down the hall to get away from Maria.

Maria took her time walking down to their room. Upon entering, she looked at Susie and said, "I need a favor."

"You're pregnant, and you need me to take you to the doctor," Susie said with glee.

"No, smarty pants, no one has gotten into my pants, yet."

"So I bet it has to do with Sir Bill," Susie said, making awful faces at Maria.

"Will you stop calling him that?" Maria could just see her popping down the hall when she next saw him and calling him Sir Bill. He would be hurt to think that Maria had told Susie his fantasy name.

"So what's the big favor?" Susie asked, as she rubbed her hands together.

"If I can't reach Bobby tonight by phone, I want you to go over to Friley Hall with me tomorrow. I need to leave him a message that I can't keep our dancing date for Saturday."

"Where are you going to be Saturday? And why are you making dates to dance with what's his name if you are so madly in love with Bill?"

"I'm going home with Bill to meet his folks," Maria said nervously, ignoring Susie's question about Bobby. It was too complicated and confusing to discuss with her razor-sharp roommate.

"You're what?" Susie said with amazement. "You are really serious about him, and he must feel the same if he's taking you home to mother."

"It's all happened so quickly that I've been caught. I've tried two or three times to get hold of Bobby to tell him I can't meet him, but no one answers the darn phone at Friley Hall."

"When do you want to go? I'll just have to save you."

"I can go first thing in the morning. When can you go?"

"That's fine with me, I don't have a class until ten."

"Thanks, Susie, I owe you one. I'm going to try one more time tonight before I start to study."

Maria went to the phone to try to reach Bobby. He was calling her at that very moment. As she picked up the phone, he said, "Is Maria there?"

"I'm so glad it's you," Maria said. "I've been trying to reach you for a couple of days, but no one in that dorm of yours ever picks up the phone."

"So what's up?" Bobby asked.

"I've been invited to a friend's house for the weekend, unexpectedly." She wasn't telling a lie, because Bill was her friend.

"Sorry we can't dance Saturday," he said. "I've been working out a couple of new routines to try with you. What about sometime next week?"

"Call me when you get a chance next week, and we'll figure something out," Maria said.

"Get ready for some fast dancing when you get back."

"I will, Bobby, thanks for understanding. Bye-bye."

Maria returned to her room. "Well, you're off the hook, Susie, and so am I. Bobby was calling me just as I picked up the phone to call him. I told him I had been invited to a friend's house for the weekend."

"Some friend. Are you sure this is a good idea?" Susie asked.

"I'm so nervous about the whole thing, I wish I didn't have to go, but Bill's in a mess that isn't his fault, and he needs me to help him out of it. I'm sorry I can't tell you anymore right now, but sometime when we work it out, I'll tell you."

"Good grief, it sounds like he murdered someone."

"No, but it involves another person who is lying about Bill."

"My, this is interesting. I can't wait to hear the next installment of this soap opera," Susie said with a grin.

"Susie, I know you are trying to make things a little lighter for me. Thanks for everything. I'm so glad you are my roommate." With that, Maria opened her book and started to read, but it was hard to concentrate. She was so tired and worried about the meeting with Bill's folks that she could hardly remember what she had just read. Was college supposed to be so full of emotions? She must have lived in a cocoon before.

7. A Romantic Dinner

If I could reach up and hold a star for every time you made me smile, the entire evening sky would be in the palm of my hand.
—author unknown

Maria shouldn't have tried to study in bed. She woke up in the morning with her book lying next to her, poking her in the arm. She sat up and thought, *Today is the day I'm going to meet Bill's parents. How am I going to make them like me? How am I going to help Bill?*

She shook her head and got up to face the day and her first class. She wasn't hungry. Maria's barometer, her stomach, was acting true to its nature. Grabbing her books, she walked to the library for a fresh place to start the day, but she just sat in a cubicle, put her head down on her books, and closed her eyes.

Oh my gosh, she thought, when she looked at the time; she had slept through her lecture. She quickly left the library to be sure to be on time for her next class; once there, the morning flew by. By noon, she was hungry. Hurrying back to the dorm for lunch, she saw Ed driving over to one of the upper-class dorm's lunchrooms where he worked at a waiter's job to make a little extra money during the year. He saw her, gave her a big smile, and waved as he drove down the road.

Why did she feel a little flutter in her stomach when she saw him? It must have been left over from all those years that she'd had a crush on him.

After lunch, Maria was confused about what to take to Bill's house. She stuffed a few things into a little suitcase. Boy, she wished she had a duffle bag. A suitcase looked so prim and proper. Why hadn't she thought about bringing one of her athletic bags with her from home? She was sure they were gone now, since her mother had sold the house moments, it seemed, after Maria left for college.

Maria was still tired from all the emotions whirling inside her last night. She lay down and fell asleep. When she woke up and realized that she was missing class, she still couldn't get up. She fell on her bed and closed her eyes again. As she drifted off, she had a moment of guilt before she was asleep.

Susie came in and made a little noise. Maria looked at her with sleepy eyes and asked what time it was. Susie said, "Five; look at the clock."

"Oh my gosh, Bill's coming in a half hour." Maria felt like she would never wake up. She lay back on her bed and tried to shift into gear. Sleeping during the day was very confusing, and she hated the feeling. She stumbled down the hall to take a shower. Maybe that would bring her into the land of the living.

To save time, no make-up, she decided. Bill didn't like her to wear it anyway, but she cheated a little sometimes. The shower felt good and washing her hair was a must, even though it wasn't going to be dry when she met him.

Bill drove up in a Ford borrowed from one of his frat brothers. He parked it and bounded up the stairs to the dorm. Maria's room had windows in the front of the building, and she could see everyone coming up the stairs if she were looking outside. She had been.

Susie gave her a thumbs up sign on the sweater and wool pants that Maria had decided to wear. Susie said, "I love your peach-colored sweater with the brown pants, but I hate the snow boots that you have on. Wear some evening shoes."

"Not on your life," Maria said. "I didn't grow up in Illinois for nothing. If you will take note, I have my nice shoes in a bag that I am clutching, along with this goofy suitcase and my purse. Ugh! Bill is going to think I'm staying for a week." On a whim, she stopped and took her Marshall Field's special with her. It was a beautiful, green, long wool skirt and matching sweater. The set had been on sale at a very special price to entice buyers into the store. She had loved it the instant she saw it and just had to have it. Spending so much of her clothing allowance on one outfit would not have pleased her father if he'd known about it. She folded them into the bag with her shoes.

"Be good and be careful," Susie advised.

"I will. I'll see you Sunday night."

Maria hurried down the hall, carrying her suitcase and bags. She felt like a bag lady. She must have looked a little flustered because Bill came over and asked, "What's the matter? Are you feeling all right? Your hair is wet."

"Ugh, you noticed? I don't feel like I am put together."

"Take it from me; you are well put together in every sense of the word."

"Thanks for the back-handed compliment, I think. Please help me with this stuff. I wish I had a duffle bag, but, of course, I left that at home. Your parents are going to think that I'm moving in for a week."

"I have lots of duffle bags at home, and you can have as many as you want to bring back to school," he offered.

Maria looked at him and thought, *He's trying to get a reading on me.* He was right to be wondering. She felt cranky because of the circumstances. He looked so concerned. She thought, *He's very alert to moods.* That made her pause and realize that he was worried about this weekend, too. *Stop thinking about yourself and think about him for a while.* He melted her heart when she least expected it.

"Let's dance," she said. She picked up her purse and shoe bag and started out the door. Out of the corner of her eye, she watched him grab her suitcase and hurry out after her. His lean body was in great shape, not to mention his muscles. She didn't think he even thought about what great shape he was in. *What does he do to stay so trim and strong?* This was just the beginning of the questions she had about him.

"What do you think of our wheels?" he asked.

"Our what?"

"The car, 'wheels' is slang for car in farm country," he explained.

"It's wonderful, and I am thrilled we're going out for dinner in it."

That statement seemed to please him. He walked around the car, opened the door for her, gave her a kiss on her nose, and smiled. "Are you hungry?"

"Is the pope Catholic?" She laughed.

"My, you are full of it tonight." He glanced at her quickly with his eyes dancing. "I never know what you are going to say; you keep me guessing."

"Well, you know what they say: 'Keep 'em guessing.'"

"So back to my original question: Are you hungry?"

"I think so, but I have been running around like the proverbial chicken, and when I'm pushed, my stomach always complains. It's just part of me."

"Well, just relax now. I'll turn on the radio, and you try to find some music other than country and western."

"What's wrong with that music?" Maria didn't like country music at all, but they had never discussed music before. Living outside of Chicago and swinging with music from the Trianon Ballroom on the radio every weekend, she loved Big Band music. Bobby, her dancing friend, had told her that various Big Band groups traveled to college campuses. He wanted to take her to the Union when one came and dance the night away to their music.

Bill said, "I grew up on that kind of music, and it is too 'twangy' for me. I much prefer the music the Big Bands play. Once in a while, when I'm lucky, I can get the music from Chicago."

"I'm so pleased that you like Big Band music. Music has always been a large part of my life. My dad use to bribe me with a nice dinner out at a fancy dining room downtown, like the Palmer House, so that I would go to the opera with him. I liked the music for a while. The deal was no complaining about how long the opera was. I usually fell asleep after the first act because I was young. He didn't care; he knew it was being absorbed into my soul."

"Your dad was very interested in a lot of things, wasn't he? He had so many side interests other than his medical profession. I would like to meet him sometime."

"Yes to your question about him, and I hope you get to meet him, too," Maria said with a little laugh.

"You are full of it, and from that laugh, I gather you are feeling better."

Driving south toward Des Moines, they were quiet for a while. The sun had set and it looked cold out there to Maria. She was glad she had her heavy suede coat to wear. Her dad had bought it for her before she left for school, plus she still got her five dollar allowance each week. Betty would have tried to subtract the cost of Maria's coat from her allowance, but her dad just took her shopping one day without Betty and bought it for her. Her dad was a sucker for leather. It was beautiful and had a silky lining. Every time she wore it, she silently thanked her dad. She loved that coat. However, it was a little impractical; there was no hood, and the silky lining, though very comfortable, was not as warm as a wool one. Luckily, she still had a warm wool coat for winter, her old high school standby.

Shivering a little, she cuddled up to Bill. She felt like she could go to the ends of the earth as long as she was with him. The little heater was pumping out warm air, but only for the front seat. Anyone who was unlucky enough to have to sit in the back in cold weather would end up with frozen feet.

Bill had on a dark leather jacket that was trimmed in lighter leather and had a fleecy lining. "You remind me of a flyer in the movies," she said.

"How so?" he asked.

"Your jacket. All you need are a pair of goggles and a helmet, and you are in business."

"And the ability to fly. I have wanted to learn to fly since I can remember."

"I'm an enchantress who has magical powers, and I just knew that about you," Maria said. "But I can't tell how you are feeling right this minute; my powers only reach so far."

"I am just fine," he said, and laughed. He was also dressed in good-looking light wool pants that looked very soft.

Maria said, "I want to feel the material. Do you mind if I run my fingers over your pants?"

He burst out laughing. "You little dickens." This was fast becoming his favorite name for her when he was surprised or delighted by something she'd said. "You can run your hands all over me, if you want."

"I don't want to cause an accident, although I don't see many cars on this road, so I will very gently pat your pant leg and feel whatever I find there."

He was really laughing now at her antics and said that she had better be very careful not to disturb the driver, or he would make her pay later.

"My, this is getting really interesting. What will you do to make me pay for my wandering hands?" she asked with a big grin.

"I think we've got this backward; usually it's the guy's hands that are being pushed back into neutral territory."

"You didn't answer my question; you ducked it," she said teasingly.

"All right, Miss Smarty; I will make you wish that we could spend the rest of our lives together." His tone had changed. He was really serious for a moment.

She touched his face lightly with her hand. She wanted to reach over and kiss him, but thought better of it. She wanted them to get to the restaurant in one piece.

Looking ahead, they could see the lights of Des Moines. By now,

Maria was completely relaxed and hungry as could be. *What a fun date they were having*, she thought.

Bill slowed down, looking for the turn-off to Drake University's campus. The restaurant was on University Drive. It was a great location for the restaurant because it was so close to the campus, making it very accessible to the professors and students.

Bill found the turn-off. He saw the sign about five seconds before she did. "You have very good long-distance vision," Maria said. "It's a lot better than mine."

He seemed surprised at her comment. "I've never really thought about it. Although, now that you mention it, when I'm hunting, I usually spot the deer before anyone else."

Suddenly, he slowed down and stopped in front of a picturesque Italian restaurant called the Italian Garden. He parked in their lot, hopped out, ran around to her side of the car, and opened the door. Maria tried not to be flabbergasted by his manners, but he really amazed her. She was not used to such gentlemanly behavior.

The cold weather was knocking on Iowa's door. She noticed the drop in temperature just since they'd left the college. When the sun went down, the temperature plummeted. Maria shivered, and Bill put his arm around her as they walked to the door—fast. She was glad.

"Hello, I'll be right with you, sir," came from somewhere across the room as they walked into the restaurant. The place was packed with people. Hurrying up to them was charming little man with a mustache, dressed in a dark suit, looking very professional. He gave them a big smile. "Welcome to our restaurant," he said in a big booming voice. His voice didn't match his size, but it was comforting, and he made them feel very much at home.

"Do you go to the university?" the maitre d' asked.

Bill said, "Which one? We go to Iowa State University."

The maitre d' looked a little confused but didn't stay on the subject. Instead, he said that he was pleased that they had come to his restaurant and hoped that they would enjoy their dinner. He looked up Bill's reservation and seated them in the corner, away from the windows and near the fireplace, which had a delightful fire in it. All the tables had candles on them, and they made the room seem to glow. *How pretty,* Maria thought.

"This is a beautiful place, Bill. You have great taste."

"Thank my mother for this one. She found it when she was here shopping one time and we have been coming ever since."

"Well then, thanks, Mom." All of a sudden, her face got red because she had never even asked him what his parent's names were.

"What's the matter?" he asked.

"What are your parent's first names?"

"Bob and Alice. Don't feel bad; I don't know what your folks' names are, either."

"Ruth and Marion," she said.

"Your dad's name is Marion? We live in Marion County. I like the name."

Their waiter came over with hot rolls in a covered basket and butter. They looked at each other and each grabbed a roll. Maria was really hungry. She ate that roll as slowly as she could because she didn't want to look like little Miss Piggy, but she wanted to stuff the whole thing in her mouth at once. She could tell that Bill was hungry, too. He took one big bite, swallowed, and finished off the roll in another bite. She loved the way he ate. He had a certain charm about him, even when he was starving.

Their waiter came back with a small dish of yellow, greenish oil and a bottle of Chianti wine. He poured them each a large glass of wine. She had wondered whether they would card her, but they didn't, and she was relieved. Maybe they thought she was older because she was all dressed up, her hair had finally dried, and she was with Bill, who looked like he could hold his liquor.

"What is that oil for in the little dish?" Maria asked. Her father had taken her to many places for dinner, but that was a new one on her.

"You don't know what the oil is for? I can't believe my little Chicagoan hasn't seen that before. Here we are out in the sticks, and we've stumped you."

She had decided that it was for dipping one's bread, but she was going to play it to the hilt. She took the dish and put it in front of her. "I know. It's for ladies to use to keep their hands from chapping," and with that remark, she started to dip her hands into the oil.

"Don't do that," he said, laughing so hard, she thought he'd choke.

She stopped and laughed, too. It was a first for them, eating out together at a lovely restaurant and with alcohol, besides.

On cue, their waiter, who no doubt had been watching them, came over with the menu. "May I suggest the lemon chicken?"

"Why don't we get two different dishes and then we can taste each other's? Do you like chicken, veal, or beef, Bill?" It was amazing that she was so in love with him and didn't know many of the basics about him, including meat preferences.

"May I suggest the veal parmesan for the other entrée?" the waiter said.

"That's fine with me," Bill said.

By the time their salads arrived, they were each working on their second glass of wine. Maria, especially, was feeling a bit giddy. She could tell that Bill was feeling the effects, too.

"Please, bring some more rolls," he said to the waiter. "I've got to soak up some of this wine so I don't drive off the road tonight."

When the waiter returned with their entrees, they were already getting full from bread and salad. He set the plates down. The food looked and smelled delicious, and they were glad that they had brought their college appetites. The waiter offered more wine, but they both waved him away. Maria crossed her eyes; she couldn't handle any more wine. Bill started to laugh again.

"I didn't know that your eyes cross. I'm not sure that I like the fact that my girl can't see. What other little problems are you hiding?"

Maria let that question hang out there, even though Bill was half-kidding, but really wanting to know her better. She thought all her warts would show soon enough.

After dinner, the waiter asked if they wanted coffee. Bill nodded, and the waiter brought them two steaming cups full to the brim. Maria needed the caffeine to keep her awake and keep Bill company. She always hated to see one person driving and everyone else sleeping.

It was getting late, around nine o'clock, when they finally got out of there. Bill had paid with cash. Maria didn't know how much the bill was, but he did not seem surprised, and he gave the waiter a generous tip. He was so smooth. His mother had taught him how to act in social situations.

The weather was getting even colder. In the car, Bill turned on the little heater and reached over to pull Maria right up next to him. He kissed her carefully and lightly, going from her mouth to her cheek to her neck and back again. It tickled and made Maria laugh.

She said, "You have magic lips."

He laughed and shook his head. "You're the magic for me."

Bill shifted the car into gear, and they went to find Route 5. The countdown was on. Maria wondered if she would measure up to whatever the family expected.

Even though she was watching as carefully as she could, Bill had spotted the Route 5 sign long before it came within her eye range. He made the turn easily. He was sure of where he was, could see like an eagle, and had the coordination of an athlete. She was very comfortable riding in the car with him.

Both of them were thinking about seeing his parents. Bill turned on the radio and was able to get the WGN radio station from Chicago. Mario Lanza was singing an aria from *Madame Butterfly*, and the words sent goose bumps up and down Maria's arms.

Bill looked over at her. "He's singing the song for us."

She cuddled up to him. "We'll have to get that record sometime, along with 'Blue Moon.'"

He glanced at her again and gave her a little hug.

With music playing in the background, Bill said, "My folks are nice people. You'll like them. They won't say anything to hurt your feelings, but I'm not so sure what will happen when Maude's family comes over with Maude. She is hurt. She thought it was a done deal with me, but it wasn't. Even if I had never found you, I was finished with that relationship a year ago. I promise I'll run interference when they come."

"It sounds like a football game we'll be playing," Maria said.

"Sort of, and I want us to end the game, winning and scoring a touchdown."

She felt like laughing, Bill was such a guy. It was obvious that his daddy had taught him well about standing up and being counted, and his momma had loved him a lot. No one could act so loving without having been shown it all of his life.

Maria put her hand up to his face and patted his handsome cheek. He put his hand over her hand and held it there for a long time. She felt him smiling. His physical touch was so soothing to her. Were they a matched pair?

Bill turned the car off Route 5 onto a gravel road which led to another gravel road. Maria was glad he knew his way; she was completely lost, and there wasn't a streetlight to be found. The stars were brighter, if that was possible, than when they'd seen them by the Ag Building. The sliver moon was hanging up there, keeping the stars company, and it was dark and beautiful—if you knew where you were; otherwise it was scary.

They had lost their romantic-music station from Chicago, so Bill turned off the static. Occasionally, Maria could see lights in a house off the road or hear a dog bark, but that was all. It was quiet out in the country, and it reminded her of nights in the mountains of Wyoming. Maria had to say something; it was so quiet and so was Bill. He was concentrating on turning into the right lane to his house. "All we need now is a coyote howling out there," she said.

"How do you know about coyotes howling?" he asked, only half paying attention.

She wondered if he was really listening to her because he was watching the road so intently. "Did you know that several members of our family were eaten by wolves in Wyoming?" Nope, she had lost him.

He was slowing down and was peering out at the road. All of a sudden he laughed.

"What's so funny?" she asked.

"Look on the mailbox; a big sign saying, 'Stay Away, We're Having a Party.' That's one or both of my brothers being smart. They are probably there, waiting to jump on me when we get to the door."

"I'm glad they are here," she said. "They will break the ice."

"If they don't break my bones, first," Bill said.

"I never had any brothers; just Don, my brother-in-law, who was too old by the time he married my sister to do stuff like that," she said.

"I can guarantee, if he'd had a younger brother, Don probably would have done some horsing around. Guys always want to fight and wrestle with each other, no matter what age they are. They are always trying to see who's the strongest. It's just instinct."

By this time, Bill had turned off the car and the lights, and they were coasting silently down the slight decline in the lane right up to the side of the house. There were several extra cars parked out there.

"Ugh, they are here waiting with my parents. Right now, my mom is saying that there will be no roughhousing tonight, and they are nodding but are ready to grab me. Let's go in through the back door, quietly, and surprise them. Don't shut the car doors," Bill said. "I'll come back later for our clothes and take care of everything."

8. Meeting Bill's Family

Where we love is home,
home that our feet may leave,
but not our hearts.
—Oliver Wendell Holmes

Maria thought that it would be fun to sneak up on Bill's brothers. He took her hand and helped her navigate around some potted plants. His border collie had come off the front porch and ran around the side to see Bill. "Come here, Shep," Bill whispered. He bent down, gave the dog a pat, and, luckily, Shep didn't make a sound. Bill was his friend. He bounded up the back stairs to go in with them.

"Are you ready?" Bill whispered and squeezed Maria's hand.

"Hold my hand tight and don't let go when we get inside," she said.

Bill nodded as he carefully opened the back door. Shep bounded past them and ran down the hall in front of them. Maria heard one of Bill's brothers say, "How did Shep get in here?" By then, she and Bill had slipped down the hall. Bill pulled her into the living room and yelled, "Surprise!" His family had been looking out the front windows and they jumped. His brothers sprung around and rushed over to Bill in a flash.

"Hold off, you guys; don't hurt the lady," Bill said, laughing.

"That's not fair; you're hiding behind the lady's skirt," the bigger brother said.

Bill's mom came over to Bill and pushed her sons away. "So good to see you again, Son," she said, as she gave him a hug. "Now, introduce me to this nice lady standing here."

Maria suddenly realized that Bill had not called before he came to warn his mother about Maria. What a coward.

By this time, Bill's dad had crossed the room and had given Bill a big bear hug. Maria saw his eyes light up when he looked at Bill. His father turned slightly and gave her a welcoming smile that was so like his son's smiles.

"Go on, Bill, introduce us," his mom said.

Bill laughed out of nervousness. "This is Maria Banks."

"I'm so glad to meet you." She smiled and gave Maria a little hug. "I'm Alice and this is Bob, Bill's dad." His dad just stood there, smiling and enjoying the moment. *Bill's parents look like they belong to each other,* Maria thought, as she felt the welcoming energy in the room.

One of the brothers said, "I'm Bob, Jr., and this is—"

"Luke, the smarter one," said the other brother, cutting in.

"Who said so?" Bob, Jr., asked. They started to push each other a little and then they said, almost in unison, "Now that we know little brother has found his way home and is safe, we've got to go. We're married, you know. We'll see you tomorrow night at the party."

"Take that sign off the mailbox when you go. I don't want the neighbors to see it tomorrow," their father ordered. "Otherwise, our neighbor, Bessie, will be over asking what kind of a party was it."

Bill's brothers said, "We'll get you tomorrow, little brother, and see who is the strongest." Then, as if their manners had kicked in, they looked at Maria and said that they were happy to meet her. Bill's mom smiled.

So, there is going to be a party tomorrow night, Maria thought. She looked at everybody and just smiled. Realizing that they were waiting for her to say something, she squeezed out a comment to the effect that she was happy to be there. She didn't know what else to say without sounding stupid.

Bill's dad said, "I'll help you bring in your things from the car. Whose car is it, anyway?"

"I borrowed it from a frat brother," Bill said, as they walked outside.

"Come on, Shep, you're not supposed to be in the house," Bob called. The dog was so obedient that he jumped up, wagged his tail, and ran out with them.

Alice put her arm around Maria's waist. "Come on into the kitchen. Let's have a cup of tea or something. Are you hungry?"

That small act of kindness made Maria feel comfortable with Alice, and Maria finally started to relax. Watching Alice working around her familiar kitchen with such ease and happiness, Maria thought that was why Bill was so calm and secure within himself. Alice just exuded love and had passed plenty of it on to Bill.

Alice was a very pretty woman, trim and tall. She reminded Maria of an athlete, the way she moved so effortlessly. She wondered if Alice had ever played any sports. Bill had her build, with plenty of muscles to boot. His father, on the other hand, was tall, but heavily built, more like a football player. Maria had many questions in her mind, but she had the good sense not to ask too much. There was a time and a place for questions. Alice was probably wondering about her, but was so gracious that she didn't pry. Alice made some tea and took some wonderful-looking cookies out of her refrigerator. She turned and smiled at Maria. *My gosh*, Maria realized, *Alice has given her beautiful blue eyes to Bill.*

"I wonder what's keeping those men?" Alice asked. Both of the women knew but didn't want to put their thoughts into words. Bob was surely questioning Bill about the new lady in his life. He was being a dad, and that's why Bill was such a man's man. He had been raised by one. At that moment, Maria loved his folks for being such caring parents.

"I'm going to go call them. It's getting really late, and I know you both must be tired. Did you have classes today?"

"Yes, but I was finished by noon, which was great because it gave me time to pack up." Maria wanted to mention what Maude had said and done the night before, but she couldn't.

"That Bill, isn't he a rascal not letting us know he was bringing you? Men, they just think that clean sheets magically appear on the beds. It's lucky that I had just cleaned up the guestroom. My little granddaughters spent last weekend with us. After they left, I checked to make sure they hadn't left any food lying around. I was afraid I'd find a piece of candy or something worse. In the country, there are a lot of mice just looking for a tasty tidbit."

Alice slipped on an old sweater and said that she'd be back in a moment. Maria heard her go down the back stairs calling to the men to come in and have something to eat. Someone must have answered to her satisfaction, because she came back in. "It's really getting cold out there, and the two of them haven't the sense to come in. I hope they aren't freezing. I think I'll make some hot chocolate. I didn't realize that it was getting so nippy out. The days have been so sunny and mild. I love the fall."

"I do, too. Bill and I have taken some long walks all over the campus in this nice weather. I hate to see winter come. Bill said that it gets below zero sometimes. If it snows a lot, the school has trouble keeping the sidewalks cleared. When that happens, he has a devil of a time getting to class." Maria shivered when she thought about it.

"This is your first year at Iowa State, I guess," Alice said.

"Yes, I'm a freshman."

"Do you like it so far?"

"It's fine. I have a nice roommate who came from the same high school outside of Chicago that I did."

"You're a long way from home."

Maria was going to respond when she heard the men coming up the back steps, laughing and talking. She knew that her name had been mentioned a time or two, but also knew Bill would never let on to her.

Alice got the hot chocolate ready, poured hot water into the teapot for tea, and added a few more cookies to the plate. The men sat down, bringing the smell of fresh air with them.

"Well, it looks like you gals have been having a hen party while we men have been solving the problems of the country," Bob said with a grin. "It feels good to be in; it's getting cold out there. I put Shep in the barn, but I left the barn door ajar in case he has to do any 'varmint' hunting."

"Let's have something to warm us up, Bill," Bob said. "What do you have, Mother? I see a plate of your special cookies. She's been swatting my hands away from them all day." Bob turned to Maria and asked if she liked chocolate cookies. "I'm sure *you* can have some, you're company," he said, as he winked at his wife.

Bill had quietly sat down next to Maria and casually put his arm around the back of her chair; this did not go unnoticed by Bob. Alice was busy pouring out the hot chocolate and tea, which distracted her from Bill's subtle claim on Maria. Bill reached over Maria to get a cookie, and he brushed her arm with his hand. That also didn't escape Bob's eyes.

"Are you ready to meet the Morgan Clan tomorrow, Maria?" Bob asked. She felt he was feeling her out a little but didn't want to appear too nosy.

"I am. I think your brothers were hilarious with their sign."

The hot chocolate was just what she needed. Even though she and Bill had eaten a huge dinner, the excitement and strain of meeting his family had made Maria hungry again. The hot liquid in her mouth and running down her throat felt so good. Bill's parents had become quiet, and she guessed that they were full of unanswered questions about their son and his new lady friend. Maria was tired all of a sudden and ready for bed. She put her hand over her mouth to try to stifle a yawn, but everyone noticed.

Alice took the cue, hopped up, and said that she wanted Bill to take Maria's things up to the guestroom.

"Which room, Mom?"

"Janie's old room." Alice said to Maria, "You'll like it. It's light and airy."

Bill grinned at Maria. "Let's get you settled before you fall asleep down here."

"There are clean towels in the linen closet. Get some for Maria, Bill."

"See you in the morning; thanks for having me," Maria said with a tired smile.

When they got upstairs, Bill put her things in her room, called to her with his finger, and wrapped his arms around her. "You feel so good." She felt him shiver slightly. He put his lips on her lips and whispered that he would come in and say goodnight to her after the folks had gone to bed.

"Fine," Maria said. "I'll be waiting for you."

She put on her flannel pajamas and was glad she had them. She wrapped her fluffy wool robe around her, slipped into warm slippers, and struggled across the hall to complete her day with some facial and dental care. Glad to finally climb into that inviting bed, she fingered the pretty yellow-and-white down coverlet, pulled it over her snugly, and waited for Bill to come.

The next thing Maria knew, it was morning, and Bill was sitting on the edge of her bed, gently stroking her hair. Where was she? What had happened last night? Boy was she groggy.

"That feels good," she mumbled. "Why didn't you come in and say good night to me last night?"

"I did, but you were sound asleep. Do you remember me tucking you in? I couldn't get your robe off without standing you up, so I just left it on."

Maria had missed out on him caring for her in such a sweet way. *What a shame,* she thought.

Bill lay down next to her on the outside of the blankets. He smelled so good. He was shaved and clean.

"Don't kiss me except on my cheek or nose. I am a mess, and I need to brush my teeth. No fair, you're all shined up."

"You look all sleepy, warm, and cozy under those covers. That is very appealing."

"Well, it's not to me, so do what I say." Maria was still feeling a little out of sorts because of all that had happened since yesterday afternoon. She had awakened in a strange room in a strange bed, however nice it was. She needed to get grounded and get used to her surroundings.

He was quick to pick up on her mood. He just laughed, kissed her on her nose, and gave her a quick hug. He said, "Just remember, I'll make it up to you tonight. You were so great with my folks last night, thanks. I'm going down and see how they are. Come when you can. I'll be downstairs or outside." He hopped off her bed, grinned at her, and went downstairs.

Maria gathered up her toilet articles and took her towels into the bathroom to have a shower. That always did the trick when she was feeling strange; nothing like warm water hitting one's skin to make everything all right.

When she came downstairs, she felt much better than an hour before. She hoped everyone wasn't waiting for her, because she hadn't felt like rushing. There was a note on the kitchen table for her. Bill was out on the farm with his dad, working on something, and Alice had run into town for a couple of things. She would be home by eleven. There were blueberry muffins in the oven keeping warm and all kinds of dry cereal on the table, plus fresh coffee in the pot.

The sun was streaming into the kitchen, the sky was clear and bright blue, and Maria was hungry again. She poured herself a cup of coffee, found the muffins, and made herself a dish of cereal. What a lovely way to spend Saturday morning.

Maria was just thinking that she would go upstairs and get her chemistry book to look over for next week's test when she heard a car pull into the driveway. She looked outside and saw a young woman getting out of the car with an adorable little boy in her arms. The woman came up the back stairs, called "Mom," and came on in.

Maria said, "Hi, I'm Maria, a friend of Bill's."

The woman put her little boy down. He ran over to Maria. "Me want a cookie."

Maria said that she had some nice warm muffins and offered him one.

He looked at his mother; she said, "Yes, sit down, and you can have one."

He pulled himself up into a chair with no trouble, turned around, and smiled at Maria.

As she was getting the muffins out of the oven, Maria asked him, "What's your name?"

He said, "Ben," and grabbed a muffin.

His mother introduced herself. "I'm Jane, Bill's sister; so nice to meet you." She helped Ben get the paper off the muffin before he tried to eat it, too.

"Is mom around?" Jane asked.

"She went to the store for a few supplies for dinner, I think. Alice left me a note because I was a slowpoke and took my time getting dressed this morning. I didn't get down early enough to talk to her."

"You know how farm people are. If they stay in bed for an extra half hour, they get all nervous that they won't get all the chores done." Jane laughed. "I think my mom is planning a get-together tonight with some of the neighbors to see Bill and now, of course, to meet you."

Silently, Maria wondered if that meant Maude and her parents were coming tonight. She said, "I'm so glad to meet you, Jane. Bill has spoken about you a lot. You're pretty high on his list."

"We have always been buds. He is a couple of years younger than me, and I used to try to dress him up like one of my dolls, but he would run away and hide. When we got older, I'd ask him what he thought of various guys I was dating, and he always gave me a straight answer. Most of the guys were low on his list until I started going with my husband, Mark. Bill knew him and liked him, so I felt good about marrying Mark. Bill is a good judge of guys."

"How about girls? How good is he at figuring out girls?" Maria asked.

"I'm not sure; he dated quite a few girls in high school and Maude Jenkins more than the rest. Have you met Maude? She is a freshman, too, at Iowa State. I told Bill she went there to keep tabs on him. She has had her cap set for him for a long time, but I was never sure how Bill felt about her. She seemed pretty aggressive to me."

Maria was all set to ask if Maude would be at the party tonight, but Ben had climbed down off the chair and was running around the room playing airplane with part of his muffin squeezed tightly in his hand.

Jane was up like a shot to grab him and sit him back down in his chair. "You can't play until you either eat your muffin or put it down. I don't want Gramma's floor covered with crumbs."

Maria asked, "Would you like a cup of coffee and a muffin?"

"Thanks, but I'm full from breakfast, and if I drink another cup of coffee, I will fly out the window."

They heard a car drive up. Jane looked out the window. "Mom's back." She gathered Ben in her arms and went out to help her mom with her bundles; she let Ben run around outside for a minute. Maria thought as she followed them, *Jane is a good mother to Ben. He's such a little ball of fire.* She also appreciated Jane's quick appraisal of Maude. Maria had learned an awful lot in a few minutes about her competition.

Alice was all smiles when she saw them. She got out of her car and grabbed Ben, giving him a big kiss. He squealed to be put down, which she did immediately, laughing at his antics.

"Give us some of the bags. We're here to help," Jane said.

"Be my guest," said Alice and waved at the backseat full of bundles.

They all took as many as they could carry and had the morning's purchases inside in no time. "So, Mom, what should I bring to this wingding?"

"Why don't you make your delicious au gratin potatoes for dinner?"

Jane said, "That's easy. When do you want us to come over? I need to arrange a babysitter."

"Seven would be a good time."

Jane scooped Ben up and started for the door. Ben began wiggling to get down, but Jane hung on for dear life. She promised him that he could play with his toy tractor when he got home and before his nap; that seemed to satisfy him.

Alice and Maria had just put the kitchen in order when they heard the men talking and laughing, coming in from somewhere near the barns. Their voices were an automatic signal for Alice to start lunch, and she took a big bowl of homemade beef soup from the refrigerator. Maria was scooping up the dishes from breakfast, Ben's muffin crumbs, and the cereal boxes when they came in with cheeks rosy from the cold.

Bill looked at Maria. When she looked back at him, she lost her concentration trying to balance dishes, crumbs, and boxes. She dropped the boxes, spilled the crumbs, and almost broke a dish or two, but Bill saved the plates in a quick move. True to form, she started to giggle and tried to recover before she made a fool of herself.

Bill's dad was watching the show and stifled a laugh as he sat down. "I see that Mother's got you working," he said.

"I've done no such thing, Bob. Maria just jumped up when I came home from the store and helped me without my saying a word to her. She's great help in the kitchen." She gave Maria a big smile.

At that moment, Maria didn't know who she was in love with more, Alice or her son. She looked at Bob, and he seemed both pleased and confused by what Alice had said. Maria felt that he was trying not to like her and was surprised when Alice paid her such a nice compliment.

"Wash up now," said Alice. "I'm pouring up the soup, and I don't want it to get cold. Maria, would you get some crackers and the fresh loaf of bread out of the pantry? I got your favorite bread, Bill. What do you want on it, boys?"

"I just like it toasted with butter, Mom," Bill said, as he got the toaster off the shelf. He plugged it in, then sat down next to Maria. He reached under the table and squeezed her hand. His touch sent shivers running through her.

Sitting next to him, she could smell the aroma of fresh air that clung to his clothes from the outdoors. "That fresh air certainly makes you smell good." After she said it, she felt that it was a silly thing to say. Maria saw Alice and Bob exchange looks.

"Jane stopped by with Ben while I was gone, and Maria entertained them. That Ben is certainly a little dickens; his mother has her hands full. I'm glad that Jane is so patient. She never seems to mind his antics."

Maria thought, *That's where Bill gets that nickname for me.*

Looking for a refill, Bob held out his bowl for more soup. "Alice is a great cook, isn't she, Bill?"

Bill gave his dad an affirmative nod.

"I think it's real important that a wife be able to cook, don't you, Bill?"

Maria saw Alice look at her husband with irritation.

"Yeah, Dad," Bill said, with a slightly questioning tone.

"Alice, who's coming to our party, tonight?" Bob asked.

Alice was up getting apples and cookies for dessert. She turned to him. "You know who's coming. I told you last week when I decided to have the party." She was definitely irked by his attitude; Maria could see it in her body language. She looked as stiff as a board.

"Well, I forgot what neighbors we are inviting," Bob said.

"Bessie and her sister, the Jenkins and Maude; she's home for the weekend too, Bill," she said, looking at him kindly. "The Olsons, the Gunners, their older kids, and, of course, our family."

"Do you want a cookie?" Bill asked, and grinned as he put one on Maria's plate. He was obviously trying to change the subject.

Maria felt edgy because Bob's conversation had a lot of hidden meaning. She wished he'd either stop or come out with it. What was he up to? Trying to stir up trouble?

Taking a big bite of her cookie, Maria complimented Alice for the yummy lunch. Maria reached over and patted Alice's arm. She was such a dear.

"Do you know Maude?" Bob asked Maria.

Maria was getting angry now. Bob appeared to be playing with all of them and ruining the lunch. They could have been talking about a lot more interesting subjects other than Maude, but he had been controlling the whole conversation with his weird comments. Maria looked straight at him disgustedly, letting him know that she knew what game he was trying to play.

"I've met her twice, and both times Maude was very unfriendly and argumentative with me. I have no idea why she was unpleasant the first time I met her in the cafeteria, but the second time she came to my room and threatened me because I was dating your son."

Bill's father looked hard at Maria and acted as if Maria must be exaggerating. He seemed to be ignoring everything she had just said.

"Great gal; Bill's known her for . . . how long, Bill? Since grade school, is it?" Bob asked.

At that last exchange, Alice jumped up and began clearing the dishes. Maria was right behind her, putting things away in the pantry. Her cheeks felt hot, and she thought that this trip was a waste of time. Evidently, Bob had the pipedream that his youngest son was going to be living near them on a farm with a little farm wife named Maude, and nothing she could say or do would change that.

"Dad, I want to take Maria around the farm in the Jeep. Would you mind if I use it for an hour or so?" Bill was as cool as a cucumber. He wasn't going to let his dad get him upset. Bill was standing up to his father.

"You didn't answer my question, Bill," Bob said.

"You didn't answer mine, Dad," Bill said, his jaw tight.

They were at a standoff. Backing down a little, Bob said that he wanted to take a short nap. "I'd like you to help me buy a part for the tractor and help me fix it this afternoon. Here are the keys to the Jeep. I'll see you in about an hour." He gave Bill a light punch on his shoulder and said to Maria, "Dress up warm; it's cold when the wind blows."

"I'll be glad to help you with the party when I get back from our ride," Maria offered.

Alice smiled the smile that her son had inherited. "Thanks so much; I can use it."

Maria felt that Alice was saying much more with her thanks than she let on. She was encouraging Maria to speak her mind and not back down.

"Mother, why don't you take a little nap with me while the kids are out driving around? You'll feel good tonight for the party, if you do." Bob grinned at his wife, and Maria could see how much he loved her. Alice patted her hair, looked a little flustered, and said that she'd think about it.

"Come on, Maria; let's drive that Jeep all over this place as fast as we can go."

Maria saw the "be careful" look that his mother gave him but didn't say a thing.

Maria and Bill ran outside like a couple of children who had escaped school and the evil principal. She started giggling as she headed for the Jeep. Bill hopped in on his side and started it. Off they went, bouncing over the bumps in the ground, relieved that they were alone and away from Bob. Maria really started to laugh, because it was so much fun, and they hadn't had any time alone together since they got there. The farm was beautiful: barns, long fences, livestock, and trees in the distance. All the buildings were painted and looked well kept.

Bill drove as fast as he dared on the bumpy terrain and yelled, "I don't want you to fall out and get hurt; you mean too much to me."

That was all he needed to say, even though he was yelling over the noise of the Jeep. He made her so happy, and this was fun. They went down to an old wooden bridge and drove over a beautiful creek to a grove of trees on the other side.

"Is this your property, too?" The trees opened up into a little clearing, and there was a picnic table and benches. "How pretty," Maria said.

"It belongs to my folks; the land goes on for quite a way beyond here." Bill turned the Jeep off, reached for her, and pulled her up to him.

"Don't squeeze me too hard; I'm full of soup."

Bill laughed. "I've wanted to do this all morning."

"Even though I fought with your father? He's not going to invite me back."

"Dad was way out of line and after you gave him both barrels, he tried to apologize in his strange way. I actually think he admired your courage. Now, don't talk; just relax, Maria."

Maria shut her eyes because he began weaving his magic by nuzzling her neck, running his lips around her throat and nibbling her skin with his teeth. He found her lips with his and began lightly kissing her. He pulled her closer to him, stopped and gazed at her with those eyes of his. He was trembling a little, and so was she. He kissed her, tongue and all. The urgency of that kiss told her that they had to stop. Bill had not given her a French kiss for a long time because of what it suggested. It was too much for both of them.

"Let's go back," she croaked. The feelings that they had generated were so strong that her stomach hurt. Bill was shaking, and she knew they couldn't stay out there another moment. Bill didn't say anything; he just put his face in her hair, breathing hard for a minute or two, and then drove them out of the trees.

On the way back, looking at the home that Bill grew up in, she marveled at the beauty of it all. The farmhouse was painted white with blue shutters; someone had lovingly planted trees all around it and several small buildings a while ago. They were now giants, protecting the house from the strong Iowa winds in the winter and keeping the summer sun from heating it up too much.

Thoughts of the party kept popping up in Maria's mind, and she felt very nervous about the whole thing. How would Maude handle the evening when she saw Maria? Maude was used to being the favored one; no matter how much Maria wished that Maude wouldn't come, she was whistling in the dark with that scenario. They had become overnight adversaries, and Maria hadn't forgotten Maude's last comment to her.

Bill was strong now because Maria was here, but what would happen during the holidays when he was alone and she was in Rock Falls?

"You're so quiet. What are you thinking about? I hope you're not worried about seeing Maude tonight. I'll be there to support you all evening."

"I'm really thinking more about the future and where I fit into your life."

"All I know is that I have never been in love like this before. It actually hurts sometimes, I want you so badly. That feeling is never going away, no matter what everyone else plans for my future. Keep that in mind tonight if you get uneasy." He stopped the Jeep in plain view of anyone looking out the side windows, turned, and gave her a wonderful hug and kiss, as if to say, *Dad, watch me now.* "Does that make you feel better?" he whispered.

Maria struggled with her answer. He was just sitting there, looking at her and waiting. She smiled at him, reached up, and put her hand on his face for a second or two. "Yes." That was the best she could do for the moment.

They drove up to the back door and got out. Bob came out, all ready to go to town with Bill to buy the tractor part. He had been watching their show.

"You have a beautiful farm and home. It was quite a sight to see when we were driving home across the land," Maria said. She wanted him to know that she did appreciate how hard he must have worked to make the farm into the thriving place it was.

Bob seemed visibly moved by her compliment. He obviously loved his farm. "Thanks," was all he could say, but Maria felt he meant far more.

Her compliment was heartfelt, but Maria was under no illusions about Bob. She knew that he wished she would just disappear so his boy could live near him with a wife whom he knew and trusted. This may have been Bob's dream, but Maria knew that Bill had his own agenda.

"I've got to go in and see what trouble I can get into. Good luck with your hunt for the right part," Maria said.

Bill waved and gave her a big grin. The men got into Bob's truck. Maria watched them drive down the road, then turned and went in to help Alice with party.

9. A Party for Bill

And in the sweetest of friendship,
let there be laughter, and sharing of pleasures.
—Kahlil Gibran

"Hi, Alice," Maria called. "Where are you?"

"I'm in the rec room, trying to decide on how I'm going seat everyone tonight. I'm down the hall on the right," Alice yelled.

Maria hadn't been in that part of the house, yet. She saw Alice standing in the middle of a room large enough to hold a billiard table and a stereo system next to a bookcase holding records and many, many books. On one side of the room, facing the fireplace and a large bank of windows, there were big, comfortable chairs, a huge soft sofa, and a coffee table. The lighting showed a woman's touch, one who loved to read because of the number and quality of the lamps. The whole arrangement reflected Alice's careful planning. She had made it both comfortable and intellectually stimulating.

"What about using the billiard table for tonight to seat people for dinner?" Maria asked. The table would be perfect if they could protect the top. Alice smiled, went over to some big closets, and started pulling out long pieces of finished wood, about three feet wide by six feet long.

"Bob made these for me a few years back just for this purpose. What I'm concerned about is that my friends and neighbors might think that they should be sitting around the dining table instead of a billiard table. Some of my friends are against playing billiards. They think it is the Devil's game."

"If we put a pretty tablecloth over the planks and add a centerpiece, I don't think they will even notice," Maria said, smiling at Alice.

"You are a little dickens, and I love your spirit, Maria. I can see why Bill likes you so much."

Maria was thrilled that Alice had said that to her. Maria's feelings were a little raw since the altercation with Bob, and she appreciated Alice's apparent enjoyment of her company.

As they walked back to the kitchen, Alice pulled a menu, written in her pretty handwriting, out of her apron pocket. She studied it for a moment and, satisfied, returned it to her pocket. She is such a cultured lady, Maria thought, and wondered about Alice's dreams. Maria hoped that Alice had had some of them fulfilled during her life.

Alice opened the refrigerator. Maria saw whipped cream and Jell-O salad, fresh fruit salad, raised rolls, and a big, gorgeous sheet cake with "Welcome Home, Bill" written on it.

"How did you do all this, Alice?"

Alice grinned. "I've been working like a little beaver for a day or so. I like cooking. There is a certain flair required to be a good cook, some creativity. I derive a great sense of pleasure from it.

"Susan and Marilyn, my daughters-in-law, and Jane are bringing most of the hot vegetable casseroles that everyone likes. I think we will have about twenty guests, and we should have a good time. Bob, Jr., Luke, and Bill are in charge of serving drinks. The men are picking up a keg of beer when they are in town and some extra ice. We have wine chilled for the adults and sodas for the children and the adults who don't drink alcoholic beverages. I'm going to make coffee and tea with dessert.

"Dad is grilling the pork roasts and chickens on our outside grill. We'll have to remind him to get the meat on in plenty of time. Most men like to grill over an open fire, and Bob is no exception. I also know he loves to cook and drink with his friends at the parties.

"I need you to help make flower arrangements for the tables with the last of the 'mums that I picked this morning. They are a combination of reds, yellows, and oranges. I have a few more things to do in here, then we can work together." She brought Maria a large selection of vases to use.

Maria worked on the flower arrangements while Alice made a few last-minute goodies for dinner, including a delicious-smelling bar-beque sauce. When Maria finished with the flowers, she took them into the dining room and rec room, placing them strategically.

Alice looked around the kitchen, turned to Maria, put her arms around her, and gave her a gentle hug. She stood back from Maria and looked her in the eyes. "Thanks for everything this afternoon. I wouldn't have finished with time to spare if you hadn't been help-ing me. I can certainly see why Bill is so attracted to you. Now you go upstairs and do whatever you want for an hour or so. I'll tell the men to be quiet when they come in, because the ladies of the house are going to rest for a little while. Would you be down to help with the finishing touches around six or so? I love your sup-port."

Maria felt blown away by her compliments and said that she'd be there. "I wouldn't miss it." Alice had touched her heart, and Maria ached for this kind of mothering. Alice stirred up many emotions in her by being so kind. At that moment, Maria wanted to sit down with her and share their hopes and dreams, but she knew that would have to come later, if at all.

"Now scoot," Alice said. "I hear the men outside, so I'm going to give them their marching orders."

Maria ran up the stairs, elated at how the day had turned out. She wanted to tell Bill how wonderful his mom was to her. He had been right when he had told her not to worry about being with Alice.

Maria looked into the bathroom and decided to take a long, leisurely bath; something that she hadn't done for a long time. There was bubble bath on the shelf by the tub and soft towels next to them. She turned on the water, then went into the bedroom to undress and get her robe. When she returned to the bath, she dipped in a toe to check the temperature, then slipped off her robe and stepped into heaven.

I'd better get going, she said to herself after the water had cooled, and she looked like a prune. It had been nice floating and dreaming in that tub, but now it was time for serious business. She had to make herself look beautiful.

Thank goodness she'd had the brains to throw her new outfit into her bag. She held it up to her, looked in the mirror, and loved what she saw. The wool skirt was jade green; the top was a long-sleeved evening sweater in a lighter shade of green with a little metallic thread woven throughout the fabric. When the light hit it just right, there was a hint of a sparkle. Maria loved that outfit. Only at Marshall Field's could one find something like that.

She put on some green and gold beads that she had found the same day as her outfit and looked at them in the mirror. They were perfect. Little did she know that she would be wearing this at Bill's house when she bought it last summer, foolishly spending most of her fall allowance for clothes on it.

Sitting on her bed in her robe, drying her hair with a towel, she heard someone thumping up the stairs. *That's Bill,* she thought. She ran over to the door, stepped back and behind it, and waited. Slowly, the door opened, Bill's head poked in, and she leaped around the door shouting, "Boo!"

He jumped back for a moment, then regained his position and grabbed her in a big bear hug. "You little dickens," he said. "What if it had been my dad coming up the stairs instead of me?"

"Your dad would never have opened my door."

"That's true. Anyway, you look like a fuzzy caterpillar in your robe."

"I know," she said. "I love it."

He went over to her bed, taking her with him. He sat down and pulled her into his lap. He put his face into her hair and didn't move for a minute or so. "I love the way your hair smells, feels, and that it's long and brown." He gave her another big hug. "I need a shower to get cleaned up. I've been working on the tractor for a long time, installing a new gear, and I feel like I've been rolling in the dirt all afternoon." He gave Maria a little kiss, and she jumped off his lap. He grinned as he said, "You are mighty quick to get away."

"You'd better get going. I don't want you be a mess for your party," she said. "Besides, I need to help Alice with the last-minute things."

"Did you like working for me this afternoon, to make my party a success?"

"I liked working for your mother, smarty."

"I knew you'd like her," he said, and with that he went out the door.

Maria turned her attention to shoes. She decided to wear her higher heels tonight. They gave her a little height, and she had danced with Bobby for hours in them. If she could do that, she reasoned, she could run around downstairs on all those soft rugs in these shoes without pain. What about makeup? If Maude came, Maria wanted to be as much of a knockout as was humanly possible. She carefully applied a little, but not too much. One final look at herself, and she thought, *so be it,* and ran down the stairs, ready for anything.

Alice was already in the kitchen. She looked at Maria and gave her a beautiful smile. "Maria, you look lovely. Green is a good color for you with your pretty brown hair."

"Thanks," was all Maria could say. Personal compliments embarrassed her, especially from older women. Being told she was a good tennis player was one thing. Being told she looked lovely was quite another. She remembered her mother as being very lost in her own world of suffering after Maria's father left. The finality of his leaving caused reverberations of loss to be continually felt by both of them, and they hadn't disappeared for Maria. Instead of joining forces, she and her mother had drifted apart. What might seem like a simple compliment from Alice's point of view took on monumental proportions for Maria, who desperately wanted to be validated by her own mom as Alice had done so effortlessly.

Trying to recover, Maria asked, "Would you like me to light the mood candles in the rec room, now? They will add a lot to the room."

Alice smiled at her and nodded.

As Maria went down the hall, she felt the dark creeping into the house as the sun disappeared. She shivered and turned the lights on in the room. Someone, probably Bill or his father, had a fire burning brightly, adding to the overall effect. Maria carefully placed the candles in strategic places, lit them, and looked at the room, satisfied. As she was standing there admiring her work, she felt Bill's hands and arms wrap themselves around her from behind and felt him kissing the back of her neck.

"What do you think?" she asked.

"The caterpillar has turned into a beautiful butterfly," he said, nibbling her ear.

"Not me, silly, the room."

He glanced around the room. "You are the best part of this room. Did you do this?" He proceeded to nibble her other ear and, picking up a curl of her hair in his fingers, he said, "Did I ever tell you what pretty hair you have? I love the way it curls and that it's long. Don't cut it off."

Turning around in his arms, she said, "I won't, and don't you ever change the color of your eyes."

Arm in arm, they walked back to the kitchen to see what Alice was up to. Bill went down the hall to set up the drink station, saying, "If you need me, I'll probably be outside with Dad."

"The candles are glowing all over the dining and rec room," Maria reported to Alice. "Who's going to choose the music? Not me, I hope."

"Maria, go get Bill and ask him to put some good records on the player. Remind him that we have some neighbors coming who are only happy with church hymns, and I don't want to make them uncomfortable. Have him play only music without words. Also, ask Bill to get the case of wine that is in the other refrigerator and bring it into the kitchen. I'll need two or three bottles opened, too."

Maria went to the back door to deliver Alice's instructions to Bill. Bob looked up, and Maria could tell that he was pleased with her appearance by the admiring glance he gave her. The old boy still had an eye for the ladies.

"I'll play mostly country and western" Bill said. "That's safe, and I'll get the wine for all the big drinkers."

Maria heard cars coming up the drive and felt a little nervous. She hoped they would like her. Lots of people were talking to Bob outside. Then the back door opened and voices were calling, "Hello, hello, we're here."

Alice said, "Come in, we're in the kitchen."

Two very pretty tall gals appeared at the door. "Here's the food for the party. You're going to love it," one of them said.

"Maria, I want you to meet my other daughters, Susan and Marilyn," Alice said.

"Hi, Maria. Bob, Jr., and Luke were gossiping about you when they were together this morning," Susan said with a grin on her face. "They said you were too pretty to belong to this family."

Maria grinned at Susan's good-natured remark, and Alice said, "Gals, please get the front door when the neighbors come. Show them where to put their coats in my bedroom."

Just then, Jane appeared at the door and looked in. "Get ready for action; I'm here."

"So what kind of action?" Marilyn asked. "You're trouble, there's no doubt about it."

"Let's see who can get the drunkest tonight," she said, looking at her mother.

"Wouldn't the neighbors have a field day with that bit of news, especially when the ones who are here give them an eye witness report," Alice said. "But we have company, now, so behave and get the front door before the bell rings off of the wall."

Someone was having a lot of fun ringing the door bell. The girls ran down the hall, yelling, "We're coming, we're coming!"

Maria could hear music playing in the rec room. *Bill has done his chore,* she thought.

He appeared in the kitchen with the case of wine in his arms. He put it down, took a couple bottles out, and uncorked them. "Want some?" he asked Maria and grinned, knowing what wine did to her.

Maria shook her head. She had to keep her wits about her.

Bill added, "I'm going out to push my brothers around for a while. Are you all right?"

Maria nodded, but she really wasn't. She was getting more and more nervous by the minute and was having a hard time disguising it.

She could hear Bob's sons talking and laughing outside with him. They were probably having a beer or two under the pretense of grilling. "Go on and have some fun at your party," Maria said to her sweetheart.

At the other end of the house, the neighbors were streaming in and chatting with Alice and her family. Everyone was ready for a party. Maria wondered if Maude was there. *Hiding in the kitchen pantry would be an excellent idea right now,* Maria thought.

Alice came back to see where Maria was and asked her to get the hors d'oeuvres out of the fridge and to put them on the table in front of the sofa in the rec room. Maria knew that Alice was using the hors d'oeuvres as an excuse to get her in the rec room, obviously to meet Alice's friends. As Maria walked down the hall, Alice put her arm around Maria's waist. "Everything will be all right." Maria loved her even more at that moment.

"Everyone, I want you to meet Maria," Alice announced. "She's visiting us this weekend. Have one of her hors d'oeuvres. They are delicious, if I do say so."

Maria felt everyone looking at her, probably wondering how she fit into the Morgan's family. One of the ladies asked if she was a friend of Jane's.

"I'm friends with both Jane and Bill," Maria answered.

Someone else asked if she went to school with Bill.

Maria said, "Yes, I do." It seemed that her answers satisfied them for the moment. They were nice and meant no harm.

One of the guys asked, "Where are the Morgan Boys? I bet they're out in back pretending they are grilling, so they can drink. Lead me to them. Come on boys; let's get some of that beer." Four guys went down the hall, stopping to fill their glasses with beer conveniently placed by the back door. Maria heard one of them say, "There you all are, you goof-offs." There were a lot of good-natured remarks passed back and forth, punctuated by much laughter. Listening to them, Maria thought that men sure had a lot of fun when they had a chance to get together.

Alice took Maria around to each neighbor and introduced her individually, first names only. They seemed very friendly to her and happy to be there. Maria wondered who Maude's parents were.

"I'm taking drink orders," Susan said, as she moved around the room. Then, giving up on remembering who wanted what, she decided to pour a lot of wine and bring some soft drinks and glasses.

Maude was nowhere to be seen. *I wonder where she is,* Maria thought, hoping she had fallen into a big hole.

Maria overheard Alice talking to a woman named Mabel, inquiring about Maude. *So that is Mrs. Jenkins, the mother of the witch,* Maria thought.

"Oh, she will be along," Mabel said. "She called from Des Moines and said that her hair appointment was later in the afternoon than she wanted, but she did want to get hair done before she came to the party. I hope that will be all right with you, Alice."

"It is fine, Mabel; we have plenty of food, no matter when she comes."

Much stomping and laughing was coming from the back hall.

"Alice, the meat is done," Bob called. "What do you want me to do with it?"

Alice and her kitchen crew all got up at the same time and went to put the finishing touches on the buffet table in the dining room. Maria felt relieved that everyone was so pleasant to her, but she was happy to be called to the kitchen.

"So, Alice, who did all the decorating in the rec room?" Marilyn asked.

"Maria did it. She worked right along with me all afternoon to put this party together."

"It's real pretty, especially the flower arrangements," Marilyn said and smiled at Maria.

"Now someone help me cut up this meat while the rest of you get the casseroles on the table," Alice commanded. "I'll bake the rolls when the oven is empty."

The men were feeling fine, full of beer and wine judging by the rising noise level in the rec room. Quiet would momentarily reign, followed by a loud chorus of laughter.

Gentle Alice became Staff Sergeant Alice when she went down the hall and announced to everyone, "Dinner is ready, come and eat," in her most commanding voice. Maria was sure she wanted to get some food into those men before they drank anymore.

It was a fun and happy crowd, who came to eat, drink, and be merry. They complimented Alice for the enticing spread of food as they filled their plates; her eyes just sparkled as she watched everyone move around the table. Pretty soon, it was quiet, except for the sounds of contented chewing.

"Girls, go see what everyone wants to drink," said Alice, "and take a pitcher full of ice water with you. Play down the beer and wine and offer water. I don't want anyone to have an accident driving home."

The front door opened as Maria was walking down the hall, ready to push the water. She knew trouble had just arrived. Maude stepped in with her new hairdo, a mass of curls around her face.

It softened her appearance considerably, giving her the look of a mild-mannered friend of the family. The gal who visited Maria in the dorm had had hair as straight as string and a highly unpleasant personality.

When Maude spotted Maria, her face registered surprise mixed with hatred. Maria felt as if the wicked witch from Oz had just come into the house. Maude wasn't dressed like the scary witch, however. She had on a long, sweeping, magenta-colored skirt. She took off her coat and threw it on a chair, then she breezed into the rec room amid greetings and compliments. She was wearing a low-cut long-sleeved blouse, and several gold chains were hanging around her neck. Her earrings were long and dangling. Being a walking jewelry case was certainly making a statement, however strange.

Maude ignored Maria completely. Maria knew it must be very upsetting for Maude to see her there; she hadn't planned on that scenario. Maude began campaigning to be the most beautiful and charming girl in the room. Everyone had greeted her as if she were a princess, and she obviously loved it. They complimented her pro-fusely about her outfit, hair, and general good looks. She was the darling of the group.

Maria watched her scan the room for Bill. Maude spotted him sitting with his sister, Jane, and her husband, Mark. He had his back to the door and, at first, didn't realize that she was there. She sat down in a chair next to him, the one meant for Maria. Maude reached over and gave Bill a little kiss on the cheek. Bill reflexively put his hand to his cheek. Maude glanced back at Maria with a confident glare and started talking a mile a minute with Jane, Mark, and Bill. Needless to say, everyone else was watching the whole show.

"I believe you are in my seat," Maria said, walking up to Maude and waiting there. Bill, looking uncomfortable, got up and brought another chair to the table, placing it on his other side. He seemed to want to keep them separated, but Maria didn't want Maude to think she had the upper hand or that Maria was afraid of her. Maria was going to hold her ground.

Maude, however, did not get up. Instead, she leaned in close to Bill. "Bill, dear, would you get me some—"

"Would you get Maude something to drink, Bill?" Maria interrupted in her most charming voice. "We would like to sit here and talk. Wouldn't we, Maude?" Maria sat down in the unclaimed chair. She knew that it would be a mistake to argue over a chair. She stared at Maude. There was a smile on her face, but her eyes were hard.

Jane and Mark were fascinated by the war being waged at their table. Bill scrambled to escape. Maria glanced at the other guests in the room; they all were mesmerized, watching.

Jane and Mark attempted to make conversation with Maude, but she was visibly upset. Maria had decided after the dorm incident that Maude would never talk or act the way she had around her again. She folded her hands and asked, "Are you surprised to see me here?" Watching Maude very carefully—she looked hurt and angry—Maria added, "I was invited by Bill."

Bill came back after a while. He seemed calmer than when he had left. With an air of confidence, he handed Maude a glass of wine. Maria wondered if he had conferred with one of his parents or brothers about what to do.

Now that Maria was in the spotlight, she gave him a quick kiss on his cheek and thanked him for being such a great host. By kissing him in front of all Maude's friends and neighbors, Maria was letting everyone, including Maude, know that Maude was no longer number one in Bill's life. Maria hoped that Maude would give up now and spare them both anymore pain.

If looks could kill, Maria would have died that very moment. Maude said, with teeth clenched, "Bill, I need to talk privately with you. Would you come outside with me?"

Bill gave Maria a quick smile and stood up. "Sure, let's get our coats; its cold out."

Maude threw a jubilant look at Maria, took Bill's arm, and left the room.

Maria was irked with Bill for being so soft with Maude. Why didn't he just say no and stay with her? That would have sent Maude a clear message that the relationship was over.

Alice came in to offer dessert and coffee in the dining room. Maria now felt like an interloper and wondered if she had stepped on too many toes, trying to hold her own with Maude. It seemed as if everyone was being very careful not to say much to her. Alice put her arm around Maria's waist as they were going into the hall and said quietly, "How's it going?"

"I've felt better, but thanks for asking." Maria's stomach was churning like she had just stepped off of a rollercoaster.

Alice's cadre of helpers, including Maria, readied the dining room table for dessert and coffee, then went back to the kitchen. Alice brought out a huge, carefully decorated cake. There was something about a cake that brought back happy memories of birthdays, weddings, and graduations. Alice put a single candle on the cake for the guest of honor.

Bob came into the kitchen looking quite irritated. He couldn't understand the hold up. He didn't like making all his friends wait and asked, "What are we waiting for? Where's the guest of honor?" He had been having so much fun with his sons and the neighbors, he was oblivious to what had been going on with the love triangle.

To Maria, it was agony to wait; time seemed to have stood still since Bill went outside with Maude. Why wasn't he back by now? Was Maude changing his mind? The whole situation was ludicrous. Maude and Bill were keeping twenty people waiting while they ironed out their differences. Why did she ever come home with him this weekend?

She began to feel sweaty and hot and was sure she was going to throw up. She asked Alice if she had some Pepto-Bismol. She hated to add to Alice's concern about her guests, but she needed help and right now.

Alice gave her a big hug. "Come with me, honey, I'll fix you up." Maria followed Alice into her private bathroom, where Alice took a spoon out of her apron pocket. Maria hadn't been in this room before.

Alice must have noticed Maria's quizzical expression. "Bob and I felt the need to add on the rec room, our downstairs bedroom, and this second bathroom a few years ago when the kids were teenagers. Bob didn't want to be upstairs with them when they were playing their music and talking on the phone half the night. Having a bedroom downstairs was much quieter. Also, as we get older, it's safer than climbing stairs. And the added bonus is the pool table in the rec room, which our big family really enjoys, especially in the winter months."

Maria sat down on the side of the tub, and Alice poured her a spoonful of Pepto. Maria swallowed it, waited a moment, then said that she'd better have another one. After popping in another dose, Alice sat down next to Maria and tenderly put her arms around her. She alternately stroked her hair and hugged her, and Maria began to felt better.

"I'm sorry to be such a boob, Alice, but I feel much better with your TLC."

Alice said, "Tonight when Maude made such a fuss and took Bill outside, I agonized over the fact that I had planned a little celebration for Bill. My friends were always asking about me about him, and I thought it would be a good way to get together with everyone and for them to see Bill, too. When you walked in with him, I wondered how all of this was going to play out. I'm so sorry that it turned out this way, but I didn't know how to stop it."

Maria started to cry quietly, hearing Alice's heartfelt concern for her. She told Alice, "I felt on pins and needles all afternoon and evening, and the tension had to come out some way."

Alice held Maria as she continued to sob. When Maria was able to get control of herself, Alice gently wiped her eyes with a hankie.

Maria thought, *I will never forget how sweet Bill's mother has been to me, even if I never see her again.* She looked up to see Jane peering in from the doorway.

"How yuh feeling, girl?" Jane asked.

Alice looked at Maria and asked, "Do you feel better, honey?"

Her tone was so supportive that Maria wanted to declare her love for Alice at that very moment, but said instead, "Yes, much better."

"Mom, the natives are getting restless and may eat someone if we don't get out there and feed them some cake," Jane said, grinning at the two of them sitting on the side of the tub.

They all trooped back to the kitchen. Alice went over to Bob and whispered something to him. Maria heard him go pounding down the hall and down the back stairs. In a few minutes, he came back with Bill, but no Maude. He glanced at Alice with a strange look on his face.

Dessert was finally served. Bill looked beat, but he put on his best face and seemed to be very pleased with his cake. He blew out the candle and everyone clapped.

With dessert over, Maria sensed that the party was winding down. One by one, people came up to Alice and Bob and thanked them for such nice evening. As everyone was leaving, Bill looked over at her with an unreadable expression on his face. Her heart took a dive.

She couldn't tell what he might be feeling. Did he still love her? Did he wish he hadn't left Maude? Maria couldn't wait to talk to him, but she was also afraid of what he was going to say.

Alice walked over to Bill and Maria and gave each of them a hug. "Thanks again for everything, Maria. Without you, I wouldn't have been ready on time. She's a wonderful lady, Bill."

"Come on, Bob, I'm tired, let's go to bed." Alice took Bob's hand and led him from the kitchen.

Bill slipped his arm around Maria's back, and they went up the stairs to her room. He lay down on her bed, and Maria slipped in beside him. Turning to her, he wrapped his arms around her; he put his face in her hair, and she could feel his breath on her neck as they lay there. Maria loved being in his arms. She could have stayed there all night. Maria heard Bill take a big breath and move a little. He loosened his grip on her. "For better or for worse, I love you. Remember that. I can't explain why I'm so drawn to you. It would have been so much easier to keep on dating Maude and to marry her when I graduate from college. That was everyone's plan, and I guess I was partially satisfied with that. But I was just skimming along, not really thinking. Then I saw you one day in the Union with a bunch of girls and something happened to me. I had to find you."

"When was that?" Maria asked. "I did have a strange feeling on one of the first days I was on campus that someone I knew was watching me. I *was* in the Union, and I looked around the cafeteria while I and my friends were getting drinks, but I didn't recognize anyone. I gave up searching, and thought I was just nutty."

"It was probably me that day. I asked my fraternity brothers about you, and they said I should drop by the Union on a regular basis to see if you came in again. No one knew you. I figured that you might be a freshman and had just arrived on campus. I walked around the freshman dorms when I had a chance, hoping to see you. I did that for two or three weeks off and on, and then one day I saw you come flying down the stairs of Stevens Dorm, running off to class or somewhere. You must have been late. I followed you for a minute or two, but I had to go to class, too. I was elated that I had found out where you lived.

"When I went back to the Farm House after class, I asked the president if we could have a get together with Stevens Dorm in the fall. He said that as far as he was concerned, it was a fine idea and would bring it up at the next chapter meeting to get approval from the other actives. At the meeting, they all said yes, bring on the girls, being the healthy males that they are.

"I wasn't sure if you were going to come, but I staked out a space in the front room where we usually have the girls sit, and I waited for you. Had you wanted to come?"

"Actually, I was undecided until the last minute. I had heard about several Greek House parties, and the girls who went to them said that they felt like meat on display. I came because you weren't Greek." Maria didn't mention the warm premonition that had given her the gentle nudge to go.

Bill looked tired from all the emotional turmoil of the night. Maria bet the talk with Maude was a gut-wrenching experience for both of them. She put herself in Maude's place—being so sure of Bill for so long and then seeing him turn away. That would be awful. Would he ever do that to her? "If you ever want to share any part of what happened tonight with Maude or anything, I'm here," she whispered.

"I can't right now, maybe never. I'm going to see my folks at breakfast and tell them as much as I can safely say without hurting anyone."

Bill unwrapped himself from Maria and sat up on the edge of the bed. "I'm going to get ready for bed. I'll be back to tuck you in."

Maria had never seen him look so sad and so beat.

She put on her warm pajamas, got under the covers, and waited for him. She had started to doze when he tapped lightly on her door and came in.

He was wearing new blue pajamas and had a grin on his face. "What do you think of these? My mother picked them out for me. She wants me to wear pajamas. I haven't the heart to tell her that I rarely wear anything in bed except for shorts. She thinks I'm still ten years old when it comes to bed clothes"

Maria laughed. "You look like a *model* for bed wear."

"Tomorrow morning, after I've finished my talk with Mom and Dad, I'll come up and get you."

Maria guessed that he wanted to spare her any more emotion if he could. "That's fine; I will study my chem notes and read some more history material while I'm waiting for you."

"I love how flexible you are." He gave her a chaste little kiss. "Please forgive me; I've got to think about things. As nice as my parents are, when I'm around them I can't express my thoughts the way I can when I'm away. Does that make any sense?"

"You have a right to your moods, whether they are up or down. Right now, we are both tired, and we need to sleep on the night's events. See you in the morning." She blew him a kiss, and he mouthed thank you and blew her a kiss back.

10. The Trip Back

Love is but the discovery of ourselves in others,
and the delight in the recognition.
—Alexander Smith

When Maria woke, the sun was pouring into her room. The light playing on the curtains and the walls gave the room a magical feeling. She lay in bed for a while, trying to imagine how her and Bill's lives were going to turn out. What Maria needed was a crystal ball.

She wandered slowly across the hall, still upset about the previous night. She took a shower and washed her hair. Talking out loud to herself in the shower, she said, "I've got to forget last night and get myself in gear. It's over, and I can't change anything. I can only control passing my tests and doing my homework."

Downstairs, Bill's parents' voices were audible, and, occasionally, she heard Bill speaking. At least they weren't yelling; that was a good sign. She felt a little left out of their lives, but realized that until this weekend, they had never even seen her. It seemed like a long time before she heard Bill coming up the stairs, but she was glad that she had made herself study. She did her best work in the morning and had a lot of ground to cover before her tests on Tuesday.

Bill tapped a little tune on her door with his fingers and looked in. She turned around, put her thumbs into her ears, and wriggled her fingers and stuck out her tongue. "Happy Halloween!"

He laughed and bounced into the room. "Stand up and get your treat." He wrapped his arms around her with a huge look of relief on his face.

"A treat? Is it tasty?"

"Are you ready for your morning kiss?"

"Is that my tasty treat? What makes it different from an evening kiss?"

He stopped to think her question over. "A morning kiss holds the promise of the day," he said quietly.

"You come up with some pretty good stuff." Maria put her arms around his neck and raised her head for her kiss.

Bill bent down, found her lips, and kissed her. Maria felt his energy radiating down her whole body.

"Okay, I give. Either you are the best kisser in the universe, or I'm under a spell."

"Just call me the magician," he said, with a grin. He picked her up and whirled her around the room.

Maria put her head back and laughed as he did it. It felt so freeing. It was like a little dance of happiness, only they whirled instead. "So why are you so happy this morning?"

"Let's go outside and walk down to the mailbox, and I'll tell you a little of what happened last night with Maude and what my folks said this morning. It's great outside."

"I'm ready, willing, and able."

"Are you hungry?" he asked.

"No . . ."

Bill took her hand and pulled her down the stairs to get their coats. Then they ran out into the sunlight.

"So why aren't you hungry this morning? I'll bet it has something to do with last night."

"I want to know your story about last night and this morning," she said emphatically, ducking his question.

"Well, when Maude insisted that we talk last night, I was dumbfounded as to what to do. I didn't want to upset her and have her make a scene. It would have been telegraphed all over the community like a shot. I also felt sorry for her because I was leaving her, but I have been telling her that it was over all fall, and she wouldn't listen. So out we went to her car to talk. When we got in, she began holding me and trying to kiss me. I liked that but knew we wouldn't get much talking done that way. I moved away and told her that I was sorry, but I didn't feel the way I used to feel about her. She began to cry and asked how could that happen. I said that I didn't know, but it had, and I'd like to be her friend, but that's all. That's when she said that she was going to tell her parents that we had been very intimate for the past two years, and now she was left alone, and I had treated her very badly. I begged her to think about what she was saying and how bad it was to lie like that about me. She said that she'd ruin my reputation if we didn't get engaged soon. My dad came out to get me to blow out my candle at just about that time."

"Oh my God, Bill. She is a mean girl."

"I talked to my folks this morning and told them what she had said to me. They were shocked, and my dad asked me if there was any truth to what she said. I told him, in no uncertain terms, that I hadn't even had one date with her this fall because when I saw you, I couldn't get you out of my mind. I said that I'd spent several weeks trying to find you, then asked you out after we met at a get-together at Farm House. The rest is history. My dad said that it was her word against mine, and it would blow over after a while and people would forget about it. I am so relieved."

"So am I. You look so happy this morning. Shall we do the dance of happiness?" At this suggestion, Bill took Maria's hands, and the couple began twirling around in a circle faster and faster until Maria started to laugh. Bill pulled her to him and kissed her with wild exuberance. Maria kissed him back and he pressed his body into hers for a second or two, then he let go. "Let's keep walking."

"Where are your folks this morning? Their car is gone."

"They went to church, and we didn't. What do you think of that?" he asked.

"I'm not a big churchgoer," Maria said, looking at him carefully as she said it and wondering if he normally went to church.

"Well, that's a relief," he said and laughed. "I didn't think you were big on church, but I wasn't sure. I stopped going when I was fourteen, and I've never missed it. To change the subject, why weren't you hungry this morning?"

"You remember everything. I got so nervous last night, it built up and up until my stomach went blah. Your dear mom gave me the Pepto treatment."

"The what?"

"Pepto-Bismol," and then Maria tried to sing the ad song; it was a mistake. "Do you like my voice?"

"You little dickens, it's terrible."

As they walked down to the mailbox, Maria saw across the road two of the prettiest horses that she had seen in a long time. She stopped, looked at them, and they ambled over looking for food. "I wish I had brought a carrot or two for them," Maria said.

"I know the farmer who owns those horses, and I'm sure he'd let us ride them around his pasture. They are expensive horses, so he wouldn't want them to leave his property."

"If I ever get invited here again, I would love to ride them any way the farmer says."

"Well, I'll have to see if you are obedient, cheerful, sexy, and whatever else the girl scouts say you have to be, and maybe I'll invite you back again."

"Where does it say in the Girl Scout bylaws that I have to be sexy?"

"I'll show you when we get back to school. For now, you'll just have to take my word for it. Let's head back." Glancing at his watch, he said, "It's eleven thirty, and we have to pack up, eat something—if you are hungry—and get a move on. My frat friend said he needed his car back by four this afternoon. I figure it will take us about two hours to get home, and dropping you off will take another thirty minutes because you have so much stuff." Bill laughed and jumped away from Maria's attempt to swat him.

Maria put her head down and bolted, getting a head start because she caught Bill by surprise. He ran after her, and she couldn't keep ahead of him, no matter how she tried. He grabbed her and held onto her. She couldn't move.

"So what was that all about?" he asked.

"You were scheduling us so precisely, I felt that I had to run to the house and pack." She laughed. "We're on a tight timetable."

"You are teasing me, and I know it," Bill said. "I'm a little over the top and need to relax a bit."

"You're right about that, my flyboy."

"Your what? Where did you get 'flyboy'?"

"You're wearing the jacket to your uniform again."

Bill had a different look in his eyes now. Having her touch on such a sensitive dream of his was very startling to him. He asked, "How did you know? I've never really felt somehow that it was in the cards for me. It's been in the back of my mind, but every time it popped up, I thought that I couldn't do that. My parents, especially my dad, are counting on me to live next door to them, running a farm like my two older brothers. I can't disappoint them. Why would I need to fly? When you said that I had my uniform on again, all my dreams came back to me about flying."

"We'll continue this conversation when we get going. Right now, we must stick to our schedule," Maria said, saluting him. She ran up the back stairs as fast as she could because he looked like he was going to catch her and squeeze her to death. She loved teasing him. Being around him gave her the most exhilarating moments that she had ever had. If Bill were with her, she felt like she could do anything.

"Are you hungry, yet? Mom left all kinds of food in here."

"You are really going to make sure that I eat something. I'm not exactly fading away. Let's have some coffee and those wonderful muffins she made."

"I'll have some coffee, but I'm still full from breakfast."

As they were sitting there enjoying themselves, Maria heard Bill's mom and dad's car pull into the driveway. Bob and Alice hurried in to enjoy a few precious moments with them before they were gone.

"Hi," Alice said, peeking into the kitchen. She looked so pretty in her blue outfit. "I'm going to change and will be out in a minute."

Bill's dad came in and nodded to them.

"Hi, Dad," Bill said.

"When do you have to go back?" Bob asked.

"We're leaving in about an hour."

Maria could see that Bob wanted to say something to them, but was having trouble framing his words so they came out right. Finally he said, "I wasn't ready to accept you, Maria, when you came here, but I am now. Mother really likes you, Maria, and her ability to know people is better than anyone I have ever known. I'm glad you came and that you are Bill's special friend. You make him very happy, and that makes us very happy." He came over and took her hand and gave it a little squeeze.

Maria looked up at him and thanked him for everything. "Being here, meeting you and Alice and your wonderful family, has been an eye-opening experience. Thank you for your honesty."

Alice appeared in the doorway and asked whether they would like some sandwiches to take back with them and they both nodded emphatically. Maria said that food was pretty scarce on Sunday evenings in the dorm.

"Let me help you," Maria offered.

Alice said, "It would be better if you went upstairs and got your things so Bill can pack the car."

"All right; I will. Thanks for everything," Maria said, and gave Alice a hug.

Alice looked at her and smiled. "I have enjoyed every minute with you, Maria. You have brought something special to our family."

Maria went upstairs, grabbed her things, and stuffed them into the duffle bag that Bill had given her. She took the spare he gave her, too, put her books in that one, ran downstairs with everything, and put it in the trunk. Alice gave them the lunch she had packed, and they were ready to go. Bill gave his dad a big bear hug, his mom a gentle hug, and opened the door for Maria to get in the car. Maria rolled down the window, waved goodbye, and off they went back to Iowa State.

Bill found some nice music on the radio, and they sat in silence for a while enjoying the music and the drive. Bill said, "You are so far over; come on, get closer to me. Or do I scare you?"

"Yeah, you scare me so much that I just may get into your lap." Maria slid over and patted his leg and put her head on his shoulder for a moment.

"So what are you thinking about?"

"The whole weekend. It was a lot to digest. I love your mother and respect your dad. Thanks for letting me into your world."

"Now, I need to get into *your* world."

"Sometime, we'll take a trip, and you can meet my family. Now tell me more about what you think about flying."

"Well, it's an idea that has been growing in me the older I get and the closer I get to graduation. I don't know why, but it's hooked up with you. Since I've met you, I find myself thinking about flying as a career. It makes no sense since I've been studying agriculture for two years. My background is farming, but recently I've felt that I want to do other things with my life. I feel that you would be behind me if I decided to go into the Air Force after I graduated."

Bill turned to look at her, trying to read her thoughts.

"I don't care what you do, as long as I'm part of it. I would go around the world in a rowboat if you were rowing, too."

"Oh, Maria, I feel like I can do anything when I hear you talk like that."

"You can," she said quietly.

She felt her hormones gearing up again. They had been on hold while she was at Bill's home because of the Maude problem.

She wanted to have Bill hold her at that moment, but it wasn't very practical if they wanted to stay on the road.

Bill looked over at her, reading her feelings. "I want to see you tonight, after we get back."

"Me too," she said softly.

They rode along quietly for a while, and Maria knew that Bill was thinking very hard about something. Finally he said, "Somehow, I can't be myself anymore when I'm home. I find that I'm on edge and am always trying to please my dad, who doesn't realize that I'm feeling this way. I want my own life, not the one that my parents and the Jenkinses have been planning for me for years. I need my independence from them. Having you there was so good for them, so they could see that I'm not staying in the old mold anymore. I have a new girlfriend; not Maude, whom I have known for a hundred years. I have grown up while my dad wasn't looking."

Maria couldn't resist. "You look darn good for being a hundred years old."

Laughing at her comment, Bill said, "I need you to help me figure it out, since I'm ancient."

They both drifted into their own thoughts again, listening to the music. They drove for a long time that way.

"Would you like a sandwich?" Maria asked him.

"That would be great. I was getting hungry. It's been a while since I ate this morning with the folks."

Opening the lunchbox was like opening a present. There were sandwiches, apples, and cookies in there. What a nice thing for Alice to do for them. Maria put a sandwich in Bill's hand, and he ate it with great gusto. "Boy, that was good. Is there anything to drink?"

A container holding soft drinks was just within reach. "Here's a beer," Maria said.

He believed her for an instant, then he laughed. "Don't I wish."

Maria crunched her apple and tried not to sound like a coffee grinder. She asked, "How about a cookie?"

He nodded and swallowed it in one bite.

As she sat there, pressed up to him as close as possible, she drifted off to sleep.

When she woke up, they were almost in Ames. "What happened to me?" Maria asked.

"You were tired from the weekend and all the stuff that went on."

"Did the trouble with Maude wear you out as much as it did me?"

"I'm fine," he said, although he didn't sound it. "And I'll be finer when I see you later tonight after we get ourselves squared away. I'll be by about seven; I have lots of things to talk over with you. Will you be able to handle all your bags?"

"I'm not an invalid, Bill. I didn't play all that tennis and not build up some muscles of my own. I can carry everything to my room."

They made good time and were back at Maria's dorm by three. Despite what she'd said, Bill grabbed her duffels, opened her door, and went up the stairs with her. Sometimes, he was *too* polite. She wondered if he really liked being such a nice guy. He gave her a quick hug and ran down the stairs to the car. "I'll see you around seven tonight."

Susie was nowhere to be seen, which made Maria relax. She hadn't felt like fielding questions from Susie. She had a lot of thinking, studying, and planning to do before she saw Bill tonight.

By six, hunger had set in, and Maria decided to go over to the cafeteria. She hadn't felt like eating most of the day because of last night, but now her body was saying, "Feed me, feed me." The cold buffet which stood in for the cook's day off was its usual uninteresting assortment of pallid food. What she really wanted was a hamburger at the Union with pickles and potato chips.

Grabbing a sandwich and an apple, she went back to her room, ready for action. She tackled her studies in earnest. She had only an hour or so before Bill would be back, so she had better get her mind wrapped around a few of these equations and history dates.

A little later, Susie bounced into the room. She had been at a meeting of some sort and was hungry.

Maria said, "I wish you had come back earlier; I would have dragged you to the Union for a hot, juicy hamburger.

Susie asked, "Is the buffet the same old"—she stopped, then decided not to swear—"stuff that we have every Sunday night?"

"Worse, if that's possible. Good luck."

Maria had a few more minutes to herself. She closed her books, took a deep breath, and began to think about seeing Bill. She wondered what he had to talk about. Maybe that was just an excuse to get her all excited. They really hadn't had time to have more than an occasional kiss all weekend. He'd be here soon, and she didn't want to think too hard about what was to come; she just wanted to be with him. She'd lost all feelings of the loneliness that had sometimes overtaken her when she wasn't with him. But she wondered why she needed a man to make her feel whole.

"So how'd it go, meeting the family?" Maria heard from the door. She looked up to see Susie holding a stalk of celery crosswise in her teeth, smiling, and waving an apple.

"It was very busy. Bill's mom is wonderful; Bill's dad was being a dad and okay; the brothers, their wives, and Bill's sister made me feel very welcome; and Maude, Bill's old girlfriend, was upset, hurt, and mad at both of us. Was that a good synopsis? Not too boring."

"Are you pregnant?" Susie asked, with an evil grin.

"We hardly had time to get close enough to each other to grab a kiss, and when we did, we were so tired that our kisses were the kind you'd give to your kid before he went to sleep."

"Why no time? What on earth was the family doing, plowing the back forty?"

"Unbeknownst to Bill, his mom and dad had planned a 'welcome home party' for him and had invited the neighbors, brothers, their wives, his sister and her husband to come. All together, they had about twenty people there. His mom and I cooked, cleaned, and set up for the party all day while Bill helped his dad fix the tractor. Maude came just late enough to upset the party by dragging Bill out to her car for a talk. We were all standing around waiting for them to come back in so Bill could blow out the big candle on his cake and we could all eat it. Bill's dad finally had to go out and bring Bill in because everyone was wondering where he was. It was not a pretty scene at the end. Maude must have left in a huff, because she never came back in the house."

"Well, it's over, and she didn't maim or kill you; that's a plus," Susie said with a bright smile.

"So how's it going with Chuck? I'm sorry to leave so soon, but I'm going to see Bill for an hour or so to talk, and I'm sure he'd like to slip in a little lovemaking."

"That's okay, I've got some work to do for tomorrow," Susie said, as she sidestepped Maria's question.

Maria thought that there was a reason for avoidance, so she said, "I'll see you later. We've been talking far longer than I thought, and it's almost seven. I've got to clean up before he comes."

11. Discussion Time

*How few there are who have the courage enough
to own their own faults
or resolution enough to mend them.*
—Benjamin Franklin

When she stepped out into the main room of the dorm, Bill was standing looking out of the window. He must have sensed that she was there because he turned immediately, came over, and put his arm around her. He whispered, "Hi there, can I have a date with you tonight?"

"What do you have to offer?" Maria asked, laughing as they were walking down the outside steps.

"I'll show you," Bill said He took her in his arms and kissed her harder than usual, until she felt like jelly.

Coming up for air, she choked out, "Okay, I'll take a chance with you. I like your style."

At least two couples walked by and heard what she said and were chuckling. "Where are we going?" Maria asked.

"Don't you want to be surprised?"

As they hurried along the sidewalk, Maria didn't like the speed they were going and the tenseness that she was feeling. Trying to keep up with Bill, Maria finally said, "Slow down, daddy long legs. We're not running from a robbery we've just committed. The cold weather has turned on your sprint button." *No more balmy evening walks until next spring,* she thought. Winter was coming to Iowa.

Silent Sam was not talking. Why the silent treatment after the big kiss just a minute ago? Breaking out in the La Grange fight song as loudly as she could sing, Maria watched for his reaction. If anything would make him laugh and talk, it was her off-key version of her alma mater's song. What had happened that was so terrible since their ride home?

Bill looked like someone had dropped a weight on his head. He stared at her and seemed surprised that she had resorted to singing. He stopped in front of his fraternity house. "What brought that on?" His tone of voice sounded rather irritated.

"Well, Einstein, what theory were you working on besides the one on relativity while walking over here? I'd like to know. Do you think because you are a great scientist you don't have to make any conversation with me, little ol' Maria?" Her eyes were sparking with anger.

"Gosh, I'm sort of in a funk about the Maude thing," Bill said as an apology. He started to enter the frat house, and Maria turned around and started walking back to the dorm. When he realized that she was not following him, he turned around and ran after her. "Wait a minute, please, Maria."

"Why? You are pretty sure of yourself; you must think that I'm made of wood. Let me explain something to you. If you want to see me and can't bring yourself to say anything, it means you don't really want to see me. When I tried to kid you out of your mood, you gave me some half-assed comment about Maude. I'm sick of hearing about Maude. She ruined the end of your party, one that your mother and I worked on all day, in case you've forgotten. Maybe you had better start seeing her again, if she is always on your mind." Maria again headed back to the dorm.

"I'm sorry that I am way too wrapped up in her and her problems. She has been calling me nonstop all fall."

"As I said before, you had better make some decisions as to what you're going to do, and when you do, let me know. Don't waste my time," she called over her shoulder.

"Please turn around and come back with me." He looked absolutely stricken and wasn't used to her voicing strong feelings. "You're absolutely right, and I'm acting like a jerk. I've almost let her ruin our date tonight, and I'm sure that's what she wants to do."

Bill stood there, looking at her, and Maria didn't know whether to stay or go. Her heart was pounding, her hands were cold, and she was sick to her stomach. Another minute of this and she'd be crying. He'd just admitted that he was a jerk. She turned toward the frat house; he took her hand, realized it was ice cold, and started to rub it. He put his arm around her; they walked in the house and straight through to the chapter room.

It was a much smaller room than their big living room, very cozy with a fire glowing in the fireplace. They sat down on a comfortable sofa across from the fireplace. Maria noticed that there was only one lamp on and with the light of the fire, the room looked darkly inviting.

"Is this where you have your frat meetings?" Maria attempted to make normal conversation to shake herself out of the unsettled feeling that their fight had given her. She didn't feel very sexy or loving at the moment.

"That's right," Bill said, moving to take her in his arms. Maria put up her hands in the stop position. That was something new to Bill. Maria had never refused his attention before. "How mad are you at me?" he asked.

"How mad should I be? You tell me. I want to settle this obsession you have for making Maude the center of our relationship. It's going to crack it wide open, and I'm going to leave you."

She hadn't given him an ultimatum before. "Maria, you have been a beacon to lead me on a new path. Please help me and don't leave me. You are absolutely right in saying that I have been a patsy around her. I should have told her last night, in front of her folks, that you are my girl and not gone outside with her. I'm not trying to make excuses, but when one is raised in a small-town atmosphere, with all the neighbors watching, it's hard to go against them. It made you sick when I did it. I'm such a fool. The other problem I have, as you know, is how to wrestle myself away from my dad and the pressure he and the Jenkinses have put on me to be their obedient son and future son-in-law."

Maria said, "When you didn't talk, walking over here after all we had been through last night, then came up with that half-assed comment about Maude, I was ready to call it quits with you. I'm waiting to see what you do before I say all is wonderful and forgive you."

"You are hitting me where I live, Maria, and it hurts, but I think I've had it too easy with you. It's good that you have decided to fight. Guys like me have to be hit over the head sometimes to do the right thing. I'm going to fight for you. You'll see; Maude is not going to control me in any way anymore."

Maria gave him a look of determination, but could tell he wanted to shift the subject away from Maude. He had just promised he was going to change the way he dealt with Maude, so she decided to relax and give him a chance. It seemed that he wanted to talk about something else.

He looked at her with those baby blues of his. "I'm sorry that I haven't said anything about a new development in my life. It's quite interesting. I was waiting until I was sure that it was going to happen. How I got so far off track when I've been dying to tell you about this, God only knows. Do you want to hear about it?"

"Of course," Maria said, giving him a little smile. It was so darn hard to stay mad at him. "We've beaten the stuffing out each other over Maude, so tell me what it is that's so exciting to you."

My Ag professor called me when I got back from our trip and said that he had been able to set up some local talks at the Grange meetings in Ames and Boone for me this week. He had been hinting for a month or so that he thought I'd be a good candidate to give these talks. I didn't think it would happen so soon.

"The Grange meetings are attended by farmers who live around here who come to listen to speakers talk on various farming subjects. I'm surprised that my professor has been able to set something up so quickly. It's something different from studying and going to classes. I'm excited about doing it because I want to get out and see what the local farmers are doing and thinking. I'd sort of put the whole idea on a back burner because I didn't think that it had a chance of succeeding. I've also been thinking about a darling girl a lot." Bill looked at her as he said this. He tentatively put his arm around her.

"I'd like to meet this darling girl so I could tell her to move over, I'm coming," Maria replied.

Bill seemed amused and relieved that Maria was joking with him again. He lifted her onto his lap, which surprised her, and whispered in her ear, "You are my little dickens, and I love you so much. Please don't be mad at me. I'm learning, thanks to you."

She turned to look at him and said with a straight face, "I'm going to tell you something about yourself you probably don't know. You are very strong. Did you know that? I just learned that when you lifted me into your lap. I'm no lightweight."

He laughed. "Maria, you mean everything to me."

"Bill, I'm thrilled with what is happening for you. You obviously impressed your professor with your ability to think on your feet. That is a great attribute," she said, and gave him a huge smile. Maria leaned toward his face until she was only three inches away, then gave him a quick kiss on the tip of his nose.

That little kiss burst the floodgates, and he started to kiss her all over her face. They laughed and hugged each other. Maria sat on his lap, looking into his eyes. "We should do the happy dance, but I'm too comfortable on your lap to get up."

Again, his facial expression showed subtle changes; apparently he was thinking of something less than pleasant. "After I tell you something that I have been keeping from you all fall, maybe you won't want to do any dancing with me. It is more about Maude. Please let me tell you what she has been doing, and then I promise I will change the whole situation."

"Okay, but make it short, because I'm sure it's ugly." Sitting on his lap, she felt so close to him; she could hear him breathing and feel his muscles tighten as he put his arms around her. He looked at her with such confusion that it irritated her. She thought they had put Maude to rest.

"First of all, I want you to know, I haven't dated her since high school, and I don't know where all this emotion from her is coming from. All fall, I have been trying to deal with her constant phone calls at all hours of the day and night. She is sometimes sweet, begging me to take her back; sometimes crying, pleading; and sometimes so angry with me that she ends up screaming because I don't see her anymore. I've been trying to reason with her, but so far it hasn't worked. I can't tell you the hours I have been on the phone with her trying to explain the new direction my life has taken with you, Maria. She doesn't want to hear what I'm saying. I hate to say this, but sometimes I am worried that she is going a little crazy."

"Why do you care so much about what she thinks she wants? You know what I think, you are afraid that she will give you a bad name in your hometown and guess what, she's threatening to do it, anyway. All your concern for her hasn't changed anything, has it? When are you going to break free of the hold that little town has on you and take charge of your future?"

Bill looked at her, dumbstruck. "I guess I've had the small town mentality, which has its good and bad points. You grew up in a big suburb and were much more anonymous, which can be very lonely, but you also don't have to answer to anybody. A small town takes care of their own, but at a price, and that price is gossip and trying to dig into everyone's private business."

Maria began to understand his silence while walking over here. He was trying to figure out how to tell her how bad Maude had become and was at his wit's end.

Maria said, "I have to share more of my own story with you to make you realize that you can't play God and make someone well who doesn't want to change. My mother went off the deep end when my dad left her, even though he had been leaving her emotionally since I was a little girl. I watched her lose control and try to hurt him as much as he had hurt her all those years.

"She would go up to his office full of patients and stand there screaming at him. I was living with her at the time, and when she came home, shaken and despondent, she would disappear upstairs, taking a bottle of liquor with her. I knew that I wouldn't see her for a day or two, and I tried in my feeble way to take care of her.

"I was fourteen, a freshman in a high school of two thousand students, and trying to keep the house together. Occasionally, I'd stop at my dad's office, and he'd give me money to buy groceries and gas, and he'd take care of the big bills. He also gave me money for my personal expenses any time I asked for it. I felt so sorry for my parents, Bill, and I have the same feelings when I hear what has been happening to you this fall. You are quite a guy for trying to spare my feelings by not saying anything to me, but this is my point. No matter how I tried, just like Humpty Dumpty, I couldn't put the family back together again. You can't change Maude, and you can't put her back together, either."

She leaned into his chest, lay her head down, and rested there, quietly, for quite a while.

"What an incredible story, Maria. You made it through, even though you had a rough few years. I love you, I'm drawn to you, and that's all there is to it."

Bill stroked her hair and rubbed her back. He whispered to her that he needed her in his life.

Maria raised her head from his chest. "It's too bad that we aren't celebrating your wonderful opportunity to help the farmers. It's exactly what you want to do. I am thrilled for you."

"I have more good news about the job. My professor said that he will try to get me a college car to drive to the meetings. The college evidently has cars available. He'll tell me more tomorrow evening when I meet with him."

"That's wonderful, too, Bill. I wish I could hear you talk."

"This may sound rather chauvinistic, but the whole place will be filled with men who think that their little women should stay home and let the men do the farming. You'd be the only woman there."

"I know, Bill. I wouldn't want to embarrass you with the farmers of America. Besides, I wouldn't be able to go because I have so many tests coming up this week and next."

"Let's try to see each other on Wednesday sometime. I will be talking Tuesday and Thursday evening this week. Oh, by the way, I'm going to get paid, too. I don't know how much yet, but I will, probably, when we meet Wednesday. It means that I will have a car to use and money to spend. It's a chance for us to get off campus, see what the area has to offer, go shopping in Des Moines." He paused and kissed her. Taking a deep breath, he said, "I've got to talk about my feelings for you. I want to be with you all the time, do everything with you. When I'm with you, I want to do much more than kiss you. It's driving me crazy.

"I'm committed to you, and I'm going to talk to my folks about what would be appropriate to give you to show the world that we are together." He paused again, then said quietly, "I wanted to talk to you about how you feel about having more intimate dates with me. We will have transportation to go anywhere we want, including a nice motel." He looked at her with love—and lust—in his eyes.

"Wow," she said, pausing so she could think about these roller-coaster feelings. "We have covered a lot of ground tonight, three big situations to think about: Maude, your new job, and sleeping together sexually."

Maria felt edgy. It had been building all evening. "You promised you'd take care of the problems we have with Maude, remember. When those are successfully resolved, then we'll talk." Maria knew Bill was hoping that she would let him off the hook about Maude, but she wouldn't, because if they didn't solve the problem, their relationship would end.

Maria didn't know what to do about their personal situation. She knew that sex had been rearing its head more and more, and she wasn't as interested in a sexual relationship as he was. She looked at their relationship differently, but she loved him and all that went with it. Doing something about it was going into areas that were new to her. They weren't kids anymore, and Bill wanted to show he was an adult.

Even if Maude hadn't been in the equation, Maria's answer to his question of whether she wanted a more sexual relationship with him was still disturbing to her. But with the Maude factor, it was difficult to say anything at all.

"I'm struggling with my emotions, too, every time we are together," Maria said. "I realize that things have changed since high school when good girls didn't have an option. Working up to at least talking about sexual dating is a start for me, but I'm concerned that we are rushing it. I also wonder if you know what I would feel like if our relationship dissolved after turning our dates into excursions to motels. I'm scared that down deep you will feel like I'm a bad woman. Your opinion of me is very important. We would be going against all the cultural attitudes of our generation."

"It sounds like I haven't done a very good job of letting you know what I think of you and how much I value you. I could never think of you as a bad woman." He kissed her cheeks and hugged her.

"That's easy enough for you to say now, but I've read too many stories of fast-talking men who say anything to get what they want. I don't know you well enough to be sure that you wouldn't decide that you didn't want to marry someone who jumped into bed the minute you said you wanted her. I'm also afraid of getting pregnant. I've never had intercourse with anyone because I have never wanted to before. The fear of getting pregnant hasn't been a problem for me up until now, but it's real now."

"Gosh, Maria, I didn't know how afraid you are about getting pregnant."

"That's the problem; we don't know anything about what each other fears or loves. Up until tonight, I didn't know that Maude had been driving you crazy. We don't trust each other enough yet to tell the other who we really are."

"I certainly don't want you to get pregnant until you want to. I'd use protection to keep that from happening. No one's ever going to hurt you, especially me. I love you, and I will be there for you no matter what. This fall, I feel as if everything that is happening between us is like a wild tornado, making me want to grab it, tame it, grow up, and be a man.

"The first thing I need is more money, and I'm going to sign on to work in the wheat fields next summer. I was thinking about that this afternoon when you were sleeping next to me in the car. I can make a thousand dollars a week by driving the heavy equipment needed to harvest the wheat. The season is about eight weeks long. I need to buy us a car and put some money in a bank, so I can take care of you."

"Bill, I love the fact that you are thinking so far into the future. I'm still here, trying to get us to deal with the problems you have in the here and now. When the Maude situation is solved, we can begin to make plans for the future. Right now, let's stay as real as we can."

"I'm going home at Thanksgiving and will get myself a job at the local equipment store selling and fixing tractors. They need people who know the equipment and can do that. When we were in town Saturday, the owner offered me a job anytime I wanted one. I'm going to work there every spare moment, for us," Bill said with determination.

Maria glanced at her watch and saw that it was ten minutes to nine. She had ten minutes to get back to the dorm or face being locked out. "Come on, Bill, we have to run back to the dorm, or I will be late. I'm so sorry that we have to stop our exploration of some very important issues, but that darn curfew is still there."

"I know," he said. They grabbed their coats and put them on as they ran down the sidewalk to the dorm.

"Please call me; I need to talk to you some more," Maria said.

152

He gave her a kiss that said more to her than any words. Maria ran up the stairs and turned for a moment to look at Bill standing there with a slight smile on his face. She blew him a kiss and ran in.

Around ten, she heard the phone ring and started down the hall, halfway wondering if it was him calling to say goodnight to her. She was right. He said, "I thought about everything you told me tonight, and I want to tell you again that I meant what I said about taking care of the Maude problem and that we were in this thing together. I've been searching for someone like you, without realizing it, all of my life. I promise you my heart, and nothing will ever keep us apart."

"Let me know when we can see each other on Wednesday. You do your part, and I'll try to do mine. I love you, Bill."

"Goodnight, my darling. I'll call you tomorrow night."

Maria still had misgivings about their relationship, because of Maude and also Bill's inability to stand up to her. What did that say about his character in general? If other women came into his life, would he take the easy way out and let them work into a relationship with him, rather than standing firm with his ideals. The shine of their romance was beginning to tarnish.

12. New Directions

If passion drives you, let reason hold the reins.
—Benjamin Franklin

After curfew on Monday night, Bill called to talk with Maria about his job in more detail. He was definitely going to get paid and have a car for personal and business use. "Isn't that wonderful, Maria? I am feeling like a guy who will be able to do something with his college degree after all."

"I'm so happy for you. When you are so excited, I am too. Are you all set with your talk for tomorrow night?"

"I can talk for hours on my subject of better farming techniques."

"I'm happy that you are so confident. Call me when you get home Tuesday night, and tell me all about it." Maria paused, thinking about the delicate subject she wanted to touch on. "Honey, I want to let you know that I have been thinking long and hard about our personal situation," she whispered into the phone. "When I see you Wednesday, we can talk. I can't discuss this on a public phone."

He said, "I certainly understand that problem with the phone very well. I love you. I'll call Wednesday, so we can set up a time to see each other."

"You are my prince charming, so go slay that dragon. Good night, my love."

When Bill called Maria on Tuesday night, he sounded very excited. "Guess what, we're in the money! The Grange supervisor told me that he had really enjoyed my presentation and asked me if I would be interested in talking around the state, periodically, at various Grange meetings." Bill paused, then blurted, "Guess what he's going to pay me?!"

"I haven't got the foggiest. I've never dated a Grange speaker before," Maria said, delighted that Bill was so happy.

"He offered me a flat one hundred dollars for each talk and said people sometimes stretch the truth a little if they get expenses. Do you know what that will mean to us in the future? There are so many possibilities; I don't know what to think."

Maria was amazed at what speakers earned. "That's a small fortune. I'm so proud of you, and, best of all, you're proud of yourself. I picked out a smart guy, didn't I? Think of it, Bill, giving talks, meeting all kinds of people, *and* making money while speaking about something that is close to your heart. I have one question, though: Will it be hard for you to get away from school to do this speaking tour?"

"I'm going to talk to my professor tomorrow and tell him what has happened. I feel sure that he will waive some of my classes so that I can do this. It's good public relations for the school. Maria, we're on our way," Bill said, almost bubbling over.

"Have you told your family, yet? I know that your mom and dad will be thrilled, especially your mom. Let me know what they think. You know, Bill, I miss Alice already. She was so good to me."

"I'm going to call them tomorrow. It's too late to talk to them tonight." Bill laughed. "They're good farmers and in bed with the chickens. Anyway, I wanted you to be the first to know because you are my best friend, and I love you." He added, "Oh, and I'm sure Alice misses you, too. She was really taken by you."

Maria decided to see how *much* he loved her and dared to ask, "Bill, have you had any more calls from Maude?"

It was quiet at the other end. Maria waited. Bill finally said, slowly and quietly, "Maude came over to the house this afternoon and made a big commotion when they said that I wasn't there. She demanded to know where I was, and the guys didn't know. Nobody is that interested. No one in the house knew quite what to do with her and neither do I."

"Well, you had better figure it out soon. Call your parents and tell them what's going on."

"I'll call them first thing in the morning, and I'll let you know what they say when I see you. I'll be by around seven, so we'll have a couple of hours together before curfew."

"My sweet, I'm beat, so I must go to bed. Do you know what time it is?"

"It's time for me to shut up and let you go," Bill exclaimed.

"It's eleven thirty, and if I don't get to bed by midnight, I will turn into a witch, and that's not a pretty sight. I'll give you a blow by blow tomorrow night of my exciting life in chem lab.

"I'm sorry it's so late. The Grange guy spoke with me for quite a while after my talk, feeling me out as to what I knew and how I would like doing the tour. Time flew by. See you tomorrow night. Get your lips warmed up for a kiss or two," Bill said, laughing as he hung up.

On Wednesday, when Maria hit the dorm around five in the afternoon, she was hungry. Peeking into their room, she made a face at Susie. "Do you want to go eat with me now? I have a hot date at seven, and I want to wash my hair before I see Bill."

Susie grinned, shut her book, and leaped off the bed, making faces back at Maria as she came out. "Let's eat and talk. I haven't seen much of you for quite a while. How goes it?"

They grabbed some food, sat down to eat, and Maria told Susie about Bill's big evening the night before.

"For a farmer, he's pretty smart. I guess I underestimated him," Susie admitted.

"Susie, shame on you; farmers feed the world."

Susie grinned. "It doesn't mean that you have to marry one; just eat the food he raises."

As they walked back to their dorm, Maria asked, "How are things with Chuck?"

Maria watched Susie's comfort level plummet as she answered. "Chuck is ready to throw in the towel and wants to transfer to Iowa University. He feels that he would have a better chance playing football for them. His whole life is wrapped up with the game, and I'm getting tired of his moods, which fluctuate depending on whether the coach let him play or not during the games." Susie started to tear up, something Maria had never seen her roommate do. "I'll really miss him, Maria. We just don't fit together anymore. If you had told me that we would break up in college after having dated all through high school, I would have said no way. But we really hardly know each other anymore." Susie wiped her eyes and tried to smile at Maria.

"Like Maude and Bill," Maria said.

"What's the latest on that front?" Susie said, relieved to change the subject.

"Funny you should ask," Maria replied. "When he mentioned her last night, he said she was becoming a real pain, and he didn't know how to deal with her. Apparently, she's been after him all fall. He's been trying to let her down easy, but she's holding on for dear life. Up until now, he hadn't leveled with me. He said it was to keep me from worrying, but I don't buy it. I think he has been having trouble saying goodbye to her. Now, since his life has begun to change away from farming, she no longer fits with him like before. We had a big fight over her on Sunday night. I told him he had to settle it with her before she ruins our relationship."

"Bill was rising on my list of okay people, but I'll have to reserve judgment until he takes care of Maude," Susie said, giving Maria a searching look. "Go take your shower and wash your hair. You smell like sulfuric acid, and that's not a big turn-on."

As Maria was showering, an idea popped into her head. Back in their room, while brushing her hair, Maria asked, "Susie, I was wondering what your plans were for Thanksgiving and Christmas? Are you riding home with Chuck for the holidays?"

"I am going with him at Thanksgiving, but he is going away on a skiing trip with his folks at Christmas. They're going to Colorado."

"Well, I have a plan to get you to La Grange and me to Chicago at Christmas time. Now that Bill has a car, I'm going to take advantage of it and ask him to take us over to Boone to get our tickets and seat reservations early, so we'll know we have seats on the train. I want us to be one step ahead of the other kids who live in Illinois and will need seats, too. I also need a round-trip ticket to Florida, because my mother has invited me down there for Christmas to meet her new husband." Maria made a face at Susie, indicating her disgust with the whole idea.

"Great," said Susie. "I'll ask my mother for the money for my ticket when I go home at Thanksgiving. Thanks for thinking of me. Did I hear you say Bill has a car now?"

"That's another whole thing that is so exciting for Bill. His car is a loaner from Iowa State for his use to drive to various Grange meetings around the state. After he talked to the farmers in Ames, it went so well that the manager of the Grange signed him up to speak a lot more. He's also going to be paid, which puts the pressure on me, because now he will have the money and the transportation to go to motels." Maria gave Susie a wide-eyed look.

Susie did a double take and asked, "What are you going to do about that?"

"That's a big problem for me, especially because of Maude. I need to talk to you—after hours," Maria said with urgency in her voice.

The phone rang for Susie, and as she went down the hall, Maria followed her and made a left turn into the front room to find Bill waiting for her in the living room. "You're early," she said, delighted to see him. The magic when they saw each other was still there.

His hand was warm, and it felt so good to touch him again. Once they were around the corner from the dorm, Bill slowed down, pulled her into his arms, and gave her a kiss of joy. Ooh, what a delicious kiss, plus he smelled so good, like shaving lotion. She gave him a gentle kiss back and felt his body grow tense. He was going for another slower and more passionate kiss when she looked at him and laughed.

"Why are you laughing?" he asked, not happy about being interrupted.

Maria didn't say anything, she just put her arms around him and started their dance of happiness. He quickly joined in with great gusto, grabbing her around her waist and twirling them around and around, laughing all the while.

"Promise me you'll never stop doing the dance of happiness with me," Maria said.

"I promise, if you let me show you other ways we can be happy."

Rolling her eyes, she said, "I'm afraid to ask what they may be."

Bill whispered in her ear that she would like them.

"All right, let's get to your house before we freeze out here," she said.

"You are full of beans tonight. You must have had a good day. Did you do well on your tests?"

"I did and I'm finished for a while with most everything except for a few lab reports. Now for you; I'm dying to hear more about your plans for speaking."

When they had reached Bill's house and hurried into the cozy room with the low lights, the house president stopped them. "I'm Dick Bailey, and I've been trying to get this fellow standing here with you to introduce us, but he's been ignoring me."

Bill said, "He's been angling to meet you."

Dick asked Maria what she thought of Bill's new speaking tour and seemed genuinely interested in Bill's success. Maria sensed that he wanted something else from her. *Spit it out,* she thought, *so Bill and I can have some time alone.*

"Bill tells me that your roommate is Susie Dunnigan. I've seen her at a few meetings that I'm involved with on campus, and she's been there as reporter for our campus paper. Does she have a boyfriend?"

Maria didn't quite know how to respond because of Susie's disenchantment with Chuck, but they hadn't separated yet. "Dick, why don't you call her some evening after hours and just talk to her. That's a good way to get to know her better."

Dick seemed genuinely pleased with her suggestion.

As they edged away from Dick, eager to be alone, he cautioned them on heating up the study too much tonight. With a straight face, he said, "I don't want a meltdown."

Like homing pigeons, Bill and Maria went to their favorite spot in front of the fireplace, which was glowing with a freshly made fire.

"Who made the fire?" Maria asked, delighted to see it.

"I did, for us. I know how much you like it, and I wanted to make our evening as good as I could."

"So tell me what your professor said about your speaking tour?"

"He said that it was fine with him; he will need to clear it with the higher ups in the university, but he didn't see any reason that would stop the tour. As I said before, it will be great publicity for Iowa State."

"Great news. Now tell me, did you talk to your folks?"

"I called this evening—I didn't have time this morning—and told them my good news. They were happy for me, especially my mother, who has always felt that farming was not for me. She said I was made to do other things, but my dad was not so thrilled. He has always wanted me to be on a farm next to his place. He liked the idea that I'll be working for Mr. Gunderson in town over the holidays, however. I also told them about the trouble stirred up here with Maude when I was gone yesterday. My folks are going to talk to the Jenkinses about Maude and try to help me out with her."

All of a sudden, Bill was done talking. She watched his face soften as he pulled her up close to him. His voice took on a sexy edge, and he asked her if she remembered what he had asked her to do last night. He gave her a sly grin.

Maria played dumb and asked in a coy voice, "Whatever do you mean? Please show me."

"You're asking for trouble, you little dickens." As he held her face in his hands, she could feel his breath coming a little faster.

Shutting his eyes, he gently kissed her lips. "Are they warming up?" he asked softly. "What's that scent on your neck?" he said hoarsely, nuzzling her. He took a couple of deep breaths and kissed her, slowly at first. Then he repositioned himself, holding her so tightly she could hardly breathe, and he pushed her into the couch with him on top of her, French kissing her until he started to tremble.

"We have to stop," Maria said, as she pushed him off her and sat up. He was breathing hard. She put her hands on his face. "That's enough, handsome." He nodded. "It's not meltdown time just yet," Maria said.

"When?" he asked quietly.

"We've got to work out a lot of details before that can happen. Don't you agree?"

"There's something that happens when I kiss you that causes me to almost explode."

"I know, Bill; this is not a game anymore. I ache sometimes after we have been together. There are times at night when I'm trying to study, and all I can think of is the feeling I get when you move in close to me and I can feel your body. But we must plan it out, Bill, carefully. There's a lot at stake."

"Oh, Maria, I'm going to work so hard for us so we can have a future life together. I am going to work this out soon with Maude."

Maria needed to talk about that big elephant waiting in the wings and scaring her to death with the thought of pregnancy. "I've been thinking that if we both use protection when we love each other, I won't be so afraid of getting pregnant. That clears the way for the big question. Can I trust you, Bill, that if we have a sexual relationship, you won't decide after a few times at a motel that you are tired of me and want to see what else is out there? Or worse yet, lose all respect for me?" Maria asked, her eyes boring into his.

With three inches separating their faces, he said, "You've been thinking. That's the first step. The ball's in your court. I'll wait for as long as it takes. You are my darling girl, and I told you before that what we have together is precious."

Maria didn't feel at all satisfied with this answer, but she didn't want to push him any further on that subject just now. She had a very prying question that had been bothering her for a while. "You may get really mad at my next question, but I have wondered why Maude has been so adamant about your relationship with her not being over. Since you were high school sweethearts, were you sexually active with her? She acts like she has a lot of history with you. Did you promise to marry her to get some sex when you were a horny teenager?"

Bill sat there and seemed stunned by her questions. He said, "Don't hold back, Maria. Just give me both barrels and see if I can survive." He was angry. "I'm going to say this once and only once; after that, I don't want to ever discuss it again." His eyes were blazing. "I did have a relationship when I was in high school, which I'll explain to you when you want, but it wasn't with Maude. As for Maude, I honestly found her to be far more aggressive when I was younger than I was able to handle. For a while, until I began to mature, she probably outweighed me. I was afraid that if I ever tried anything with her—not sex, just petting—she would tell the whole town and embarrass me and my family. I think she liked the idea of saying I was her boyfriend more than actually being my girlfriend. She seemed way too masculine for me. When she was in one of her moods, she would threaten me with the same stuff as she has this fall. Coming here this fall, she enjoyed telling everyone in our hometown that she was following her boyfriend to college.

"As far as Maude's latest threat to ruin my reputation with the town's people, my folks assured me not to worry. People have known me all my life in my little town and won't believe what she says about me. Since I talked to you, and you shared your mother's story with me, I've realized that I will never get her to act rationally. We will just have to go about our business and ignore her as much as possible."

"No, Bill, that won't work, just ignoring her. She will always be there like a sliver in our foot, hurting every time we try to walk. Have you called her and talked to her since the incident?"

He looked a little sheepish. "No."

"Are you afraid of her? Go call her right now, and tell her not to come around the house anymore. Explain to her that you are through trying to be friendly. Tell her to stop bothering you or something like that. You'll know what to say. Go on, so we can enjoy the rest of the evening. Don't wait for her to call, you take control and call her."

He hadn't been gone long enough to talk to her like Maria wanted him to when he came back with an ashen complexion. He looked at Maria and said in a shaky voice that Maude's roommate had found Maude in the shower, crumpled over and bleeding. She had slit her wrists. "They called an ambulance and have taken her to the hospital in Des Moines."

Bill sat on the sofa next to Maria, not moving or saying a word. Finally, he said, "It's all my fault."

Turning to face him squarely on the sofa, she said emphatically, "No, it isn't. It's no one's fault. When people are depressed, they do terrible things to call for help. Maude wanted to get your attention. That's why she did it. It was bound to happen. Remember what you said about trying to reason with her. Sick people are unreasonable. She needs professional help.

"Look on the bright side, she will get help now. It is out of our hands and into a doctor's hands who specializes in this kind of problem. She will be able to relax and let all the pain that she had been feeling for so long slip away. Her parents have been encouraging her to keep after you, hoping that they could get her married off to you. Then she'd be your problem, and they would have all your nice land, besides."

Bill had been listening to Maria intently. Then he said something she had never heard him say, "God bless you, Maria. You make me feel so much better. I was feeling so guilty, but as you say, she will get help now, and maybe it will lift her out of pain."

Maria looked at him. Tears were rimming his eyes. He and Maude went back a long way and she knew he felt sorry for her, which was such a kind way to be. She hugged him, and neither one moved for a few moments.

After a while, Maria softly said, "Maude will get better and maybe really start to live. In any event, it's not your fault." She kissed him lightly. "I'm sorry for being so mean with the way I demanded you tell me some pretty personal stuff. I won't do that again."

Bill said, "Now that you've gotten mad and asked me about Maude and our dating, can we can get on with *our* future? I hope I never have to deal with her again. It would be a relief."

Maria sidestepped this and excused herself for a moment. She found Dick in the living room watching the fire. She told him what had happened, and he immediately asked if Bill was all right. Maria said, "He's a little shaken but fine."

Dick went to spread the word, so that no one would say something stupid to Bill—joking or serious.

Maria returned to Bill, feeling good at having talked to Dick. "It's time to go, handsome," she said, smiling widely.

Throwing on their coats, they went out the side door. When they reached the steps to Maria's dorm, Bill said, "Thanks, Doc, for the help. You're a pretty smart cookie, and there must be a reason why we are dating." His kiss goodnight had a different quality to it. It produced a warm and loving feeling that encircled Maria's body and stayed with her for a long time after she had gone up the stairs. Bill called out to her, "I'll call you tomorrow night after my talk in Boone."

When he said Boone, she thought, *Darn, I meant to ask him for a ride to Boone.* Maude's attempted suicide had turned the evening upside down. She would talk to him tomorrow night about it, not tonight.

In their room, Susie was propped up on her bed, writing an article. Maria sat down on Susie's bed to get her attention. "Guess what? Maude slit her wrists in the dorm shower tonight, and her roommate found her."

Susie said, "I know. I saw the ambulance pull up and take Maude out after you left on your date."

"Bill knows because I insisted that he call her tonight and set the record straight with her. He's been acting like a patsy and letting her dictate what happens. He was shaken to his roots when he came back and told me. He seemed better when I left him, but he felt that it was his fault. I spent the rest of the evening convincing him that she would get help now. By the way," Maria smiled, "guess who was asking about you tonight?"

"Who?" Susie asked in a halfhearted way, glancing back at the article she was writing.

"Only the president of Bill's fraternity, Richard Bailey. Do you know him?"

"I've run into him at campus meetings. He's cute, I'll give him that."

Maria was tired from a big day of classes and helping Bill feel better that evening. As for Richard, she didn't want to mention that he might call Susie in case he didn't. She crawled into bed and was drifting off to the Land of Nod as she thought, *Tomorrow has got to be easier than today was.*

13. Maria's Decision

Hear reason,
or she'll make you feel her.
—Benjamin Franklin

On Thursday night, the phone rang around eleven, and Maria ran down the hall to get it so as not to wake any goof-offs who might be sleeping instead of studying.

"How did you know it was me?" asked Bill.

"You're the only night caller that we have here."

"No kidding. What's the matter with the guys? They're missing opportunities," he said.

"Maybe they like to sleep and aren't as nutty as we are. So how did things go tonight at the Boone Grange? Did you wow 'em?"

"I don't think wowing is quite the right word when you are talking about agricultural farming practices," he said, laughing. "My professor came along to hear how I performed, and he talked to the Grange organizer. I'm all set for the tour. The big boys love the idea that I will be talking around the state."

Maria knew he was high on his good news. "So let's talk about Saturday night," he said. "I can borrow my college tour car if I want to. It's fine with the powers that be." Bragging a little, he said, "I have the keys to a new Ford in my pocket right now." She heard the tinkling sound of keys over the phone. Bill laughed. "That noise means freedom for us and more, Maria."

"I can tell you are ready to go exploring. So am I. We can take all kinds rides around the area and see things that are just waiting for us to find," Maria said.

"Things are changing for us pretty fast, and I have you to thank for lighting a fire under me. Let's take a test drive tomorrow night. I'll get you after dinner around seven? Friday night's curfew is ten o'clock, giving us an extra hour," Bill said.

Maria hoped that investigating the location of motels wasn't included on the evening tour, but she knew in her heart that they would be. She had better ask Susie to take a little stroll with her over to the clinic soon to see if they offered contraceptives for women college students and what the cost was. She could feel Bill's sexual urgings and all that it entailed rolling into her life at a faster pace than she had anticipated. Without Susie, she would be at a loss to know exactly what to do. If the clinic didn't include information and actual products, she'd have to see a local doctor, and that would really break her bank account.

"Ah, Maria, where'd you go?" Bill asked. "Did I say something that upset you?"

"No, honey, I was just thinking instead of talking. Sorry, I guess I'm tired."

"It's late, and I've been keeping you up this week. I'm just so excited for us."

"Me too. See you tomorrow night my love," she said. She knew why *he* was excited; she hoped that she could feel the same way when the time came.

"Sweet dreams, sweetheart," he said.

The next morning, Maria was on her way to breakfast when the hall phone rang. She picked it up, casually, and heard Bill asking to speak to her.

"It's me. What's up?"

"You must have been waiting by the phone all night; now that's love," he said, chuckling at his joke. Maria didn't say anything; it was too early in the morning to be that happy. Bill said, "I got the bright idea of picking you up this afternoon instead of tonight. We can see a lot more during the day. Last night, I wasn't thinking straight; I was so hopped up from things going so well for us with the car and my job. When are you finished this afternoon?"

"I'm done by four today. No labs on Friday—yeah."

"Great, I'll be by a little after four to give you a chance to run home," he said with a laugh.

"Thanks a lot. Do you mind if I stop to catch my breath during my run?"

"Not too many times; we have lots of exploring to do."

Maria thought about how wonderful it would be to get off campus. Iowa State was a great school, but she didn't like being stuck there all the time.

That afternoon, Maria decided to slip out of class early, because the professor had also slipped out of his lecture; he had asked his assistant to give it, and the guy was boring. Besides, she wanted to see Bill. When she returned to the dorm, Bill was there waiting in the nicest-looking car she had seen for a while. New cars were still rare. After the war was over, everyone's car looked old because they were. New models were finally being made again.

She went up to the driver's window and asked, "Can you give a girl a ride?" She knew she had surprised him because he jumped.

"You are such a little dickens. Get in and get ready for our new adventure."

Maria threw her books in the back seat and hopped in beside Bill, giving him a big, satisfied smile, and relaxed. The car was almost brand new and had that wonderful new-car smell. They drove down Lincoln Way out onto the highway to Ames. She knew that having this car for personal and college use was an answer to Bill's prayer.

"So where would you like to go this afternoon?" he asked. "I was thinking of driving around Ames in the daylight to see all its roads and stores."

"That would be my first choice, too."

They were like a couple of kids let out of school, going to get an ice-cream cone.

"Let's check out the restaurants, stores, hotels, motels, and anything else that crosses our path," he said.

After about an hour, they had seen all there was of little Ames. Although it certainly beat Dog Town, Maria really wanted to explore Des Moines, Iowa's capital. She had heard that it had a nice cultural center and great shopping.

Bill looked over at Maria and pulled her to him. "I want to make future plans for us and find a nice motel that you like." He stopped by the side of the road and kissed her. When he began to tremble, Maria said, "We're fogging up the windows, handsome. What about the motels in Des Moines? I'd like a little distance from the campus."

"You're right, a little distance would be good," Bill said. "How do you feel about the two of us, you know, getting together?"

Ignoring his question, Maria said, "We should go back to school now for dinner. On the way back, I'd like to throw another couple of ideas in the pot for tomorrow. I have been wanting to go on the Boone Scenic Valley Railroad Ride. It has a fifteen-mile ride in antique railcars through the Des Moines River Valley. How does that sound to you?"

"I love railroads, in general, so that sounds like a winner to me. Where did you find out about it?" Bill asked.

"Someone had a brochure about it in the dorm, probably from the Chamber of Commerce. I saw it lying around, picked it up, and saved it for us."

"You are a clever little dickens. You know what I like about you, you are aware of lots of things. I have dated girls who never were any help figuring where to go and what to do. They expected me to do it all. What was your other idea?"

"I also talked with a gal today who comes from Boone, and she told me about a state park called Ledges just about five miles south of Boone. She said that Boone has a Chamber of Commerce on

Story Street that will have lots more information about that area, plus maps."

"Great," Bill said. "Tomorrow Boone," he grinned at his exciting girl.

As they drove back to school, Bill seemed absorbed in his thoughts. Maria wondered if he was thinking about all the things they had discovered that afternoon and their plans for tomorrow. Maybe he loved to explore just as much as she did.

Suddenly he blurted out, "I'm so happy I met you, Maria. Your dad was a good travel teacher."

"You're right. My dad loved to travel, and a lot of his curious nature rubbed off on me. I think you're like him in that respect." Maria hoped the comparison ended there; she certainly didn't want Bill to leave her as her father had left her mother. She glanced at Bill and asked, "What about traveling the world together?" She felt he would be a wonderful traveling companion because he craved adventure and excitement. But would he also crave women, or would he settle for her and monogamy?

"I'd love to take you to the ends of the earth with me, Maria. Comparing me to your dad is quite a compliment, too, I might add." Turning in by her dorm, Bill said, "I'll call you tonight after dinner to decide what we want to do first tomorrow." He pulled her close to him and kissed her gently. "Thanks for being you."

When she least expected it, he said the most thoughtful things. It always pleased and surprised her. She couldn't top his heartfelt compliment, so she hopped out of the car, ran up the stairs, then turned and threw him a kiss. She went into the dorm to freshen up, then headed for the dining hall. She spotted Susie eating and slipped in beside her.

"Where have you been?" Susie asked.

"I've been riding around in Bill's new loaner car, looking over Ames for the first time since I got here. It's a cute town. We found a bunch of motels, the library, grocery stores, a bank, and drugstore."

"Did you say motels? As in looking for a place to do the deed?" Susie gave Maria a smart-assed look. "So, go get some food before it's all gone. This stew is pretty good."

"Okay, I'll be right back. Wait for me. It won't take me long to eat."

Susie waited until Maria finished, then they walked back to their dorm in the darkness.

"Susie, I want to ask you something, but it's so personal that I've got to wait until we're in our room."

"So shoot," Susie said, when Maria had closed the door behind them. "What's the big question?"

"You may be shocked by this, but I have to tell someone and you're my best friend, so here goes. Bill has been getting more and more . . . um . . . well, he's getting really sexy and pushing me in that direction. You know. He hasn't actually said, 'Let's go to a motel,' but he's been pretty frank about wanting to do more than just kiss. I know he doesn't want to wait much longer. Like you said, he was checking out places to 'do the deed.' So, do you know much about what kind of contraceptives I should use and where to get them?"

"What do you think Chuck and I do on our dates? Or did. When you date a football player, it's part of the drill. We've been going together for a couple of years."

My very 'with it' mother took me to her 'gyno' doctor to get me protected, and he fitted me with a diaphragm. My mother said not to trust a guy to use protection when the time came. Having your own protection is the only way to go; then there are no slip-ups."

"What's a diaphragm? I came from a family who pretended babies were brought by the mailman. My sister wouldn't discuss what she used if her life depended on it, and I have always been too shy to ask her or my mother about the whole sex thing."

"It's simple. A diaphragm is a small ring that you insert in you before you have intercourse, and it stops all the sperm getting to the egg, if you are ovulating." Susie said this with a self-satisfied look.

"Do you use one?" Maria asked shyly.

"All the time," Susie said.

"Could you tell me where I could get a diaphragm?" Maria surprised herself with her newfound boldness and hoped Susie could help her.

"I'll take you to the college clinic. I'm sure you can make an appointment with a gyno to be fitted for one."

"Does it hurt to get fitted? I'm such a chicken about pain."

"No. Haven't you ever been examined by a gyno?"

"In my family, I was lucky to have my teeth cleaned by the dentist. My mother was so into herself and mad at my dad for divorcing her that she didn't give a moment's thought about anything as important as this. And what is a gyno, anyway?" Maria asked.

"'Gyno' is short for gynecologist. It's a doctor who specializes in women's reproductive organs," Susie explained.

"Thanks, I understand—I think. Will you go over to the clinic with me next week, sometime?" Maria asked.

"Just check with me about my classes. Actually, I don't mind skipping one or two. They are so boring." She looked at Maria and asked, "So you've never done it before?"

"No, because I haven't had a boy friend that I liked well enough to try it."

"So, Sir Bill is the one, eh?"

"I'm crazy about him, and I'm sure he feels the same way about me—if he doesn't speak with forked tongue," Maria said, giggling.

"As long as you don't get pregnant or catch VD, there's no harm done, and sex is fun," Susie proclaimed.

"What's VD? Does it stand for venereal disease?"

"Yes; there's hope for you yet," Susie quipped.

"In my house, Susie, I swear we have never talked about periods, sanitary products, deodorants, or anything that had to do with the human body. As I said before, my mother was into herself. She was a decent mother when she was in an up cycle, but those didn't last very long. I always asked my friends about anything that was personal, and they loved telling me all they knew, which was a lot more than I knew."

"Well, you came to the right person on this one. We'll get you all set for Bill," Susie said, rubbing her hands together.

Around nine o'clock, Bill called to set up their plans. His voice was vibrant with excitement, obviously anticipating tomorrow's trip.

Ignoring the charge in his tone, Maria calmly said, "I have one class first thing in the morning, then I will be home around ten."

His only comment was, "Great, I'll pick you up around ten thirty."

"One more thought, let's have a picnic outdoors unless it's too cold. We'll find a sunny place and eat our lunch on a big rock. Do you think there'll be rocks?"

"We'll find out, won't we?" he said.

"Before we hang up, have you heard anything further about that third person who shall remain nameless?" Maria asked.

"No, but I called my folks before I called you to let them know what 'nameless' had done. They were shocked, especially my dad. He always thought I was exaggerating about her behavior because I know he didn't want to believe it. If he knew how unstable she really was, it would ruin his fantasy about her and me getting married. However, my mom wasn't surprised at all. She said that she had had her doubts about Maude for a long time as far as being right for me, especially after meeting you, you little dickens. My mom said that you were one of a kind, Maria, because of the way you have been raised, and that I wouldn't find another one like you."

"How's it going for you as far as nameless is concerned?" Maria asked. "I saw how upset you were after you found out what she'd done. I know you and she have had some good times together."

174

"I'm okay about her. I'm resigned to the fact that I can't go back to the way it was in high school and an undergraduate in college, even though that's what she desperately wants for us." Bill sounded pensive.

"One can never go back. I learned that when my folks' marriage broke up," Maria said quietly and with finality. "See you tomorrow; we'll have fun."

"Get ready to have a ball tomorrow, cutie," Bill said and hung up.

14. Explorations

Pleasure is a freedom song. It is the caged taking wing.
—Kahlil Gibran

Saturday morning dawned clear, crisp, and sunny. Maria watched the sun stream through their windows and thought, *It couldn't be more perfect.* She got up and dressed quickly, had a quick breakfast, and headed for her morning class. She fairly flew back to the dorm after class to get ready to see Bill. She put on the old ice-skating jacket that she loved and took her small duffle bag with her. She ran down to Bill's car parked by the dorm, slid into her seat, leaned over, and gave him a kiss on his cheek. She knew he loved it when she did that. "So hi," she said with a big smile.

"You look happy and cute as the devil," he said. "Ready for everything?"

"I think so, depending on what everything includes."

"Off to Boone on US 30," Bill said, shifting the Ford into gear.

"Would you like me to read to you about Boone? I have my little brochure with me."

"Sure, fire away," he said.

"Okay, here goes nothing. Boone has a population of ten thousand and is the county seat of the Des Moines River Valley. It boasts of Ledges State Park, six miles south. The tall ledges rising above Pease Creek give it its name." Maria looked at Bill and asked, "Ready for more?" He nodded, so she continued reading, "The Scenic Valley Railroad has a fifteen-mile round-trip ride on antique railcars through the scenic Des Moines River Valley. So what do you think of our options?" Maria asked.

"They both sound good. Let's see what we feel like after we get there. I think I'd like to try the railroad first."

"That's fine with me." Maria thought to herself that she didn't care what she did as long as it was with Bill.

"I'd better check the times the train leaves for its little run. Hmmm . . . it says here on the brochure that the train goes at two thirty every afternoon. I guess we'll have to do something else first," she said.

"Let's drive around Boone a bit, and I'll show you the Grange Hall where I spoke the other night."

"We could look for the Chamber of Commerce, too. There is a phone number to call for directions on my brochure. They could tell us more about Ledges State Park and where we could go for some food for our picnic."

"You are just a great little tourist guide, aren't you?"

"I aim to please." She gave him another little kiss on his cheek, delighted with him and life at that moment.

"That's not fair. I'm driving, and you are taking advantage of me. I owe you one or two," Bill said and gave her a big grin.

"Promise?"

"I'm keeping a tally, so watch it, young lady."

They drove into Boone, a quiet little town with a business area and only a couple of motels on the outskirts. Bill stopped at a gas station and found out where the Chamber of Commerce was located. Maria thought it was nice to be with someone who had a good sense of direction. The Chamber was very happy to give them lots of information on many points of interest. She loved collecting information for possible future trips. Maria asked, "Which way to a grocery store and the Grange Building?"

When they got back in the car, Bill wrapped his arms around her. "It's pay-back time," and proceeded to pay her back.

When she came up for air, Maria said, "Look at the people in the Chamber office watching us out their front window."

He glanced up over her shoulder and then laughed and laughed. "You got me, you little dickens! I believed you. Their windows are so dirty, they couldn't have seen us out here if they wanted to, which they don't. Let's go and get some food, and I'll show you the Grange on our way out to Ledges State Park. We can walk around there and have a picnic. By then, the train will be getting fired up and we can go for our scenic ride. What do you think of that plan?"

"I think you are brilliant," Maria said with tongue in cheek.

"Well, don't get carried away; an idiot could figure that one out. You're feeling really frisky, aren't you? You're playing with fire, young lady. I'm going to get you. I don't forget."

Maria shivered at this last statement. She felt the implied meaning.

Bill found the grocery store easily. It was small, but it had everything they wanted for lunch. Bill whipped out his wallet, paid the clerk for their food, then Maria put it all in her duffle bag.

"You like that duffle I gave you, don't you?"

"Yes, and we're going to take it everywhere with us when we travel. Also, thanks, handsome, for buying our lunch."

"I see you're making some plans of your own about our future. Let me in on what's going on in that very busy mind of yours." He stopped talking for a moment and looked at her with those big blue eyes full of mischief. "I'm keeping a tab, and we will settle up tonight."

She rolled her eyes at him. "Let's go explore."

Off they went to Ledges State Park, which was a short drive from Boone along the Des Moines River. It was a very pretty drive. Everything was green, but the trees were being singed by frost, which etched the edges of their leaves in reds, yellows, and oranges.

Maria thought Bill was oblivious to the landscape; he seemed too thrilled with his car. She had been watching the magnificent view out her window when Bill announced, "I love driving this car. It is so smooth. Hey, do you have a driver's license?"

She was jolted out of her reverie by his question and stammered back, "Am I my father's daughter? The first thing he did when I turned fourteen was to take me out on the back roads and teach me how to drive. He was a great teacher. I still hear him in my head, telling me to watch the cars because it isn't the lights that hit you. I used to say to myself, if he says that one more time, I will scream, but it has stuck with me since as a good bit of advice.

"Before I started driving a car, he showed me how to drive his little Ford tractor on his dry farm. I pulled something behind the tractor in the fields to do something to the dirt, but I don't know what the thing was called or what I was doing. All I know is that I drove it in a straight line up and back, up and back a million times and loved doing it."

Something she said made Bill start laughing. "I love your description of your tractor work in the fields."

She gave him a prissy look. "I did the best I could."

"You are a very interesting young woman. Your dad did a great job teaching you so many things."

"My daddy treated me like a boy in a lot of ways, and I will be forever grateful that he never said I couldn't do something because I was a girl." All of a sudden, Maria started to tear up. She couldn't help it. Down inside, she had never come to grips with the fact that he left her when she was fourteen. There was a lot of pain tucked away inside her about the unfinished business Maria still had with him. "I used to wonder," and her voice wavered as she quietly asked, "how could he leave me?"

Bill pulled over and stopped the car. He hugged her, stroked her hair, put his face in her hair. It smelled so good. He told her she was his precious girl and waited while she recovered. Drying her tears, Bill asked quietly, "Do you feel better?"

Maria nodded and thought what a kindhearted guy he was. Bill scored a lot of love points at that moment.

The big green sign on the right-hand side of the road said that Ledges State Park was one half mile ahead. "We're almost there,"

Bill said, checking on her again. He drove into the park and stopped at the ticket booth. He rolled down his window, paid the ranger, and headed into the main parking area. There were more cars there than they had expected. People were still enjoying the park because it was sunny, even though the temperatures were getting nippy.

Bill turned to her. "I'm sorry your folks split up while you were still so young." He put his arms around her, put his face in her hair, and whispered ever so softly, "I'm going to be your buddy forever."

"You'd better watch it, or my waterworks will turn on again." Maria was so touched by his understanding manner that she was having trouble keeping it all together. "Let's go and see this place before it gets any later."

Bill grabbed her duffle bag and put it over his shoulder while she scrambled out of the car.

"What do you have in here?" he asked, as he looked inside. He reached in and pulled out her Brownie camera. "What a good idea to bring it with us. You are always thinking, aren't you?"

Maria gave him a big smile. "Thank you, kind sir, for your compliment."

They started walking toward the Ledges Trail marked on the map.

"It looks like the trail winds around and follows the general direction of the river, high above it in the ledges. What fun it will be to see that. Can I take some shots?" Bill asked.

"Go for it; that's why I brought the camera. I'm glad you want to use it. It has black-and-white film in it, which makes the pictures much clearer than color with this little camera."

Bill bounced along like an excited kid, following the trail and using the camera. Maria wondered if he had ever just taken pictures of the outdoors before. She walked along in the sunshine, watching him climb up on the various ledges, jumping from place to place, getting different angles and shooting pictures. It was fun, seeing him having so much fun, and she thought he was having a chance to explore many new paths, literally and figuratively. *He's going to be very successful someday,* she thought, *and with that success, he will be happy.*

"How many pictures are on the roll?" he asked.

"There are thirty-six, possibly thirty-seven. Sometimes, you get an extra one."

"Do you care if I use up a roll?"

"My buddy can do anything he wants. Look in the duffle, there are two more rolls you can use, too."

"Gosh, honey, you are so generous. I'll get them developed by a friend of mine who does it on the side in one of the labs. It won't cost us anything." Suddenly, he turned, pointed the camera at her, and took her picture.

"You didn't let me pose before you shot it," she said.

"I wanted to catch you with your hair blowing and the sun pouring down on you. I think it will be a beautiful picture. You are very beautiful, you know."

"I'm glad you think so. I've got you fooled," she said, but her heart was beating extra fast with his compliment. Bill didn't say things like that to her, and she often wondered what he thought about her looks. Covering her obvious pleasure, she asked, "What about finding us a place to eat our lunch? I'm getting hungry. You know me; when I'm happy, I get hungry."

"There's a big flat rock over there in the sun, just like you imagined. How about that?" Bill asked.

"It looks like a winner to me. Give me the duffle, and I'll make us a couple of sandwiches."

Overlooking the river way down below them, it was a magnificent place to eat. Maria felt that it was a magical moment, sitting there in the sun with Bill, eating their lunch and looking at the view.

"Guess what?" Bill said. "We won't be able to make the train ride today. Do you know what time it is?"

"No, I've lost track of time, because I left my watch in my room. What time is it?"

"You'll never believe this: it's three o'clock," he said.

"This is an enchanted forest where time moves twice as fast as any other place, Bill. I'm just sure of it."

"We'll have to come again, maybe tomorrow afternoon, if the weather is nice and you want to."

"I'd love to. Let's start back to the car. By the time we get there, the sun will be getting pretty low in the sky." Maria shivered when she thought of losing the sun's warmth.

"You're right, it's time to go." They walked hand in hand, much more slowly than the hike up. The setting was so ancient, Maria wondered if the Native Americans had come there to hunt and enjoy the rocks and ledges many decades ago. If she squinted, she could almost see them.

Driving home with the sun at their back was easier than it was coming over to Boone. They were quiet and thinking about their great day. Finally, Bill broke the silence. "I haven't had so much fun in a long time. Thanks for being you."

"You've said that a couple of times, and it is one of the nicest compliments that you could give me." Maria gave him a big smile and moved as close as she could to him, so close that she could hear him breathing and feel the warmth of his body next to hers. She snuggled in, with her head resting on his shoulder, and closed her eyes. She felt the car stop and she knew they were back. It was close to five in the afternoon.

Bill walked up the dorm steps with her duffle on his shoulder, holding her hand. Maria felt loved. He was a comforting kind of man.

"I'll be over about eight tonight. That will give us some time to regroup," he said.

"That's just fine with me. See you then."

He gave her the duffle, bent down, kissed her nose, and went out the door. She strolled back to her room, ready to rest for a little while. Susie had left her a note saying that she was out with Chuck for dinner and would see her later that night. *Good,* thought Maria.

I can take a little nap and then eat dinner. She set her alarm, lay down, and was out like a light. She heard her alarm and wondered why it was ringing. When she finally came to, it was dark outside.

After a quick bite, Maria took a shower to help her wake up. The water worked its magic on her skin, and she felt good. Thinking about their day, Maria realized that she had discovered more about Bill than she thought possible in one brief outing. He was so joyful at Ledges State Park; he obviously loved to take pictures and was curious about everything. What a natural for *National Geographic* magazine someday. She didn't know why *National Geographic* had popped into her head, but it felt right.

Maria had almost an hour before Bill was due, so she cracked open her English textbook. There was a big test coming up, but luckily she liked English literature, so it didn't matter. It was one of her most favorite classes. She was lost in thought when she heard someone yell her name. "What is it?" she yelled back.

"Bill's here in the front room," someone answered.

Oh my gosh, she thought. She threw on her fall coat, ran down the hall, but put on her brakes when she got to the double doors. She walked calmly through them, seeming very poised, and stood with her hand on her hip, looking at Bill.

"So what kind of a pose is that?" he asked.

"I've been reading English literature while I was waiting for you to come, and I just finished a story about Queen Elizabeth. She inspired me."

"Okay, my queen, Sir Bill is here."

"You're a mighty handsome knight. Would you like to come to my chambers tonight?"

"What time?" Sir Bill asked, raising his eyebrows, then winking at her.

"You're pretty eager."

"I'll do anything my queen wants me to do. It's my duty as a royal subject." He grinned as he said it. "Come on, my queen, the evening is flying away."

"You must have had English lit, too. Or you have read too many comic books about Prince Valiant."

"I am a big Robin Hood fan. When I was little, I asked for a bow-and-arrow set for Christmas. I was going to be an archer like Robin Hood. I really practiced hard. My dad set up a row of hay bales out behind the barn, and when I could, I'd go out there and shoot arrows."

"I bet you were good. Did you keep it up when you got older?"

"No, I discovered BB guns. My dad gave me one for Christmas, and I was suddenly a big hunter tracking bears in the woods."

"I'll bet you were a little rascal as a youngster."

"I got into my share of trouble, but luckily, it wasn't life threatening." They'd quickly arrived at his frat house. "Time flies when you are talking about yourself," he said.

Inside, they stopped to talk to some of Bill's friends, who were funny and nice to be around. Maria could tell that they really liked and respected Bill. After a few minutes, Bill was tired of talking to the men and guided Maria away into their favorite place. One of the guys called, "Don't heat it up too much in there."

Maria noticed that every time they had been in there, no one ever bothered them. The younger actives seemed to idolize Bill and keep out of his way.

"I spent the time away from you tallying up what you owe me, and the total is very impressive. I don't know how many kisses it's going to take to work off your debt, so we'd better get started." He was funny. He sounded very businesslike, sort of like a banker negotiating a loan.

Sitting there looking at her with his face only a couple of inches away from hers, he looked so smug. His eyes were sparkling as he watched her.

"Did you ever hear of being in somebody's space? Sir Bill, you are in my space," Maria said with her nose almost touching his.

"If I could get any closer in your space, I would do it. I'm working on that angle very diligently." His voice was deep and sexy.

"What big words you use. You must be in college."

Bill reached over and turned off the light by the sofa. There was only the fire throwing out light. "Now, it's so dark, you can't tell whether I'm in your space or not."

Maria's heart turned over as he slipped his arms around her. "I've got to have a little payment on your debt," he whispered in her hair, then brushed her lips with his lips. He started breathing harder as he kissed her, pressing more and more. She didn't stop him. What incredible feelings he gave her. Kissing her neck, he moved his lips down the front of her blouse and opened her blouse a little. Very gently, he kissed her body above her breasts, moving down closer and closer to them. By the time he reached her bra, they were both gasping. She wanted him to go on, but knew she had to stop him.

She took her hands and put them on his face and raised his chin. She looked at him and whispered that they had to take a breather. He nodded. He put his arms around her again. "I love you so much and want to show you how much by making love to you."

Maria changed her tone, trying to get some distance from the subject. "I have something to talk to you about before we go any further." He sat there so still, listening to her and looking upset. Her heart went out to him. "We can't go on like this much longer. It's much harder on you than me, and I don't want you to have any problems with your genitalia. My brother-in-law was a great teacher about male sexual problems. I think I told you that he is a veterinarian and very much into bodily functions, but basically he's a good guy. He's always treated me like his little sister. We had a few discussions about males and sex. Don't worry, my sister was always there, too. Don told me that there is something called 'blue balls' that happens when a guy gets too aroused too many times and has no way of ejaculating. It hurts the testes. They get very sore and have to be iced down until they return to normal."

"Gosh, Maria, I'm so thankful that you brought up this subject. I didn't know what you knew about guys, having no brothers, and I didn't want to shock you. I haven't had any symptoms yet, but I'm sure it will happen if we don't do something. If we are going to continue seeing each other, we have to decide what we are going to do. Do you want that? I want to kiss and love you so badly I ache after I leave you."

"I talked with Susie about what we—and especially you—are going through every time we go out. She volunteered that she and Chuck have been having sexual intercourse for a couple of years. They have been going together since high school, and there was no way they could keep seeing each other without some release.

"I asked her what kind of contraceptives I should use, because I really didn't know. Thank God for Susie. She told me she uses a diaphragm and Chuck uses a condom. The combination is almost foolproof against pregnancy." She looked at Bill's face, and he was so absorbed in what she was saying, she thought she could have pricked him with a pin, and he wouldn't have felt it.

"My sister and my mother acted like any information about protection from getting pregnant was taboo. Bless Don; he, at least, talked to me about male problems. He never talked about women using contraceptives, probably because he didn't think that it would be appropriate coming from him. I really wish he had, though.

"So, my sweet, Susie said she'd go with me to the clinic at the college and help me make an appointment to see a doctor. He will have to examine me, check my blood to make sure I don't have any venereal disease, and fit me with the right size of diaphragm so it is tight and won't let any of your special sperms get near any of my eggs until we're ready for children. What say you, knight of wonderful possibilities?"

Bill's eyes were clouded with so much emotion, he seemed overwhelmed by what she had just described. "I want to go with you instead of Susie. It was awfully nice that she wants to help you, but it's my place to stand up like a man and be there for you. This is a partnership, and if I'm going to be your partner, I am going in to talk to the doctor with you. Will the examination hurt? I hate to think that you have to be examined, but I guess he can't fit you properly without an exam. You are gutsy, Maria. There's a lot to this whole thing."

"Bill, are you sure you're ready for this? We can't have two people in jeopardy of fainting. I'm a mess in doctors' offices. The other thing is, I'm afraid the nurse or desk attendant will tell me that they don't give out diaphragms to students or, worse yet, ask me a lot of personal information about why I want a contraceptive. That's been on my mind ever since I started down this path. It really bothers me, so you are going to have to be patient with me. Shall we get this over with? Do you have time on Tuesday? When's your next talk?"

"Yes, yes, and not for a while. I won't have any more talks until after Thanksgiving weekend, and I have a good handle on what my next subject will be. I'm sorry to put you through something that is so personal and embarrassing to you. I really think we would be all right with just me using protection that I can get at any drugstore."

"I'm paranoid about pregnancy and scared about doing *it*, too. I've got to be honest with you," Maria admitted, quietly.

"I promise I will not do anything unless you give me the go ahead. I don't want to scare you in any way. What kind of a guy would I be if I forced myself on you? That's rape in my book. If I'm not a good lover, I don't deserve you. We'll take it slow. If you don't enjoy it and have a bad experience with me, you'll never want to do it again with me, and that isn't what I want."

"I still think that I want to have a diaphragm. Help me through all this stuff, Bill. I'm groping my way along. I'd like to go over to the clinic first thing on Tuesday and get an appointment."

"Just tell me what time, and I'll be there. You're my gal, and this is very important to me."

She could tell he was a little worried about this doctor thing and her exam, but he was determined to have a sexual relationship with her, so she knew he'd do what he had to do to make it happen.

"Whew," Maria said. "I'm glad we've got the sex talk over now."

"Not so fast, we have a couple more things to think about: when and where," Bill said. "Obviously, over a weekend would be the 'when.' I will check out the best motel for us. Leave that to me. It's the least I can do after what you have to do." He put his arms around her, and they sat back on the sofa, holding each other.

Maria said, "I have a couple of other ideas that I want to run by you, now that we have the big one taken care of. I was watching you taking pictures. From what I saw, they should turn out pretty good. You seemed so happy, so I got the idea that you would be perfect working for *National Geographic* magazine someday."

Bill looked at her as if she were floating out in space. "That's a stretch for me. I do like photography, but a lot of things have to happen before I could consider that as a profession."

Maria ignored his practical answer. "I also thought about you working for the *Iowa Progress*, writing a column all about farming and answering the sort of questions that you are asked every week by farmers at those Grange meetings. You are a natural for this one. Save all your talks, all the material you use to write the talks, and the questions the farmers ask. They could be the basis for your columns. Also, you have a great rapport with your professors here; they could be a source for material, too. You are a good writer, I bet. Tell me, do you like writing? What do you think of that idea?"

"You are full of ideas for me to pursue. I am overwhelmed by how your mind works, and your observational powers. You're moving a little faster than I'm comfortable with, but you are truly the best thing that has ever happened to me. I'm very interested in both ideas for future work, especially writing for the *Iowa Progress*. I have never thought of myself as a writer, but I do like to write and inform people about farming. I will save all my material and sometime, when I feel it is the right time, I might go to the paper and pitch my idea—pardon me, *your* idea—about a column. We'll see where it goes."

Maria felt a certain lassitude overtaking her body. "It's late, and I've been ready for bed since about an hour ago. I don't have the stamina that you seem to have."

"You're right; it's almost curfew time, my love. I've got a lot of thinking to do. Our sex life and the possibilities for our future are all tied up together."

As Maria thought about offering up one more idea, she feared that Bill might want her to just shut up. She winced a little. "I almost forgot to mention flying. You could go over to the ROTC building on campus and find out what you have to do to sign up for the Air Force. I think it would be a great chance for you to fly."

"Well, you've been thinking overtime, haven't you? I'd had this idea, too. There may be another war in an Asian country called Korea by the time I finish school next year. I want to be able to choose what I do if my draft number comes up. I wouldn't get a deferment like my brothers, because they are established as farmers, I'm not." Suddenly, he changed subjects. "I almost forgot, you wanted me to remind you of something. What was it?"

"Oh, that's right. Susie and I need a ride to the bank and the train ticket office in Boone to buy tickets home for Christmas. We don't need to go tomorrow, but sometime soon. We need to get them early if we don't want to end up sitting on our bags."

"Just say when and I'll drive you over. Come on, let's get you home, so that I can do some thinking. You are something else, you know that don't you?"

"Yes, and when you know what your plan is for the rest of your life, I'm interested. I hope I fit in there somewhere."

"None of it will amount to a hill of beans if you aren't with me."

Maria glanced at Bill. He wasn't smiling or joking. He meant it.

They got back to the dorm just as the Campanile started to gong midnight. "I'll call you." His tone of voice suggested to Maria that she had shaken him up.

Bill didn't kiss her. He just held her in his arms and said that he was the luckiest man alive.

She ran up the stairs, turned, blew him a kiss, and darted inside.

Maria and Susie stayed up talking late into the night. Susie said that things were really deteriorating between Chuck and her. He wasn't happy at Iowa State, and a lot of his unhappiness was rubbing off on their relationship. He was going to talk to his folks at Thanksgiving about transferring to Iowa University in Iowa City. He liked their curriculum and football program better.

"What are you going to do?" Maria asked.

Susie said, "I'm going to get busy with Chi Omega's rush program for next semester, for one thing. Also, several of my clubs want me to run for office. And I'm on the VIESHA Spring Festival committee.

"What's VIESHA?"

"Each letter stands for a program of studies at Iowa State. V stands for veterinary medicine, for example. I'll probably need your help later next semester."

"I would like to help out, Susie, but I want to know what my other options are in regard to volunteering activities." Maria had been given some awful jobs in high school that other members of various committees hadn't wanted to do; she didn't want that to happen again.

"Don't worry, roommate, I won't steer you wrong," Susie said. "S-o-o-o, how did things go with Sir Bill?" She looked so wide eyed with her pretty brown eyes.

"We went over to Boone and had a picnic at the state park there. It was so much fun to get away from the campus. It's like a breath of fresh air to see people who aren't carrying books around and scurrying along sidewalks, struggling to get to class. The state park was built along the Des Moines River. Did you know that? I didn't even know there was a Des Moines River."

"It must be nice now that Bill has wheels. It opens up a host of possibilities not available to you before."

"You are so right. We had a lot of fun finding our way around. You'd think we were going on a thousand-mile journey the way we were discussing it. Bill is very good at looking for signs, keeping cool, and asking for help—unlike some guys. When we got to Boone, he hopped out of the car and went into a gas station to ask someone where the Chamber of Commerce was.

"We may go back tomorrow and take a little scenic ride on an old-fashioned train. It only goes fifteen miles round trip. We'll be back before we get started, but it should be fun. Bill really likes trains, and so do I.

"You know, Susie, with Maude in the hospital, we feel like a big weight has been lifted off our shoulders. It has made Bill act like a normal guy, not like the one who's been giving me sad, strange looks the last few weeks. It used to scare me. I'm sure he was thinking about Maude a lot. She was right between us all the time. Now he is free."

"It's getting late. We should get our beauty sleep. By the way, are we still on for Tuesday for the clinic?" Susie asked.

"Oh, I forgot to tell you. I talked to Bill about the whole contraceptive issue, and he said that he wanted to take me. He said he was the one who was involved in this with me and wanted to help me. Isn't that terrific?"

"Yes, if he wants to escalate your relationship, he *should* go with you. If he acts like a man, I'll consider moving him up on my scale of nice guys who try to do the right thing."

After that comment, Maria passed out in her bed, never moving until Sunday, late in the morning.

Sleeping in on Sunday morning and waking up to the music coming from the Campanile was very energizing. As Maria stretched, she thought, *Ah, first a shower, then I have to hit the books for the rest of the morning.*

By noon, she was getting hungry. "Susie, are you ready to eat?"

Susie looked up from her books and thought a minute. "Let's do it. Sunday lunch is usually pretty good and a great way to give me a break from studying."

When they came back from lunch, the unlucky girl who had the floor phone outside her room said, "Someone called you a few minutes ago, Maria. I told him that you probably were at lunch, and he said he'd call back in a few minutes."

"I hate when that happens. I'm going to be ready when Bill calls back, because he may want to go catch a ride on that antique train this afternoon."

Sure enough, when Bill called, he wanted to go, so he said he would pick her up in fifteen minutes. Maria quickly packed her duffle with her camera, a couple of apples she had taken from the lunchroom, and some napkins for their sticky, juicy fingers. Maria was waiting on the steps when Bill pulled up. "Don't get out," Maria said, and slid into her seat. "Are you ready for your exciting 'choo-choo' ride? You won't be scared, will you?"

"Listen, Missy, I'll show you how old I am, so you'll know I won't be scared." He kissed her until she felt like her toes were sizzling.

"I give, I give," Maria struggled to say when he let her up for air. "I take it all back."

Bill was laughing so hard as they pulled out, she thought they might run off into the ditch.

"What we need is a little music in our lives," she said, as she turned on the radio. "Ah, I've found a good station." She settled back to listen. "What's your view on dancing with me sometime?"

"I've never heard it put quite that way, but I love dancing with you."

"A big band is coming here a week after we get back from Thanksgiving. I would like to hear them and dance around in your arms. Are you a good dancer, or will you embarrass me on the dance floor?" Maria asked with a straight face.

"You liked it when we danced a couple of times at the house. I haven't grown two left feet since then. And, as I recall, you had no trouble with me stepping on your feet," Bill said, grinning as if he had gotten the better of her in that exchange.

She looked up from adjusting the radio. "I don't remember any-thing like that happening," she said in her most reserved manner, looking the other way. He was so much fun to tease.

"Boy, that was quick," Maria said as she saw that they were in

Boone. "The conversation and the music must have been good today."

"There's the sign to the 'choo-choo' rides," Bill said. "Get ready for excitement."

Parking was easy; hardly anyone was there for a ride. Maybe the weather was too cold. Bill bought their tickets, took her hand and her duffle bag, and they climbed aboard. "Did you remember your camera?"

She gave him a confidant smile that said, of course, she remembered it. Maria reached into the duffle and pulled it out, then handed it to him.

"Good girl. I think I'll take you out again."

Inside the train, the benches were covered in a velveteen material that looked reminiscent of that used in upholstery in the1900s. The car reminded her of a set in a western movie. Leaning close to Bill, she said, "Please protect me, kind sir. Did you bring your gun?"

"Dadblast it! I knew there was something I forgot when I got dressed this morning."

Maria muffled her usual hearty laugh, because there were a couple of ladies who looked like they were out of the 1880s, sitting in very prim positions, watching them. "You've been holding out on me, Bill, hiding your accent," she whispered in his ear.

"I have lots more things that I have been hiding, but gradually I will show them to you," he whispered back, twirling an imaginary mustache.

"We're moving. Get our expensive camera ready for action," Maria said quietly.

He nodded and began looking around. After taking several shots of the railcar interior, he said that he was going out on the platform. She followed him out and watched him climb up on the railing, lean out and take some pictures of the train as it curved around the river bed. *He's a natural photographer,* she thought as she watched him hanging by a toe, taking pictures. What balance that guy had, plus all those muscles, he could hang on the side of the train like an acrobat.

"Looks like you're getting some great shots," Maria said, thinking, *Here comes Mr. National Geographic.*

He looked down from his perch and smiled that wonderful smile. "We'll see how great they are when the film's developed, but it's fun. What do you think of that river down there? It's pretty, isn't it? I'm glad we came, aren't you?"

"It's been a fun ride on our 'choo-choo.' I'm glad you like to take pictures."

They stayed out on the platform to get a better view of the valley, and the ride was over before they knew it.

Bill exclaimed, "Boy, that was fast trip. We'll have to find more 'choo-choo' rides to take."

Maria nodded and got ready to get off the train. "I'm glad I wore my sweater and jacket. It's getting cold."

Bill put his arms around her to warm her up and asked, "Are you hungry? I'm starving."

"Being an acrobat hanging on the outside of the train used up a lot of your breakfast, I bet."

As they pulled out of the parking area, Bill said that he had noticed a mom-and-pop restaurant on the way to the station. "Want to try it?"

"Fine." Maria didn't care where they ate as long as they ate together.

As they parked, Maria saw a lot of cars outside, which was a good sign. She looked over at Bill and said with a smile, "It looks good to me."

As they sat down in the warm atmosphere of the restaurant, Bill said, "You are a good sport. Did you know that? You are game to try anything. I'll bet your dad had a hand in making you so flexible, and you never complain."

"I've got you fooled," she said, her eyes sparkling.

"You have, eh. I'll have to investigate that further when we're alone." He twirled his imaginary mustache again and grinned at her.

After observing several orders of pot roast being served, Maria said, "That's for me."

Bill said, "I love the fact that you like old-fashioned food and aren't fussy."

"Being fussy about food wouldn't have done me much good while growing up, because my mother only cooked once in a while. She had so many demons inside her, she tried to drown them with alcohol for long stretches of time. As a kid, I was delighted when I came home and found her in the kitchen. I didn't care what it was, I was ready to eat it."

"I know I have said this before, but you were really out there on your own a lot of the time. That's partly why you have such a great attitude about things. You seem so appreciative about life in general. It's one of the reasons that you interest me. I see things differently because of you."

"Here's our food, yum-yum," Maria said. She was glad to have the interruption, because she was feeling a little funny about how she came across to Bill. His description of her made her sound like a gal in the comics named Daisy Mae, Li'l Abner's goofy girlfriend; she was always happy, too.

"This is pretty good, but I'm so hungry I could eat anything with gravy on it," Bill said. "My mother used to say that if she served shoe leather with gravy, we'd all eat it without even noticing."

Maria laughed. "Your mom has a great sense of humor. I saw that when I was visiting."

They ate like two undernourished orphans and, finishing quickly, were ready to go. Bill paid, as always, and Maria said, "I could get used to you picking up the tab all the time."

He looked at her. "There's no free lunch. Don't you know that by now?" He grinned from ear to ear at his not-so-subtle message.

Maria found some good music on the radio and sat in the car—full, happy, and completely satisfied with the afternoon. She thought that they certainly got along well. Since she was in a quiet mood, she liked the way that Bill had quiet moments, too, when they were together. It was very restful not to have to keep answering questions or listening to a boring guy talk about himself until she was ready to scream. Maria had experienced both situations with many of the guys she had dated in high school.

They pulled up in front of her dorm, and Bill asked her if she wanted to come over to his frat house for a while that evening. He wanted to talk about a couple of things with her.

"I'm fine with that. I love our fireside chats," Maria answered.

"I'm not Franklin Roosevelt, but I'll try to make my chat interesting. I'll come back in an hour or so." He leaned over and kissed her cheek.

Maria ran up the stairs, turned, blew him a kiss, and returned to the real world again after her afternoon of fantasy.

15. Making Plans

Energy and persistence conquer all things.
—Benjamin Franklin

On the way to her room, Maria decided to call her sister, something that she had been putting off for days. She had to reverse the charges, and she hated to ask May to accept her call, but there was no other way she could make a long distance call from the dorm. It was school policy; otherwise, kids might run up huge bills and not be able to pay them when they came due. Although Thanksgiving was still a couple of weeks away, Maria needed to let her sister know when she would be arriving. Maria gave herself the excuse that she had been too busy with school to call earlier, but the real reason was Bill. He made her crazy, she was so in love with him.

May accepted Maria's charges. "It's about time I heard from you. How are you anyway? When are you going to get here for the holiday?"

"I'm fine, and I'm not sure what time I'll be there." Maria worried that May sounded irritated, maybe because of the added responsibility of Maria's visit. "I'm coming home with Ed and a bunch of his girlfriends. He's dropping them off in various towns along the way. We may stop for food, if anyone gets hungry, and that will slow us up some. Don't worry about me, though; I'm in good hands with Ed."

"Thanks for calling and letting me know your plans. Have you met any nice guys this fall?"

"I'll give you the rundown when I see you. Don't wait up for me; just leave the garage door open, and I'll creep in. Am I sleeping on the pull-out couch in the rec room? I wouldn't want to get in the wrong bed at midnight."

"My little sister has grown up, getting home at midnight. Don't get too carried away with Ed. Yes, you are sleeping in the rec room, as always."

"Ed has so many girl friends, he hardly knows I exist. I've only run into him in the Union once this fall when I was with Bill."

"Who's Bill? Is he cute? Do you like him? We'll have to talk," May said, with interest.

"I'll tell you when I see you, yes, and yes," Maria laughed. "I have to go. Bill is picking me up soon. I just wanted to be sure and call you now, because you are usually home on Sunday evenings. Sorry I haven't called before. Thanks for accepting the phone charges. Bye."

"Bye, yourself. See you at Thanksgiving. Your head had better be peeking out of the covers in the rec room when I get up Thursday morning."

As she ran down the hall to their room, Maria thoughts were with her sister. Absence, even from a relative, sure makes the heart grow fonder. Maria burst into the room, thinking a million different things, but pulled up short. Susie was sitting on her bed, looking dejected. "What's the matter, Susie?"

"Chuck seems to be saying goodbye to me. He's acting distant and preoccupied."

"I'm so sorry that he's being a jerk these days. I bet he's feeling strange about changing schools in January, even though he isn't saying so," Maria said, trying to comfort her friend.

"I'm sure that enters into his attitude, but it doesn't make it any easier for me. I honestly don't think he is in love with me anymore and wants a clean break."

Maria could see the sadness on Susie's face. Susie and Chuck had grown up together. This was a hard time to have her boyfriend going in a different direction, especially with the holidays coming up.

Maria sat down next to Susie and looked at her. Then she made a face at Susie.

Susie retaliated and threw her pillow at Maria. Susie laughed. "I wish you could make it all go away. Make it like it was for us in high school."

"I wish with all my heart that I could," Maria replied, feeling Susie's utter despair.

"Maria, Bill is here in the front room," someone called from the hallway.

"Susie, I have to go. I'm sorry that I have to leave you right now. Take a soothing shower, call your mother, go see some friends, or eat if you're hungry. I'll be back at curfew and we can pick this up then, if you want."

Maria flew down the hall and out into the front room. She hadn't had time to clean up or make herself look pretty.

"What's the matter? You look jumpy. Do you feel all right?" Bill asked.

"Susie is feeling bad because Chuck is acting weird. He is transferring to Iowa University to go in a different direction in hopes that he will get more of a chance to play football there. He's leaving next semester.

"They have been going together since high school, and at one time probably thought they would get married. I'm glad that I never found anyone who interested me enough to get that attached in high school."

"You're lucky. I wish I had ended my relationship with Maude in high school, before I ever came to college. I was a chicken and thought she'd find a new guy, but she didn't."

They left the dorm, and it was cold outside. Maria turned her collar up and put on her gloves. "Let's walk fast."

That was all Bill had to hear. He took off, which meant Maria had to almost run to keep up with him, but it felt good to move.

When they got to his house, she was slightly out of breath, but not Bill. He had amazing lung capacity.

The house was quiet. Everyone was out or studying. They sat down on the sofa by the fire and hugged each other. "Are you using me to get warm?" Bill asked.

"Yes, I'm cold, but now I feel better. Are you complaining?"

"Are you kidding? I have an opportunity to feel your body, so no complaints from me. Shall I give you a nice rub down? Just to warm you up, of course."

"A likely story, but it's a good idea," she said, a little mischievously.

He stopped, looked at her, and took her face in his hands. He said, softly, "We haven't kissed all day." He carefully pulled her close, so their lips were almost touching, and he smiled and asked in a sexy voice, "How about it?" He kissed her, got another breath, and kissed her again. He took a quick breather, then gave her a French kiss that she felt down to her toes.

"Enough, enough, my sweet. We've got to come up for air," Maria whispered.

Sitting there as close as they could, Bill said, "Just remember I love you, and we will get through this. Now, before I tell you something I don't want to, when do you want me to pick you up Tuesday morning to go to the clinic?"

"Around nine, I think. They open at eight, but I want to let all the folks with cuts and bruises get fixed up and gone before we arrive. So tell me what is bothering you, handsome?"

"My folks called me early this morning, before I picked you up for our outing, to tell me that since Maude got home after her suicide attempt, she has spread the rumor far and wide that I'm a very bad guy. That we have been having intimate relations all fall, and that I insisted upon it if I was to stay with her as her boyfriend.

"Her mother and father went to see the minister about the situation, and the minister made a visit out to see my folks about it. My parents were so mad after he left. He believed the Jenkinses' story and wanted my folks to make an appointment for me to talk to him when I get home. He said that he had to protect Maude and help in any way he could to make me stand up, be a man, and do the right thing by Maude. My folks asked him what he meant by the right thing, and he said that I should give her an engagement ring at Christmas with the intention of getting married as soon as possible.

"My folks defended me and said that it was her word against mine. They said that I hadn't even dated Maude this fall because I have a new girlfriend, whom they met last week when you came home with me. They told him we had been dating for a while and were in love with each other. The minister said that he would have to talk to you, Maria, and decide if he believed this. He intimated that you were trying to break up my relationship with Maude. The minister said that it was my fault that Maude tried to commit suicide."

Maria sat there dumbfounded. She finally said, "Maude is delusional. Don't they see that? What do you want me to do?"

"Absolutely nothing but love me. I have been giving this a lot of thought. When I go home for Thanksgiving, I'll meet with the minister and see what I can get worked out. I absolutely will not allow you to be put through some kind of interrogation."

When he said that, Maria thought of the Spanish Inquisition. When that picture popped into her head, Maria couldn't help but laugh. "Do you think he would hang me from my thumbs until I confessed that I was trying to steal you? I can see it all now: Your minister is trying to hoist me up on the rack. I'm too heavy and he's too little, so we fall to the floor together with him on top of me. I lean up and kiss him. He gets so excited, he kisses me back and tries to have sex with me, but you come in and discover him fumbling around with me. The minister is so upset about getting caught, he runs away." She laughed even harder after finishing this little scene.

"Did you get into the liquor cabinet before I picked you up? I think you should join the drama club or write short stories. That mind of yours never quits. Actually, the picture of the minister is really funny, and when I go see him, I'm sure I'll think about your story and probably laugh inappropriately. The whole thing is stupid, anyway," Bill said, disgustedly.

"If you give me your sister's phone number, I'll call over Thanksgiving to give you the latest details in this soap opera. I'm only going to support my parents. Otherwise, I wouldn't dream of giving Maude, her parents, or the minister the satisfaction. By the way, the minister *is* a little guy, not much taller than you." Bill laughed out loud when he realized that.

"My parents have to live there and are surrounded by a bunch of gossiping people who must not have much to do. They have some friends whom they enjoy, but for the most part, they don't agree with attitudes of a lot of the people in their church. I will never go back to that church again."

Bill sighed. "Let's change the subject. I won't be able to see you tomorrow at all because I have to meet with my professor and work out some details on my future talks with the Grange people. I also have a house meeting, where Dick is going to talk to the actives about my new job with the Grange. He wants me to explain what I'm doing and how it came about. I think he's using me to inspire some of our less-interested students, so that they can see how their studies might help them get a job. I'll call you after the meeting is over. It will be about ten or eleven, is that okay?"

"When has that ever stopped you before?"

"You are a little dickens." He kissed her lightly on the nose and gave her a big hug.

Hugging and touching physically was very comforting to both of them, especially because of the nasty little situation that Maude had brought about. *When will people wise up and realize that Bill wouldn't do all the things that Maude's saying about him,* Maria wondered. Sometimes, people loved to make a situation worse by believing the gossip.

Maria said, "Together, we're going to lick this small-town type of attitude or go down fighting."

He looked at his watch. "When I'm with you, the time goes by so fast. We've got to go."

They jumped up and ran out the side door. It was cold. It took Maria's breath away. As they were walking at a brisk pace, Bill said, "I forgot to tell you again how much fun the 'choo-choo' ride was. Today was a perfect day, except for Maude."

"You amaze me. You never let on that something was bothering you during the scenic ride. I think you are pretty darn strong not to let problems stop you from having a good time. By the way, are you sure your parents didn't steal you from the gypsies or circus people? You were hanging from your toes and balancing like an acrobat on that train."

He gave her a surprised look. Without missing a beat, he said with a straight face, "I'd always wondered why my parents acted so strange when they took me to the circus. Perhaps they thought they would be recognized, and my real circus acrobatic parents would take me back."

"We are a pair; our stories are getting wilder and funnier than ever. Let's write a children's book, together."

Maria was almost out of breath from walking so quickly. When she mentioned their possible book writing, she started to laugh. The cold air made her cough, which made her laugh—and cough—even more. Finally, she had to stop for a moment. She stood there, doubled over with laughter. It was infectious, and Bill started to laugh, too. By the time they got to the steps they were a sight, coughing and laughing, but their laughter released a lot of anxiety. They had made it back to the dorm with a couple of minutes to spare. Where did the warm weather go? No more balmy strolls until next spring. She was already thinking about the spring, and winter hadn't even started.

"Let's hug and save our kisses for the car or the house," Maria said. "My lips are getting chapped."

He gave her a sly look, fished around in his pocket, pulled out a beat-up ChapStick, and began painting her lips with it. "No chapped lips excuse from you will let you escape my kisses." Maria had the urge to laugh again, but Bill covered her lips with his and kissed her until the Campanile stopped ringing. He stood back, held her at arm's length, looked at her lips, and pronounced her cured of chapped lips. "Talk to you tomorrow night," he said.

Maria hated to leave him, they were having so much fun, but he gave her a gentle push and sent her up the stairs. She did her little performance, and he stood there looking up at her, grinning.

Being with Bill was the most fun Maria had ever had. No one she knew had ever loved playing and joking the way he did. What a wonderful day. They just clicked. It was so easy being with him. Maria thought that she was a very lucky girl as she opened their dorm room door, peeked in, and saw Susie sound asleep. Maria was glad. Maybe sleeping would make things better for Susie. Maria knew Bill wasn't going to call her tonight, so she did her bedtime routine, jumped into her cozy nest of blankets, and the next thing she knew, it was early Monday morning.

16. Susie's Troubles

My heart is ever at your service.
—William Shakespeare

Six o'clock in the morning—Maria hadn't been up this early for months. *Great,* she thought, *I can get a shower before anyone and have plenty of hot water.* She flew down the hall to the showers, cleaned up, and dressed. She was studying when Susie woke up, sat up, looked at Maria, and threw her pillow at her.

"This is getting to be a habit with you, this pillow-throwing stuff," Maria said.

"You taught me, and you look too well put together for so early in the morning. I wanted to change that," Susie said, grinning. "I'm going to get dressed and go for breakfast. Are you hungry? I am. I didn't feel like eating last night, but I'm ready this morning." With that comment, Susie grabbed her clothes and a towel and headed for the showers.

In the dining hall, after they had coffee and some food, Maria asked Susie, "How are you doing?"

Susie said that her mother had called the night before, sensing that something was wrong, to find out what was the matter. "Talking to my mom made me feel better; I was able to study afterwards and slept quite well." Maria reached over and gave her little pat, as if to say, "'atta girl."

They grabbed their books and headed to class. Maria said, "I wish we had some kind of school-bus service around this big campus.

Iowans may want to be hardy and brave the cold, but this is ridiculous. There's nothing about this in the brochures. It's a conspiracy, I say, to get students here without telling them about the cold, the size of the campus, or lack of bus service. If potential students knew those things, they would never come. Ugh! How did you like my rant so early in the morning, Susie?"

The sidewalk split in two directions. Susie said, "I agree with everything, but here's where we part company, partner."

"You sound like an actor in a two-bit western. See you tonight for dinner, unless I freeze solid out here somewhere," Maria said.

"I'll send out my St. Bernard for you with a cask of beer around his neck."

"Make that whiskey, I'll need it," Maria called over her shoulder.

As Maria was walking along, she thought about her dad's continual concern that she needed more exercise. *Well, Dad, you'd be happy with this campus.* She would call him from May's house at Thanksgiving and tell him how far she walked every day.

Suddenly, she felt a little wave of sadness wash over her as she thought about her dad. Maria missed his gentle ways. She wished that he and Betty hadn't had any children. Being tied down with two little girls made it impossible for him to make any impromptu trips to see her. Having a trophy wife, thirty years younger than he was, may have seemed exciting at the time, but he was already getting old when he married her. He'd told Maria that he thought he and Betty would be winging their way around the world, that he finally had a travel partner, but Betty apparently had other ideas. She surprised him with her plans to have a family. Maria thought, *I'll bet Dad didn't think he would end up feeding babies in the middle of the night at his age.*

Maria was miles away, hardly noticing her walk. When she surfaced, she was in front of her destination, the chemistry building. She shivered and was glad that she could go inside and warm up. She decided right then that she was going to buy a longer, warmer coat when she went to her sister's house for Thanksgiving. Right now, she felt confident, thinking she would borrow Don's car, ask for money for the coat, go to Sterling, and get it. However, that was still a couple of weeks away. She might chicken out when she was there in front of Don, but she was freezing in her old coat. When the wind blew across the Quadrangle, it was *cold*. If it was already like this in early November, she hated to think what *winter* would be like.

If she hadn't met Bill, she would be very unhappy about being out here in Iowa, away from everything she had grown up with in the suburbs of Chicago. Why hadn't she thought this through a little better? She hadn't even visited the campus when her sister was here, because she was seven years younger than May and hadn't been thinking about college. Her big concern was racking up Girl Scout badges, and, besides, her folks were fighting all the time, so neither she nor May were ever center stage with their parents.

Another thing, Maria wasn't sure that she liked any of her science curriculum. When she'd realized that she had to take physics, math, and a whole bunch of chemistry courses, she'd thought, *Oops, what did I do?* She was an art and English lover. What was she doing out here, freezing to death, taking courses she didn't like?

At La Grange High School, the principal's office handed out applications to the kids for any colleges that they were interested in. One day, Maria asked for an application to Iowa State. The secretary handed it to her. It was just that simple, or simple-minded, depending on your point of view. She had a terrible reason for choosing this school:, her sister had come here and met her future husband, who was in the vet med program.

Maria was lost in thought again. *Wake up and get going with your chem experiment,* Maria chided herself. She hated chemistry this morning. Everyone was busily getting their test tubes ready, reading their lab books, as if they really liked this stuff. She wondered what they really thought about chem lab.

She finally trudged back to the dorm for dinner. She had spent three hours in lab, had to walk back to the dining hall for lunch, then back to campus for English and history. She must have walked three miles each way. At least, that's what it felt like. She had been so peppy this morning, but she was worn down now, with the sun dipping farther on the horizon, and the cold seeping through the cracks in her clothing.

"Boy, Thanksgiving break can't come soon enough. It's almost all I can think about. How about you?" Maria threw her books down on her desk and looked at Susie. "This cold is very depressing."

"Another fun day in the chemistry lab, I presume," Susie said, as she grabbed Maria's arm and hustled her out the door to the dining hall.

"That's another thing I hate about this place, we have to go outside to another dorm to eat. I didn't notice it so much when it was warmer, but it really is awful in the cold weather," Maria whined.

"That's another good reason for you to pledge Chi Omega next semester. The cook lives there, and the dining room is in the house. I have built you up to everybody, so they think you are an answer to a prayer," Susie said, as she pushed Maria into the dining hall ahead of a gang of girls.

"Where did you learn to be so aggressive?"

"Good ole La Grange High, same place as you.," Susie grabbed a tray and gave Maria one, too.

"I think you are so mad at Chuck, you are fighting back, and the people who cross you are going to get it as stand-ins for Chuck. I love it. Did your mom give you a pep talk?"

"She did, and she made me realize that I have a lot to offer to the right person, and Chuck will be the loser for leaving me."

"Amen to that. What a great mom you have. I'm so glad she called," Maria said, putting enormous amounts of food on her tray.

"Are you sure you can eat all that? Did you ever hear of portion control?" Susie asked, with a big grin on her face.

"Yes, and I see that you are going to have trouble carrying your tray, too. It's so heavy with all those desserts you are carrying."

Walking back to their dorm, feeling very full and tired, Susie said, "I'm glad that we ended up together, but I was a little worried about you being my roommate after I came to visit you and met your mother last fall. She scared me."

"My mother scared me and my other friends, too, so join the club. I never felt comfortable having kids over to our house, because I never knew whether she would be sober or not. My friends soon learned to invite me over to their homes for overnights. No one ever said anything to me about my mom and my home life, but I'm sure they knew that she had big problems. They probably also guessed that my dad had left her, since she and I were living alone in that big, old house.

"You are so lucky to have such a charming mother, Susie. I remember when I met her for the first time. She was sitting in your cute little living room in your apartment, talking to your bird, who was sitting on her finger. She got up, came over to me, gave me a great big smile, and said that she was happy to meet me. She turned to you and said that I was cute. Do you remember that?"

"Yes, and she was wrong about that, but that was the only mistake she made that day," Susie said, laughing. "My mom has been good *to* me and *for* me. She holds a big job in Chicago with the American Cancer Society. That's why we went to Chicago from South Dakota. The only thing I wish were different is my dad's interest in us. He has a new family, and he doesn't see my sister or me much anymore. I miss him."

"That sounds like my story. Why do fathers forget their children when they remarry? Is it the sex that they are getting again? I wish I could ask my dad, 'Are you so busy in bed that you can't think about anything else? Will Betty cut you off if you dare to mention your other two daughters?' Anyway, it's good that we are roommates, because we have a lot of things in common. Enough going over the old stuff for one night," Maria said. "Isn't there a house meeting tonight in the front room?"

"Oh my gosh, I almost forgot. Good work, roomie. One good thing, Maude won't be there. I guess we can stand it." Susie made a face. "Come on, let's get this show on the road and see what trouble we can cause at the meeting."

After the meeting, Susie said, "Well, that was boring, except when Maude's snippy little friend stood up and questioned why people were being allowed to slip in after curfew. I wonder who she was referring to? She looked at you like you were an evil spirit."

Maria laughed. "I didn't know I had such an audience."

"You know something, Maria? I haven't thought about Chuck for at least two hours."

"Good, keep feeling mad and not sad," Maria said as positively as she could.

They had just reached their room when the phone down the hall rang. Maria turned and ran back in case it was Bill. "Hi, how did you know it was me? I'm always amazed when you answer the phone."

"I told you, I'm magical. You just don't listen," Maria said.

"Are you all set for me to pick you up around nine tomorrow morning? "Bill asked, knowing the answer.

"Yes, that's fine. How did the meeting go? Was everybody impressed with your talk?"

"You're just a bundle of questions, aren't you," he said, obviously pleased with her interest.

"Yes, now shoot. What did they say?"

"The guys were great. They kidded me a little about having wheels and how convenient that was for us. And I got the general impression that everyone was pleased about my new job." He paused, and his voice changed in tone. "So tomorrow, we'll take the first appointment we can get with the doctor, okay?"

Maria was learning something very charming about his personality. It was one of the reasons that he was admired as a leader among his friends. He didn't like to go on and on about himself. He let his actions speak for themselves.

"I wonder why someone's so anxious to get this contraceptive," she whispered into the phone.

"You are a little dickens. Sometimes, I don't know whether I want to squeeze or kiss you," he said with a laugh.

"I'll see you tomorrow morning, bright eyed and bushy tailed, but tonight, I must say goodnight. I am beat, and I'll bet you are tired, too. I love you, sweets."

"I hope you're never bushy tailed. That's one thing I don't think I could live with, but I love all the rest of you. See you tomorrow."

17. The Next Step

The most powerful symptom of love is a tenderness.
—Victor Hugo

When Maria woke up, her mind was whirling and she felt queasy. Nineteen years old. Was she ready for this? Bill's sex drive was pushing her into it. It was time, wasn't it? So many unanswered questions were driving her crazy. There was a lot of commitment involved with her decision. Time was ticking away while she was doing her soul searching. She groaned because she had to get ready to meet Bill in less than an hour.

Susie was coming back from the shower as Maria was running to get one, "Wow," Susie said as Maria blew past.

"I'm late. I've got a lot to do, and half an hour to do it in."

When Maria came back, Susie asked if she wanted to eat something before she met Bill.

"No time. Besides, you know me, Susie. I can't eat when I'm nervous."

"What's so bad about making an appointment?" Susie asked.

"I don't know what the person who is making the appointments is going to ask me. I'm afraid she is going to lecture me on being intimate before marriage. Maybe ask me some personal questions that I won't be able to answer, or embarrass me in front of Bill."

"No way," Susie said. "I can guarantee it. Those nurses don't care what you are doing. They've seen it all. It's all very cut and dried to them."

"I hope so," Maria said, looking out their front window for Bill's car. "He's here. I'll see you later."

Susie stuck out her tongue to make Maria laugh. "Relax," she said.

Maria met Bill coming up the steps, and he swung around when he saw her coming down.

She gave him a weak smile when he opened her car door.

"How are you doing?" he asked, as he gave her a little hug. Maria looked like a ghost, she was so pale.

"Let's go. I'm nervous, and I know it's silly, but that's me," she said, shivering.

They got there fast, driving instead of walking. *Darn,* she thought, *I needed more time.* She felt a little sick to her stomach. "I wish I had some peppermints. They would really help right now."

Bill said, "I'm sorry to put you through this. I didn't realize how sensitive you were to this whole thing."

"Well, you are getting to know me better and better. I have a lot of traits, and this nervous one is less appealing than some of my others. It seems that anything to do with doctors sets me off. My dad is a doctor, and he was always very good to me. He never did anything to cause these nerves, but I have them nonetheless."

"What would you like me to do? Should I take you back to the dorm, and we can try another time? I wish I had some peppermints for you." He reached over and pulled her to him so he could give her a hug.

"I just need to take some deep breaths and maybe get a drink of water, if they have some. Then I think I will be fine. I feel so goofy acting like this."

They sat in the car for a bit, Bill's arms hugging her and her face buried in his shoulder. She took deep breaths, trying to settle her stomach. Bill was so calm and patient, he made her feel better.

Finally, Maria said, "Let's go in and see what we can do about an appointment."

Bill came around the car and opened her door. "If it makes you feel any better, you look very pretty this morning."

He just melted her heart sometimes with the things that popped out of his mouth. "Thanks, but I don't believe you for a moment. I know I'm as white as a sheet. Come on, let's get this over."

The receiving room of the clinic was big and barnlike but clean. A lady in a white uniform, looking very official, looked up at them from her desk—first at Maria and then at Bill. She didn't smile. She was overweight and had a sour, edgy way about her. Even the way her hair was tightly pulled back made her seem unpleasant.

"What can I do for you?" she asked in a brusque manner.

"You'd think she had a hundred people waiting to be admitted, like in a Chicago hospital emergency room, the way she's acting," Maria whispered to Bill.

Bill said in a calm, but rather stern, manner, "We'd like to make an appointment to see a doctor."

The nurse asked, "Are you two married?"

"No," Bill said. "My girlfriend here wants to discuss getting a diaphragm to protect her from getting pregnant. I want to meet with the doctor, too."

"Well, I guess that's plain enough. No beating around the bush with you, Sonny."

Maria thought, *Hurray for Bill.* He had backed the nurse down, somewhat, with his very authoritative manner.

The nurse looked over the schedule, flipping the pages back and forth. "You'll want to see an OB/GYN for a fitting," she said, looking at Maria with her little beady eyes. "He's on vacation and won't be back until after Thanksgiving, three weeks from today. He's booked solid at his other office in Ames after that, and as far as I can see, the first available appointment here will be December 16 at three in the afternoon. Do you want it?" She looked straight at Maria without a hint of a smile.

"Sure, that will be fine. By the way, what's the doctor's name?"

"Dr. Summers, and his partner is a she, Dr. Summers, also. They're married." The nursed grinned as if she'd just told a joke.

Walking out the clinic door, Maria said, "Thanks so much for what you did."

Bill said, "We're in this together. Since you have to go through this with a doctor, and I can buy condoms at the drugstore with ease, I want to help you through your part in our new relationship."

Here was one more reason why she was so in love with this guy. He stepped up to the plate, so to speak, and supported her by taking the lead; facing that cranky nurse down, for example. He didn't hesitate. It was like it was second nature for him. What a wonderful family he had; they had taught him how to be a real man. Maria had the feeling that this would be the way he was always going to be with her during their lives together.

"Guess what? I'm hungry," Maria said. "Do you have time to go to the Union for a little food to celebrate?"

"Sure! This is how I love to see you—with a smile on your face." Bill flashed his amazing smile at her.

After their stop in the Union, Bill offered to drop her at the science building. Maria took him up on his offer so fast that he laughed. But on the way over, Bill looked quite sober.

"Why the long face?" asked Maria.

"Well, I hate to do this to you, especially after this morning, but I probably won't be able to see much of you for the next couple of weeks. The professors really like to ramp up the exam schedules before the holidays, and I'm going to be swamped with schoolwork. Can you forgive me?"

Maria sighed. "You know, it's probably just as well. We have to wait so long for the doctor's appointment that this will put temptation at arm's length for a while." She smiled halfheartedly. "I'm going to be pretty busy with exams and labs, too, and I really need to be able to concentrate without a certain someone always in the background." Maria nudged him gently in the ribs.

"I'll call as often as I can, and I'll come by for some hugs and kisses after dinner. That will have to last us for a while. Here we

218

are," he said, as they pulled up to the building. He started to get out to open her door.

"I'm fine, don't move. I'll just pop out. Love yah."

As Maria walked up the stairs to her classroom on the second floor, she reflected that she and Bill had reached a new level of knowing each other. The initial superficiality of their first meetings was necessary to attract each other's attention, but now the layers were beginning to peel back, and something much deeper was happening between them. They were learning to read each other's signals and were forming a tighter and tighter bond.

Maria had been woolgathering again, and when she looked at the numbers on the doors, she realized that she had walked past her classroom. She was doing that more and more these days. She backtracked, making the excuse to herself that all the darn doors looked alike.

As she sat down, opened her notebook, and tried to prepare herself for a lecture on covalent bonds, she thought instead about this morning with Bill. He had seemed to know that he needed to talk to the nurse and give Maria a chance to get herself together. That was an example of this new type of bonding. Maybe they were covalent bonds. Anyway, it sounded good to her.

As the day wound down and she was making her way across the Quad, she thought about Bill and the minister. Maria had no fears that Bill would come out all right from the skirmish, but she wondered what kind of pressure Maude's family would try to exert on him. It would be a long few weeks to wait to find out.

Her dear father had always tried to tell her how it was, from his point of view, no matter what the subject. His number one rule on any subject was that when people were involved, follow the money. She wished she could get his point of view on this problem. Maria planned to call him to wish him a happy Thanksgiving while she was at May's. She would ask him about the situation then. She needed to hear what he had to say about the land gift from the Morgans to Maude and Bill when they married. Who stood to gain from this marriage?

Maria hurried to her dorm, threw her books in her room, grabbed Susie, and went off to eat.

"How did it go this morning?" Susie asked. "What did Bill say? When are you going to see the doctor?"

"Good," Maria said, laughing at Susie.

"What do you mean 'good'? That's no answer. Give me the particulars," Susie demanded.

"We'll talk when we get back to our room, too many ears here. Do you see Maude's friend sitting over there, leaning back and trying to catch our conversation?"

"Gosh, I didn't. Sorry. I was just so upset with how you felt this morning that I thought about you all day and wanted to know if you were okay. Nothing like having a big mouth," Susie said.

They had just settled in their room and Maria was explaining how funny and cranky the nurse was, when they heard the phone. "Darn, just when we get to the good part, Bill has to call," Susie said.

Maria ran down the hall, just in time to see that same friend of Maude's from the dining hall pick up their phone and speak into it. Maria was incensed but knew her reaction was ridiculous. Maude's friend was probably just passing by the phone and was doing a good deed by answering it. Anyway, the phone call obviously wasn't for Maria. Maude's friend continued talking to whoever it was. As Maria watched her, she thought she heard her say, "You're a damned liar!" She looked angry enough to hit someone.

Maria turned and was starting back to her room when the girl called to her. She turned to see what that pest wanted, and the girl held the phone out to Maria with a taunting look on her face.

"It's for you. It's lover boy, himself," she said in a most insulting manner.

Maria grabbed the phone and gave her a vicious look.

The girl just stood there, watching Maria. "Hello," Maria said into the phone. She put her hand over the receiver and said to the pest, "Is there something you are waiting for?" Maria wanted her to go away so that she could talk in private.

"I'm a friend of Maude and Bill's," the girl said with a malevolent look. Then she moved irritatingly slowly down the hall.

"What's going on over there?" Bill asked. "Are you ready for kisses and hugs?"

"I'll tell you about the phone thing when I see you and a definite yes to the second question."

"See you in fifteen minutes or so. I'll have my ChapStick with me in case I run into any opposition," Bill said with a chuckle.

When Maria came back to their room, Susie asked, "What was going on at the phone station? I was talking to Jeannie, our friend across the hall, and I saw that girl from the dining hall giving you a hard time."

"I'll be darned if I know. I think I heard her call Bill a damned liar. Those cohorts of Maude's are planning something, and I'm sure that she was down here to harass me. She probably overheard me say that Bill was going to call me when we were chatting at dinner."

"Well, that little stinker," Susie said, emphatically.

"Which one? They are lining up, it seems. Anyway, I can't think about it now. I've got to at least get my face washed before I see Bill. I haven't had a chance to do that since lunch."

Feeling full and now refreshed, Maria put her coat on and went out to the front room to wait for Bill. He came bounding up the stairs. He threw his arm around her shoulder and they headed out. "It feels like snow," he said, opening her car door and grinning at her.

Maria pulled her coat up around her neck. "Darn," she said. "I've left my scarf in the room. I was a little rattled by the phone fight. What I need is a coat with a hood."

"Do you want to go back and get it?" Bill asked as he leaned over and lightly kissed her.

"I'll be just a minute." Maria leaped out of the car and disappeared up the stairs. When she returned, she not only had her scarf wrapped around her neck but a hat on her head. "Now the snow can't get down in my coat."

"You look cute in your hat. I don't remember seeing you in one before."

Bill started the car and eased out onto the road. He was quiet for a moment, then said, "The desk nurse or whoever she was reminded me of a dog we had on the farm. Her bark was worse than her bite. I could never get my dog to stop acting like someone was going to fight with her and keep her from landing the first punch."

"Speaking of fights, do you want to hear about my little phone fight?"

"Sure, I couldn't figure out who was talking to me when I called. I knew it wasn't you or the gal whose room is next to the phone. We've gotten to be pretty good friends. When she said it was Isabelle, it finally dawned on me that it was Maude's best friend at school. She lives in our little town and has known both of us for a long time."

"I heard the phone and started down the hall to answer it in case it was you, but she had already picked it up and was having a conversation. I thought, 'well this isn't for me' and headed back to my room. All of a sudden, I heard her call my name, so I went back to the phone stand. She held the phone out to me, almost as if daring me to take it from her. When I took it; she stood there, not moving away so that I could talk to you privately. I finally had to ask her to move, and she gave me a look far worse than our crabby nurse did. She said that she was a longtime friend of yours and Maude's. Then she slowly sauntered down the hall like she owned the place."

Maria looked at Bill and asked, "Did she call you a liar? I thought I heard that."

"She may have. She and Maude are very close, and she'll say anything in Maude's defense. Don't give it a thought." Bill smiled at her, but Maria saw that old fleeting look of concern cross his face.

A few snowflakes were hitting the windshield as they drove slowly around the campus. "Oh, it looks like winter is coming," said Bill. "I should buy some chains for my car before we get a big snowstorm."

He obviously didn't want to discuss his small-town "friends" anymore, and she didn't blame him.

When they arrived at the Farm House, there was a fire crackling in the study. Maria went up to it and put her hands out to warm them. "I love a fire," she said. The fire was the only light in the room.

"It's just for you," Bill whispered and took her hands. He put her arms around his neck, held her close, and put his face in her hair. Speaking softly, he said, "I love you." He began kissing her, pulling her more tightly to him.

Maria knew things were heating up pretty fast, and she wanted them to calm down. She pulled back. "We'd better sit down and relax a little. It's almost curfew time, and we've got to go soon," she said weakly. Maria was always so surprised by how strong he was.

"We aren't going anywhere until you kiss me some more." He closed his eyes and waited. She moved a little, and he tightened his arms around her.

"Okay, you asked for it; here it comes." She leaned into him and could feel the warmth of his body on hers. She kissed his eyelids and then leaned back.

He opened his eyes. "Is that it?"

Maria nodded, a big smile on her face.

"This is how you do it, in case you didn't know." Bill put one hand behind her head and pushed her face gently into his. He kissed her with such sweetness, Maria melted.

She put her hands on his face. "We've got to go, handsome. You've worked your magic long enough for one night."

She straightened her clothes, gave herself a mental shake, and was ready to face reality again.

He held her coat open. "Slip this on, cutie. One thing I want to say about you is you've got class and make me feel like nothing is impossible in the future."

Maria loved his sexy gallantry and hated to leave him.

It was nice to be spoiled and driven to her dorm instead of having to walk in the cold. The snow had stopped. There was just a light cover on the trees and road, and it sparkled under the street lights.

When they got back to the dorm, he parked away from the other couples standing by the steps. He turned to her and held her in his arms, putting his face in her hair. He didn't move for a few moments. He found her lips and kissed her. He was a great kisser, but the Campanile began its incessant gonging, forcing them to take a breather.

"I'll try to see you once more before we leave for Thanksgiving break," Bill said, squeezing her hand.

Maria got out of the car and ran for the steps. She blew him a kiss and went into the dorm.

18. Recruiting

It is when you give of yourself, you truly give.
—Kahlil Gibran

Maria was alerted to the fact that they had company in their room by the laughter and giggles she could hear through the door. Stepping into the room, she saw her roommate, who was a ham at heart, entertaining two girls.

"Hi, I'm Maria, Susie's roommate. Who's going to introduce themselves?" Maria asked.

A tall, willowy, very pretty blond girl smiled and said, "I'm Janet, and I live on the third floor."

The other girl said, "I'm Marianne." She was the opposite of Janet in stature, very petite, but equally pretty. She seemed the shyer of the two.

Looking at Susie, Maria waited to be clued in. Susie said that she had been telling the gals all about the Chi Omega sorority and possibly rushing during winter semester.

"Your roommate is so funny," Janet said. "We've been having so much fun talking with her. She's been telling us all about Chi Omega, and she's going to give us a tour of the sorority house after we get back from Thanksgiving break."

"So what have you been saying to these girls?" Maria asked, with a wry look. She wanted to say "innocent girls" but held back.

"Chi Omega is a great sorority, and the gals are outstanding in their achievements in grades and volunteering in college functions.

Their cumulative grade ranks second among all the sororities." On and on Susie went with her propaganda. Maria decided to block out the sales pitch and do something constructive.

"I'm going to get organized for exams." She hoped the others would take the hint. "I'll just move around here quietly." She gathered books and checked her schedules. Looking at everyone with a big smile on her face, she thought, *If Susie doesn't shut up, I'm going to stuff a sock in her mouth.*

Janet and Marianne had glazed looks on their faces; they were obviously tired of Susie's sermon, too. Maybe they were going to barf. Maria giggled silently to herself.

While Susie was looking for the words to the Chi Omega loyalty song, the two girls saw a chance for escape, hurried to the door, and said that they wouldn't forget the evening. Maria thought, *I bet you won't.*

Susie gave them assurances that they were at the top of her list of potential members for Chi Omega. She was good at making people feel important. She was something to watch in action. *Maybe Susie should consider politics as a career,* Maria thought, *and forget all that icky math and physics.*

After Janet and Marianne left, Maria and Susie exchanged looks, then made faces at each other. "Good job, Chi Omega booster," Maria hailed her. "Sign me up, even though you made me want to barf. You piled it on higher and deeper tonight."

"They probably won't take you, even if I beg them to, with that attitude," Susie said.

As Maria grabbed her towel and soap, she said, "They'll love me," and walked out the door, heading for the showers.

After they had both climbed into bed, Susie asked her how the appointment meeting had gone.

"Nurse Crabby was obnoxious, but Bill was magnificent. We have to wait, get this, until December 16 for an appointment."

"Do you want to look up a different doctor in the phone book and see him instead?" Susie asked.

"No, these two doctors, husband and wife, practice together. I like the idea that the university has hired them. They must have pretty good credentials. The controller of the appointment book told us that they are taking an extended Thanksgiving leave, they teach one day a week at Drake University, and have a practice in Ames, besides working in the clinic at Iowa State. That's why we have to wait so long."

19. The Thanksgiving Ride

A good conscience is a continual Christmas.
—Benjamin Franklin

The next couple of weeks flew by. Maria was so wrapped up with exams, labs, and final papers that she barely had the energy to think about Bill. He called most nights, but it was almost a relief to have a little breather from the physical aspect. However, by Thanksgiving week, she was really starting to miss holding and kissing him. So when Bill called on Tuesday morning to ask if he could see her that evening, she practically shouted "Yes!" into the phone.

When Bill picked her up, she was happy he'd brought the car again. What a godsend it was in this cold weather. She raced to the car as soon as she saw him pull up and jumped in. He hadn't even started to get out to open the door for her.

Bill immediately leaned over and kissed her. "Oh, Maria, I've missed you so much. Being apart from you is almost like torture."

She greedily kissed him back, surprised at herself. Then she shivered. "Brrr . . . let's not waste time sitting here in the cold when we could be curled up in front of a cozy fire."

Bill grinned. "Your wish is my command."

Once they were happily situated in their favorite spot, Bill got down to some serious catch-up kissing. When he started to tremble, Maria knew they had to stop. She gently pushed him away. "Whoa! I need to breathe! Plus, remember what we talked about—no blue balls."

Bill laughed, which helped release the tension, and seemed content to just sit there and cuddle for a while.

It felt so good to be back in Bill's arms that Maria was sorry they were going to be parted again for the long weekend. "When are you going to get away, tomorrow?" she asked.

"I'm not sure. I have to wrap some things up with my professor about the talks I'm giving when I come back after Thanksgiving."

"Are you going to stop by the *Iowa Progress* on your way home?"

"Yes, I'm going to try to make an appointment for Friday. If I have to wait until after I get back to school, well, I'll do what it takes. We could go down to Des Moines and you could go shopping or something while I'm giving my pitch."

"It would be fun to see Des Moines. I was wondering if you had talked to your professor about possibly writing that column. He may know someone who could get you an appointment."

"Honey, that's a great idea. My professor is well known around here and probably has contacts at Drake University, too. You are always looking out for me, and I really appreciate your caring." He put his arm around the middle of her back and the other one under her legs, then lifted her up on his lap—easy as that. "Now shut up and kiss me some more," he said, grinning.

Maria was happy to comply, but she kept it gentle. She didn't want Bill getting all excited again, especially since it was almost curfew. After a few minutes, she said, "Bill, I hate to say this, but it's time to go."

He sighed. "I know. Hey, you need to give me your sister's number so that I can call you over Thanksgiving."

"Yeah, I really want to know how that 'chat' with your minister turns out."

Bill dropped her off outside her dorm. He gave her one last kiss. "Have a great holiday, cutie. I love you."

"You too and me too, Bill. I hope everything goes well."

Maria dashed up the stairs. She was exhausted. She did the bare minimum necessary before falling into bed and was asleep in an instant.

The next thing Maria knew, it was morning. She thought, *I have four and a half glorious days off from school, starting at one o'clock today when Ed picks me up. I'm so ready for a break from the whole class and lab routine.*

Susie sat up in bed and looked at her with sleepy eyes. "Do you have any classes this morning?"

"Unfortunately, yes, I have one: a history lecture. He's going to give out a reading assignment to complete during the break, so I can't skip the class. Are you hungry? I'm starving."

"Let's go as soon as possible. I have some loose ends to tie up, including Chuck, this morning," Susie said.

"Good, it sounds ominous for Chuck."

After breakfast, when they were walking back to the dorm, Maria asked, "Susie, when are you leaving?"

"I'm not sure, seeing how difficult Chuck is being. If he doesn't take me, I'll catch a ride with Janet. You remember, one of the gals you met a couple weeks ago. She lives in a 'burb outside Chicago, too."

"Give Chuck a kick in the butt from me. I'll see you for lunch, anyway, before we all hit the road." Maria gathered her books and walked out the door with Susie. Susie went one way and Maria went the other.

At lunch, Susie told her that she was successful in locating Chuck and getting the promise of a ride from him, which made Maria happy. It was a long way to Chicago from Ames, Iowa.

Around one o'clock, Maria started looking out her front window, waiting to see Ed's car. She wasn't disappointed. There he was, right on time. Two girls were in the front seat with him. Maria ran down the stairs with her duffle bags banging against her legs but still trying to look smooth for the girls watching her. Ed was standing by the car, waiting for Maria.

He stuffed her bags in the trunk. Maria almost reached for a bag, flirting with the idea of reading her history book on the way.

Silly girl, she'd look like a study geek doing that. Maria climbed into the back seat and settled down for a long ride. She introduced herself to the gals in front, both of whom were dark haired and very pretty. She thought, *That's Ed. He doesn't waste time on girls he's not interested in.*

They stopped near an upper-class dorm, and two more nice-looking gals appeared with their bags. Ed's trunk was large, but would it hold all that luggage? Ed struggled a little back there, but he got it all in. What a sight they must have been, one guy and all those girls. *Ed and his harem,* Maria thought. *Either he's the luckiest guy in the world or the craziest.*

"Hi, I'm Maria," she said to her two riding partners in the back seat.

They introduced themselves as Jane and Peggy. Both were upper classmen and were well on their way to finishing up their degrees. Maria wished she were in their shoes.

Maria could hear Ed regaling the girls in the front seat with stories about his work. There was much laughter and teasing. He was certainly performing for them. Maria wondered if that was the real Ed. She had always felt that he had a very deep side but covered it with jokes and laughter.

This is fun, she said to herself. *What was I thinking? I could never have concentrated on a history book. With five women in a car, it would never have been quiet enough to read.* The real question on Maria's mind was how had Ed met and befriended all these gals?

After an hour or so, he took a side road, pulled up by a house, and one of girls got out of the car. As she left, she said, "Thank you so much, Ed," and called him her handsome waiter. She gave him a blazing smile as she left.

Ah-hah! Maria thought, *He waits tables in their dorm, at least for one of them. Maybe that's how they all knew him. Or were some his girl-friends? No, he wouldn't be so stupid as to put girlfriends together. Not smooth, sexy Ed. Maybe just one is his special friend, the one sitting next to him in the front seat.*

After another hour, the sun was going down. How short the days were getting. Ed pulled into a gas station and said that he would be leaving again in ten minutes or so. Maria knew he was politely giving everyone a chance to go the bathroom and reminding them not to dawdle. The gas station was huge and looked like it did a big business. They piled out of the car as fast as they could. It felt good to stretch and walk a little. Maria couldn't help thinking that they must have looked like those cars in the circus that kept letting people out, it seemed, by the dozens. She followed the other gals to the bathroom, which was inside the station, not outside in some obscure place.

When Maria came out, Ed was standing by the car with a cup of coffee in his hand, smoking a cigarette. She realized that he hadn't smoked until now. His car smelled new, and now she knew why. No smoking by anyone inside. Thank goodness for that. All that smoke in a closed car would have given them headaches.

She was seeing a generous side of Ed: taking all of them home, not smoking in the car. *What nice things to do,* she thought. All those years of seeing him at her brother-in-law's house, and she really didn't know him at all. He was much older than her, so that set them apart, but now the gap didn't seem so wide. Don must have seen a lot of potential in him, taking him on as an apprentice. Her dear brother-in-law knew what he was doing as far as guys were concerned.

As the other girls returned to the car, Maria watched Ed being charming and funny with them. That was another side of him that she had never had the chance to see, his charming side. She wondered if his other riders were thinking about him as date potential. Did he look like more than a friend to her? She spent some time quietly thinking about this whole turn of events, all brought on by a simple ride.

By the time everyone else had been dropped off, Maria was in the backseat alone. With each drop off, Maria had noticed that Ed had not given anyone a hug. After driving for a while, he seemed to remember that she was there and glanced over his shoulder. "Hello, back there. Do you want to sit in the front seat with me? Or do you want me to be your chauffeur?" he asked with a chuckle.

Maria had begun to feel lonely back there, but hadn't known how to remedy it. She said, "I'll hop in front with you." She didn't know what possessed her, but she put one leg over the front seat and the other one followed.

"Well, you're a surprise. I thought you were a well-mannered little freshman, not this acrobat up here in the front with me." Ed seemed genuinely amused. "I would have stopped and let you in through the door."

Maria blushed from embarrassment, but it was dark, so Ed couldn't see her face clearly. *I'm an idiot,* she thought. As they were riding along, she recalled when she had first met Ed. She was a sophomore in high school and he was an apprentice, working for her brother-in-law, a veterinarian in Rock Falls, Illinois. Ed was in veterinary medical school at Iowa State, and Maria was in awe of him then. Some of that awe carried over into the present.

After a little while, he asked if she was hungry. He had an unusual look on his face.

Maria wondered what that look meant. He was a hard person to read. She felt there were many layers of Ed that maybe even Ed didn't know.

"Sure," she said, in her tongue-tied way. She found herself acting in a whole different manner with Ed than she did with Bill. Why was that? The car was dark and warm inside. They were alone with each other, and she began to feel her heart pulsing. It was if they were a million miles from the rest of the world, hurtling along on the road stretching away in front of them, every mile bringing them closer and closer to each other. Did Ed feel it, too?

As he pulled into a dark parking lot outside a brightly lit diner, he turned and looked at Maria with his big brown eyes. Neither of them spoke. She knew he had felt it, too. He touched her shoulder, and it made her jump. A current raced through her. "How's this place?" he asked, quietly. "Sorry, I didn't mean to startle you. I just had the urge to touch you, to see why I feel the way I do."

Maria looked over at him and said hoarsely, "It's fine." What was happening between them? As she started to get out, she remembered her coat in the back seat. She leaned way over to grab it and felt like Ed was undressing her as she did. Her rump was up in the air for a moment, and she could feel his eyes on her body. *How unsmooth can I be,* she thought. When she got out and started to put her coat on, she felt him come up closely beside her and help her into it. Maria felt that unexplainable current between them again and said to herself, *Just relax, he isn't going to do anything.* Then she thought, *Maybe he will.*

The jukebox was playing one of her favorite songs, "Somewhere in the Night," when they walked into the nicely decorated restaurant with the aroma of good food in the air. *Boy,* she thought, *I'm hungry.* They found a booth and slid in, he on one side and she on the other. Frank Sinatra was crooning in the background. The words were very romantic, but she tried to ignore them. Instead she picked up the menu and began to study it feverishly.

"(I Love You) For Sentimental Reasons" started playing, another romantic one. Why didn't someone play "Smoke! Smoke! Smoke! (That Cigarette)" or "Boogie Woogie Stomp"? Reading the menu, Maria saw the dinner prices and wanted to offer to pay for her dinner, but it was hard for her to talk to Ed about it for some reason. She thought she'd wait until the check came and offer then.

Ed looked at her and grinned. "So what looks good to you?" He was smoking a cigarette and offered her one. She didn't know whether to take it from him or not. On the one hand, it might make her look smooth, but on the other, he might think women shouldn't smoke. Then she said to herself, *Why do I care what he thinks?* It shouldn't have mattered, but it did.

"Okay, I'll try one," Maria said. "Don't laugh if I choke. I've smoked once in a while with Don or some of my friends, but not very often."

Ed handed her a cigarette, touching her hand as he did, looking at her reaction. The jukebox was playing, "Smoke Gets in Your Eyes" and to cover her feelings, she commented on the coincidence of the song title with her attempt at smoking, while thinking, *Oh sure,* now *they play a smoking song.* "Let's hope that doesn't happen, though. I don't want red eyes." She halfway swallowed her words because he took her breath away.

The waitress came over, gave Ed a big smile, and took their order. Ed held out a match and lit Maria's cigarette, all the while looking at her as if he had never seen her before. It was very unsettling. As Maria was trying to smoke like a pro, she wondered what these looks signaled. Was she imagining it? Was she being a little naïve, or was Ed really coming on to her?

Clearing her throat from the harsh smoke, Maria asked him if he was tired after driving all that way.

He laughed and said that driving was one of the easiest things he could do. He mentioned that he was going to do some work for Don while he was home. "After a day with the doc, I'm tired. He gets his money's worth out of me. So what are your plans for the weekend?"

"I need to look for a warmer coat in the stores in Sterling. If I can borrow a car and maybe some money from May or Don, that is. My bank account is pretty depleted. I hadn't realized how cold it was going to be walking across the Quad, and it is only going to get colder."

Ed said, "Tap the old man; Don owes you a lot. What did he pay you when you spent the summers babysitting all their kids?"

"He never paid me. I didn't realize at the time that it wasn't fair not to make a little money. I started out visiting them when I was young, and everyone sort of took my help for granted. I liked being with them, but as I got older, I could have used the money. My dad gives me a little allowance every week, but it isn't enough for things like clothes. My mom lives in Washington, D.C., with her new husband. She may help me out a little when I see her at Christmastime, but help is spotty."

Ed seemed a little surprised about her financial situation.

236

"Well," he said, "I'm buying your dinner. It would probably take your whole week's allowance to pay for it otherwise."

At first, she thought he was teasing her, but he wasn't. He meant it. He was very kind, and he knew the value of a dollar. Don had told her once that Ed paid all of his college expenses himself. No one helped him through vet school. That was why he worked every minute he could, both at school in the dorms and at home. Maria began to see a guy who stood completely on his own, and it impressed her.

Their food came, and it looked delicious. Maria put out her cigarette and started to eat as carefully as she could. He was across the table, talking and watching her. She didn't want to look like a little piggy. As Ed ate, he was smiling and enjoying his food and hopefully her company. She didn't understand why his opinion meant so much to her, but it did.

"Do you like beer," he asked? "I don't think we should drink and drive, but sometime if we are just going to be local, would you like to go out and have a beer and dinner with me?"

Maria couldn't believe her ears. He had always acted as if he didn't even notice her. She could feel her hormones starting to flow. What was the matter with her? She just left her darling Bill, whose last words were that he loved her. Ed didn't really know her and certainly didn't love her.

He was waiting for her answer and smiling at her.

"I like beer within limits, and of course I love to eat, as you must have noticed tonight," she said.

"Good, we'll figure something out. If you're done, let's go. We've still got a ways to drive to Rock Falls." Ed paid the bill.

Maria thought of her plan to offer to pay for her dinner but couldn't say anything, especially since he'd commented on her lack of funds and already offered to pay for her dinner. He helped her on with her coat and draped his own over his shoulder. On the way to the car, he casually put his arm over her shoulder.

All Maria's hero worship of him was surfacing. She was tongue-tied, and she didn't know what to say anyway. She should have said

237

something to let him know that she wasn't available, but she didn't. To tell the truth, she was flattered by his attention. She had an unsettling thought: *Maybe he picks someone on every trip to make out with*. She was stirred up and not thinking clearly.

He unlocked her side of the car and before he opened the door, he turned around and gave her a quick kiss on the lips. Then he walked around to his side of the car, unlocked it, and got in. She could feel her heart pumping from that kiss and was feeling shaky when she got in the front seat. Maria said to herself, *He knows I'm an easy mark*. She stayed in the middle of the car seat, not quite on her side but not on his, either. She tried to get herself under control, but was becoming more nervous by the minute. *He's older, nice, sexy, and very used to making love,* she thought. She wasn't afraid of him; she was afraid of her own feelings.

"We have another couple of hours of driving," Ed said. "Are you tired? If you want to lean up against me and close your eyes, it's fine with me," he said softly.

What a smooth operator he is, she thought. If she sat close to him, what message would that send? She was torn about what to do. She couldn't let this situation get out of control. He probably had a glove compartment full of condoms.

She said, "Thanks, but I'm not sleepy. Do you like music when you are driving? I can try to tune in a Chicago station and get some nice music."

"Sure, that's a great idea. I love music." He gave her a glance that was heart melting.

Maria quickly found some dance music. She started tapping her fingers to the beat of music. Although she wanted to sing some of the lyrics, she refrained, because no one likes to have a song ruined by a sing-along.

"Come on over closer to me," Ed said. He reached over, put his arm around her, and gently pulled her nearer to him. He began stroking her arm with his fingers.

She knew he was playing with her, but she sat frozen, her heart beginning to beat like mad. *Just tell him to stop,* she thought, but she couldn't. What was she getting herself into? She didn't want to say, "Don't do that." She was embarrassed by the lust that was taking over her body. That's all it was, lust; she freely admitted it.

"How are you feeling?" Ed asked her a little hoarsely. Maria thought that he was probably feeling very sexy. The music was playing a beautiful love song and the car seemed full of electricity. "Maria, I want you to know that I have been watching you grow up into a woman, getting more appealing every year. When I asked you to ride home with me, I didn't know if we would hit it off. We've never even had a date, because I felt you were way too young, and, of course, Don was my boss. I think he would have killed me if I'd dated you then. Tonight, when we were sitting across from each other at the diner, I felt feelings that have been there for years, ever since I first met you. I can't explain the draw, but it's there."

Maria said, "When I was a kid in high school, I had a huge crush on you, but I felt it was very one sided. You were this distant but nice guy who didn't have any interest in a teenager like me. I was dating all kinds of boys my age, but when I knew you were coming over to get Don or have lunch with the family, thoughts of them flew out the window. I would be overcome with excitement when you came into the room."

Ed said he was surprised by her feelings about him. "For a teenager, you were very cool around me when I was in the house or waiting for Doc. I couldn't figure out what you thought of me. Well, I guess we've cleared that up, now." With that, he pulled off the highway onto the breakdown lane and took her in his arms. "Now that I know that the feelings are mutual, I want to explore our possibilities." Without pausing for breath, he French kissed Maria with such intensity, she felt like she couldn't stop what seemed to be happening to her. Ed put his hands up under her sweater and began rubbing her breasts.

Maria knew then that if she didn't stop him, they'd have sexual intercourse right here or in the back seat. As hard as it was to stop, especially when she started shaking with desire, she pushed his hands away and pulled her sweater down. "Ed, I can't do this tonight," she choked out, breathing so hard she could hardly talk. "I'm not ready, although you may think I am. I can't believe what kind of a reaction you set off in me. As you can feel, I'm shaking, and I'm just barely in control. Please help me to get us back into neutral territory. It isn't fair to you for me to get you so worked up and have nowhere to go with your feelings. Let's have a cigarette and take a look at our feelings about each other."

Ed nodded without any enthusiasm. He got out his cigarettes, lit two of them, and gave her one. He took a big drag on his. "What just happened sort of surprised me too, especially the intensity that I felt from you. I didn't realize how passionate you were. It was thrilling to kiss you."

"Ed, tonight you've made me feel so sexy and surprised the heck out of me. I'll level with you, though; I am so afraid of getting pregnant that I have to consider the consequences if the condom failed. It would ruin me, and I couldn't take the chance, as much as my hormones wanted me to."

He took another drag on his cigarette, sitting there in the dark, then said softly, "I don't want to hurt you in any way."

Maria reached over and patted his face. "Thanks for stopping. Let's go so you can get home before the night is over, especially if you are going to work for Don tomorrow."

Ed pulled back onto the highway, and soon they were moving along at a fast pace. He leaned over and gave her a light kiss to let her know that he wanted the same thing she did, no babies.

Moving on to a less intense subject, Ed said, "I'm graduating in May, and I need to put all my efforts into getting started as a veterinarian. I want to build a clinic and be self-sufficient as soon as possible. My biggest problem is getting backers for the clinic. Doc has offered to invest, and I have a few other people who are willing to take a chance on me, but it's going to be a struggle. It took your brother-in-law the better part of ten years to get enough money and backers to build his clinic."

"Would your backers own part of your clinic, or would you just take out loans with them?"

"I have many options, and I'm going to explore them all," Ed said.

"I'll bet Don would vouch for you with the bankers in this area. I'm sure they know him. Where are you planning to start your practice?"

"Doc gave me the idea of looking in the St. Charles area."

"I know St. Charles; it is a wealthy farm area a ways out of Chicago where there are lots of horse farms. My dad has a dry farm in St. Charles. It's where he goes to get away from his practice— and maybe Betty and the babies."

"Your dad has little kids now? Poor devil, isn't he getting up there in years? Why start over with a family again after already raising a family?"

"Ask Betty. She is thirty years younger than he is and got pregnant soon after he divorced my mother. She more or less trapped him, I think. I wish they had just lived together and traveled together. My dad loved to travel. Now he's getting up at night to deal with babies."

Maria could see that talking about her dad's problems didn't interest Ed anymore. He changed the subject. "What are your plans for next summer?"

"I'm going to apply at the King's Ridge Resort in Galena as a waitress or hostess for the season. A friend suggested that I look there. I'm tired of taking care of my nieces and nephews and not getting paid for it. Do you suppose we could stop there on the way back to school this Sunday to take a quick look at the place? I would appreciate it so much. Maybe I can get an application and a name of someone to send it to."

"That's a great idea for a summer job. Sure, I'll pick you up an hour earlier than I'd planned so that we can stop and see it. I'd like to see where it is, too. Maybe I'll come up and take a swim with you in the summer. I'll bring a beer or two, besides," he said, grinning. "Would you like that?" Ed abruptly changed tack. "I know this is very personal, so don't answer me if you don't want to, but have you ever thought of getting some advice about female contraceptives from a doctor?"

Maria was taken off guard by Ed's question. Ed was much older than Bill and was an animal doctor, but still a doctor. Obviously, he was well aware of female anatomy, and not just in animals. That must be why it was easy for him to talk about contraception. She wanted to kid him and ask him if he had an ulterior motive, but she was afraid of where that might lead. "I have considered that very thing and will probably do something about it when I get back to school," Maria said.

"You'll feel safer. If you have an intimate relationship, you will be controlling your own destiny. If I were a woman, I know I would do the same thing. Women have too much to lose if they don't take care of themselves."

Maria appreciated Ed's candor about using protection in sexual relationships. His plans for the future obviously didn't include marriage and children. He hadn't even mentioned them, so they evidently weren't in the picture. Bill, on the other hand, was all ready to commit to her for a life together. How could she be so drawn to two completely different guys at the same time? There was no question in her mind that Bill was the man for her. What had happened tonight must not happen again. She couldn't do that to her and Bill's relationship.

They rode along quietly in the dark, thinking their own thoughts and listening to the music. She was surprised when Ed said, "We're here, Maria." It was amazing how time flew when there was so much to think about.

"Thanks so much for giving me a ride home," Maria said. "I feel like I finally know you a little better after all these years. I'll probably see you tomorrow." She reached over and gave him a kiss on his cheek. "Thanks for being such a considerate guy tonight."

He responded by giving her a sweet kiss on her lips and throat. Maria got out of the car and so did he. He took her duffle bags out and asked where she got them. They said Avillia High School on them.

"Oh, just a friend. He had plenty of extras."

Ed asked, "Was it the guy I met in the Union with you?"

"Yes," she said. Maria turned to go into the house, but he held her and gave her another hot and gut-wrenching kiss that seemed to last forever. She couldn't resist the guy. She let him kiss her until they were both panting. She could hardly breathe from the intensity of it. Once again, Maria was feeling such intense electricity between them that she was stunned. She finally wiggled away and whispered, "Good night." She ran for the garage. She was afraid that if she didn't go in now, she wasn't sure what she would let happen.

20. Home for the Holiday

Your hearts know in silence
the secrets of the days and the nights.
—Kahlil Gibran

Maria's sister had pulled out the sleeper couch in the rec room, as promised, and had put sheets, blankets, and a couple of pillows on it. *Thanks, May,* Maria said silently as she lay down. She was so tired, so emotionally drained, so confused with events of the evening that she didn't even wash her face; she just fell asleep.

Someone was stomping around in the rec room. What time was it? It seemed like it was in the middle of the night. Maria heard her brother-in-law talking to someone, and they were laughing. What were they doing in the rec room? She put her head under the pillows to shut out the noise and felt someone poke her.

Don said, "You're in there, I can tell."

Maria thought she'd ignore him, the big tease. Maybe he'd go away. Good grief, she heard Ed's voice. That smooth, handsome man was in the same room with her. It must be morning, and they are going out to make calls on the farmers. Maria heard the roar of a truck and then blessed silence, and she drifted back to sleep. The next thing she heard was her sister, May, padding quietly around in the kitchen.

"I'm awake," Maria said as she sat up, rubbing the sleep out of her eyes. She stretched and generally tried to regain her sense of balance after the last twenty-four hours.

May came over, sat down on the edge of the bed, and said gently, "Good to see you. When did you get in last night?"

"I think around ten or eleven. I'm not sure because my watch is broken. Ed had so many riders with him, that he had to drop off all over Iowa, it took us much longer than if he and I had driven straight through alone. We stopped for dinner too, which took some time because the diner was busy, and we had to wait a while for our food. Thanks for making my bed. I just crawled into it and fell asleep, within seconds, I think."

"How was Ed?" The tone May used for this question was quite interesting. What information was May looking for? Was she was fishing for something specific? Maybe she had a secret crush on him, too. That wasn't hard to imagine. Maria gave herself a mental shake, *Boy, I'm getting paranoid.*

"He is fine," Maria said. "I hadn't seen him all fall, but I got a chance to talk to him after the other riders were gone. I got to know him a little better." The fact that they did a lot more than talk was nobody else's business.

"Do you want some coffee? I just made a pot. Are you hungry?" May was playing big sister, which would be nice while it lasted. In a few minutes, May would move on to something else that needed her attention. When there were five kids to look after, the maximum time of mothering anyone besides her children got was five minutes.

"What can I do?" Maria asked the dreaded question. She knew May was waiting for her to ask and was probably ready with a list of chores. May was a great manager. She hated to deal with anyone's emotions, but she could organize a household like a pro. Maria knew that it would impossible at this point to have a proper conversation with her, so she just got dressed, folded her bed into the couch, and turned the "bedroom" back into a rec room. She had learned the drill years ago.

Preparing breakfast had first claim on Maria's time. Don and Ed would be back soon enough, and they'd be hungry. *Ugh,* she thought, as she pulled the cold, slimy pieces of bacon apart, lay them in a pan, and watched the fat start to bubble up. It was all she could do not to gag. She turned away, swallowing hard. She dug the orange juice concentrate out of its can, plopped it into a pitcher of water, and breathed a sigh of relief. The hard part was over.

Besides food for the men, her little nieces and nephews would be slowly appearing for their breakfasts, too. Like all young children, they got up early, and Maria was looking forward to seeing them.

Maria knew that as soon as she finished one job, May would have another lined up for her to do. It was never ending. At least when she went to work at King's Ridge Resort next summer, she'd get paid. If there had been any doubt in her mind about her plans, today cleared it away.

One of May's brood, Tommy, came running down the hall. He stopped when he saw Maria and asked, "Aunt Maria, when did you come to see us? Are you going to stay all day? Will you play with us? Please, please, please." He wrapped his five-year-old arms around her legs and hugged her. She knelt down and gave him a hug and kiss, which he recoiled from. Tommy obviously thought that he was too big for a kiss from his auntie, even though he still wanted attention from her.

"I hear daddy's truck," Tommy said. He ran to the window and waited for Don's truck to pull into the driveway. "Who's in there with him?" He ran to the door and peeked out. Don and Ed came in with blood all over their coveralls. "What happened, Daddy? Did a cow die? Hi, Uncle Ed. Are you staying to eat with us? Can I see your cigarette lighter?"

"Enough questions, Tommy. Go get ready to eat," Don said, picking up his boy and tickling him. Tommy shrieked with glee and struggled to get down.

Not to be put off, Tommy asked, "Did a cow die?"

"No, I had to operate on her and fix something inside. She's fine," Don said. "Give me your coveralls, Ed. I'll throw them in the wash. These whites are nice to look at but a pain in the butt to keep clean. I must have fifteen pairs of them, and even that isn't enough sometimes. We'll get another set when we go out after breakfast."

Don looked over at Maria, who was cooking eggs and waffles, and grinned. "So where were you guys last night? I can't believe it took all that time to drive from Iowa State to here. What were you doing?"

Ed waited for Maria to answer. "If we were doing anything, you'd be the last to know, you old letch," Maria said. Then she turned to Ed, "Now, what do you want for breakfast? We have eggs, bacon, juice, coffee, toast, and waffles." Her eyes sparkled, but only Ed could see it.

"What about me?" Don asked. "Doesn't your old, hard-working brother-in law get some breakfast, too?"

It seemed that May had been listening to this banter and was a little irritated, judging from the look on her face when she reappeared. Maria guessed things weren't humming along quickly enough for her, or perhaps she didn't like the attention Maria was getting from Don.

"Sit down, Don, and eat," May ordered in a very businesslike manner. Mornings were not May's best time, not with the responsibilities of the day looming out there. She handed Don a big plate of food and some coffee. "How about you, Ed?"

"Maria's already asked me," he said, looking at her and then at Maria. The long, slow look he directed at Maria gave her the shivers.

Ed was still looking at Maria when she handed him his plate of food and sat down across from him with a cup of coffee for herself. May didn't join them. She had the tendency to stand in the kitchen, feed everyone else, then eat breakfast after everyone had gone. Maria used to follow her sister's lead and act like a servant, too, but not anymore. If she was a guest, she was going to sit down. If she was a waitress, she'd stand and get paid. While May bustled around, Maria talked with the guys.

Don asked, "Well, little sister, how's your love life? Have you met any sexy men yet?" He grinned and lit a cigarette.

Maria thought the sexiest guy around here was sitting right across the table from Don. "I'll say this, life has been very interesting this fall. Oh, by the way, I've decided to pledge Chi Omega. They are one of the best sororities on campus, and they have their dining room in their house."

"Is that the main reason you are joining?" Don asked.

"No, they have a smoker in their basement where I can smoke and play cards."

"Two very good reasons to join a sorority." Don laughed at her smart remark. "Do you want a cigarette, now?"

"No, but I do want to borrow your car to go to Sterling to look for a warmer coat. And maybe get some money to buy it?" Maria grimaced. "I'm broke."

"Didn't Marion give you any money this fall for clothes?" Don asked.

"He bought me a couple of things, but I need more things than I'd expected, like gloves, scarves, waterproof boots, and a warmer coat. Dad pays for my tuition, room, and board, which is very generous, but I only get five dollars a week for everything else. Betty keeps him on a very short leash when it comes to me. That brings up another subject." While Maria had been talking, she was watching Ed's reaction to her comments. He seemed pleased with her new attitude. "I've decided to work at the King's Ridge Resort next summer, and maybe holidays, so I can make some money for myself. No more free babysitting for you guys," Maria announced firmly.

"My, my," said Don, "one semester out in the world, and little sister has declared her freedom. How much do you need for your coat?"

"Forty dollars should do it and the use of your car for a couple of hours."

"It sounds okay with me. What do you think, May?"

"I've got to go shopping for the kids. Maria can go with all of us," she snapped. May gave Maria an angry look.

Maria groaned inwardly and was irritated that her sister had turned *her* shopping trip into *May's* shopping trip. May probably felt slighted that Maria hadn't asked her for help and instead approached Don. Maria hated going shopping with her sister. May had to look at everything in the store before making up her mind what to buy. Maria usually ended up running all over the store after the kids. May drove Maria crazy with her indecision, but May expected Maria to be quick with her own decisions, when she gave Maria thought at all. Nothing had changed at the Dawsons'.

May didn't seem to value Maria as a living, feeling person, just saw her as a good cook, waitress, and nanny. Maria knew her attitude stemmed from the long-standing belief that she was doing Maria a big favor by allowing her to stay with the Dawsons for the summer. She probably felt that Maria owed her, and that she was justified in working Maria from morning to night.

Now that their mother was living in Washington, DC, with her new husband, Maria needed to have a place to stay during school holidays. Her home in La Grange was gone for good. Perhaps King's Ridge would be the answer. Then she wouldn't have to rely on May's "hospitality" and feel obligated to her.

Having had almost a full semester on her own at college, watching how confidently Susie operated, being treated like a special person in Bill's life, and observing how most of the girls in her dorm acted, Maria had begun to believe in herself. She attributed a lot of her newfound spunkiness to Susie, who had become the sister Maria had never really never had.

Maria knew that May believed that Maria had siphoned off any bits of love in their childhood home, especially from their mother. Maria wondered if May was jealous of the relationship that she'd had with their dad, too. Growing up, May always kept Maria at arm's length, and Maria couldn't remember a single time when

May ever took her with her to do something fun, like getting an ice-cream cone or going to a movie.

Maria could have used a friend in Betty, too, but she was very protective of her new life with Marion and didn't encourage any contact from either Maria or May with their father. Betty's way of keeping Maria at arm's length was to not provide any sleeping arrangements for her in their new home addition.

They had bought an older home that was too small for them. Since they now had two little girls, they added on another bedroom but not a guest room, which would have given them a total of three bedrooms. On Maria's first visit to stay with them, she'd nearly fainted when her dad showed her where she was going to sleep. He had taken her up into the attic, where Betty had instructed him to put a mattress on the floor between the joists for her bed. Maria had been so shocked and hurt that she went downstairs and out for a walk, trying to figure out what she was going to do. Did they actually think it was all right to put her up in a stuffy attic? How dare they! She was particularly disappointed in her father. She felt like Cinderella and vowed never to go there again. What a change in her father's behavior toward her. Since his marriage, Maria's life had been turned upside down by Betty.

Maria snapped out of her reverie when she heard the guys getting up from the table. She looked around. "Hey, where are the kids? They never came for breakfast."

"I fed them separately," said May. "I didn't want them underfoot in the kitchen today."

The sisters spent the rest of the morning cleaning up from breakfast and getting things ready for Thanksgiving. Maria made a couple of pies, one apple and one pumpkin, while May made beds, washed loads of clothes, and cleaned. As part of a nice holiday tradition, Maria helped her little nieces, Anne and Mary, make baskets out of paper and filled them with nuts for each place setting. The girls were so cute. They worked feverishly to make the table favors and were very proud of them. When they were done, Maria and her two nieces looked at their handiwork decorating the table, and they laughed with glee.

Don and Ed came back from their second round of farm calls. They had finished early because of the holiday. They sat down in the living room, and Don got out his favorite game, cribbage. A little while later, Maria heard a yell of anguish from Don, who was losing to Ed and being skunked. Ed was laughing as he finished the game, then got ready to leave.

Acting as if he had been mortally wounded, Don said, "At least give me a chance to win back some of that loot you just took from me."

"I can play one more game, Doc, and then I've got to go home and do some things around the house for my folks," Ed said. May had invited him for Thanksgiving dinner, but he had declined.

As they played, Maria caught Ed watching her occasionally as she was cooking in the kitchen. Every time their eyes met, she felt a surge of excitement. What was she going to do about him?

After finishing the second game and uttering a few bad words, Don laughed and paid Ed a penny a point, threatening to win it all back the next time. Ed pocketed his winnings and grinned at Maria as he put on his jacket. On the way out, Ed popped his head into the kitchen, smiled at her again, and left. It would have been fun if he had stayed for dinner, but the chore of getting the turkey into the oven on time and preparing the rest of the Thanksgiving feast took Maria's mind off her mild disappointment. Besides, she was pleased that he was so good to his folks. Maybe he wasn't so alone in the world, after all.

Don's partner, Gill, and Gill's wife, Joan, were going to be joining the Dawsons for dinner. *Thank goodness,* Maria thought, *another woman to talk to besides May.* Gill and Joan had no children of their own and enjoyed Don and May's brood in small doses. When the pair arrived, the kids crowded around, trying to outdo each other with all kinds of entertaining antics. May stopped that with curt orders to go get washed up for dinner.

There was a stampede to the bathrooms, with each child trying to get there before the others. Maria hoped that no one was going to end up crying. They all came back fairly clean, with no tears, and scrambled for the prize positions next to the company. The boys won because of their agility and size. When everyone was finally seated, May brought in the turkey, followed by Maria carrying the veggies, rolls, and potatoes.

Maria wished she had brought her camera to take a picture of that cute group. Just as she sat down, May leaned over and asked more pleasantly than usual, "I hear Baby June. Please go and get her so that she can eat with us, Maria."

Typically, May had fallen back into her familiar role and expected Maria to play nanny. Actually, Maria enjoyed the baby and went down the hall to get her. When she opened June's door, she saw June, who was just over a year old, trying to climb out of her crib. Maria picked her up and June put her little arms around Maria's neck. They returned to the festivities. The baby said, "Woo, woo," as Maria settled her into her highchair.

The conversation was interesting, with five adults around the table. The children added a word or two but basically were busy eating and jostling one another. They finished before the adults and went into the rec room to play. Maria was sure that the boys would end up wrestling each other, and the girls would play make believe.

Tommy came back soon enough, exclaiming, "I'm hungry for pie."

This brought May and Maria reluctantly to their feet to clear the table to make room for the pies. The pie orders were simple: the kids wanted apple and all the adults chose pumpkin. The adults savored coffee with their pie; the children had ice cream with theirs.

Later that evening, after Joan and Gill had left, May said that she was going to put the kids to bed and go to bed herself; she was tired. This was music to Maria's ears; she'd had enough of her cranky sister for one day. Maria pulled out her bed, made it, and climbed in. She was tired, too, and reading history would be the perfect sleep potion.

Maria heard someone moving around in the rec room and wondered why. It was Don, and it was morning. She couldn't believe it. How could morning have come so fast?

Don was talking to Ed, who had come in to get some more coveralls. Maria put a pillow over her head and tried to go back to sleep, but Don came over and gave her foot a tap. He just couldn't walk by her and not to touch her in some way.

"Go away," she said from under her pillow and heard him laugh and go out. He was the brother she'd never had and had unwittingly taught her a lot about men by just being himself.

As usual, May wasn't far behind. She came through the rec room on her way to the kitchen. Maria said, "You don't have to be quiet. Don already woke me up."

"What is the matter with him? He doesn't use good sense," May said in an irritated manner.

Maria wished Don would back off a little, so May would be easier to live with. Maria hadn't asked for his attention. "He's just a big tease, like a big brother," Maria replied, hoping it would seem less offensive if she put Don in the brother category.

Ignoring Maria's assessment of her husband, May announced, "Today, I want you to help me sort out the kid's clothes, so I know what they need before we go to Sterling to shop. I'm going to make a list for each one before we go. If I don't, I will end up with all the wrong stuff."

Maria said, "I need time to shop for my coat," feeling more irritated by the moment.

"Oh, don't worry, Miss College Student, I'll give you time," May yelled with a venomous tone. "You know, I don't appreciate your attitude. You're flirting with my husband, planning a shopping trip with *my* car, and you have the nerve to ask for money, as well. I don't think I want you to visit at Christmas. You're getting too out-spoken for your own good. Where did my sweet little sister go?"

As Maria listened to her sister rage, she knew that it was definitely time for her to stand up for herself, go off to work somewhere, and make a new life. May was trying to put her back into the position that she had lived in for years. It reminded her of Bill's complaint that his father was always assuming that Bill would stay the same and do exactly what his father wanted him to do.

"Don't yell at me just because you are tired and feel overworked. *I'm* tired of being treated like an unpaid nanny and cook. If you and Don had ever paid me for all the work I've done for you, I wouldn't have had to ask for a few bucks from your husband now. And I'm *not* flirting with him!" Maria yelled back, walking up to May and getting in her face as she spoke.

"You ungrateful wretch! What would you have done if I hadn't taken pity on you and let you stay here all those years?" May stood with her hands on her hips, so furious that her face was red and blotchy.

"For years I tried to please both you and our mother. When I was left at home alone with her, both of you managed to take advantage of me. Well I'm not letting that happen anymore. You got married and escaped, Dad slipped away to marry his trophy wife, and I was left taking care of our alcoholic mother. You and Mom never gave me a second thought all those years." Maria said all this quite calmly. She had been thinking about it for months. It felt so good to get it all out, and she felt freer than she had in years.

May's back was to the hallway, so she didn't see the kids coming down the hall, no doubt awakened by the fight. "Mommy, Mommy, why are you and Aunt Maria yelling at each other?" Anne asked.

May hissed at Maria, "Now see what you've done. You've upset the kids."

"And, of course, they always come first, don't they?" Maria said, pleased that her feelings were out in the open. She walked around the kids and said over her shoulder, "I'm going to call Dad, wish him a belated happy Thanksgiving, and ask for more money to live on every week." Maria decided not to mention the primary reason she was calling him. The less May knew the better.

"Okay," May said, sounding a little deflated. Maria wondered if May was suddenly realizing just how badly she'd been treating her little sister. With a somewhat conciliatory tone, May said, "Let's make breakfast for the men and kids. Don will be back in an hour."

Still standing in the hall with the kids looking at her, Maria said, "Didn't you hear me? I want to call Dad. You can fix breakfast or not, I don't care. I'm going to phone Dad now." Maria looked at her sister, whose mouth was hanging open, then walked down the hall to May's bedroom where the phone was. Maria felt elated that she had finally started to stand up to her sister.

Don and Ed appeared right on time and quickly made the exchange from dirty to clean overalls. Don insisted on wearing white coveralls because he felt that they were more professional looking than blue denim. The guys looked like they had been working hard, judging by the state of their dirty uniforms. They sat down at the table, laughing and joking, as Maria returned from the bedroom. She had been unable to reach her dad. Betty had said, with no love in her voice, that he would be back that afternoon. Maria sat down across the table from Don and Ed.

Her brother-in-law blew smoke at her. "The food and coffee at this restaurant are good, and the waitresses are cute."

Maria coughed and waved the smoke away, laughing at Don. Maria sipped her coffee and looked at Ed over the top of her mug. Catching her eye occasionally, he telegraphed his feelings. He was on the hunt and she knew it.

Ed offered Maria a cigarette, and when she took him up on it, Don gave her a quick look. Ed lit her cigarette and poured her another cup of coffee. He said, "I like to take care of good-looking waitresses." He got up, came around the table, sat down next to her. He put his arm around her shoulder and gave her a little hug. Don's mouth opened in surprise.

Don gave Maria an insipid grin and leaned over to her. "It's against the rules of the restaurant for the waitresses to fraternize with the customers."

Maria reached out and tapped her cigarette ash into Don's saucer. She gave him a big smile. "Be careful, or the next tap will go into your coffee."

"Well, little sister, you *are* growing up," he said. "How much money do you need for that coat?"

"As I told you before, I think forty dollars should do it." She wasn't going to beg.

"I'll add that to the money I'm giving May for the kid's clothes. How much do you need, May?"

"I think two hundred and fifty should do it. Shall I write a check, or are you going to give me the cash?"

Maria thought how generous Don was with money. He wasn't going to make May account for every penny like some guys did. Maria turned to Ed, who gave her a look that said, "See, Doc has plenty of money." She smiled at him and nodded slightly.

May dished up breakfast, dropped their plates in front of them, and huffed out of the room. *What now?* thought Maria.

Don rolled his eyes. "Eat up there, friend," he said to Ed. "We've got extra to do today because of the holiday yesterday." He and Ed quickly finished and were on their way. Don called to May on the way out, "Don't worry about lunch for us, we're going to be too far away. We'll catch a bite at a restaurant."

May seemed delighted and said, with a big smile, "I'll treat us all with lunch out." She came up to Maria. "Truce? Perhaps I'd better think about what you said today."

Maria gave her sister a little smile. "Perhaps you should."

By the time the children were fed, washed, and dressed, they were bubbling with excitement. When May told them they were all going out for lunch, it made them even wilder. "We don't go out to lunch very often, Aunt Maria," Brett yelled.

He's growing up, Maria thought. He was the eldest, and probably the smartest, kid in the family; he was also a nice-looking little fellow. Maria had always had a special affinity for Brett, ever since he was born. She loved him best but never let on, because she didn't want to play favorites. Sometimes, though, she wished she could be more forthcoming with him.

The kids were much more rambunctious than usual, and May finally said loudly, "Now everyone settle down. After lunch, you are going to see a kid's movie while Aunt Maria and I shop. Brett will be in charge, and everyone has to mind him."

After lunch, May bought tickets for the movie, put them all in their seats, and said sternly, "Don't move until the movie is over. Everyone stay together. We will be right across the street, and we'll pick you up after the show."

Maria handed each of them their very own box of popcorn. The place was packed with children of all ages, which obviously made May feel better about leaving them.

"I'll be back to check on you," May said, "and you had better be in your seats when I do, or you won't get to come again." With that threat hanging over their heads, they promised to stay together and not leave their seats. The kids might fight at home, but they were the best of friends when they were in strange situations. Brett looked very pleased at being left in charge and was already giving Tommy a hard time.

May and Maria took baby June with them, of course, and hurried through their shopping as fast as humanly possible. May said, "Well, Maria, you'd better go look for a coat. How long do you need?" When Maria answered, "An hour," May's face got a brittle expression. She took the baby in the stroller and went the other way.

Maria found just what she was looking for, and it was her lucky day. The coat was marked down from fifty dollars to thirty-nine because of a "Day after Thanksgiving Sale." Her new coat was made out of a synthetic fabric designed specifically to keep out the cold and wind. It had a hood that was trimmed with real fur. Checking herself in the full length mirror, Maria decided that she looked like Nanook of the North, but she didn't care. Having a hood was an essential in Iowa in the winter, plus the coat was a pretty shade of blue.

When she found May knee deep in kid clothes, Maria gave her the slip for the coat. May added it to her bills and paid for it all with one check.

"Thanks for the coat, Sis," Maria said.

They crossed the street to collect the kids, who were streaming out of the theater. The children spotted their mom before May saw them.

"We saw a show about puppies, and we want one," Mary cried out.

May ignored the plea. "On the way home, we'll stop and get some ice cream." She was a good mother and knew what distractions would work.

When the family got home, the men were still out. May sent the boys to the grocery store for a couple of things for dinner. The grocery store was just a couple of streets away, and in that small town, everyone felt safe. Maria fed the baby her dinner, while May started dinner for everyone else.

After the baby was fed and settled in her playpen, Maria slipped into her sister's bedroom to see if she could reach her dad. *If Betty answers,* she thought, *I'm going to hang up.* Maria didn't want two conversations with her in one day. Before Betty entered the picture, Maria's dad had been very generous, but everything changed after Betty arrived. Luckily, Maria's dad answered. Maria said, "Hi, Dad, how are you? I wanted to call and wish you a belated happy Thanksgiving."

"Tritti," he said, using her childhood nickname, "it's so good to hear from you. Where are you? At Don and May's?"

"Yes, it's just like old times being here. Not much has changed, unfortunately. All I do is follow May's orders. I know that she's very busy with five kids, but I'll be glad to go back to school." She knew her response wouldn't please him, but she didn't care anymore. He was so removed from her now, and had been for a long time. She loved him, but she found it hard to relate to him.

When she was little, she had loved her nickname; it made her feel special. She had asked her dad what it meant, and he'd said it meant "love." Maria loved hearing his voice again. It brought back nice memories. "I'm sorry I haven't called you more often, Dad, but you know I can only call collect from the dorm."

"You can always call me if it's important or you need help, Maria. Otherwise, it's fine to just wait, like you did this time."

Huh, if it's "important," Maria thought. Her father had never thought that it was important to call just to get support from one's family. When she heard all her dorm mates talking to their families, it made her feel lonely; she wished she were talking to her parents, too. Maria had felt completely abandoned by her dad after he'd married Betty.

Trying to reconnect with him in some small way, Maria said, "Dad, first of all, thanks so much for sending me to school and paying for everything. I really appreciate it. I don't tell you that enough. But I have a problem now that I hope to be able to remedy next summer. I find that I can't quite make my weekly expenses on five dollars a week. Would it be possible to put ten dollars a week in my checking account? Next year, you won't have to give me any spending money, because I'm hoping to get a summer job waitressing at a big resort complex in Galena, Illinois. I'm going to apply early, so I will be first in line."

"Working like that will be good for you. Let me know if you get the job. Tritti, I appreciate your being so aware of this chance to get an education. I promised myself that all of my children would be offered a college education if they wanted it. How are your grades? Are your courses hard? I hope you like going to Iowa State."

"I am doing fine in school, even though it's hard. Thanks for asking." He hadn't said that he would up her allowance, but at least she'd asked.

"You're okay physically?" her dad asked. She was sure he was wondering if she were pregnant, but he was too kind to put her on the spot.

"I'm fine in every way," she said to allay his fears, "but I have a college friend who needs some advice. He had a girlfriend all through high school, but like a lot of young lovers, they went their separate ways when he left for college. Before they parted, the girl's family had offered a section of their farmland as a present if my friend and their daughter were married. My friend's family felt that they needed to match the land gift and offered the same amount of farmland to the marriage. My friend's land has been enriched by good farming practices and is very valuable.

"Although my friend has been dating another woman, if the girl's family were to somehow pressure him into marriage, what safeguards should his family employ so that they wouldn't lose the farmland gift in the event that the couple get divorced or either one of them dies? My friend is thinking of going into the Air Force after he graduates to become a fighter pilot. God forbid that anything were to happen to him, but there's always the possibility that he could become a war casualty."

Maria's dad was quiet for a moment or two, then he said, "Remember what I always told you about following the money? Well here's a perfect example. The girl's family is pushing the marriage because they stand to gain the more-valuable farmland from the deal. They see an opportunity to get their hands on a sizeable fortune. Does that make sense?"

"Perfect sense, like always, Dad."

"So your friend must have his father and mother go to a good lawyer to draw up an ironclad deal, specifying that in the event that anything happens to either partner in the marriage, meaning death or divorce, the land will revert back to the original owners. To establish an airtight deal, they must get both parcels of land surveyed, recording their exact location, so there can be no monkey business with plot plans. A good lawyer will know who to recommend and how to put it in the correct language so that the document will stand up in court should the girl's parents try to contest it.

"Now, in the event that a baby is born from this marriage, the property will go to the child unless there is a prenuptial agreement or provision that makes that situation null and void."

As her dad was finishing up with his advice, Maria heard Don coming down the hall. She hurriedly said, "Dad, thanks so much for the wonderful advice. I hope you'll feel like calling me sometime at my dorm so we can talk again. Call after nine in the evening and just ask for me; one of the girls there will get me. I'm in Stevens Dorm, in case you've forgotten. I love you, Dad. Bye for now."

"Bye, little Tritti," he said, "I love you, too."

"Who were you talking with so earnestly?" Don asked upon entering the room. "Your college boyfriend that you haven't mentioned to us yet?" Don had a big grin on his face.

"Thanks for letting me use your phone" Maria said. "When you see the charges, just remember all the work I have done for you and May over the years."

"Anything for you, little sister," he said with more conviction than was necessary.

"I've got to go help May with dinner. Oh, by the way, thanks so much for getting me my new coat."

"I didn't get it for you; I just paid for it," he said with a smirk on his face.

"Okay, smarty, whatever you say." Maria walked down the hall to the kitchen to face May again.

"So where did you go, just when I needed you?" May asked.

"I wanted to call Dad and wish him a belated happy Thanksgiving."

But May wasn't listening to anything Maria had just said. Instead she asked, "Would you set the table in the dining room? Ed may come and join us for supper. Our kitchen table isn't big enough."

Maria was irritated all over again that May never seemed to pay any attention to her. No comment on their father as to his health or general well-being. She was completely engrossed in every mundane thing going on in her home and nothing else. While setting the dining room table, Maria realized that Don might mention her phone call in front of Ed to stir up trouble. Don had assumed that it was a guy, and Maria hadn't said anything to change that impression.

Maria helped the kids get washed up and seated in the dining room. Every meal around there was a big production with five kids to feed. Maria knew for sure that she didn't want to have more than two children after dealing with this busy crew. Ed didn't take Don up on his offer of supper. Maria was relieved that he was busy. Now, she hoped, she wouldn't have to explain anything to anyone.

The kids were tired from their big day and so was Maria. After the children were in bed, she set up her bed in the rec room and got out her books. She wanted some quiet time to think, and the books made it look as if she were studying. That would keep May and Don from asking her any questions. Thinking over what her dad had told her regarding Bill's situation, she was as ready as she could be to talk to him about the land deal if he called. Maria had all kinds of questions for him about his talk with the minister, also whether he had gotten an appointment with the newspaper.

Around ten, the phone rang. Maria picked up the extension in the rec room, but Don had answered it. He was used to getting emergency calls at all hours of the night. Maria heard him say, "Hi, this is Doc Dawson."

Maria was about to hang up when she heard Bill on the other end saying in a very strong voice, "Hi, Doc, this is Bill Morgan. I'd like to speak to Maria, please.".

"I'll get her," Don said with a surprised tone to his voice.

"I'm on the phone, Don," Maria said. "Just hang up, please; no listening in."

She heard him laugh, then a click when he hung up. "Hi," she said to Bill. "I think it's safe to talk. I'll be able to tell if anyone else picks up the phone."

"How are you, sweetheart?" His voice was soft and loving, and he had called her sweetheart. He must miss her.

"I'm fine, and I miss you." She meant it, even though Ed had been on her mind, too. How could life be so cruel as to hand her two incredible men at the same time? She shouldn't even be thinking about Ed, but she was. She felt guilty because of Bill's complete commitment to her, and up until Wednesday, she hadn't thought about anyone else.

"I stopped in at the *Iowa Progress* on my way home on Wednesday and was able to speak to two different people about my proposal for working for them. They were in different departments, but both said that my idea to write a daily or weekly column was a great new way to give the farmers advice they needed. Thanks so much, Maria, for coming up with such a wonderful idea. I feel it is going to work. They said to be sure to come back, and I made an appointment with the assistant editor in charge of columns and such for next week."

"I am thrilled, Bill. You're going to be a newspaper man." Maria didn't want to bring up the bad stuff on the heels of this wonderful piece of news, so she just waited.

After a little pause, Bill said, "Do you want to know what happened with the minister?"

"I do if you feel like talking about it. I'll bet you were great." She didn't quite know what to say to him about the awkward situation Maude had put him in. There were times when Maria wanted to strangle Maude.

"Well," he said and paused again, "the minister started out by trying to be my friend and acted sort of goofy about it. He said that he wanted us to bond as brothers. I just listened, trying to figure out where he was heading, and he quoted some scriptures on the sanctity of women and why it was important, as brothers, to do the right thing with women that we love. I know he was nervous and wanted me to talk, but I wasn't ready to volunteer anything. After clearing his throat and coughing for a while, I thought, who knows what he might say. I figured I could wait him out."

"Bill, you are so tough in a very quiet way and good at making people sweat."

"I don't know about that, but it's foolish to shoot your gun until you know where to point it. Anyway, he finally got tired of trying to draw me out, so he could argue with me, I suppose, and looked at his watch. I waited, and he said that he had been asked to talk to me about my plans to marry Maude. I asked by whom. He said that her mother and father had come to him and voiced their concerns about how I was treating Maude. I asked him what he meant by how I was treating her, and he got all red in the face and started coughing again. I thought the poor guy was going to have an attack, he was so nervous.

"He looked at me, then looked away. He went over to the window and sort of talked to me over his shoulder. He said that he knew Maude and I had been intimate before marriage, which his church did not condone. He asked if I would do the right thing. I asked him what he thought the right thing was. He said that I must make her an honest woman and give her an engagement ring with the intention of marriage, thereby making things right in the eyes of God."

"What did you say?"

"I'd think about what he said, but I wanted to clear up this mistaken idea that Maude and I had been having a sexual relationship. In fact, I said, I hadn't even dated her because I had fallen in love with a fairy princess who had cast a spell over me."

"You didn't say that, did you?" Maria asked with a laugh. "You are too much."

"Yes I did, and I asked him if he believed the story that Maude's parents had thought up, with Maude's help I'm sure, although I didn't say that. If he believed that tale, then he should believe mine about the fairy princess, which was just as far-fetched. Then the minister told me that he had to go to a meeting and had to end the conversation. I didn't believe that for a minute, but I was almost as glad as he was that our meeting was over. We both tore out of there like a couple of athletes running a marathon."

"How are your parents taking this?"

"They are fine, but they have stopped going to church for now. My dad is so mad about the comments that people in the community have been making, he's about to pop."

"Have your folks talked to the Jenkinses about this whole thing? Maybe that would help."

"My folks have made repeated attempts to contact them, and the Jenkinses have ignored them completely," Bill said. "Enough about me. What have you been up to?"

"I called my dad and asked him his opinion about your situation. I hope you don't mind. My dad is very wise on matters like this. His ability to understand women isn't so good, but he gave me some good advice about your problem. I just asked him what he thought about your situation. I didn't tell him that you were my love, and he didn't ask. I just called you my friend as I was describing the problem to him."

Maria related everything her dad had said, and was especially emphatic about the prenuptial agreement regarding a possible heir.

"Okay, I want to get this straight. What is a prenuptial agreement?"

"It is a contract drawn up before a marriage with provisions to protect everyone's assets. If one person has lots more than the other person and wants to make sure it doesn't get divided up in the case of divorce, the agreement takes care of that," Maria explained.

"That's the reason for all of this," Bill said, with realization in his voice. "The Jenkinses want my folk's land because theirs is so run down."

"It's always the money," Maria stated. "They are sort of using Maude for their own purposes, encouraging her to get you back into the fold, so to speak. I'll bet they have been rubbing their hands with glee for some time thinking about your parents' land becoming part of their daughter's estate and therefore theirs, too."

"So is this what happens to you when your mind isn't bogged down with chemistry labs? I can't get over how much effort and thought you have given this problem of mine. You truly are my sweetheart. I would like to meet your dad and, of course, Doc and your sister sometime. They all sound like wonderful people," Bill said.

"We'll do it when we can find the time next semester. And guess what? I bought a warm, wonderful coat for the winds of Iowa State this winter. I can't wait to wear it. You won't recognize me because I'll look like Nanook of the North in it. It has a hood with fur trim to help keep the winds out," Maria said excitedly.

"Don't worry, Nanook. I'm so in love with you, I'll always recognize you," Bill replied. "Thanks for all your concern. We will be all right. Things will quiet down here or they won't, but it won't matter to me. When will you be back on Sunday?"

"I don't know. The guy that I'm riding back to school with is going to pick up a few other riders along the way. That takes a lot of time."

"Well, I guess I'll see you when I see you. It was great to talk with you and also very informative. I'll try your dorm after curfew on Sunday. If you get in early, please call my house so I can come over to see you. Promise?" Bill asked.

"I promise," Maria said, but not as convincingly as she might have done.

"Just remember how much I love you. Hope to see you Sunday evening. Bye," Bill said.

"Bye," said Maria and hung up the phone. She fell into bed and breathed a sigh of relief. *What a phone call,* she thought. It was so pleasant to talk to Bill. He never seemed agitated with her, and he always listened. She loved him for it.

21. Maria's Awakening

The hottest fire has the coolest end.
—Socrates

Saturday morning was a repeat of the previous two days. Maria was sleeping so soundly that she couldn't believe that the voices she was hearing were the men getting ready to make morning calls. It was so early. *What a life,* she thought. When they finally drove off, she settled down to sleep some more, but May was up and puttering in the kitchen. Maria put a pillow over her head and said to herself, *I'll be glad to be back in school.*

"Maria, I hear you moving around in there. How are you doing?" May asked.

"I'm still sleeping." She hoped May would take the hint and leave her alone for a little while longer.

"Maria," May said with an edge to her voice, "it's time to get up and help me with breakfast."

"I know, I know," Maria snapped back. "I'm going to take a shower and wash my hair, then I will be ready to help you." She knew May handled breakfasts when Maria wasn't there. She just couldn't stand having Maria in bed when she was up and working.

Maria took her time in the shower. She was so tired of May's attitude toward her. How had she stood it all those years? Her irritation level was rising on this trip.

When Maria sauntered into the kitchen, May was fuming. As she spit out orders for Maria, Maria was reminded of their mother when she needed a drink or some pills. The women in her family sure didn't show much love for each other. Maria had taken refuge with her dad whenever she could. Now, she could look forward to being with Bill tomorrow night. She breathed a sigh of relief that the weekend was almost over and smiled at the thought that she would be away from May and with her darling Bill.

By the time breakfast was ready for Don and Ed, the kids were straggling in for their breakfasts. The girls still looked half asleep, while the boys came out at a dead run. Maria heard the baby beginning to make her presence known and went into the nursery to get her. June was warm and happy to be alive. She gave Maria a big smile, reached out her arms to be picked up, and gave Maria a tight hug. At that moment, Maria felt a little ping inside her. It was the first stirrings of mother love. She changed June's diaper, carried her down the hall, and put her in her highchair. Maria kissed June's cute little face and began feeding her some soft pieces of fruit.

She was still feeding the baby when Don and Ed came in, looking hungry. Maria looked up and smiled.

Don said, "Now isn't that a picture. You'll make someone a great wife and mother."

"I am not in the market for marriage right now, for your information. I want to have some fun, make some money, figure out what profession I want to go into, and go for it."

"Well said, little sister. You have found your voice now that you're in college." He sat down, took a sip of his coffee, and said that he had a favor to ask.

"What is it?" she asked, hoping it wasn't babysitting for tonight. They always did that, tapped her for free babysitting.

"We have a big party of vets getting together in Sterling at the Marriott for drinks, dancing, dinner, and a speaker tonight. I figured your new coat was payment for an evening of babysitting," he said with a big grin on his face.

As Maria realized that Don had trapped her once again, she glanced at Ed to see what he thought about this conversation. He seemed slightly edgy. He took a cigarette and lit it, took a drag on it, and looked at Maria. He wasn't smiling.

"Okay, you've guilted me into it. But this is the last time I'm doing it. The only reason I'm agreeing now is because you have good kids and I love them. What time are you leaving for the big evening?"

"When are we going, May?" Don asked. "The boss decides when we do these things."

"We need to be there by six for drinks; dinner is at seven, so you vets don't get too drunk," she said with a touch of irritation in her voice.

"Ed, are you going? Are you bringing that cute girl you brought the last time?" Don asked, looking at Maria and her reaction to his comment.

"Actually, Doc, I hadn't decided whether I wanted to go or not. I'm not interested in the topic, all about pigs and their breeding," Ed said, rather stiffly.

"You may need that information sometime when you are talking with a farmer about his pigs," Don said.

"I'll take my chances, Doc," Ed said with a grin.

"Thanks for the delicious breakfast, girls. Come on, Ed, we've got to make tracks to help that mare have her baby. See you for lunch. I'll call when we're getting ready to come home."

Maria spent a long time getting the kitchen shined up. When she finished, she asked May, "What do you want me to make for lunch?"

"We're going to have BLT sandwiches and slip some turkey slices into the men's. I want turkey soup for lunch today and tomorrow, so make that, and make some creamed turkey for dinner tonight while you're at it." Just like that, May barked out her orders.

Oh great, another two hours gone. Maria found herself more and more irritated with the way May talked to her. She wished she hadn't come home at all for Thanksgiving. Maria thought about Alice Morgan and how sweet she was. Alice didn't have to be so kind and caring, but she was. Maria wished she could have spent Thanksgiving with the Morgans, not to mention her darling Bill.

While Maria was using her skills in the kitchen, the phone rang, and she heard May answer. It was Don; they were on their way home for lunch. Maria had the soup hot and the sandwiches ready by the time Don and Ed were back and had changed into clean clothes.

"Well, little sister, what's for lunch? It smells really good," Don said.

Maria was just about to answer when May interrupted. "Call the kids, will you, Don, and tell them to wash their hands. Also, I need to talk to you privately," May said.

Maria and Ed glanced at each other. He had that same look in his eye that he'd given her on Wednesday night before he kissed her. She felt a little shiver run through her.

When Don and May were out of earshot, he said, "I'd like to come over tonight and help you babysit, if that's all right. I really wanted to take you out on a date tonight, but when Doc guilted you into babysitting, I knew that plan was shot."

So that was why he had looked so edgy at breakfast. He had wanted to take her out. He was so sexy, Maria couldn't get him out of her mind, especially when he talked like that. What was she going to do? She was afraid of her emotions, and she knew whatever happened between them was going nowhere.

"Okay, but only if you promise to be a good babysitter," she said as lightly as she could.

Maria was glad when the kids appeared for lunch; it broke the tension.

"Mommy and Daddy are fighting in the bedroom," Tommy announced.

Brett gave him a shove. "Be quiet, you little snitch."

"Come and sit with me," Ed said, patting one of the chairs in the dining room. "I'll tell you what we did when we went on calls today."

While they were eating, Ed told the kids some cute stories about the little colts and baby cows that he had seen that day. The little girls and Tommy were so entranced by his tales that they hardly ate a bite. When Ed finished a story, Maria reminded the kids to eat. Ed gave Maria a very sweet smile. It was far different from the looks he had given her before. He was a very complicated person.

Don and May came back, looking angry. Don sat down quietly. Maria served him a sandwich and some soup, and he smiled and thanked her. "Did you make the lunch, little sister? You are a good cook." May glared at him. Immediately he looked down at his lunch and just ate; he didn't say another word.

Maria realized in a flash what their fight had been about. It was about her. May was actually jealous of the attention Don had been showing her. Damn, May was an idiot. She reminded Maria so much of their mother at that moment that Maria felt sorry for Don. He was going to have to live with her and her moods for the rest of his life, unless he decided to make a change.

When they finished lunch, Don said, "Ed, how about a quick game of cribbage before we go back to work?"

"Sure, Doc, set 'em up."

They played for about an hour, then headed back out to work.

"May," Don yelled, "we'll be back early this afternoon so I can get cleaned up for our big date tonight. Get your dancing shoes on so we can show all those vets how good we are on the dance floor."

May was either taking a nap or was still mad at Don, because she didn't answer him. Maria hoped she was taking a rest, for all their sakes.

"See you later, little babysitter. Have a nice afternoon."

"I'll be here," Maria said, as she thought to herself, *Unless I can think of a way to escape.* She went into the rec room to lie down and rest for a little while. She knew she was going to be busy with the kids tonight, so she had better gather her strength now.

Around five o'clock, the men came home. The boys came running to see their dad, and baby June toddled down the hall as fast as she could. Don's boys were five and ten, and Brett had already started helping his dad on calls to the farmers.

"Can we go over to the park and play ball with the kids for a while, Dad?" Brett asked.

"Yes, that's fine, just be home by six thirty for dinner. Is that all right with you, Maria?"

"Fine," she said, delighted to get the boys out of her hair while she made dinner.

The girls were four and six and loved playing with their dolls. She could hear them in their bedroom, scolding their dolls because they hadn't washed their hands before dinner. They sounded just like May. Children imitate their parents.

Baby June was hungry, so Maria put her in her chair and strapped her in. She didn't want any accidents on her watch. She gave June some Cheerios, which the child loved to pick up one at a time and eat by herself. She was very dexterous and getting more independent all the time.

As Maria was preparing dinner, she heard May and Don coming down the hall, ready to go on their big outing. May was looking rested and very pretty in her fall dress; Don was all shined up in a sports coat and tie. They did make a handsome couple. "You look wonderful, both of you," Maria said in a generous moment.

May smiled, and Don said, "Thanks, little babysitter. Here's the number to call in case you have an emergency. They will get me in the ballroom. Veterinarians are always on call and the hotel recognizes that."

"Have a good time, and don't worry about us. I've been doing this for years with your crew." Maria put a few more Cheerios on June's tray.

She watched them leave, and Don even opened May's car door for her. Would wonders never cease?

Maria wondered what time it was. She really needed to get her watch fixed. Shouldn't the boys be back by now? *Darn,* she thought, *maybe I'd better go to the park and get them. Don should get Brett a watch.*

Maria heard a car in the driveway. It was Ed. She was surprised he had come so early, but was delighted to have his help for an evening of babysitting. *Great,* she thought, *he can go over and get the boys.*

Ed popped into the kitchen and held up a cold six pack of beer. He put it in the refrigerator and asked if he was in time for dinner.

"You have to earn your creamed turkey by going and getting the boys at the park. They're over there playing ball without a clue as to what time it is."

"We're having creamed turkey?" Ed made a face. "Could I have a turkey sandwich, instead?"

"Picky, picky, picky," Maria said and laughed. "Go get the boys, and I'll see what I can do."

On the way out, he called, "Let's have a beer, too."

When Ed got back and the kids were eating, Maria got two cans of beer out of the refrigerator. She sat down and took a sip right from the can, as she handed the other beer to Ed. It tasted good. "Thanks," she said. "I've really wanted a beer for quite a while."

Ed grinned at her, took a sip, lit a cigarette, and took a drag from it. He looked very contented. "Not too much beer. You're babysitting, remember?"

"Let's eat, Doc," she said, kidding him with his future title. As she put his sandwich in front of him, he touched her hand, and gave her an indescribable look. Maria got a scary, exciting feeling in the pit of her stomach. She distracted herself with eating.

Everyone had finished dinner, and the kids were getting restless. Maria said that if they were very good, she had a delicious dessert for them.

Of course they screamed, "What is it, what is it?"

"Fudge sauce."

"Ice-cream sundaes!" they yelled in unison. "Thanks Auntie Maria."

"Do you want one too, Ed? Or is your beer good enough?"

"I'd like something else for dessert, but I'll get it later, I hope."

Maria felt a little tickle run around inside her again, but managed a prim look.

After dessert, Ed regaled the older kids with more farm stories, while Maria put June to bed. She made sure the baby was clean and dry and had a bottle of watered-down apple juice to drink. June wasn't a fussy baby and was very happy to be put down for the night. Maria kissed her and covered her before she left the room.

Ed was in the living room enthralling his audience. Maria signaled him to wrap it up. He nodded and started to wind down his latest tale of danger.

"It's time to go to bed, after you both take a shower," he said to the boys.

"Do we have to?" they whined.

"Yes, and I'm coming in to make sure everything is washed."

"Gee, Uncle Ed, Dad never makes us shower before we go to bed."

"I'll bet your mother does, so get going."

Meanwhile, Maria put the girls to bed. "Gee, Auntie Maria," Anne said, "it's fun to have you take care of us. We love the way you laugh and make jokes with Uncle Ed. Would you read us a story before we go to sleep?"

"Sure, I'd love to. Get the book that you want me to read."

Mary picked a book called *The Little Duck;* Anne chose *Cinderella*.

"Okay," Maria said, "I'll read both if you promise, cross your hearts, that you will go right to sleep afterward."

They both solemnly nodded yes.

Mary was asleep before long, and Anne was struggling to hear the end of *Cinderella*. Maria kissed them both goodnight and turned out the light. "I'll be right down the hall, if you need me, Anne. Good night."

Maria met Ed coming out of the boys' bedroom as he closed their door. "Wow," he said, "kids take a lot of time to put to bed. I never realized that before."

"Didn't you ever babysit when you were a kid?" Maria sat down on the rec room sofa.

"No, I grew up on my dad's farm and helped out in the fields all the time. I also milked the cows, so I was pretty busy." He went into the kitchen and brought back a couple more beers. "Want a cigarette, babysitter?"

"I would like that," Maria said, taking off her shoes and tucking her feet up under her. "What time is it? My watch doesn't work. I think the stem needs to be replaced because I can't wind it. My dad gave it to me for graduation, but just repairing it costs a lot."

"It's eight thirty by my watch. I'm impressed by the way you handled the kids tonight," he said.

"Don't be too impressed. I've been sort of forced into it because of my circumstances. I really love my little nieces and nephews, but enough's enough. I'm going to pop if I don't get out of here. I hope we like King's Ridge Resort tomorrow."

"I'm not going to work there, so I don't think I have a say in it," Ed said, pulling her over to him.

"But I respect your opinion, Ed. I really do hope you'll like it, then it will be easier for me to sign on for next summer."

"You respect my opinion, ay? Come here and let me show you what my opinion is about kissing you."

Maria had been expecting this. She knew she should stop him, tell him about Bill, but she couldn't.

Ed lifted her onto his lap. "Here," he said, "straddle and face me. That way, you can't get away." Ed grinned.

Maria found herself so close to him, they were like one. He gently put his hand behind her head and pulled her to him. His lips were almost touching hers, and when he kissed her, he reached under her sweater and undid her bra. Maria was shocked and thrilled at the same time, and she didn't do anything to stop him. He had begun to caress her breasts as he was kissing her, and his breathing was getting ragged. She could feel him getting very excited, and she was going out of control with all the touching.

"Stop," she squeezed out. "We've got to talk about what we are doing." She wiggled off of his lap and stood up to catch her breath. She refastened her bra.

She stood in front of him and looked into his big brown eyes. He sat there, his legs sprawled out in front of him, smiling at her. Maria said, "This is not going to work, Ed. You obviously want more from me than I am prepared to give right this moment. I hardly know you."

He held out his arms to her. "Come sit by me. I will take it easy with you. I got a little crazy. Please forgive me."

Maria couldn't resist him, he was so calm and sexy sitting there. She sat back down. Ed snuggled up to her and said quietly, "You may not believe me, but I can't explain why I am so ready to make love to you. When Don and I were talking this fall about me working for him during Thanksgiving vacation, he also asked me if I would call you and offer you a ride home. I said that it would be no problem and would be glad to do it, thinking of you as a nice kid, but I was fooling myself. As I admitted at dinner on Wednesday, I have had thoughts about you for a long time.

"When I ran into you in the Union with Bill this fall, I figured that he was your guy and he seemed nice enough. But I was really surprised by the wave of jealousy I felt as I watched you two together. I had been dating several girls at the time, and one in particular was my main interest. At least that's what I thought until I saw you again.

"Then on the ride here, when you hopped over the back seat, I felt something happen. You were giving off some wonderful invisible scent or something, because I found myself getting aroused even with you sitting way over on the edge of the seat, as far from me as possible. I wondered if you were afraid of *me* or your own feelings. When I pulled you over to me, I was amazed that I couldn't keep my hands off you. I don't usually act that way just because a girl is in the car with me, especially if she's Doc's sister-in-law.

"Then at dinner, I couldn't even think straight. It was like you had enchanted me. All I could think about was wanting to make love to you. Did you feel it, too?" Ed asked softly, his voice hoarse with desire.

"I couldn't believe that my emotions were going wild. I had just said goodbye to my boyfriend, whom I've been dating all fall. We had even planned our next date before I left for Thanksgiving vacation. He had just told me that he wanted to be with me the rest of his life, and I thought I felt the same way.

"When I was a teenager and would see you working with Don in the summers, I had a crush on you big time. I thought you wouldn't be interested in me. You were much older than I was and probably had a dozen girl friends. So I put my crush in my back pocket and left it there.

"I want you to know, too, Ed, that Bill and I have not had sexual relations because of my fear of getting pregnant. Like you, I don't usually get in someone's car and automatically feel the urge to make love with him. I think we are both surprised by the depth of our feelings." Maria reached up and touched Ed's handsome face with her fingers, running them over his cheeks and lips.

That almost put Ed over the edge. "Let's have another beer. When in doubt, drink, I say." He laughed, but he had to get up. He was so excited, he was having a tough time controlling his emotions.

"Don't open one for me," Maria said. "I'll just have a sip of yours and a cigarette. I'm loopy from the two I've already had."

"Now that we've bared our souls to each other, what's going to make this incredible urge go away?" Ed asked as he handed her a cigarette.

"I don't know, but do you want to know what my roommate thinks about having sex?"

"Sure, if it's positive."

"She said it's fun, and as long both people want to do it and don't make any babies, why not."

"I like her attitude, but it's not the attitude of most women," Ed said.

"I don't want our evening to end like this, but I am afraid to let you start anything," Maria whispered haltingly.

"Does that mean you considering my offer? If I can convince you that you won't get pregnant, will you give me a chance? I sound awfully crude, but I want you to know that I'm not celibate, and I've never gotten a woman pregnant. I'm not exactly thinking clearly, but I won't hurt you in any way. I didn't know you were a virgin when we were first drawn together, but I get the feeling that you are interested, just a little scared.

"Now that I know this will be your first time. I'll make it so you'll have fun and satisfaction is guaranteed," he whispered into her hair as he began kissing the back of her neck. He felt her shiver and pulled back her sweater collar so that he could kiss her throat.

Maria took his head in her hands, gently stopping him. "Take it easy, handsome. I know you are confident that the condom will do the job. And, come to think of it, you are almost a doctor of veterinary medicine, so you probably know more about my anatomy than I do, but I'm still not sure."

Ed said, "I want you to remember this night as a wonderful experience. I don't want you to ever be disappointed in our evening together, even if our future together is uncertain. I want to make love to you tonight and show you how much fun good sex can be." As he was talking, he began rubbing Maria's back very lightly, then slowly moved his hands around to her breasts and began stroking them very intimately. He whispered, "If you take your clothes off, I'll massage you some more."

He was driving her wild with his careful build-up. She was getting hot and sweaty and could hardly think straight. Good grief, she was so excited by him she found it was easy to talk herself into agreeing with him. Would she really have fun and always remember tonight? Maybe it would be a good idea to do it with a guy who was so absolutely sure of himself and knew how to do it with her. He wouldn't hurt her because he said he wanted her to enjoy herself, too. But when all the reasoning was over, he was hot and so was she, and that was the bottom line.

Maria had made up her mind. She closed her eyes and whispered, "Okay, I can't stand anymore of this. I think I'm ready."

They both got up. Ed didn't waste a moment, pulling the convertible sofa out into her bed. Maria turned out the lights. Ed walked over to where she was standing in the shadows and took off her sweater.

"You take my shirt off," he whispered. "I want you to undress me as I undress you. I don't like the idea of you having to be naked while I still am dressed, especially the first time."

"Okay," she said and tried to pull his T-shirt over his head, but he was so tall that she couldn't do it. She started to giggle nervously and said that he would have to leave it on, unless he bent over so she could get it over his head. He did and she said, "Phew, we're over that hurdle," as she flung it on a chair.

Maria felt a little ridiculous and couldn't stop giggling, which then gave her the hiccups. Still hiccupping and laughing, Maria said stupidly, "I didn't know you had a chest full of black hair." She had never seen him without his shirt on, even in very hot summer weather. Ed ignored her giggles. He had a one-track mind, and Maria knew what track he was on.

He said, "Undo my belt and unzip my pants." She hoped his pants worked the way hers did. She fiddled around with his belt, trying to figure it out. It didn't have a buckle, it had a clip. She couldn't get it open and broke into gales of nervous laughter again.

Ed said, "You're hopeless, you know."

Maria ran to the kitchen to get a drink of water, leaving Ed standing in the rec room trying to maintain an atmosphere of sexual excitement. "We can't do it with me hiccupping," she said, drinking gulps of water. She stood quietly for a moment and waited. The hiccups had gone, and she went back into the darkened rec room. She started to giggle again when she saw Ed standing there in just his shorts. They were silky and had designs all over them. She said that she liked his taste in underwear.

He grinned at her and said that it was great that she was so relaxed that she could joke about his underwear. He put his arms around her and slowly undid her bra, pulled it off, and put his hands all over her breasts.

It was show time. She was going into orbit, and he knew it. He said that she had beautiful breasts and kissed them. Then he reached down and undid her slacks, which dropped to the floor. She thought she'd be embarrassed standing there naked, but she wasn't. He was so cute and serious. To break the tension, Maria asked him if he liked what he saw. He was getting so excited that he could hardly smile. He went over to his pants and pulled out several condoms. Then he went into the kitchen.

She couldn't resist saying, "What are you doing in there? It isn't the time for a snack, yet." She was choking with gales of laughter and was completely out of control. The excitement was almost too much. She thought, *Oh why don't we just have a quickie and get this over with. Then all this buildup wouldn't be necessary.*

Ed came back with some olive oil. He was smiling; he wasn't nearly as tipsy as she or at all nervous.

"What kind of a snack is that?" Maria asked.

"You are a little devil. I didn't bring any lubricant with me because I forgot." He said it as casually as he could, "But olive oil will do."

"I thought we were going to drink it like a toast before we did it," Maria said, laughing so hard that she had tears in her eyes. "I noticed, though, that you didn't forget your condoms; hoping, no doubt, that you might run into a willing subject."

That was too much for Ed. He grabbed her, pulled her down on the bed on top of him, and started to laugh, too. There they were, trying to do that magical act, and they were hysterical with laughter.

"I wonder if the kids have heard us laughing and when we look up after our passionate encounter, we'll see them all standing there watching us," said Maria.

Ed jumped up like a shot and ran down to hall to see if everyone was asleep. He came padding back in his bare feet and said that they were all zonked.

"Are you baby proofed?" she asked. "There can be no slip in without that step."

"I'm all set. That's what the oil is for; condoms need to be oiled."

Maria had calmed down a bit now, the laughter having been replaced by anticipation. She was about as relaxed as she was ever going to be. Lying naked next to Ed was exciting to the point of insanity. Ed was rubbing her gently all over, and she knew what the next step would be. She started to laugh again. She couldn't help it; nervous laughter was something she couldn't control.

Ed whispered hoarsely, "Take a deep breath, Maria. Don't be afraid." He kissed her and held her. "You're a very desirable, beautiful young woman." He kissed her neck and breasts and caressed her nipples.

As her temperature began to rise, he asked gently, "Are you ready for me to make love to you?" He held her close and looked into her eyes. "I'll stop if it starts to hurt too much or you want to wait for a while—or forever."

Maria choked out, "Let's try it."

"Maria, I'm going to say it again. We don't have to do anything more. Are you sure you want me to make love to you?"

She nodded and he kissed her again. He oiled himself up and began to carefully make love to her. He was a careful lover and took his time. Watching her face intently to see if he needed to slow down, he saw that she was a little uncomfortable at first, but she didn't stop him. He had done such a good job of getting her into a passionate mood that she began to really enjoy it as the intensity of it grew. Ed waited until he felt she was almost there and took her to a place where their energy exploded. They were so in sync that release came almost simultaneously. It was an incredible experience. Ed was bathed in sweat, and Maria's mind was reeling. They pulled the covers over them, because now that the passion had cooled, so had the room. It was late November, after all.

After Ed's breathing returned to normal, and Maria knew that he wasn't going to expire on the spot, she said, "I'll never forget what happened between us tonight. You are a wonderful lover."

They hugged each other and Maria said, without thinking, "I'm so glad I didn't chicken out. Sex games are thrilling!"

Ed smiled. "Sex is what makes the world go round."

"What time is it? I don't know how I would explain you away if May and Don came home right now. I could say that you just wanted to see how the couch in the rec room felt. Or that you were looking for me everywhere and found me in bed, but I don't think Don would buy it."

"It's ten o'clock. They won't be home yet. The speaker is just warming up."

"I'm sorry about laughing while you were trying to help me trust you." She kept hugging him. "You must admit that there were parts of this experience that were funny. Through it all, you never lost it. You are one sexy guy. Thanks, it was wonderful. I would heartily recommend it to my friends—if you are the one doing it. I could hire you out to all first timers. Think of the money we could make."

"I'm not that hard up, yet. You'd turn me into a real stud, wouldn't you? Wouldn't you be a little jealous?" Ed laughed as he said it.

"You're right. I have to share you with too many girls as it is."

Ignoring her comment about other women, Ed said, "Maria, I still can't explain this incredible urge I had to make love to you. You are so passionate and adorable. The whole evening has made me rethink a lot of things. You also say the funniest things without even realizing it. Teach me to be like that," he said, looking at her with those deep brown eyes full of electricity.

Maria didn't know what to say to him except that she would try.

To lighten things up a little, she said, "How about a shower before we get dressed? We are all gooey, sweaty, and oily, so let's clean up. We can take one together in the kid's bathroom, so Don won't get wise to the activities of the babysitters."

They scooped up their clothes and padded down the hall to their next first-time experience: showering together. Maria was still thinking about how it felt to lose her virginity. She was actually proud of everything they had done together. She felt like she had been taken through a rite of passage by a really nice guy.

When she opened the shower door and looked at Ed, she thought how strong and muscular he was. She didn't quite know how to tell him that she liked his body, so she decided to make a little joke out of it. "Where did all those muscles come from, chasing girls?"

He laughed and doused her with water. He took the soap, lathered up his hands, and started washing her body, lingering on her breasts. When she gave him a look, he laughed again and pleaded innocent.

"Now, it's my turn," she said, she took a washcloth, soaped it up, and started working over all those muscles. "You have a lot of surface area for me to wash," Maria said as she scrubbed away. "Am I ruining your skin?"

"No, I love to scrub or be scrubbed, if I'm lucky. It feels good."

"So, you like to have the top layer of your skin removed whenever you shower."

He pressed her up against the shower wall. "You had better not make any more smart remarks, or I'm going to make love to you right here in the shower."

"No condoms, no sex," she said, and slipped out of the shower, making a face at him.

Maria put on her pajamas so she would be ready to jump into bed when he left, and he took a second look when he saw her in her bathrobe and slippers. "You look all fuzzy and warm. I wish I were going to sleep with you."

She cocked her head. "That would never work with the two of us. We'd be exhausted driving back to school."

"I'd take that chance," he said.

She padded back to the living room with Ed right beside her. He looked at his watch. "Oh boy, I'd better get going."

Maria said, "That's a good idea, because I wouldn't want to explain to Don why you were here so late and me in my pajamas."

"I'll pick you up tomorrow around noon. How's that?" Ed asked.

"It's fine, and I'll make some sandwiches. Do you mind more turkey?"

"Anything will be fine. Thanks in advance."

She put on as serious an expression as she could. "I'm sure that we were meant to be together for some reason." She paused thoughtfully, then grinned. "It was to have sex."

Ed laughed and took her in his arms. He gave her a wild kiss. "You're right," he said, smiling as he went out the door.

Maria hurried to bed before Don and May came home. She thought, *What a night.* She actually didn't feel as if it were her who had been on this wild ride. It was as if it had happened to someone else. It was so darn sudden. She had gone from being afraid of sex on Wednesday to losing her virginity on Saturday. Who was she? She constantly amazed herself. It had seemed so right at the time, but now she was wondering what had happened to her since she was let loose upon the world. Nineteen and madly in love with one guy and having wild sex with another guy. While Maria was pondering this, it was suddenly morning.

22. Back to School

In real love, you want the other person's good.
In romantic love, you want the other person.
—Margaret Anderson

When Maria woke up, it was the first quiet morning since she had arrived. Don evidently had Sunday off. His partner, Gill, was on call. As Maria was stripping the sheets off her bed, she had a terrible thought. What if Bill had called just as she and Ed were in a mad passionate embrace? Boy, was she lucky.

She had the coffee started, bacon frying, table set, and orange juice made when she heard someone coming down the hall. It was May, and she looked happier than Maria had seen her the whole weekend. "So how was the evening and the food? Did you have fun?" Maria asked.

"It was a very nice get together, and we had a lot of fun. We haven't been out like that in several months. We danced, Don didn't get tipsy, and we talked with a lot of interesting couples. You know how Don loves to tell his stories," May said, laughing as she rolled her eyes. "How were the kids? Did they behave? I told them that we would be mad if I got a bad report."

"They were perfect. I love your kids; they are so great. I made dinner, and Ed stopped by for a little while. He brought the boys home from the baseball field. The girls were adorable and easy to deal with. I read them a couple of stories, and they were out like lights."

"Thanks for babysitting and getting breakfast started." May looked quizzically at Maria. "You seem awfully chipper this morning. Anything happen last night to provoke this breakfast-making flurry?"

Maria played innocent. "No, nothing out of the ordinary."

"I'm sorry that you want to have a job and won't be with us next summer. I will miss your help and your company," May said.

"Thanks, May. I'll miss you and the kids, too. But I need to fly on my own now. I won't be far. I'll come and visit." Maria thought, *She actually sounds pleasant for a change, but it doesn't change my decision.*

"I'm making sandwiches for Ed and me for the drive back to school. We're going to stop at King's Ridge Resort this afternoon so I can take a look at it and get an application for work next summer. I'll let you know what happens."

By noon, Maria was packed and had her duffle bags by the door. Things seemed very peaceful between May and Don. Maybe getting out for the evening had put May in a good mood.

She heard Ed's car pull into the driveway, and she felt a little ping in her stomach. Don, May, and the kids came to say goodbye.

"Keep out of trouble, little sister," Don said. "Ed, I'll keep in touch regarding your new assignment."

Maria thanked him again for her new coat, kissed the girls, and smiled at the boys. Then she reminded them, "I'm still planning to go to Florida for two weeks over Christmas, but if anything changes, I'll let you know. I'm hoping I can still come here for a week before I go back to school."

Once they were on their way, Ed turned to her. "How do you feel? More to the point, are you sore?"

"Nope, are you?" She couldn't resist teasing him, even though he was trying to be thoughtful.

He burst out laughing. "When did the folks get in?" he asked, changing the subject.

Maria had felt that Ed was acting a little reserved, and the minute she had gotten into the car, she had sensed the charge that immediately occurred between them. Maria looked at Ed, who was obviously trying to decide what to say next.

"Maria, this thing that has happened between us has taken me off guard. I want you to know that I have a girlfriend whom I've been dating all fall, but we don't seem to be on the same wavelength anymore. She's planning to go to law school after she graduates this spring, and that may be part of the reason. She's more of a thinker than a feeler."

"After you left, I thought about Bill and how this 'thing,' as you call it, happened. I don't know how I could love him, yet have sex with you. Also, and don't tell me if it's a secret or something, but what did Don mean about 'your assignment?' It sounded as if I had sex with a spy."

Ed laughed. "Your imagination never stops, does it? In February, if all goes well, I'll be going to the University of Kentucky's equine center to work with race-horse breeders. I want to show them an artificial insemination program that Doc and I have developed and take any courses that will help me with the breeding and care of race horses. A while back, Iowa State contacted Doc to see if he wanted to go, but because of family commitments and his vet practice, he recommended me to go in his place. I'll get paid while I'm there, have a waiver from Iowa State for the courses that I will miss, and still be able to graduate in May. The grant covers February through April. That isn't a prime time for breeding race horses, but was the only time I could get off from school."

"My gosh, that's exciting for you. I am in illustrious company today. Congratulations, Ed. You've worked long and hard, and it is paying off now."

He smiled, obviously pleased at her reaction. "I owe a lot to Doc. He has been in my corner ever since I started working for him. To change the subject, however, would you read where this place is in your brochure? We're almost to Galena."

"It's six miles east on U.S. twenty. I'll start looking for a sign to King's Ridge." Almost immediately after she said it, a big green sign loomed up ahead with an arrow directing the way to King's Ridge Resort, four miles north on King's Ridge Drive.

"That seems pretty straightforward," Ed said, as he made the turn. "There it is. It's definitely big, over a hundred rooms, I'll bet."

Big old oak trees lined the driveway that looked like they had been there forever. A tip of the golf course ran parallel to the road for a ways and added a certain charm to the whole place. They drove up to a large, well-maintained two-story brick structure with a covered entrance. Maria couldn't tell how far the building went back or to the sides because of the way it was nestled into the landscape.

There was a circular driveway with a spur leading to a huge parking lot. Ed pulled into the parking lot, turned off the car, and looked at her. "What do you think of it so far?"

"I like the outward appearance; now for the inside," she said. Her stomach was doing a nervous little dance.

Ed put his hand on her face, smoothed it with his fingers, lifted her chin, and gave her a little kiss. "That's for good luck," he said with a smile.

He opened her door, took her hand, and they walked up to the entrance of King's Ridge Resort. He looked very professional dressed in a coat and tie. Maria was a little surprised but pleased that he had done that for her. He pulled hard on the heavy, wooden double doors that opened into an entry hall. They had to go through another set of doors to reach the desk.

"I'd like to see the manager," Ed said.

The manager asked if anything was wrong with the accommodations, thinking that they were staying there.

"We aren't guests. My friend would like to talk with someone in charge of hiring for next summer," Ed said, glancing at Maria.

"Certainly, sir, just step this way."

Ed waited for Maria to precede him, then followed her down a beautiful hall that had thick carpets on the floor and oil paintings on the walls. The walk was intimidating and quite long. Finally, the manager stopped and knocked at a heavy carved wooden door.

"Come in," they heard. The manager explained why they were there, then left.

A nice-looking older gentleman with stacks of paperwork in front of him was seated at a beautiful oak desk. He smiled at them and said, "Please sit," gesturing with his hands. He took off his glasses. "My name is Mr. Glenmore. How can I help you?"

"It's nice to meet you, Mr. Glenmore. My name is Maria Banks, and this is my friend, Dr. Ed McDermott." Maria smiled brightly. "I would like to work here next summer as a waitress, hostess, or in any other capacity for which I might qualify. I will be twenty next summer and am currently a freshman at Iowa State University."

"I'll give you an application to fill out. Please list your work preferences. I will need three references from you, and the application must be signed in front of a notary. If you can get a bank manager as one of your references, it would be very good. I will need the material by February first of next year. We are always looking for college students, because they are usually intelligent and work well with our clientele.

"I am going to put a star next to your name on the application. That is my little signal to myself that I met you and liked your presentation. If your references check out, we will notify you by no later than March 1 that you have a job. You will start on May fifteenth and have a couple of days of training. We will include the details in your letter. If you do not hear from us, we will not be hiring you, but I don't think that will happen in your case. The customers like to have pretty college students taking care of them." He stood up, shook Maria's hand and Ed's, then said to Ed, "You're a lucky young fellow."

"Thank you so much for taking the time to see me. I really appreciate it," Maria said, giving him another big smile.

When they got back to the car, Ed unlocked her side first. He hugged her and gave her a light congratulatory kiss for being so smooth in there.

"Nothing to it," she said, waving the application envelope in his face. "Piece of cake."

"What was with the Dr. McDermott title? I wondered who you were talking about."

"That place smelled like money, and people who run those places like to think that their clientele are all wealthy doctors and lawyers. I was stretching the truth by a few months. By the time I'm working there, you will be Dr. McDermott."

They climbed into the car.

"You know, Maria, with strangers, you come across cool and tough. The soft side never shows unless you feel safe. Am I right?"

"I've been found out. You're quite clever, you know. I try to put up a good front, and it is easy for me. I've had a lot of practice with my mom, May, and Betty. Thank you for being so supportive. I must admit that I was a little nervous before I went in." She leaned over and gave him a kiss of thanks on his cheek.

He looked into her eyes and said that he had another idea how she could thank him. "Remember the diner where I couldn't keep my hands off you. Well, next door to it is a nice motel. We could stop off for an hour or so. What do you think about that?" He took her in his arms and put his lips close to her ear. "I want to make love to you so badly. I couldn't get to sleep for a long time last night, even though I was tired. I couldn't get you out of my mind. I don't know where this is going, but loving you seems so right."

Maria was slightly surprised by his request. She was still basking in her success of the previous night. *Do all virgins have an orgasm the first time they do it,* she wondered. Ed was one sexy guy. Jokingly, she asked, "Is lunch included in this service?" Her eyes were sparkling.

Ed shook his head in disbelief and laughed out loud. "Am I way out in left field, or do you feel that I'm asking for payment?" He hadn't started the car, he just sat there, waiting.

"Well, the thought crossed my mind, but if you want my more honest reaction, I am rather flattered that you suggested it. I'm probably guilty of being too innocent, but I actually believe you. If I'm wrong, that's the price I'll pay."

Off they drove to find the motel and the diner. Maria sat as close to Ed as possible. She asked with a straight face, "Do you think you will have trouble finding the place? Should I look on the map."

He grinned. "How can you be so funny? You make me feel happy and free. It's very hard for me to keep my cool with you. You don't realize it, but you have become very important to me. And the most amazing thing is, you aren't expecting anything from me except some fun."

"And lunch, don't forget," she said, giving him a poke in his ribs to emphasize the joke. "I'll try to find some romantic music to get us in the mood for our afternoon interlude. That rhymes, mood/interlude. You are bringing out the poet in me, besides more adult things."

"Is it me, or are you this funny with everyone?"

"When I am happy, funny things pop into my head. I am not very funny when I'm in chemistry lab."

"I need to lighten up, Maria. It has been a hard climb for me to get where I am now. I'm too serious and I'd like to laugh more."

The music was coming in loud and clear. Someone was singing a beautiful love song, and Maria loved the way music made her feel. She wanted to respond to Ed's comment without sounding trite. "How about reading joke books or funny comic books? Some of them are really good." Maria looked at Ed's expression and realized that those suggestions didn't strike a chord with him. It's a hard thing to help someone lighten up. *Once he graduates and gets his clinic going, he will laugh more,* Maria thought.

They rode along with the music filling the car. Ed had awakened a love and passion in her that she hadn't known existed. She realized that she had put darling Bill on a back burner. She had a few pangs of guilt but not many. She wondered if the pressures of looking after her mother had bottled up all her teenage feelings, and making love with Ed was letting them all out. Whatever the reason, she was excited and looking forward to doing it again with Ed.

"We're here," Ed said, quietly and lovingly, as he turned to her and gave her a light kiss. He went into the motel's office. In two minutes, he was back, waving the key in front of her nose. He seemed as happy as she was. He took their duffle bags out of the car and led her to the room. "After you, honey," he said at the door.

Maria felt his eagerness as he melted her with his tender touch. He put his hands around her face and kissed her with such passion that she began to tingle. He stood there hugging her, then whispered, "Right this minute, I'm so happy to be your lover, I don't know what to do." His attitude toward her had changed somewhat, still lusty but more caring than before.

Ed turned up the temperature in the room. He helped Maria off with her new coat and hung it up. Maria reached up and undid his tie; she slowly pulled it off, all the while looking into his eyes and telegraphing desire. He raised her arms and gently lifted her sweater over her head. Listening to him breathe faster, she undid his shirt while he undid her slacks. It was more fun undressing him this time, and she was far less nervous.

"You can take off your own belt and pants. I'm not going through that rigmarole again; once was enough," she said, giggling a little. She was cold and to hurry up the process, she shrugged out of her undergarments, stood there naked for a moment, then dashed to the bed and dove under the covers.

Ed climbed into bed with her. "You have a beautiful body, Maria." He touched and kissed her breasts.

She couldn't resist teasing him. "So, you're a breast man, are you?"

"Are you turning this into a comedy?" he asked, smiling at her. Then he picked her up and placed her right on top of him.

She squeaked a little from his fast move but lay still as he began kissing her face and neck. His breathing became more ragged with each kiss. With skilled hands, he began barely touching her, tickling her almost unmercifully. As she rolled around, squealing with pleasure, she saw a radio across the room. She jumped off him, ran shivering across the cool room, and turned it on.

Ed asked, "What's the matter? Did I do something to upset you?"

She couldn't resist. "I've changed my mind."

He couldn't believe it. The look on his face was priceless.

She burst out laughing and dialed the radio to some romantic music. She found a wonderful station and ducked back into bed. "I got you going, didn't I? Now, where were we?"

"Which should I do, squeeze the daylights out of you or make love to you? You choose."

Maria kissed him as her answer, and that did it for him. He disappeared beneath the blankets, and she felt him working his way up her body in the most delightful manner. The more he kissed and touched her, the more the two of them wanted. Finally, they couldn't stand it one more second. Ed's lovemaking was much more passionate this time. Maria responded differently, too, with complete abandon. She clung to him as he moved into an exotic rhythm. Ed was a terrific lover and was careful to wait until she was ready to drop over the edge in a climax with him. They were lost in a sexual trance that held them in its timeless grip for what seemed like forever. Shaking from the experience, they lay in each other's arms, not talking, just breathing and waiting for the trembling to stop.

"My God, Maria, I can't believe what just happened," Ed finally whispered.

She looked at his handsome face; he was so different now. She had seen a side of him that she would never have known existed if she hadn't been his lover. She loved being in his arms, both of them all sweaty and sticking together. It was very sensual. She could see how a good sexual relationship could top anything. She also realized that what Ed had said was right: a good experience for the girl was absolutely critical.

Ed reached out with his free hand and picked up his pack of cigarettes. "Do you want to smoke with me?"

"Sure, but how will you do it with only one arm?"

"Smarty!" He got up and went into the bathroom. When he returned, he lit two cigarettes and got back into bed, handing her one. He took a drag, blew out some smoke, and asked, "It was more fun this time, wasn't it?"

"Fun?!" Maria blurted out. "It was a whole different experience. You are a great lover; you know my body better than I do. Is it from your anatomy courses or personal experience?" she asked, grinning at him.

"You don't expect me to answer that, do you?"

"It was worth a try," she said, trying to decide what to do with her cigarette. She really didn't like to smoke, and now the darn ash needed to be gotten rid of, but she didn't want to move.

"By the way, I checked the condom I used last night, and it was in perfect condition. I'll check this one when we get up."

Maria hugged him. "You make me feel so much better. I know you don't want a little Ed or Edwina running around." She put her head on his hairy chest and took a little puff from her cigarette. "I've got to be careful with the ash. I wouldn't want to burn one little hair on your chest." After a while of enjoying the peace that came with the sexual release, she said, "Well, a deal is a deal. It's time for a nice meal." She had completely forgotten about the picnic lunch she'd packed.

"Let's take a shower together, first. You can scrub a little more skin off me, and I can check your breasts."

"Are you giving me a breast exam or taking a shower? I want to know." She laughed.

"You'd better be careful. I get awful sexy in the shower," Ed said.

"You're absolutely amazing. How much testosterone flows through those veins of yours? And besides, you know the rule, no condoms—"

"No sex. What if I told you I had a boxful in my duffle?"

"You really don't mean it, do you? How can you after all the energy you put into doing it a few minutes ago?" Maria stepped into the warm water of the shower. "Just don't drown me while we are doing it." She was feeling absolutely wild at the moment. How could she have more sex? Then she thought, *With Ed it's easy.*

Ed had a delighted grin when he poked his head into the shower. "Keep those feelings. I'll be back in a moment." Ed returned baby proofed. He had a little shower stool onto which he lifted Maria. He grinned. "You will enjoy this much more if you are up higher. Besides, I won't drown you this way."

The warm water tickling their bodies had provided the foreplay, and Ed found a very willing partner in Maria. Holding on to each other for dear life, their bodies moving together in a constant rhythm, Ed brought her with him to that incredible, indescribable, and completely satisfying place. When it was over, they stood with the water running over them, hugging.

Ed nuzzled her neck. "I won't forget this." He shut his eyes, his lips felt for hers, and he tenderly held her.

Maria wiggled free and picked up a cloth to wash his back and break the spell. "You're going to be exhausted tonight," she said as she lathered him up and scrubbed his body. She knew he loved it. He stood stock still as she moved all over his body with her hands. When she finished, he kissed her thank you.

"Now, it's your turn." He lathered his hands and washed her back and down her legs. Then he turned her around and caressed her breasts with his hands. "This is the best part," he said.

Maria grabbed his hands. "That's enough!"

He grinned at her. "I'll continue that at a later date." He carefully washed the soap off every square inch of her, saying, "I don't want you to have itchy skin."

They got out, wrapped themselves in towels, and she grabbed a bottle of free motel lotion and offered some to him.

"Maybe, but let me put the lotion on you," he said, still enjoying her nudity.

Maria said, "I was afraid of that." She gave him as stern an expression as she could muster.

"I'll be good." He took the lotion from her and began rubbing it all over her, and gave just a little extra attention to her breasts.

"You couldn't resist, could you?"

"I love your breasts. They are beautiful. I wish I could lie down with them next to me every night. I definitely *am* a breast man."

"We'd better get dressed, have lunch, and pick up your other riders before it gets too late."

The diner was fairly crowded when they went in, but they found a seat. Hungry after all the energy they had expended, especially Ed, they ordered and ate fairly quickly. They headed out to the car. Ed looked like he wanted to say something, but seemed to change his mind. He opened her door and hugged her. "Get in, you little lover."

After driving for a while with Maria cuddled up next to him, Ed said, "We have to pick up two gals in Cedar Rapids and one in Marshalltown. Claudia doesn't need a ride back because she has another friend who is picking her up. We could be back by eight o'clock, if everyone is ready."

"It's very nice of you to take the girls back and forth to school."

"They've been a lot of laughs when I've waited tables for them these past couple of years. Fortunately, I don't have to do that my final spring at school. If all goes well, I'll be away for three months and back just in time to finish up before graduation."

"I'll bet Don and May will come out for your graduation."

"Don't count on it. Doc is awfully busy in the spring with new calves, colts, and pigs. All the farmers want their babies born in the good weather."

"Well, I'll come and cheer on my sexy lover," Maria said as she fiddled with the radio. She found a nice station, pulled her legs up under her, and leaned against Ed. All the sexual tension was gone for the moment, and they were very contented.

Suddenly, Ed said, "Oh, yes, I almost forgot to tell you some bad news."

"What?" she asked. "Don't tell me the condom broke or, worse yet, both of them failed."

Ed looked at her and burst into laughter, "Nope, I can't do it. I was going to string you along, but you look so worried."

"So, Mr. Tease, you're beginning to sound like me. I guess that's good. I've been a good teacher."

They rode along listening to the music. After a while, Ed said that he would be happy to take her to Ames to get her application form notarized. "I know the assistant manager of the bank there."

"Thanks, Ed, I would certainly appreciate your help. When do you want to go?"

"Late Thursday afternoon after classes would be good for me. How does that sound to you?"

"That's fine with me."

"Let's have dinner and a motel stay, too," he said, looking at her and grinning.

"You are really thinking ahead, aren't you? I call it blackmail." She thought that she was crazy, dating Bill every chance she could and sleeping with Ed. Talk about sowing some wild oats. She'd sown a field of them that weekend.

"Well, I want to make sure I make the most out of the time I have. I won't be able to see you the following week because I'll have a ton of vaccinations to do for the local farmers."

"And the week after that will be taken up with final exams; then we'll be going home for Christmas vacation."

"So next Thursday will probably be the last time I see you until I pick you up from Doc's in January. How are you getting to Boone to catch the train?"

Maria lied and said that Susie's boyfriend was taking them to Boone.

"If something happens to him, and you are in a pinch, give me a call. I'll get you there."

"You are a sweet guy, thanks so much. It's the thought that counts."

He pulled into a filling station. "I've got to get gas before we pick up the gals. How about a cigarette before we hit the road again?"

"Sure," she said, "I'm going to the ladies room first, though." Maria sensed that Ed had something more to say to her.

After gassing up, Ed moved the car away from the pumps. He lit two cigarettes and gave one to Maria. She loved looking at his profile when he lit up. That slight overbite and the dimple in his chin got her every time.

Ed said, "I know I have said this before, but I just want you to know that what happened between us this weekend was completely unplanned. I found myself feeling and doing things with you that I couldn't stop. I'm sure you're thinking, 'Yah, yah, yah, he says this to all of his girls,' but I don't. I've had to keep my nose pretty clean to survive these last five years of vet school. I wish that I knew how things were going to turn out, so I could make some plans with you. I'm afraid that by the time I get a clinic up and running, you will be gone. But that's a risk I'll have to take." He took her cigarette from her, then kissed her with such passion that she felt it clear down to her toes.

Maria finally had to push him away because of the intensity of it all. She cleared her throat. "This has been a real awakening for me, sexually and emotionally. I have changed this weekend, gotten wilder than I ever thought possible, loved our lovemaking, and wanted more. No one ever forgets their first time, and I certainly have good memories."

It wasn't really an answer to his implicit question, but he seemed satisfied with what she said. They finished their cigarettes and got back on the road.

They made good time. He picked up and deposited everyone else before he took her to her dorm. He grabbed her duffle bags, and they ran up the stairs to the living room. "Thanks for the wonderful weekend," she said. They had said their goodbyes back at the filling station. He smiled and was gone.

23. Returning to Bill

Love is the irresistible desire to be irresistibly desired.
—Robert Frost

Maria walked down the hall to her room feeling like a different person from when she ran out of there Wednesday afternoon. How could she have changed so much in such a short period of time? She was very tired and wrung out emotionally. She didn't want to talk to Bill before curfew, because she knew he would want to come over. Guilt about what she had done was raging.

She opened the door and looked for Susie. She wasn't there. Aimlessly, Maria took her books out of the duffle. She couldn't understand her mood change. She had been so high, and now she felt lethargic and depressed. Why had she been so irrationally wild with Ed? She knew she needed to get ready for Monday's classes, but all she wanted to do was lie on her bed and try to make sense of the weekend.

She looked at her assignment book, then shut it. She needed to sleep. Maybe it would be easier after a nap. The next thing she knew, Susie was shaking her. "Wake up, Bill is on the phone."

"What time is it?"

"It's about nine thirty. I've been in for about a half hour. I was going to cover you up and let you sleep all night, but now Bill has called."

Maria stumbled down the hall and grabbed the phone. "Hi, Bill, how are you?"

"I missed you so much, Maria. You sound sleepy."

"I am, and I missed you, too," she said, weakly. The nicer he was, the worse she felt. If only he had been irritable, she could have cut their conversation short.

"Are you all right, Maria? You don't sound very good."

"I'm just tired from the trip. It's a long way from Rock Falls, Illinois. And while I was there, I was busy helping to take care of my nieces and nephews. I was asleep when you called."

"I'm sorry it was so hard on you. I hope you will feel better tomorrow," her sweet Bill said.

"I will, I'm sure. How was your weekend?"

"I'm sorry I didn't call you Saturday night. I was in the midst of a big discussion with my whole family about what to do about the Maude situation. I told my folks everything you said, and they called my brothers and sister so we could all figure it out."

There was something so appealing about Bill. She loved his voice. He was so vulnerable and innocent, in a way. He had a wonderful family behind him, and that made her feel less guilty. "So what happened at the meeting?"

"My mom and dad are going to follow all your suggestions. They are fired up now. Thank you so much for helping us and getting that advice from your dad. They'll thank you themselves when they see you again."

"I'm so happy your folks are so 'with it,' and are going to get everything protected. They are very intelligent people."

"Maria, when can I see you? I have a chapter meeting tomorrow night, but I want to skip it and see you. We could go to the library and whisper to each other in there for a while or go to the Union and have a Coke or something. I have that appointment on Wednesday to see the assistant editor of the *Iowa Progress*. Could you take part of the day off to go with me?"

"I would love to go with you. What time?"

"One in the afternoon. How does that sound?"

"It sounds good. I won't miss much that I can't make up if we leave about noon."

"Okay. That will give us time for a quick lunch. My mother told me about a great short-order place to go. We'll talk more about it tomorrow night. I'll pick you up around seven. I can't wait to see you."

"I can't wait, either. Sweet dreams, my love."

"I love you, Maria."

She walked back to her room, feeling more in love with Bill and even guiltier than before. He had a charming way of weaving a web of happiness around her, but she still wasn't very comfortable at the moment. Deceiving him wasn't a pleasant feeling. Her dad used to say, "Act in haste, repent in leisure." She had left as a girl at Thanksgiving break and come back a woman.

Susie was perched on her bed, looking over her notes for tomorrow's classes. She looked up at Maria and asked, "So what's up with Bill? Is he still mad about you?"

"He's fine. It's me who's confused." Maria didn't know how much to share with Susie. She was afraid Susie might think that she was horribly unfaithful by having sex with Ed.

Picking up on her mood, Susie said, "Does this have anything to do with Ed?"

"Yes, and it gets worse," she said, looking at Susie with an expression of guilt and pain.

"You had sex with Ed, didn't you?"

"Yep, and I can't explain how I am drawn to two guys at the same time, so don't ask. With Ed, it's pure lust, although I've had a crush on him for a long time. I'll say one thing in his favor, he's a terrific lover."

"How do you feel about Bill now?"

"I love him, and he loves me; we are good together. I'm going down to Des Moines on Wednesday with him. He's going to see one of the editors at the paper about a part-time job. But get this, I'm going to go with Ed on Thursday to Ames to have my job application for Kings Ridge notarized. Ed offered to take me to see the bank manager, whom he has gotten friendly with. He wants to take me out to dinner afterward and make a motel stop. And you know what? I'm looking forward to that, too."

"My advice to you is to go for it. I told you how I feel about sex. It's fun. As long as no one gets hurt, enjoy yourself."

"I guess I was brought up in a culture that said that dating two guys at once and getting intimate, physically, with either one was somehow very wrong."

"Me too," Susie said, "but I've gotten over it. By the way, whatever changed your mind about not having intercourse until you had a diaphragm?"

"Ed did. He was so darn sexy without being pushy in any way. I couldn't resist him."

Susie's advice was just what Maria needed to hear. Susie had erased a lot of the guilt that Maria felt. Susie's matter-of-fact attitude about sexual intercourse was perfect. She took things as they came and did not dwell on anything she couldn't change. Maria began to feel much better the more she thought about Susie's philosophy. *But I have to be very careful about not hurting someone, too,* she thought.

"Thanks, my friend, for your help. I will sleep well tonight. See you in the morning," Maria said dreamily and closed her eyes.

On Monday, Maria thought about seeing Bill for most of the day. Getting back in the routine of school and paying attention in class was hard. It was much more fun to think about Bill. She hoped he wouldn't sense anything different about her. *Honestly, Maria,* she chided herself, *stop worrying.* She wasn't wearing a scarlet A on her clothes, but in her heart she felt adulterous.

Maria was overly anxious that evening, so she was in the front room, ready to go, a little early. She saw Bill park his car, jump out, and take the stairs two at a time. All the feelings of love rushed back into every pore of Maria's body when Bill smiled at her. She didn't care who might be watching; she flung herself into his arms and gave him a big hug.

He laughed and rushed her down the stairs. When they got to the bottom, he kissed her with such hunger, her emotions become unstable once again, and the evening had just started. They hadn't said a word to each other. He held her at arm's length and just gazed into her eyes.

"Come on, handsome, you are doing a number on me. Let's go to the library and talk."

He nodded and opened the car door for her, but he held onto her like a life preserver. She waited.

He laughed. "I've got to let you get in, don't I?" After he started the car, he said, "I didn't know how much I'd missed you until I saw you standing there, waiting for me."

"I have something to tell you when we find a quiet spot in the library," Maria said.

"I hope it isn't bad news." Bill got a sudden worried look on his face.

"No, just a change in me," she said, taking a deep breath and wondering how she was going to tell him.

"Here we are," he said, as he jumped out to open her door. His face still registered concern.

Maria took him to a second-floor room that she had found. It had a table and chairs and a beat-up sofa. It was used for small conferences during the day but was always empty at night.

As soon as they shut the door, Bill said, "So what's wrong between us? What happened while we were away from each other?"

Maria went cold. Could Bill somehow know that she had been with Ed? Could he sense something? She sat down on the sofa and patted the seat next to her. "Why do you assume it's bad? Sit down, and I'll tell you what I decided over Thanksgiving break." She ignored her nerves and sounded very upbeat.

When Bill sat down and put his arms around her, he looked at her with such intensity that Maria almost became tongue tied. She shut her eyes for a moment to think, then said, "I want to have us make real love, physically." She couldn't say the word "intercourse" to him for some reason. She felt so awkward; she blushed and shut her eyes again. When she opened them, he was gazing at her with those blue eyes of his, melting her into a pool of jelly.

He smiled delightedly and buried his face in her hair. "I won't hurt you, I promise. This is the best news you could had given me. Don't be nervous; we will be just fine together."

Maria pulled away and squeaked out, "Neither one of us can stand this much longer, and I'm taking the chance with you." She couldn't quite understand why she was so embarrassed to talk about being intimate with him; it was so easy with Ed. Maybe it was because Bill was younger than Ed. Maria wondered if he'd had much experience.

Bill said quietly, "I was so afraid you were going to tell me that you had somehow changed your mind about being my girl and wanted to break up. You seem different than you were before the break. I can't tell you how I feel now that you've told me something that I've been dying for all fall. You are going to let me make love to you, Maria. I promise that you will always be my darling, and I will take care of you until the end of time. I'll do everything I can to keep you from getting pregnant until we want kids, but if something ever goes wrong and you do get pregnant, I will take care of you and the baby with everything I've got in me."

"Don't even *think* about me getting pregnant, let alone say anything about it."

Bill was looking at her with such innocent love that if she hadn't been upset by his comment about her getting pregnant, she would have kissed him for his promise to stand by her and take care of her. She wanted to believe his every word.

It's funny, she thought, *we should be yelling with glee about our decision to have sex, instead of being so serious.*

"Do you want to drive over to the Union to celebrate our new relationship?" Bill asked.

In the Union, Maria put her hands around a cup of hot chocolate to warm her fingers. She breathed in its aroma, then took a careful sip. "There's something so nice about having a hot cup to wrap your hands around when it's cold out."

Bill took a sip of his coffee and smiled. "Nothing like a cup of coffee when you need it. I've got to finish preparing my talk for tomorrow. I'm sure the farmers of Marshalltown will be absolutely enthralled listening me tell them about cover crops." He laughed. "It's really just a night out for the men and boys, more than anything. I've also got to make some plans as fast as I can, so we can try out our new relationship." He grinned at her and took her hands in his. "Here's to us."

"Let's make our plans for Wednesday now," said Maria. "I feel so 'out there' when we are talking on the dorm phone. I wish that it had a little private cubicle. Anyway, let's go for lunch, like you suggested. Before your interview, I would like to meet the assistant editor. Then I'll make myself scarce for an hour or so by going shopping in the big city. Afterward, we can find a motel that looks appealing and spend the afternoon there. How does that sound to you?"

Bill blinked in surprise, then grinned. "I know the perfect motel."

"When you stop by the drugstore for your supply of condoms, would you get me some gel? You have wheels to go anywhere, and I don't want to buy it in Dog Town; it's too close to home."

"Wow, you've really thought this out. Don't worry, I'll take care of everything in that department." Bill had a sexy grin on his face.

Maria thought, *Well, I've let Pandora out of her box. I hope I know what I'm doing. There's no turning back now.*

When he stopped the car in front of the dorm, Bill said, "By the way, I really like your new coat. Now the campus won't feel like the frozen tundra to you." He put her hood up, pulled the fur close to her cheeks and kissed her. "Good night, Nanook, my darling."

She laughed and ran up the stairs. She turned and blew him a kiss. He blew one back and then he was gone.

As Maria returned to her room, she realized that she hadn't

asked Susie anything about Chuck and their vacation. She chided herself, *You've been quite self centered lately. You need to show a little concern for your roommate.* But when she opened the door, Susie was nowhere to be found. *Oh well,* Maria thought, *I'll do some planning for Tuesday's classes.* She was looking over all her notes when Susie walked in and said, "I have something to tell you."

"Have you been signing up girls left and right for Rush Week in January?" Maria asked.

Susie nodded in an offhanded way. "Yeah, but that's not what I want to talk to you about." Susie paused, her eyes filling up with tears. "I'm pretty sure that Chuck and I are finished. He said that he'd come back to see me after he transfers, but I doubt it. I'm sort of ambivalent about the whole thing, now that I have been home and had a chance to properly talk to my mom. I guess it's time we both move on, but I don't want to. I keep remembering all of the great times that we had in high school together."

"It's tough to see you having a bad time," Maria said, ducking the pillow Susie threw at her. Maria knew that Susie wanted to throw more than a pillow, maybe a brick, and she wanted to throw it at Chuck. "Susie, as long as you brought it up, could I give you some help on the relationship? It sounds like the best part of it was in high school. Both of you have outgrown that. It's dead. Chuck knows it, your mother knows it, and you will feel better when you can say it's over and really believe it."

Susie wiped her eyes and nodded her agreement. She couldn't talk. Susie left the room, taking her shower bucket.

Maria thought, *Susie is doing what I do. She's washing away the pain.*

Maria had just finished a history chapter and was stretching and yawning when Susie come back all pink and shiny.

"Thanks for being such a great friend," Susie said. "I want you to come to Chi Omega with me next year."

"Why, because I throw a mean pillow and you would miss our fights?" Susie ignored her goofy comment, and Maria got more serious. "The more I think about it, the more it appeals to me.

Having a boyfriend this fall has made me quite preoccupied. But now I have been giving it some real thought."

"Sex will do that every time," Susie said. "Great for the brain cells."

"As a matter of fact," Maria said, "I've decided to try it with Bill, now that I've gotten my feet wet, so to speak."

"So when are you going to slip him into your sex schedule?"

"Wednesday afternoon after his interview. He's delighted that I have loosened up."

"I'll bet," Susie said with a laugh. "Then you'll be faced with making comparisons."

"I'm not even going there, for your information." Maria was trying to think of a smart retort when someone knocked on their door.

"Hi, we hope we're not bothering you, but we wanted to add our names to your list of people who are interested in Rush Week with Chi Omega next semester."

Susie jumped up and asked them to come in. She started her pitch about Chi Omega.

Maria gathered up her books. "I'm escaping."

Yawning over her books after an hour or so, Maria decided that if the girls were still in her room, she'd make a lot of noise getting ready for bed. Maybe they'd take the hint. If that didn't work, she would say, "Lights out time." That should get their attention, especially if she turned out all the lights.

Maria opened the door, and Susie was in bed, fast asleep. *Good,* Maria thought, *no extreme measures required.* She climbed into bed.

Tuesday was a washout from beginning to end. She couldn't concentrate on her classes and chem lab was a disaster. All she could think about was Wednesday's rendezvous with Bill. She thought about what Susie had said about making comparisons. *What if Bill is inept at making love and it is a bust?* After Ed, Bill would need to be very good to match him. How would she feel with Bill, even if he was a real Don Juan? Would she feel sexy or turned off? How would she respond to his lovemaking? *Oh god, I hope I won't freeze up.* One minute, Maria felt good about going to bed with Bill, and the next minute, she wondered if she should have been so eager. The questions just kept pouring into her head until she wanted to scream.

Maria felt like a zombie, lurching along through the day. She finished up her lab, making a halfhearted job of it, and walked home in the chill wind. It was getting dark so early now. Thank goodness for her hooded coat. She was still cold, but not as cold as she would have been in her old coat. Anyone who didn't have a hood was nuts in frigid, windswept Iowa.

Ah, she could see the dorm. She picked up her pace. She entered her room and looked around. Where was her roommate? No doubt, she was working on more recruits for Rush Week. Maria wished she'd come back so they could eat dinner together. She was tired and hungry, and she didn't feel like eating alone.

Maria heard Susie laughing with someone. She was glad Susie was her roommate, even if she was obsessed with finding a lot of pledges for next semester.

Susie appeared at the door with several girls. She said, "I've invited these nice girls to have dinner with us, Maria. This is Josie and Emily. They are interested in Chi Omega and Rush Week."

Maria wondered if Susie was using Rush Week for Chi Omega as a way to stop thinking about Chuck. It was probably a good idea. However, she had wanted a private dinner with Susie. "Wonderful, nice to meet you gals," Maria said, gritting her teeth. "Are you as hungry as I am?"

Everyone was ready to eat. The cold weather really kicked up the appetites. They headed off to dinner, where Susie could play hostess to the girls and charm them with tales of Chi Omega. Maria was bored and wanted to talk to Susie about tomorrow afternoon, but she doubted she would get a chance.

Once back at the dorm, Susie went off recruiting. Maria got her books out and sat at her desk on the hard chair instead lying on her soft bed. Hopefully, it would make her more alert so that she could use her time wisely. She began to read, for the third time, the same history material. *Tomorrow, you won't have time to study, so get busy,* she told herself. If she wanted to maintain her 3.0 average and be able to pledge next semester, she had better concentrate.

She was making headway with her long history assignment when Susie appeared at the door. "What did you think of Josie and Emily?"

"They seemed like nice prospects for Chi Omega. How are their grades?" Maria asked.

"That's a problem with both of them. They have never had to study like this before. They were both cheerleaders and just made the cut for instate students. We'd have to set up a study schedule for them. I'll have to see how their grades turn out for this first semester." Susie gave Maria a questioning look. "You seem more preoccupied than average tonight. What's the matter with you?"

"I don't know how I feel about making love with Bill tomorrow afternoon."

"So why don't you want to? You've been dying to do it with him all fall. You're all broken in, thanks to Ed," Susie said, laughing hysterically.

"I know, that's why I feel so weird. I am scared to go through with it with Bill. I don't seem to have any sexual juices flowing right now."

"Let me tell you something. Once you are with him and you feel his testosterone flowing, you will be a goner. Right now, you are tired and all frozen up, but you will thaw out in a flash when he kisses you—guaranteed," Maria's wise roommate said.

"Susie, I'm going to pledge Chi Omega—guaranteed," using her big word right back at her, "so I can get counseling from you. What's your price?"

Quick as a flash, Susie said that she wanted Maria to be on the executive board of Chi Omega when she became the president.

"You're going to become president of Chi Omega? What will all the other actives think about that?"

311

"They'll love me and my photographic memory."

"I'm glad my roommate is so modest. You have no ego problems, I can tell," Maria said grinning from ear to ear. She realized all of a sudden that she had been laughing and having so much fun with Susie, which seemed to happen easily with them, that she had forgotten her nerves. Susie was very charismatic without really trying. Maria looked at the clock and saw that it was eleven. Bill would be calling soon. "Thanks, Susie, for being so good to me. Maybe I can return the favor sometime."

"You can. Remember what I said? I want you to be my right arm when we are actives."

"It's a deal, Susie." Maria got up, casually so as not to alert Susie, and quick as flash, grabbed her big pillow and threw it straight at her.

Susie caught it right in the face and gave Maria an evil look. "You had better watch your back, because I'm going to lie in wait, just like a lion, and get you when you least expect it," Susie snarled.

Maria opened her mouth to say something in return, but stopped as she heard her name being called from down the hall. Maria smiled at Susie and ran. "Hi, it's so good to hear your voice," Maria said with delight.

"I love the hero's welcome that you give me every time I call. You sure know how to make a guy feel good. Did I ever tell you how smooth your voice is? It's not high and squeaky or just dull. It's sort of musical," said Bill.

Maria thought that he should have heard her voice a few minutes ago, when she was fooling around with Susie. "How did your talk go?" she asked.

"It went fine, and now I want to change the subject to a much more interesting topic. I was thinking that instead of just stopping off for an afternoon at some motel, I would like to take you to a beautiful place for our first time together. It's sort of a pre-honeymoon type hotel; it's my folks' favorite place. It's called the Berkmar Hotel, and it's right in downtown Des Moines. It is the best hotel there, and we're going to stay overnight. They have a room called the Invitation Suite, which comes complete with free room service, a hot tub *in the bathroom,* and a living room/bedroom combination with a king-sized bed."

"You sound like a salesman for this place. You've sold me, but how is the price fitting into your finances?"

"Let me worry about that. I've made plenty of money this week, so I can afford a special occasion," Bill said emphatically.

"I'll have to scurry around a little in the morning to cover what I will miss in classes. Let's not go so early and instead have lunch *after* your appointment with the *Iowa Progress.*"

"That's fine with me, we'll have a great lunch. I know a restaurant near the hotel, rather than the short-order place." Bill's tone shifted as he said seriously, "I'm glad you are going to go with me. It will be great to have your support when meeting Mr. Addison. Then afterward, I will give you an experience that you will never forget. That's why I didn't want to settle for a two-bit motel."

Whispering as quietly as she could, with her hand cupped around the phone, Maria said, "Besides the gel and condoms, would you buy some nice Italian bubbly wine for us to drink? I think it would make me more relaxed."

"We'll get the wine from room service. I definitely want to wine and dine you. My folks have had dinner at the Berkmar, and they've raved about it. As for lunch, Kaleidoscope at the Hub, right near our hotel, has a bunch of restaurants to choose from. I have a little one in mind, but that's all I'll say. I want to surprise you."

"You really know your way around Des Moines. I'm impressed."

"Remember, I've lived here all my life. I would be an idiot if I didn't know a few things about our fair capital of Iowa."

"I was feeling a little shaky this afternoon, thinking about our adventure. I was cold and hungry, I guess. Susie made me feel better about our trip," Maria whispered. "When you called, she had me laughing about how silly I was being. Now talking with you, I feel really good, and I know it is going to turn out all right. Just first time jitters, I guess." She thought, *I'm only lying a little. It will be the first time with him.*

"Thank Susie for me for giving you a pep talk. I promise that you won't have to do anything you don't feel comfortable doing. I don't care. I don't want you to remember our being together with any bad memories. You are too precious to me. I can wait, if you get scared. I want you to know that. We can always try another time."

"Oh, Bill, you are just about the best there is. Right this moment, I love you so much. I know this may sound silly, but ever since I've been dating you, I've felt so valued."

Bill whispered hoarsely, "Maria, I can't imagine being any other way with a woman like you. I feel honored that you love me. I love your jokes, your brains, and the way you love me." He paused and said ever so quietly, "I have never known such a passionate woman in my life."

"Well, handsome, you have woven your magic around me again. I feel great. I will go to bed thinking about our day and night together tomorrow."

"Will you be able to make it by, say, twelve fifteen? That will give us just enough time to get there before my interview." Bill said.

"Yes, I'll be waiting for you. Sleep well and so will I. Love you, honey."

"Good night, my dearest girl."

When Maria got back to the room, Susie was fast asleep, and that was just as well. Maria crawled into her bed with a light heart.

24. The Invitation Suite

I love you, not for what you are,
but for what I am when I'm with you.
—Roy Croft

The next thing Maria knew, it was morning, and she had a lot to do before she met Bill. Whispering quietly over breakfast, Maria told Susie her plans, and asked Susie to help cover for her. Maria hurried across campus to see her professors in their offices. She crossed her fingers and smiled as she lied to them. She explained that her relatives were arriving that afternoon to see her and visit Des Moines. "I'd like to be excused from my classes to show them around, please. They will bring me back tomorrow afternoon." Her love life was putting her in a precarious position, but she didn't care. Maria felt really free for the first time in her life.

The teachers bought her excuses with their blessings. They gave her assignments for the next several days and said to have a good time. Little did they know.

Maria went to her morning classes, relieved and getting excited. When she ran back to the dorm, she was delighted that she still had a half an hour to get packed and ready for Bill. While folding up her green outfit from Marshall Fields, it dawned on her that she didn't have any fancy underwear. *I can't do anything about it now,* she thought. *Maybe I can buy some in Des Moines.* If she knew Bill, he wouldn't be worried about her underwear anyway.

It was almost time, and she was dying to get going. Walking out to the front area wearing her nylons and high-heeled shoes, she felt like she stood out like a sore thumb. When she looked out the front door, she saw him. Bill had parked and was bounding up the stairs. Maria burst out the door and met him on the stairs. He smiled with surprise as she fled past him down the stairs as fast as she could go. She wanted as few girls as possible to see her leaving with an overnight bag. He turned quickly and was right behind her.

Laughing when he caught up to her by the car, he said, "You look like you're running from the devil himself."

"With the lies I told this morning, I probably am," Maria said, catching her breath. "I don't want half of Stevens Dorm to see me leaving with a bag and my boyfriend." She opened the door quickly and flung her telltale suitcase into the back seat. "Let's make our getaway, Bill."

"Should I wait until you're in or just go?" Bill asked, grinning at her.

Maria stuck out her tongue and got into the car. The sun was pouring in, making it very cozy. Maria unzipped her coat as Bill hopped in and took off. "Was that fast enough for you?"

Breathing a sigh of relief, Maria said, "Yes, thank you." She leaned over and gave his cheek a little kiss. "You smell good. Do you have on aftershave?"

"Yes. I'm not sure I like it, but if you do, that's good enough for me."

Maria turned on the radio and found some nice music. She settled back and listened to the melodies. It was very soothing. Bill just drove, not saying anything. He was probably concentrating on his upcoming interview. She didn't want to disturb him.

"My, you've been so quiet," said Bill.. "Are you happy? You look so cute with your eyes closed, listening to the music. I've been thinking about how to let Mr. Addison know that I'm capable, intelligent, and hardworking without exactly saying it. That's going to be hard."

"I'm glad I pass inspection." Maria smiled. "Why don't you just act normal when you're with him? He'll figure it out soon enough. I'll do all I can to impress him, but I promise I'll be smooth about it. Now just relax; you'll knock him dead."

Bill grinned at her. "I love having you in my corner. I want this interview to go well because it's our future that I'm working on."

They arrived with time to spare and decided to wander around a little.

"I feel a little jumpy," Bill said, "and need to let off a little steam before I go in to talk to Mr. Addison."

They walked along quietly while Bill gathered his thoughts for the interview. As usual, Maria had trouble keeping up with him. "Slow down, partner," she said.

Bill stopped and smiled. "Sorry, partner," he said.

They turned around and retraced their steps. As they went, Maria caught their reflection in a large window. Who was that handsome devil in the glass? Bill had certainly dressed the part: suit, tie, and a good-looking overcoat.

Inside the *Progress* building, Bill stepped up to the receptionist and said that he had an appointment with the assistant editor, Mr. Addison.

"He was just asking about you. He's around here somewhere." The receptionist called his office and spoke to his secretary. "He's on the way down to meet you. Ah, here he is now," she said in a cheerful manner.

Mr. Addison was as tall as Bill, had a full head of white hair, a ruddy complexion, and a big smile on his face. He stuck his hand out to shake Bill's, then looked at Maria with another big smile. She liked him immediately.

"So who is this pretty lady, your wife?" asked Mr. Addison.

"She's going to be, but we are just engaged. This is Maria Banks, Mr. Addison."

Maria noted that Bill stretched the truth the way she did.

"Well, don't let her get away. Take it from me, this kind of lady will have lots of admirers. So nice to meet you, Maria."

"I don't intend to let her out of my sight," Bill said with a grin.

"I'm going to be out of your sight while I go shopping," Maria said. "Where are the shops, Mr. Addison?"

He pointed her in the right direction, and Maria said that she would be back when she had bought out the stores.

"That's the ticket," Mr. Addison said. "Keep this guy on his toes."

Maria left with a very light heart. She felt as though Bill's interview would go well. God bless you, Mr. Addison.

Maria easily found the shopping area. It reminded her a little of Chicago with its upscale boutiques. *This will be fun,* she thought. She tried on a lot of cute outfits but finally decided to stop in the lingerie department to get a new bra and pants. *Oh my,* she thought, *I'm going to be late, but it was worth it.* She hurried along the avenue to the tall newspaper building.

When she entered the lobby, the receptionist said, "Mr. Addison and your fiancé are waiting for you on the top floor of the building. Please take the elevator. They want to show you the view of the city from there."

As Maria stepped out of the elevator, she spotted the men, talking and laughing. Mr. Addison waved her over to them. "Your young man is very smart and has made a great pitch to me for his column. I'm very impressed with his ideas about how to further help the farmers. I want you to know, I'm looking forward to a long and exciting future with him."

Giving Mr. Addison her warmest smile, Maria said "I'm delighted. I knew you men would have a successful time together."

Mr. Addison's eyes were sparkling when he said, "One of the reasons that I'm hiring him is because of his taste in women. Anyone who could attract you must have something that will make him very successful in life." He smiled gently. "I hope I haven't been too forward. My darling wife of thirty-nine years is always scolding me about the personal comments I make to pretty ladies."

Maria said, "You must be a great guy to call your wife 'your darling' after thirty-nine years of marriage." She stuck out her hand. "Congratulations to both of you."

Mr. Addison shook her hand. "You've got yourself quite a woman, Bill."

Exchanging handshakes with Bill, Mr. Addison said, "Our handshake seals the deal. Now let's show Maria our fair city."

Maria walked up to the large picture window and looked out over the capital city of Iowa. It was well laid out, and she could see a river running through it. "It's quite a view from up here," she said.

Bill took her hand, and they all moved toward the elevator.

"By the way, folks, call me John," Mr. Addison said as they stepped into the elevator. Getting off at the floor of his office, John's tone changed to being the boss. "Bill, get me those employment papers filled out, signed, and dropped off on my desk by Friday."

"Will do," said Bill and waved goodbye. As they left the building, Bill sounded very pleased as he said, "That went very well. I'll tell you more about it, but let's go to the little luncheon place I have in mind. Are you as hungry as I am?"

"You know me, I'm always hungry when I'm happy, and at this moment, I couldn't be happier. I'm with my darling fiancé, and he has landed a job with the *Iowa Progress*."

"You like the word 'fiancé' don't you?" he said with a grin.

"I like the ring of it, yes." She glanced at him to see if he got her joke. "You were the one who said we were engaged, remember?"

As they drove to the restaurant, Maria was pleased that Bill knew his way around the city. She didn't have to mess around with a map.

"Here it is," Bill said.

Maria saw a charming-looking building with the name La Petite Auberge lettered on its sign. A sophisticated hostess came up to them when they entered and said, "Bonjour, mes amis," with a beautiful smile. "Where would you like to sit?"

There were a few people enjoying a late lunch, but basically, they had the pick of the tables.

Bill said, "Bonjour, Madame Chantelle, we would like to sit by the window."

"Très bien, it's lovely with the afternoon sun coming in now."

Snowy white tablecloths lent an air of lightness to the room, and little vases of fresh flowers added a delightful touch. "I'll order some wine with lunch to celebrate a successful interview," Bill said. "Our hotel is just around the corner, so I think we can safely drive over there after one glass of wine." Maria knew that Bill was teasing her about her low liquor threshold.

Anticipating Bill's order, a young waiter came over to them. "Oui, Monsier, what would you like to drink?"

"We'll each have a glass of chardonnay, and what do you suggest for an appetizer?"

"The goose liver pâté is very nice today."

"Would you like to chance it?" Bill asked Maria.

"I'll try anything once," she said, although her face registered skepticism.

"Bring us some," Bill said, giving Maria a glance of amusement. Then he reached across the table, took her hands in his, looked at her with those big blues, and asked, "How do you like this place so far? I want everything to be right today. This is a pretty big occasion for us. It's the beginning of our future."

"If the food is as good as the atmosphere, it couldn't be better. There's a feeling of lightness in here, and I feel like I'm floating, so I fit in here very well," Maria exclaimed.

"I'm glad I picked this place. If you're happy, so am I."

The waiter brought their menus with the wine; French hard rolls, butter, goose liver pâté, water crackers, and ice water soon followed.

"Here's to us," Bill said, lifting his glass, then he touched it hers with a little click.

She took a sip of the chilled wine and rolled it around her in mouth, enjoying the tart taste. It slipped down very easily, and she nodded to him in a pleased way. In the background, music was playing very softly. She recognized Debussy's "Clair de Lune." She shut her eyes, listened, had another sip, and enjoyed the whole experience.

Bill covered a cracker with the pâté. Just as Maria opened her eyes, he ate the cracker in one bite and declared, "It's good."

"How would you know? Your taste buds never had a chance." Maria took a cracker and spread a little pâté on it. The aroma was sickening, but she took a bite and shivered. "I don't like this."

Bill grinned at her and said that it was an acquired taste, just like caviar.

Maria took another sip of her wine. "So, Mr. Cosmopolitan, I hope I can keep up with your food tastes. What do you recommend for lunch?"

"I'm not going to get trapped into any recommendations for you. I don't want the responsibility," he said, handing her a menu.

She studied the menu and decided on the quiche Lorraine and some more wine. She was beginning to feel very warm and fuzzy. "What are you having?"

"I'm going to have the scallops in wine sauce, some more wine, and a lot more than a bite out of you." Looking up at the waiter, he said, "We're ready to order. The lady will have quiche Lorraine, and I want the scallops."

"Oui, Monsier, do you care for another glass of wine?"

"Yes, please," Bill said, handing him their menus.

Maria watched him relaxing more and more, sending her sexy signals. "Are you feeling the wine? I'm getting loopy. I'd better slow down so I don't walk like a drunk when we are signing in at the hotel desk. How are you doing?" Maria took a roll out of the basket to help blunt the effect of the wine.

"I'm fine. I've eaten so much liver pâté that the alcohol can't get through to my bloodstream," he said, looking happy. She could almost see the testosterone pumping through his veins.

When the waiter brought their orders, she was very ready to eat. The quiche smelled delicious and tasted homemade. She loved it.

Looking at Bill's scallops, she said, "Would you like to trade a bite of scallops for a bite of quiche?" She waved her fork full of quiche under his nose.

Bill carefully ate it. "It's nice, but I like my scallops." He speared a scallop for her on his fork, reached over, and carefully put it into her opened mouth.

She gazed at him and licked her lips, slowly chewing the scallop and watching him.

Bill leaned over toward her. "If you keep looking at me like that, I won't be responsible for my actions. I think your wine is beginning to show. We'd better go while you can still navigate."

They grinned at each other. Bill finished the last sip of his wine, paid the check, and left a generous tip for the waiter. He helped Maria stand and tried to slip her coat on her, but a sleeve was twisted, and he had a slight wrestling match with it. All the while he was struggling with her coat, she didn't move or help him in any way.

"You're potted, aren't you? Please lean on me and let me get us out of here without embarrassing you." Bill slung his own coat over his shoulder, took a firm hold of her, and walked her out to the car with his arm tightly around her waist.

Bill drove around the corner and stopped in front of a beautiful old hotel, the Berkmar. A doorman opened Maria's door and helped her out. Bill got out, took Maria's arm, and steered her into the hotel lobby. They stepped up to the front desk. "My name is Bill Morgan. We have reservations for the Invitation Suite for tonight." Bill waited for the clerk to find the reservation, all the while holding Maria close to him.

"Here it is, sir. Would you please sign the register? We require half the bill in advance; it's policy here."

As Bill was registering, he glanced at Maria. She gave him a bleary look and smiled a silly grin. Bill carefully took away his support and leaned her against the counter. He took out his wallet and peeled off several tens. Maria started listing, and he immediately put his arm around her again.

The desk clerk smiled at them. "Thank you very much. Here's your key; it's room number eight thirty. Have a wonderful stay, and please feel free to call the desk if there's anything you need."

"Do you want to come out to the car with me to see where I'm going to park?"

Maria was coherent enough to realize that Bill didn't want to leave her alone in the lobby in her condition. Talking a bit loudly, she said, "Sure, if I have to make a quick getaway, I wouldn't know where to go." She giggled as Bill took her arm and hurried her out to the car; she thought everything was so funny.

After driving down a ramp and under the hotel to a huge parking garage, Maria swayed a bit as she got out of the car. "Let's make sure we know where we parked." She tried to find a slip of paper to record the level, while Bill waited and watched her fumble around. Finally she said, "Forget it, I'm too fuzzy to do it."

He breathed a sigh of relief as he took their luggage and her hand and went to find the elevator. When the door opened on the eighth floor, they were pleasantly surprised by the plush rug runner that went the length of the hall.

"Here's our room number," Maria said, swaying a little and pleased that she hadn't walked by it.

Bill opened the door, and Maria was all set to walk in, but he stopped her. "What's the matter?" she asked. "Are we in the wrong room? I must be really drunk if I can't read the room numbers." She started to giggle again.

Bill put the luggage down on the floor, smiled, and picked her up. "I'm carrying you over this threshold, emotionally and physically. It's our start in so many ways. It's an 'engagement carry,' taking us to a new place." With that, he walked through the opening with her in his arms. When he put her down, he kissed her very gently. "Welcome to our new world."

"Were you thinking about carrying me over the threshold when you were driving us down here?" She couldn't stop giggling and was trying hard to stand without swaying.

"No, but I wanted it to be special. The idea came to me in the elevator," Bill said, as he gathered their luggage from the doorway. He shut the door and went to the phone. "I would like some Italian white wine, a bubbly type please, and bring it in a cooler full of ice." He smiled at Maria. "There, now we are all set. When the waiter leaves, we can relax."

Maria thought, *In a pig's eye. Knowing Bill, we're going to do more than relax. He's just human, and he's been waiting all fall for today.*

"I'm going to check out the bathroom," Maria said. She looked at the hot tub, turned on the faucets, and watched it fill. It would take a long time to fill that baby. It looked like it could a hold a convention of people. *We're going to be able to swim in that one,* she thought. She looked at herself in the mirror, and a rather drunk girl looked back. *Oh well, who cares, it's a special occasion.* Maria laughed and stuck her tongue out at herself. She was still swaying as she thought, *Pandora is out of the box.* She was glad she felt so fuzzy. It kept her from feeling nervous. While she waited for room service to come, she sat on the edge of the hot tub, watching the water and trying to clear her head.

"Maria, the waiter has gone. Come out and have some bubbly." Bill was holding a glass of wine for her as she reappeared. "Here, enjoy. It tastes a little like ginger ale."

Maria took her glass and put it on the table. She thought that she had better take it easy. She'd had more wine today than she'd had all fall.

Bill found some great music on the hotel radio, then he joined Maria on the sofa and took off his shoes.

Maria knew he was subtly watching her. She could read his mind; he was waiting for her to make the first move. "I'm filling the hot tub," she said. "It's going to take a while because it's a big one. I brought my bathing suit." She looked at Bill and gave him a drunken grin. "You'll love it, it's cute." She saw Bill do a double take, but she kept a straight face until she took a sip of wine. Then she burst out laughing. Maria laughed until she thought she'd choke.

"You are the biggest tease in this world," he said. He took her glass out of her hand and placed it on the table. He gathered her in his arms, then gently pushed her down on the sofa. He proceeded to tickle her ribs, stomach, and anywhere else he could reach.

Maria squealed with delight and rolled and wiggled, trying to get away. He laughed and relented, then gazed at her with that look she knew so well and kissed her.

That broke the ice. He picked up her wine and held it in front of her nose. "Open wide and take your medicine."

"I'll make a bargain with you. Let's take off each other's clothes, and I'll let you pour it down my naked throat in the tub. How do you like that?"

He laughed harder than he had all day and quickly let her up off the sofa. He went into the bathroom and turned off the water. "Okay, that's a deal."

Maria said with a sensual tone in her voice, "You go first, take something off me." She could see that he was aroused, slightly intoxicated from the wine, and feeling the intensity of the moment. She waited.

He played it safe and took off her earrings and necklace and carefully laid them on the nightstand. "Now, it's your turn." He stood there smiling at her and watching every move she made.

Maria felt more comfortable with Bill than with Ed, but not as wild. Bill and she fit together so well, but Ed's sexual intensity sent her into uncharted areas when they made love. She couldn't help but make the comparison.

"Let me see," Maria said, as she walked around him. She decided to take off his belt. It was a regular belt with a buckle on it. She said to herself, *This will be easier than that belt Ed had.* She undid the buckle, pulled the belt out of the loops, and put it on the table. Maria gave him a satisfied smile.

He unbuttoned her sweater and took it off her, one sleeve at a time, watching her all the time.

Does he think I'm going to bolt? Why the intense scrutiny? Maria undid his tie and put it with his belt.

He turned her around to undo the little buttons at the top of her blouse and gently lifted it over her head. His eyes were glued to her bra.

"What's the matter, are you at a loss for words because of my boobs?" she asked.

He stopped the game, put his head down, and starting kissing her neck and the top of her breasts that were peeking out of her bra. He was starting to breathe faster.

Maria realized that they would never make it into the hot tub. Undoing her skirt and letting it fall on the floor, she knew the game was over. He couldn't take any more playing around. She stood there in her silk hose and underwear while he pulled his pants off and stepped out of his jockeys. He took her in his arms, undoing her bra and letting it fall on the floor. His fingers slipped her out of her stockings and panties. As she stood there completely naked, he pressed his naked body to hers and held them tightly together. Releasing her, he quickly went into the bathroom. When he came back, she had climbed into their big bed and was under the covers.

"Are you baby proofed?" Maria asked.

"You bet, my darling girl. No babies will be made today, just love." Bill moved under the covers and began very gently rubbing her body with his wonderful fingers. There wasn't a place he missed. "Are you ready for more," he whispered.

"I need to do something first," she said, as she got out from under the blankets.

"Where are you going?"

He was so surprised when she got up that she giggled. She ran into the bathroom to grab the gel. "We need to use this. It makes everything much better."

The light dawned and he looked a little embarrassed. "I'm sorry, I had forgotten about the gel in the heat of the moment." He put it on both of them.

The excitement of the moment had stalled, but he kissed her with a long French kiss, then moved down to her neck, using tiny little kisses that tickled like fury. Finally, he carefully began to make love to her. He was an extremely confident lover, and Maria relaxed into the rhythmic movements he used, holding onto him as the intensity built. She let herself go and became completely lost. When she began to tremble, Bill murmured, "Here we go, my darling," and they went over the edge together, falling, falling, falling. . . . The experience shook her so much that she knew in her heart that he loved her. They were meant for each other. She had read that the mind controls whether one has an orgasm or not, and she had experienced one down to her toes.

As they lay glued together trying to recover their senses, he breathed, "Am I mashing you?"

"No, I like the feeling of it just now." After a few minutes, she pushed him gently, and he rolled off and over on his back. She put her head on his chest and just rested there, feeling as if she never wanted to leave that space. He had not disappointed her. It had turned out better than she had ever dreamed.

She compared the way she had felt with Ed, and it was entirely different. Bill's love for her turned their lovemaking into a magical, almost spiritual, experience, if that were possible. He wasn't as controlled as Ed or as intense, but he was gentle and very sexy. She had contributed to their lovemaking in a more relaxed way with Bill than she had with Ed. With Ed, she couldn't control herself the way she could with Bill, and that helped her keep her sense about her.

"Maria, I didn't know what to expect from you, especially because it was your first time. You were so passionate that it made it easy for me to help you reach a climax. You are something else, you little dickens. How I love you."

Maria had to suppress some guilty thoughts, but if her darling Bill knew what she had done over Thanksgiving, they would be through. Bill also knew more about her anatomy than she dreamed possible. She wondered where he had learned his sexual confidence. She moved her head to the pillow and looked at Bill just as he rolled over and did the same thing. "I can't believe what we just did so well together," Maria said. "You are one passionate guy and a great lover. Did you know that? We were in another plane or dimension. Let's go and get in the hot tub and let the warm water make this experience even nicer."

"That's a good idea. Come on, my little passion flower." He got up and pulled her to him. He put his hands on her breasts. "I've been wanting to touch and hold these ever since the first time I saw you. You have beautiful breasts. When we lie down tonight, I'm going to put my face right between them."

"That's fine with me, but when I want to sleep on my stomach, you'll have to move. Come on, let's get into that warm water. I'm getting cold out here naked as a newborn baby." She ran to the tub and climbed in. It was still nice and warm, and it felt so good to sink down into the water. "Where are you, Bill?"

"I'm coming with the wine for us. Also, I want to check my baby proofer to make sure that it is still in perfect condition before I get rid of it." He was busy at the sink for a couple of minutes, then smiled at her. "We have no worries." He poured them each a glass of bubbly and, stepping into the tub, smiled. "Ah, that feels good, but something else tops it."

The bathroom was warm and steamy, and the water was blissful. Maria thought, *I could get used to this.* "This was a wonderful idea, staying together tonight. Having an overnight with my darling boy-friend is fantastic." She smiled at him and knew he wanted to say something but was having trouble.

"A guy always wonders how the woman who he is crazy about is going to react to him when he makes love to her. I was pretty sure that we would make wonderful love because of the way we were on our dates, and I wasn't disappointed." He looked at her shyly. "Were you satisfied, or do I need to do more or be different next time?"

"Don't tell me you couldn't tell how I felt. You just want to hear me praise you. I was shaken down to my toenails. You are one incredible lover." Pleased with her answer, he leaned over and gave her a big thank-you kiss.

Maria could see that he was getting aroused all over again, but she needed more time to recover. "No more kisses for you until I rest up a little. Just drink your drink, my sexy, darling man, and let me do the same."

He laughed. "You're right, honey." He settled back and sipped his wine. Then he said, "Would you like to get dressed and go out for a ride? I'd like to show you a park that has a real waterfall and a reflecting pool. There are also about twenty miles of roads to drive on along the Raccoon River.

"That sounds like a lot of fun. Let's go." Maria climbed out of the tub and began drying herself off. Bill asked if he could dry her. "You will freeze," she said.

He shook his head. "Nah, I'm tougher than that."

"All right, go for it."

He rubbed her all over and spent a little extra time around her breasts. He seemed mesmerized by her naked body. "You have a beautiful body, you know. Your legs, hips, and breasts are in perfect proportion, and you aren't very big. How tall are you? I didn't realize how little you were until I saw you naked in the living room. Now I see again how small you are. Somehow, when you are walking around with your clothes on, you seem bigger."

"Let me tell you about you, since we are discussing body types. I like your body. I love your long legs and slim but muscular build. I love the color of your hair, but the thing that drew me to you the most were your blue eyes. Somehow, when I look into them, I get the feeling that I will never know the depth of them. There is a world of old experience in there." She looked into those bottomless eyes. "Nothing tops your sexiness, however."

Bill laughed. "It's pretty easy to please you, just be a muscle-bound guy." He was making light of what Maria had said, but she knew he was pleased.

She attempted to put on some lotion, but Bill asked if he could do that, too. "All right, be my personal massager, skin protector, and, most of all, lover." He smiled as he rubbed lotion all over her, especially working it into her breasts. "More on my back, please; my boobies are fine."

"What did you call them? Your boobies? That's pretty funny."

"I'm glad you think so. Now I have a big question for you. What should we wear? The same things we had on earlier or something different? I did bring my fancy green dress, but if we get out of the car, I think I'll want something warmer."

"I'm going to put on my suit because jackets are required for men at dinner here."

"It's much easier for men; they can always dress so simply and comfortably."

"We're just smarter than you gals." He jumped out of the way of Maria's hand as she tried to whack him.

All right, she thought, *I'll just put on what I took off. That's easy, no decisions.* Maria rummaged around in her bag, found her new bra and pants, and put them on. "Like 'em?"

Bill looked her over. "They're pretty. I'll get you some more when you tell me what size you are."

"I'll feel like your mistress if you do that—and actually, that's not all bad. Mistresses don't have to have children, cook, clean, or work. They just have to look pretty and have plenty of sex with the old boy."

Bill shook his head at her comments and laughed. "I never know what you are going to come up with."

He helped her into her coat, grabbed his own, and out they went to find their car and explore Des Moines.

It was getting dusky and cold out. Maria decided that she didn't want to get out and walk around. She had done her share today, plus spent the afternoon in a much more physically intense but pleasant manner. Bill pointed out the park, and she could see the waterfall and reflecting pool from the car. They took a short drive along the Raccoon River. "Let's come back sometime during the day and drive along the river," she said. "It's getting too dark to see properly now. Thanks for trying to be a good tour director."

Back at the hotel, Bill suggested, "Why don't we go into the bar, get a drink, and dance a little before dinner to warm up?"

"You are a human dynamo, you know. I'm ready to just sit down and rest a little. Let's go into the bar and get you a beer. I'll just have a sip. I have had enough alcohol today."

"That's fine with me. I don't want to wear you out the first time we spend a day and night together." Bill put his arm around her waist. The strains of music from the hotel's café and bar grew louder as they stepped into a lively scene of drinkers and dancers. Bill ordered a beer.

The bartender asked, "How about your lady?"

Maria piped up, explaining she was on the wagon.

The bartender leaned over conspiratorially. "I have the same problem. I go to AA meetings all the time," giving Maria an understanding look.

Bill took his beer and led the way to a small table on the edge of the dance floor. As he sat down he laughed. "So, I'm dating an alcoholic, am I? You are a little dickens, letting that guy think you were just like him."

"He wanted me to be an ex-drinker; I didn't have the heart to correct him. And besides, maybe I *am* a drunk. We haven't talked about that subject much yet." Her eyes were sparkling.

"The answer to that is a no brainer. You can barely take one drink and not get shaky. Here, take a sip of my beer and have some nuts." As Bill held the glass for her to take a taste, she looked up and saw the bartender shake his head "no" at her.

Maria started to laugh and choked on her sip. Bill said, "That's it for you. Let's dance." He got up, took her in his arms, and away they went. Bill was a great dancer; he had perfect rhythm and the grace of an athlete. During the slow dances, he put his chin on top of Maria's head, as he had when they'd first danced together. He said, "Remember the first time we danced? I was so excited to hold you in my arms, I had trouble controlling myself. I was so aroused, I was worried that I would embarrass myself."

"I was thinking that I might step on your toes. I was worried sick that I would be clumsy out there, and you'd take me back to my seat and leave."

"Not on your life. I took one look at you and knew that this was my chance to meet the girl I had been chasing around campus. You danced well, by the way, that night. Now, do you want some more fast dancing?" He didn't give her a chance to answer. The rhythm of the music was picking up and Bill responded by tightening his hold on her as he moved faster and faster across the dance floor. He guided her with his body and arms, pulling her in and twirling her out, completely in control. They moved quickly around the room, and several couples had stopped dancing and were watching them. Bill was really dancing fast now and taking her right along with him. He was strong and capable, so she just relaxed and danced her feet off.

Maria thought, *Wow, he is a fantastic dancer. Why didn't he ever mention this skill before?* As the music came to an end, Bill bent her back until she thought she was going to fall on her head. But he was so strong, he easily pulled her back up and gave her a big kiss. The onlookers clapped exuberantly at their dancing exhibition.

Bill grinned at Maria, and she said, "You've been holding out on me. How many surprises do you have in there?" She knocked on his head.

"Let's go in and have dinner. I'm hungry. How about you?" His eyes were sparkling with happiness.

"It sounds wonderful to me."

He put his arm around her waist, bent over, and whispered in her ear, "I love you."

The dining room was beautiful in an old-fashioned way that Maria loved. Long white tapers everywhere—on every table, on the side boards—burning brightly and turning the room into a magical place. Each table was covered with a white tablecloth and had napkins folded like fans stuck in the water goblets at each place setting. As they walked in, the maitre d' came up to Bill and asked if they were guests at the hotel. When Bill said yes and gave him their room number, he raised his eyebrows and put them in a choice spot in the center of the room. Maria had the feeling that he was showing them off to the rest of the clientele. The waiter for their table gave them menus that were so tall, she could hardly see over the top.

"If I didn't want to talk to you, I could just hide behind my menu," Maria said.

"What looks good to you, Maria?" he asked.

"I don't know. What looks good to you?"

"I asked you first." Bill was tapping the table with his fingertips in time with the music that was coming from somewhere.

Maria recognized Nat King Cole singing a love song. She thought the music was a wonderful addition to their dinner. "I think I'll have the shrimp cocktail, because I love shrimp and haven't seen one in ages. I'll also try the grilled salmon with lemon sauce and a green salad. I like fish and rarely get any in the school cafeteria. You were smart to have scallops at lunch."

"I'm glad you think I'm smart about something. I'll have the same thing," Bill said.

He raised his finger and signaled the waiter. They placed their orders and got rid of the gigantic menus. "This is some place. I'm glad we're here."

"This is the best time I've ever had," Maria said. "Somehow, I feel like we are on our honeymoon." Maria wondered what Bill would say to that, but he seemed to ignore her remark. "By the way," she asked, "why did the maitre d' give you that look when you gave him our room number?"

"Maybe because it is the number of the Invitation Suite. But to get back to your honeymoon feeling, I was thinking the same thing."

"Good, we're on the same wavelength. I hope this vacation isn't too much money for you to spend. It must be an expensive suite, right?"

"I take the fifth," Bill said, looking at her with his eyes dancing. "It is worth every penny."

"Can't you give me a little hint?" Maria teased him, rolling her eyes.

"No, I want to keep you in my debt."

"Wait, what are we talking about? I thought it was about the cost of the suite."

"I've skipped past that, and I'm on to another subject."

Just then, the waiter came with their first course: a tray of hot rolls, butter roses, and shrimp cocktails. After serving them, he took the napkins out of the goblets, shook the napkins and placed them in their laps with a flourish. He was a character, and Maria liked him. He filled their goblets with ice water and asked if there was anything else he could do.

Bill looked amused. "I think you've done it all."

Maria was really hungry now. It was after eight, and it had been a long time since lunch. Everything was delicious, but she forced herself to have lovely manners and take little bites. She had to remind herself quite frequently not to eat like a piggy.

They were eating with a dedicated purpose when out of the blue, a big guy was suddenly standing by their table. He was well dressed, rather fat, and very drunk.

He said, slurring his words, "I know you. I've been watching you from my table. You're that little prostitute who ran out on me, taking my money when I was in the bathroom. You're a little slut, and you deserve the beating I'm going to give you." He looked really ugly and reached over and grabbed Maria by the shoulders. Thinking that he was going to punch her, Maria was so surprised and frightened that she couldn't even scream.

Bill instantly leaped to her defense and knocked the guy to floor. Bill yelled, "Go get the security guards in here right now and call the police."

Maria saw the maitre d' running to the front desk for help.

The man was big and strong, outweighing Bill by about a hundred pounds, but Bill had him in a wrestling grip, holding the guy's arm up behind his back, keeping him pinned on the ground. That caused the drunk quite a lot of pain, and he began screaming and swearing, yelling that he was going to sue. He struggled mightily, but every time he moved to escape, Bill yanked on his arm.

Two security guards came running into the room and said that they had called the police. "What happened here?"

Maria explained what had happened to her, but she wasn't sure they believed her. *What a pair of idiots,* she thought.

Everyone in the room was watching the scene, frozen in their chairs. The security guards, obviously trying to seem important, said that they would take care of the guy and for Bill to let him up.

Bill said incredulously, "You've got to be kidding." The guards didn't look like they could fight their way out of a paper bag. Bill didn't move except to readjust his hold on the drunk, who had stopped struggling by now and was just lying there, panting.

Then the next act began. With guns drawn, the police came running into the room. They saw Bill holding the guy down, and one asked, "What are you doing, fella?"

Bill gave them the same look as he had the security guards.

Maria screamed at them to do something. "Can't you see that this guy is a dangerous man? That monster on the ground tried to take a punch at me, and hurt my shoulders when he grabbed me."

The other patrons in the dining room took up the cause, shouting at the police to help Bill restrain the man. One lady said, "That nice young man leaped over to protect the young lady. What a brave young man. Do something!"

The police finally got the picture, apologized to Bill, and put handcuffs on the drunk before Bill let him up. They apparently weren't taking any chances. They still had their guns out as they helped the guy stagger to his feet. They asked Bill if he would bring his wife down to police station to make a statement about the incident.

"Can we finish our dinner first, officers?" Maria knew he was being sarcastic with them, because he was so mad at the whole situation.

"Of course, just stop by in the next couple of hours. Sorry that he bothered you like that. Are you all right, Mrs. . . ?"

"I am, but I wouldn't have been if Bill hadn't reacted as fast as he did. He kept an ugly situation from developing in here."

"Your husband is to be commended," the police officer said over his shoulder as he and the other cop were marching the drunk out to the police car.

Maria turned to Bill. "How can you think of eating after what you did?" Her stomach doing an acrobatic dance. She thought, *He's just putting on a brave front. He must be upset, too.*

"It's easy. He wasn't half as hard to bring down as my brothers. I've practiced that move since I was little, but I was too light then, and spent most of my life being pinned by my brothers. I didn't perfect the move until I went out for wrestling in high school. Then the tables were turned on my brothers." He was actually laughing. Bill was really tough at his core.

Maria shook her head. She was learning yet another side of Bill, one that she knew would help him become a success. He was a man's man and yet so lighthearted about his accomplishments.

"How do you feel?" Bill asked. "Did he really hurt your shoulders? If he did, I'll kill him."

"No killing, please. I don't want you in the penitentiary. I need you to be with me. I'm fine, just a little shaken after watching you fight that guy."

The waiter came over and asked if they were ready for the rest of their dinner. Bill said, true to form, "Bring it on; we're really hungry now."

When their delicious, hot dinner arrived, Maria couldn't eat much. The fight had really upset her. She felt like crying and knew that she would have if she were in Bill's arms, but out in the middle of the dining room with everyone watching them, she swallowed them away. Thank God that Bill was so strong.

Bill watched Maria pushing her food around her plate as he made his way through his dinner with gusto. "Damn that drunk; we were having the time of our lives until he appeared," Bill exclaimed, popping half a roll in his mouth.

Someone approached their table. "Good evening, I am the manager of the hotel, and I want to apologize for the incident that your wife had to suffer. I'm returning your payment for the room and, while you are here, all your expenses will be taken care of by the management."

Everyone around them heard what he said and cheered and clapped loudly.

"Even the gift shop?" Bill asked, looking at the manager with a smirk on his face.

As the manager assured them everything would be covered, Maria thought, *Bill's such a rascal, thinking that up so quickly.* How she loved him.

"So what are you planning to buy?" Maria asked.

Bill dodged the question. "The lengths we'll go to for a free meal and gifts," he said, his eyes sending her sexy messages. Bill finished his meal. "Let's go and get the police station visit behind us. Wait here while I get our coats."

Maria had been drained by their experience, and she dreaded going to the police station, but she didn't want to let on to Bill. When he came back with the coats, everyone started clapping again. He smiled, looked around the room, and realized they wanted him to say something. He raised his hand to get their attention. "Thanks for helping tell the police what happened. I was a little busy at the time and couldn't do much talking."

Someone yelled out, "You are a very brave man."

Bill just stood there, seeming at a loss for words. He looked so handsome and acted so humble. Maria was proud of him. "Thanks everyone," he said again and waved a silent thank you to the restaurant at large. The patrons clapped and whistled as Maria and Bill walked out.

Getting into their car, Maria shivered. The cold outside was a shock after being in the nice, warm hotel. At the police station, they helped each other fill out the forms as quickly as they could. Maria noticed how fast Bill could read and respond to the questionnaire. *He will make a great reporter for the paper,* she thought.

As they drove back to the hotel, Maria watched Bill's expression get brighter and she knew why. He wanted to make love again tonight, and so did she, especially since he was such a wonderful lover. Good lovemaking was very exciting and, at the same time, very soothing. It took away the hurt and made everything all right.

When they were back in their grand suite, Maria sat down on the bed and took off her clothes. Once naked, she got under the blankets to keep warm and waited for Bill.

He jumped into bed. "You're all naked already. I wanted to undress you, but you beat me to it."

"I'm not a toy doll that needs to be dressed and undressed all the time."

"I feel like we belong to each other. I want to do everything for you and to you," Bill said.

"That comment sounds a little kinky, if you know what I mean." She grimaced.

"Yeah, there might be a little kinkiness in there, but not much. I wouldn't do anything to you that you didn't want me to do. I love you too much."

"You don't seem at all tired, even with all that fighting tonight."

"No, growing up on a farm, wrestling the farm animals, wrestling my brothers, and wrestling on the team in high school was a lot harder than what I did tonight."

Maria just nodded. She didn't want to talk anymore. She slipped out of bed, found some romantic music on the radio, and jumped back under the covers, shivering.

Bill hugged her to him. "Let me warm you up." He moved from hugging to caressing her all over with his magic fingers. He whispered that he wanted it to be really exciting for her. It was like he had an animal instinct about the timing and began making love

338

to her with such care, she couldn't believe he could have such self-control. When they both felt the explosion of electricity pass through them, they clung to each other. Bill was sweating from the exertion and his sweat stuck them together long after they had finished.

Maria was shaken by the intensity and didn't move. "You are some kind of lover," she said weakly.

He gently massaged her shoulder. "I can't believe how passionate you are, Maria. I feel like I am the luckiest guy in the world. It makes it so easy to make mad love to you, because you actually like it."

She hugged him and put her head on his chest. "It makes me feel like I couldn't be any closer to you than if I were actually attached to you."

"I know, I feel the same way. We are twins." Bill cleared his throat and looked away for a moment.

Maria needed a shower in the worst way, although she felt herself falling asleep. Pushing Bill gently, she said, "It's time for a shower."

Bill nodded. They dragged themselves out of bed, and each took a short, hot shower. As they stood together, brushing their teeth, Maria envisioned them doing that for a lifetime.

The next morning, Maria rolled onto her side and watched Bill sleep. *He looks so handsome,* she thought as she shut her eyes and drifted off again. The next time she opened her eyes, Bill was awake and watching her.

He said, "You look so pretty when you are sleeping."

"You just want more sex; flattery will get you everywhere. What time is it?"

Bill reached over to the night stand for his watch. "It's early, seven thirty. What time do you want to head back?"

"I should show up for lunch and my afternoon classes. How about you?"

"I want to check in with my professor about tonight's talk and keep working on a couple of projects that I have to finish before Christmas break."

"Well, guess what? That leaves plenty of time to try lovemaking in the morning!"

"You know, guys love it when the gals initiate sex. They feel like they aren't the only sexual beings in the partnership."

"Good."

"Just 'good.' Is that all you have to say?"

"Yes, I've said it all." Maria hopped up, put her fuzzy robe on, and ran to the bathroom. She brushed her teeth and got herself ready for love. She hurried back to bed to get warm "Brrr . . . it's winter out there. Would you turn up the thermostat before you come back to bed?"

Bill did his morning routine and set the thermostat before he hopped back in bed. "Where are you?"

"I'm in here."

He peeked under the covers and found her. "I've got a little mole in here with me." All of a sudden, he dove under the covers and wrapped his arms around her. "I've gotcha!"

He moved so quickly that Maria let out a little yelp. "I can see why you were such a good wrestler. You move fast."

"You're right, and don't you forget it. I'll catch you every time."

"Promise?"

He started kissing her everywhere. She felt like they were in a cave under the covers. It was exciting, but she needed more air. It was getting steamy and she struggled to get to the surface. Bill stayed under the covers, kissing and caressing her all over.

"You're going to get the bends if you don't come up soon," Maria said. "Then you won't be able to make love."

"Don't count on it. I can hold my breath for a long, long time."

"If you come up, I promise you will like it," Maria said giggling.

Bill slowly slithered up her body. When he got to the top, he gave her a gentle, exquisite French kiss. He whispered, hoarse with emotion, "What is your promise?"

"That this is the beginning of a long and happy sexual life for us," she said.

"Maria, I'm so glad we met and are here now."

Making love in the morning was a new experience for both of them, and they weren't disappointed. He held her in his arms and his breathing slowly calmed down, as did her trembling.

She whispered in his ear, "Three for three. I'm going to make a plaque for you, and it's going to say, 'I satisfy my customers.'"

"Customer? I thought you were my lover."

"Well, I guess the plaque could say, 'Guaranteed Results,' instead." She jumped up to escape his arms and ran for the shower.

He was right behind her. "Let's take our last shower together. I want another shot at those boobies of yours."

"You like that word, don't you?" She turned on the water and waited for it to get warm.

"It's a great word," he said as he put his arms around her from behind and put his hands over her breasts. She pushed him away and climbed into the shower.

When Bill came in, he asked her why she was standing on the stool.

"It will keep me from getting drowned."

"Oh yes. That's a good idea," he said, as he started to rub her body.

"No more playing, my sexy friend. We have to hurry, or we or we won't have time for you to pick out something for me at the gift shop, courtesy of the house. You see, I'm just full of good ideas. Ask me anything, and I will give you an idea about it."

"That's what I'm afraid of," Bill said.

By the time they had gotten out of the shower and Bill had put lotion on Maria, they were hungry.

"It's all the physical activity we've been engaging in; it uses up the calories. Especially for you, my busy guy," Maria said.

"I'm not complaining," Bill said. "I'll never turn you down when you want some loving."

"As if I didn't know that," she said, smiling at him with kisses in her eyes.

They dressed for action and threw everything else in their bags so they'd be ready when it was time to go.

"It's nice that we have until eleven before they kick us out of here," Bill said.

The hotel's breakfast room was designed with large windows to overlook the gardens and trees at the back of the hotel. It was another sunny day and beautiful but cold outside. Seated near the windows with sun streaming in, one could be fooled into thinking the weather was hospitable. After bringing Maria and Bill cups of hot, delicious-smelling coffee, the waitress took their orders. They sat there, sipping their brew, each with their own thoughts about their whirlwind trip.

"I wish this was just the first day of a trip to the coast and back," Maria said.

"Which coast?" Bill asked

"The West Coast. I want to drive on an ocean highway, if there is one, all the way from Washington through California."

Bill got a faraway look in his eyes. "I've always wanted to see the West Coast, too." He took her hands in his. "We'll go; I promise you that."

"So what were *you* thinking about?" Maria asked.

"How good everything has turned out for us on our mini trip." He lowered his voice. "I never dreamed we would be so good for each other. And I'm pleased with my interview and job offer from Mr. Addison."

Their food came, and Maria almost let Miss Piggy out but restrained herself.

Bill said, "I'll bet you're hungry. You hardly ate a thing after the big brouhaha last night."

When the waitress came with the check, she asked what their room number was.

Bill told her, and she looked at a note on her pad. "Oh, you are the couple who were assaulted last night. There's no charge for your breakfast. May I ask you a question, sir? Are you a police officer?"

"No, I'm not. Why?"

"Well, everyone said you knew exactly what to do when that man tried to assault your wife."

Maria smiled when she said "wife."

Bill said, "I was just lucky, I guess."

"Well, everyone is talking about you. It's a pleasure to wait on your table. I hope you will stay here again."

Since the meal was free, Bill left a generous tip.

"Let's see what you can find in the gift shop while I sign us out at the desk," Bill said. "Maybe we'll have time for a quick drive along the Raccoon River before we start back. What do you say?"

"I'd like that." *Anything to prolong our trip,* she thought

In the gift shop, Maria found a locket that opened out into four panels, making room for four tiny pictures. She had to have it.

Bill came up beside her at the jewelry counter, and she could feel his warmth. She showed him the locket, and he said, "What are you waiting for? Buy it; it's cute, and you can put my picture in it." His eyes danced with pleasure. "Oops, it's on the house; I almost forgot. That makes it better yet."

As they drove along the Raccoon River, Maria couldn't resist taking out the locket and looking at it again. "You know what this means, don't you?" she asked.

"I get unlimited sex." Bill ducked instinctively at the wheel, as Maria whacked him with her glove. "Don't abuse the driver when he's driving. It means I can scout a motel for Saturday night for us," he said gleefully.

"None of the above. It means I need to take a good picture of you, my mom, and whoever else I decide to put in it. I'm going to wear it next to my heart." She paused, then laughed. "Except in the shower! So, do you need a map to these motels, or are you like a bloodhound? I suppose where sex is concerned, you're better than a bloodhound."

"I certainly am that," Bill said. "I have a couple of places in mind for us to check out on the way back to school. I've been thinking along these lines all fall."

Maria was looking at her map, thinking about different attractions to go to on future trips. "Bill, do you like zoos?"

"I can take them as long as long as there is a breeze, especially during the summer," Bill said, not very enthusiastically.

"We'll save that trip and take our kids there someday. I'll find you some air shows and train rides," Maria said with a laugh.

"Did I hear the word 'kids'?"

"I was just checking to see if you were listening. I knew that would get your attention."

"Okay, we've reached the end of our drive. Now what's the road number connecting here to take us north?"

"It's U.S. 35 toward Urbandale. At Hickman Road, we'll continue north on 35 to Ames."

"Thanks, my little map reader. I was pretty sure that was the way to go, but it's been a while since I was last here. You're fun to have along, besides your map-reading ability. I'm going to keep you."

"There's a price for everything, including my services." She smiled at him.

"That sounds pretty sexy. I like it."

"Let's watch your pennies and just find a place that is clean for next time. It doesn't have to be fancy."

"We've got to stay more than two hours. I want to get my money's worth." Bill gave her a sexy grin.

"Now who's teasing whom here?"

"Just checking to see if you are listening."

"That's my line; no fair using my material. Oh, there's a Quality Courts on the right-hand side and a Midwestern on the left. From the outside, I think I like the one on the right better than the other one. Would you like to pull in and see what we think?"

They had a look at a room.

"So, do you like it?" Bill asked when they got back in the car.

"It was clean and good for what we want it for. It's not the Berkmar, but neither is the price."

Bill relaxed. "We should make good time back to school, now."

Maria turned on the radio, found some nice music, and settled back for the short drive.

Bill pulled up in front of her dorm. He leaned over and gave her a light kiss. "I'll call you after my talk, all right?"

Thinking fast, Maria said, "I might be asleep after such a busy day. I will call you in the morning if that happens." She didn't know what to do about Ed. She hadn't planned on such an extraordinary time with Bill. She felt terrible about meeting Ed after her wonderful overnight in Des Moines, especially knowing that Ed wanted to see her for more than dinner. But not terrible enough to call him and cancel her date. How did she get into this triangle? She was flattered by Ed's attention after all the years when he had seemed so unobtainable, but she was thrilled that she and Bill were so close, too.

Bill looked concerned. "What's wrong, Maria?"

Quickly covering her guilty conscience, Maria said, "I was just thinking about all the work I have to do to catch up, but I wouldn't have missed being with you for anything. Hope things go well for you tonight, my love. I'll be waiting to talk to you." She gave him a kiss, lingering a moment longer than usual. "I'm also sad that our overnight is over. I'd better go so you can have lunch, too."

Bill got out of the car and retrieved her little overnight case from the back seat. He gave her a quick hug and watched her run up the stairs. Maria waved and disappeared inside.

25. Maria Makes a Choice

As we must account for every idle word,
so must we account for every idle silence.
—Benjamin Franklin

Maria watched Bill drive off and went to find Susie. Maria saw her coming down the hall for lunch. Susie whooped when she saw Maria, moved into a faster gear, took Maria's bag, and ran back to the room with it.

"I was waiting for you just this once," Susie said as she dropped Maria's bag. "Let's go eat." On the way to the dining hall, she whispered, "How was everything? Are you still madly in love or ready to kill him?"

"Bill was great, the hotel was perfect, and I'm worried as the devil about meeting Ed this afternoon. This is crazy, what I'm doing. When Ed offered to drive me to his bank, I had just come back from a wild weekend with him, and I said yes without really thinking it through. I'm really in a mess."

They shut up when they hit the buffet line to choose their lunches. Maria was glad when they sat down alone. Susie usually attracted girls to her like bees to honey.

"Do you want my take on this?" asked Susie very quietly, almost covering her mouth with her hand.

"Yes, I do. I am so worried that somehow this is all going to come out and ruin Bill's and my love affair."

"Remember this, you might have an hour of physical fun with

Ed, but you're not promising anything and neither is he. It's just part of nature, no more, no less. Will you remember this evening with Ed in ten years or with the same intensity as now? I don't think so. It's the long journey and how you walk on it that is the important part." Susie paused. "The main thing is to do what your heart tells you to do. Always listen to that little part of you in situations like these. Don't do something that makes you uncomfortable."

"Susie, thanks for your advice. My problem is that he flattered me, and I did feel an incredible draw toward him, and I know he felt it too. I do actually feel a little sorry for him, although he'd die if he thought I felt that way. He doesn't seem to have any family support, just my brother-in-law and maybe some professors and business people who have been impressed by his work and determination." Maria looked up. The place had emptied out while they were talking. "Let's go get ready for class. Thanks for your good advice. This is getting to be a habit."

"One more thing, Maria. Don't ever have a sexual affair with a guy because you feel sorry for him. And remember this, my services aren't free; when you become a pledge, I will make you work to pay for my counseling." Susie was almost laughing.

Maria grinned at her and picked up her notebooks for class. "See you later, maybe. If I'm gone when you get back, please cover for me tonight. Tell everyone I'm sick or something and need to sleep. I'll try to be back by curfew, but if I miss it and Bill calls, just say I'm asleep and will call him in the morning." Maria laughed at her complicated directions to Susie. "It's a good thing you are Phi Beta Kappa material, so you can manage all my instructions."

Boy, she thought, *I never planned on back-to-back lovemaking sessions with two different guys. Maria, you've really gone wild. Weigh the consequences.*

Susie said, Don't worry, I'll cover all your bases. Remember, it's got to be what you want."

As they went their separate ways to their classes, Marie thought about how much she loved Susie and would never forget their friendship.

Maria concentrated on her classes as well as she could all afternoon and ran home after her last class to make a few repairs before Ed came. When she saw his car pull up, she desperately wanted to get away before one of Maude's cohorts saw her with Ed. He was standing by the car and she nearly knocked him over in her hurry. She jumped into the car as fast as she could, scrunched down in the seat, and called, "Let's get out of here."

Ed got in, smiling. "Hi, nice to see you, and who's after you?"

Clutching her purse and giving him a simple-minded grin, she answered, "I just don't want any nosy neighbors getting into our business. Sorry, if I'm a little jumpy. I promise I'll relax and enjoy the afternoon and dinner with you."

"Just dinner? I was hoping for more with you. I thought we had an understanding," he said, reaching over and pulling her next to him. He kissed her face quickly as he drove, and Maria could smell his aftershave and his masculinity. "I've missed your teasing since we got back," he said. "I've found myself thinking of all the laughs we had together. In fact, you've interfered with my life." When he uttered those words, he looked at her in dead seriousness.

"Well, I'm glad I'm good for something," she replied, feeling her skin getting all tingly.

"You do a lot more than you realize." His facial muscles tightened.

Maria felt her stomach roll and thought, *I've got to lighten up this conversation.* "That's the way to do it. A few more lessons, and you'll be my star pupil." She forced a little chuckle.

"How many students do you have?" His deep mood seemed to be disappearing.

"I don't know. They come and they go."

"Is that what's going to happen to me?"

Maria was at a loss of how to wiggle out of this conversation, so instead asked, "How about some music on our ride?"

Ed's posture changed. He just looked at the road and drove like the wind as the music filled the silence. In a businesslike tone, Ed finally said, "We'll have to continue our conversation after we do our bank business." He pulled into the bank's parking lot and turned off the car. "It's too cold to smoke outside. How about a cigarette inside the bank?"

"Why not," Maria replied, wishing that Ed wasn't so upset. What had set him off? They hurried into the bank lobby, sat down, and lit up. "This place is nice and warm. Good idea," Maria said as she blew smoke at him, trying to get him to laugh.

The darn cigarette was burning her throat. She shouldn't smoke. She took another little puff, and it made her cough. She thought, *That's it for me. No more smoking. I really hate it.* Was she trying to impress Ed? She should just tell him that she didn't like to smoke. It seemed like second nature to try to do what she thought a guy wanted. *That's ridiculous,* she thought and ground her cigarette out in the ash tray. Ed gave her a look, and she said, "It burns my throat."

Ed took a big drag on his cigarette. "Then don't smoke. I've been trying to quit for years."

He leaned over and said quietly, "I have an appointment with the bank president after we get your application notarized. I'm going to give him my pitch on investing in my future clinic. Wish me luck." He gave her a tense smile. "I hope you bring me luck. Let's go find the bank manager."

They went up to the manager's desk, and Ed said, "Hi, John. This Maria Banks. She needs to have her job application notarized, please."

John said, "Do you have any identification with you?"

Maria got out her Illinois driver's license. The manager took her application, gave it a quick once over, and asked her to sign it, which she did. He signed, too, and used his press to notarize it.

"What do I owe you?" Maria asked.

He waved her away, saying, "Nothing. Ed has banked with us for five years and because of that, your notarization is free."

Maria sat down to wait for Ed. He was with the president for a long time. She wondered if the length of the meeting meant good tidings for Ed. She hoped so. Her mind drifted to the subject she had been ignoring all afternoon: going to a motel with Ed. It seemed so ludicrous now, even though it hadn't when Ed had brought it up on Sunday. She snapped out of her musings to see Ed standing in front of her, smiling. His body was more relaxed. She wanted to ask him how things went, but decided against it, especially inside the bank.

"Let's go," Ed said. "I want to get you something that you need, but it doesn't have anything to do with drugstore products." He had a slight smile on his handsome face.

"Well, that's a relief. Where are we going?"

"It's a surprise."

As they walked outside, Maria buttoned her coat and put up her hood. It was really getting cold as the sun slipped away. They stopped at a small jewelry store.

"Come on," he said, "let's go in. I want to get you something."

Maria was dumbfounded. What in the world was Ed doing?

He took her over to the display of watches. "I would like to get you a Minnie Mouse watch."

"Really? I don't believe it. I've wanted one of those since I was in high school. All the kids did, but only the wealthy kids got one. My dad said he wanted me to have a more lasting kind of watch, but I was disappointed. You remembered that my watch was broken. You said that you would fix it for me, but not right then. As I remember, you had other things on your mind."

He laughed and seemed so pleased that she remembered what he had said. "I think you need a Minnie Mouse watch. It fits you somehow."

Maria had never been given anything like a watch from a boyfriend. Except for the free locket Bill got her today, the biggest present she had ever received was a chocolate sundae. Boys in high school didn't have much cash, or if they did, they spent it on cars or sports.

"Do you like it? You're mighty quiet. I expected some smart remark to come out of that cute little mouth of yours."

"My dad told me to accept gifts with appreciation. So I will. It is darling, and I love it. Thanks so much for being so thoughtful." She had the sudden urge to kiss him but refrained. It might send him the wrong signal.

"Do you want to wear it, miss?" the sales clerk asked. "I can wrap it up if you wish."

"I want to wear it, thank you."

The clerk put it on Maria's wrist and fastened the little leather strap. Maria held out her arm to admire her cute, new watch.

Ed paid for it, and they hurried to the car in the cold, dark, early evening. Ed turned the car around and drove west out of town on U.S. 30 toward Boone. "There's a nice restaurant near the center of Boone that I think you will like."

"I'm starving, as usual. Are you hungry, too?"

"I'm hungry for more than food," he said and pulled her close. This time, he turned on the radio and found some nice, romantic music. He put his arm back around her shoulders and began gently massaging her, driving with one hand.

Maria couldn't believe that her hormones were revving up again and beginning to run away with her. There was such a mysterious air about him. He exuded testosterone. She had just made love in the morning with Bill, and now she was getting all steamed up over Ed. She began to question her sanity.

The lyrics to the song talked about a kiss of fire. Maria stole a glance at Ed as he concentrated on the road, his profile barely visible in the dark. She loved his slight overbite and the way his hair curled up on his neck. She couldn't help but wonder what he was thinking. Probably what the bank official had said to him. Perhaps she'd never know. Ed kept his own counsel.

Maria shut her eyes and made a decision, although she was torn. Bill represented all that was good and had given her a fantastic time at the Berkmar. It was out of the question for her to have sex with Ed again, even though he was so darn sexy.

Bill was committed to her and probably would pin her or give her a ring after Christmas, she told herself, not really believing it. She tried to convince herself that he just needed to go home and talk things over with his parents.

She was glad she had made a decision, but how she could tell Ed? Pushing up her sleeve, she looked at her new watch. Minnie made her smile, and it was fun to know what time it was again without having to ask someone. "I really like my watch, Ed. It's so cute. Every time I look at it, I'll think of you."

Ed looked at her, but in the dark she couldn't tell what was on his mind. He didn't say anything. When they pulled into the restaurant parking lot, he turned off the engine, squeezed her tightly, and asked, "How would you like to repay me for your watch?" Without waiting for an answer, he found her lips, and gave her a small kiss. "Mmmm," he whispered, "you taste like peppermints." He deepened the kiss, exploring her mouth with his tongue.

Wriggling away, Maria said, breathlessly, "We've got to go in, or we're going to be in trouble."

"I know, Miss Peppermint. You must be hungry if you had to eat candy on the way here."

The restaurant was doing a good business, judging by the cars outside. Maria saw a lot of little candles twinkling through the windows. When they ran into the warm, inviting atmosphere of the place, she saw that each table had a candle.

As they waited for a table, Ed held her hand and absentmindedly began squeezing it slightly. She wondered what he was thinking.

After they were seated, Ed moved to sit next to her rather than across from her. "How are you feeling, my cute little Minnie Mouse?" He lit two cigarettes, handed one to Maria, and took a deep drag on his, blowing the smoke away from her.

Maria held hers for a moment, then put it down.

"You're not smoking yours," Ed said.

"You forgot," she said, barely three inches away from him, "I don't want to smoke, anymore." She put out the cigarette in the ash tray.

"I was thinking about other things with us," he said, searching her eyes.

"I know; so was I."

The waitress came over and broke into their intimate moment. She asked in what seemed a provocative manner, "Are you hungry? We've got good pot roast tonight." She was looking only at Ed.

"Give us menus, and we'll get back to you," Ed said, irritated at the interruption.

"Suit yourself, but you're missing out if you don't try our pot roast." The waitress walked away, swinging her hips.

When she was gone, Ed put his arm around Maria and asked, "What are your plans for this evening?" His voice was soft but serious.

"Let's get our order in before we have any more discussion, shall we?" Maria said, angling for time.

Nodding slowly, he took his arm away and straightened up. "I'm ordering breakfast, because I didn't get much this morning. The farmers kept calling the vet's office on campus today, asking for me, specifically, to come out and help them with their animals. I've been swamped with work."

Maria felt as if he were making an attempt to apologize for not trying to see or at least call her since he'd dropped her off on Sunday. "You are a good vet," she said, "and the farmers know it. Are you happy that they want you?"

"Yes and no. I make some money on each call, but it interferes with my personal life more than I want." He gave her a devilish smile.

The waitress came back, looked at Ed, and asked, "What would you like?" in a way that suggested she was up for a lot more than food, if he was.

Ed grimaced and looked at Maria. "What would you like, Maria, my little cupcake?"

Laughing at his endearment, she answered, "The same as you, honey." She looked straight at the waitress as she said it. Maria wondered how many times this sort of thing happened to Ed. There was no question about his good looks. They were outstanding.

The waitress's attitude hadn't gone unnoticed, Maria knew, when Ed said, "Waitresses are fine, but they aren't the kind of gals I'm interested in. I like to go with women who can understand what I'm talking about. It also doesn't hurt if they are sexy, like you."

Maria laughed. She found him quite interesting, when he felt like talking, and appreciated his candor. She admired his ability and brains. No one could get through the veterinary medicine program and not be right up there at the head of the class. She noticed that Ed had a certain way of holding his chin when he was about to say something he thought was important. He was doing it right now.

"I wanted to tell you what the banker said this afternoon," Ed said. "He wants to see the old sheepskin before he commits any money to my clinic. He did intimate that he was ready to invest in its future, which really pleased me, but he asked me to come and see him after I graduate."

"That's terrific, Ed. I'm glad you feel good about the meeting."

"It was fine. I'll feel better about it when he gives me some money."

Maria wanted to ask him how he and his gal were doing, but felt that wasn't any of her business. He never asked her about Bill. She thought, *Let him tell me what he wants; don't question him.* She didn't like to be questioned, either, about personal stuff. Maria knew that Ed wasn't making any commitments at that time; he just wanted to have fun. But he had said that he had a lot of strong feelings for her, and as far as she knew, he had never lied to her. Perhaps he could date two people at once, but Maria couldn't. Her feelings

355

had changed now that she had experienced a new level of intimacy with Bill. There was no room for Ed.

Their food came piping hot, and the waitress asked, "Is that all, sir?" giving him another big smile.

"Yes, that's all," Maria said. She wanted to add "and please get lost."

Having breakfast for dinner was a welcome change. It was comfort food and light in her stomach, which was doing flip flops at the moment. She especially appreciated the coffee; it would help keep her awake later on tonight. She needed to study and catch up with the lessons she'd missed while spending time with Bill.

Ed was eating and watching her. He had a deep intensity about him that was hard to understand. A lot was going on in that handsome head of his. Maria wondered if anyone would ever be allowed to know his more personal thoughts. Bill, on the other hand, was much more open and had told Maria much about himself already. Of course, to be fair, Ed and she hadn't seen much of each other until just recently. She was probably expecting too much in such a short time.

Maria noticed Ed ate differently from many other men. He handled his knife and fork like surgical instruments and was very quick and precise about the way he cut his food. Although his hands were big, they were graceful.

Concentrating on her meal, Maria was slightly embarrassed when she realized that Ed had finished and had lit a cigarette. He took a drag and sat watching her, giving off an air of quiet sexiness that she could feel. Maria said to herself, *I have to tell him that I want to go home after dinner.* She stopped eating, her appetite suddenly gone. She pushed her plate away and smiled at Ed. Her stomach was in a knot from the anxiety of what she was about to say.

"I see you liked dinner," Ed said with a wry look on his face. "One thing about you, Maria, you love your food. I'll get the waitress, and we'll be out of here in a couple of minutes."

She could feel the intensity of his desire building. He could hardly wait. She took a deep breath. "Thank you for my darling watch, a nice dinner at this cute place, and helping me get my application notarized." Her hands were clammy and her stomach was nervous, but her voice was steady.

"You are such a great gal, and so appreciative of the littlest things that are done for you. You make me feel like a good guy."

He had made it even harder for her to tell him what he wouldn't want to hear, but she was determined. "I have to go back to the dorm tonight, Ed." To her surprise, he said that he understood.

"You do?" she said, amazement written all over her face. What a relief.

"When I kissed you out in the parking lot, that incredible draw to you was still there, strong and hot as it always is. But I realized earlier that I was being an incredible jerk to expect you to drop everything and fall into bed with me when I haven't even taken one minute out of my last few days to touch base with you. I wish with all my heart that it was two or three years from now, and we were sitting here. I know that if I felt then like I do now, I would be slipping a ring on your finger."

"I'm flattered by your future intentions, but I can't spend the next two or three years wondering if you are still interested in me." Maria was irritated by Ed's continual single-mindedness about stopping his personal life while he built his professional one. "It's time to go, while we are still enjoying each other's company."

Ed's face changed after her stinging comment. He paid the check and helped Maria on with her coat. As they walked out of the restaurant, he put his arm around her. "I'm sorry you feel the way you do, but I'll keep in touch with you anyway. I don't want to lose track of you."

Maria felt the tears welling up in her eyes. One minute she was mad at him and the next she was moved by him. She must have a split personality, whatever that is. She said, "I'll always want to know where you are and how you are doing. I'd still like to know you better. You are quite mysterious to me. Maybe, someday, you'll feel comfortable enough with me to let me in on the private world of Ed McDermott."

They headed back to Iowa State. Now that they had spoken their true feelings to each other, there was an air of understanding present for the first time in their relationship. When they pulled up in front of Stevens Dorm, the Campanile was gonging eight.

"How about one for the road," Ed asked, reaching for her.

Maria couldn't resist him. He exuded a lustiness that was intoxicating. She felt somehow that they were saying goodbye instead of good night. She moved over to him, put her arms around his neck, and gave him a gentle kiss.

He responded with such passion that he melted her with the intensity of it. She pushed him away and looked into his deep, tender eyes. "Remember, you were my first. You awakened in me such incredible passion, I will never forget it."

As Maria got out of the car, Ed said, "I'll call you later." She saw him wait to leave until she was inside.

Maria ran into the dorm in a confused state, having just left a guy who made her feel wild. Ed was so sexy, a bad boy promising nothing. But hiding under that veneer was a feeling, thoughtful guy. She had misread him and realized that she hadn't had a real chance to know him.

"I need to take a shower and relax," she said under her breath when she opened the door to her room. She quickly gathered her shower essentials and walked to the bathroom, anticipating some soothing moments to relieve her frustration and guilt over Ed.

When she reluctantly turned off the water and was looking for her bath towel, Maria heard her name being called for the phone. It was cold standing out there in the hall, and she was irritated. It was too early for Bill's call and she had just said goodbye to Ed, so who could it be? She hurried to the phone with her big towel wrapped around her. She was going to make it short before she froze to death.

It was Ed. "When I got to my room, I had to call you because I felt I couldn't leave things the way I did. I was so intent on getting you back to the dorm, Maria, and a little angry. I've realized that I was awfully quiet. I have trouble letting down my guard, and I know it shows. There's a lot more to our relationship than I'm willing to admit, and I think we could build it up into something good. It just has to have time to grow, and I don't have the time right now. I won't see you after tonight because my schedule of calls is packed until I leave for Christmas vacation. I also have to keep my courses going. I'm sorry that I'll be so busy, but I want to spend more time with you in January."

Maria was amazed that now he was using work and his courses as reasons for not seeing her. *He's afraid of seeing me,* she thought. *Well he'll just have to stew in his own juices, as my mother used to say. He may never be ready to commit to a woman.* She didn't care and couldn't do anything about it anyway. *He'll have to get really lonely before he comes to terms with his problems.* "Ed," Maria said, "what I said tonight, I meant. I have no claim on you. You have been up front with me all the way. I have strong feelings for you that come from somewhere deep inside me. Otherwise, I wouldn't have dreamed of doing what I did with you over Thanksgiving. Thank you again for our nice evening. I'm so pleased that you understood my change of heart. Good luck with all your work. You are such a hard worker and a wonderful human being. I admire you a lot. Sleep well, good night. I'll see you in January 1949.

26. Going to Ames and Boone

Where sense is wanting, everything is wanting.
—Benjamin Franklin

Maria ran to her room to get her fuzzy robe. She had left her pajamas in the bathroom when she went to answer the phone, and now she was cold. Susie was sitting in the room getting ready for bed when Maria grabbed her robe and ran back to the bathroom. As she was coming back down the hall, the phone rang. She picked it up, and it was Bill. Immediately, her feelings for Bill came flooding back. She said that she was so happy to hear his voice and really meant it. She felt so safe with him.

"You always make me feel so good, Maria. I love calling you. I can always count on your happiness. I got home early from my talk, and I wanted to call you as soon as I could so that you could go to bed."

"How was your talk?" She asked with real interest. She loved to hear any little tidbits.

"It was good, as always. The farmers love me, but I don't want to discuss that now. I wanted to let you know that I can pick you gals up around two tomorrow to go buy your train tickets. We'll start out at the bank in Ames, go to Boone to get the tickets, and, guess what, I want to take you and Susie out for dinner tomorrow night."

"That's so sweet of you to help us get our tickets and also take us out for dinner. I'll tell Susie when we hang up. I can't wait to see you, handsome. Sweet dreams."

"It's the least I can do for you, Maria. Tonight, driving home, I kept thinking about our incredible night. It was something I had been dreaming about all fall, and you were everything I had hoped for. You are very special to me, and I love you so much. Until tomorrow, sleep well." The phone clicked, and he was gone.

When Maria got back to her room, she danced in, smiling. "We are all set to cash our checks from home and buy train tickets tomorrow. Bill is going to take us to his bank in Ames, then drive us to the Boone train ticket office. Isn't that grand?" She jumped onto her bed with an extra flourish.

"I didn't know you were such a dancer. You're just a bundle of surprises. So when are we departing for the grand tour?"

"Two o'clock, and I didn't tell you the best part: Bill is buying us dinner." Maria gave her rear end a little shake and twirled around the room with her arms flying. "He's been paid for his latest speaking engagement, and he feels rich."

"Terrific. Rides, money, food, and if you could add sex, it would be perfect."

"Anybody listening would think you were a nymphomaniac."

"I've been accused of worse things." Susie was grinning from ear to ear.

"Now that we've got that settled, I've got to study and catch up for tomorrow." Maria went to her desk, opened her history book, and settled in for some concentrated study. She was tired, but she promised herself that she would study for at least a couple of hours.

"Oh, no," Susie said. "No studying until you tell me about your date with Ed. Did you or didn't you?"

"I didn't. It was hard to resist that terrible draw we have for each other, but we did. When I asked to come home after dinner, he said that he understood completely and felt he had been acting like a jerk to think I'd just go to bed with him without having heard a word from him since Sunday. I didn't have to go into any of my reasons. I just left it at that and we zoomed home—and I mean he drove *fast*. I'm sure he felt bad, and that was the only way he could make himself feel better." Maria looked at Susie. "That's the whole truth, nothing but the truth, so help me, God. Now I have to study, unless you have more questions."

"Good for you, you did what your heart told you to do. Turn out the lights when you go to bed; I'm going to sleep." Susie put a sleep mask on her face and rolled over.

When the Campanile gonged midnight, Maria folded up like a piece of wet tissue paper and fell into bed. The next thing she knew, her alarm was ringing in her ear. *Oh my gosh, is it time to get up already?* She felt as if she had just gone to sleep.

Susie had heard Maria's alarm and was attempting to get up, too. They both stumbled out of bed, showered, dressed, and ran to breakfast like robots, hardly saying a word to each other.

After breakfast, they went back out into the cold, Iowa winter, the wind blowing up a storm around them. They were all bundled up and looked like two penguins lurching along to class.

After lunch, Maria decided to skip her one o'clock and take a nap instead. She was cooked.

From a haze, she could hear Susie stomping around, and Maria realized that Susie was trying to wake her up. When Maria opened her eyes, Susie was standing by her bed, waggling her fingers in her ears, crossing her eyes, and sticking out her tongue.

"What a pretty sight to wake up to," Maria said.

"I knew you'd be touched."

Maria quickly got up. "Come on, you goofball. Bill will be here in a few minutes. Are you all set? Thanks for waking me up. I'm confused, don't mind me."

"I'm always ready," Susie said, twirling around the room.

"What a pain to room with," Maria said, teasing Susie. Maria ran to the bathroom to splash some cold water on her face. She was delighted that they were going to have so much fun this afternoon and evening. If she didn't have to study, college would really be great.

Bill pulled up at two, and the girls were so intent on getting to the car, they almost tumbled down the stairs, which were slippery with the snow that was just beginning to fall.

"That was close," Susie said. "Aren't we glad we are so light on our feet and fast at grabbing the railings?" Susie waved at Bill. "Hi, I'm Susie. I've spoken to you on the phone, but never met the voice."

Bill smiled. "Hi, girls. Glad to meet you, Susie." He opened the doors for them.

Susie said, "I'm impressed. I like your car, Bill."

"It's just on loan to me from the school, mainly for my talks, but it's nice to have for personal use, too."

"We're happy about that, too," the girls said in unison.

"We've been living together too long," Maria said.

As they were driving to Ames, the snowflakes were getting heavier and collecting on the windshield. "I think we're in for an Iowa snowstorm. It won't get bad for a couple of hours. We have time to do what we need to do," Maria's handsome prince announced.

When they parked by the bank, Maria realized that they might see the same bank officer that she had with Ed. *Goodness, I wish I had clued Susie in beforehand.* The girls quickly popped out the car, so Bill didn't have to come around and play doorman.

As they walked in, Maria held Susie back and whispered, "Think of something to divert a creepy little guy from the bank if he comes over to see us. He notarized my application when I came in here with Ed. I really hope he doesn't notice me." Maria was sure that Bill was wondering what she was whispering to Susie so intently.

They walked over to a teller's window, and Maria gave the lady her endorsed check. The teller looked at her hard and, with a very serious face, asked if she had an account there.

Bill stepped up next to Maria. "Hi, I'm Bill Morgan, and I have a savings account here. This young lady needs her check cashed, as does her friend here, and I vouch for them both." He handed his passbook to the teller. "I can cover both checks if they bounce, but I assure you, they won't."

"Right, Mr. Morgan," said the teller, giving him a big smile. "I just need to get the bank officer to okay it." She walked over to the little weasel whom Maria had been trying to avoid. She showed him Bill's passbook and Maria's check, gesturing toward Bill.

Of course, he came over to check Bill out and saw Maria. Susie immediately stepped up to him and said, "Would you okay my check, too, while you're here? I'm also with Mr. Morgan."

"Well, Mr. Morgan, you certainly attract the girls. Just yesterday, when my friend, Mr. McDermott, was here with *you*—" He was looking straight at Maria.

Susie interrupted. "No, Mr. McDermott was here with me," she said with conviction. "Don't you remember?"

The little weasel looked confused because Susie sounded so sure of herself.

"Here's my check, sir. Please okay it so I can buy a train ticket to Chicago to see my sick, old mother." Susie waved it in his face.

The guy kept looking at Maria and then at Susie. He nodded to the teller, finally, and went back to his desk.

The teller counted out their money while Bill waited. He looked a little confused, too. When they were all back in the car, Bill asked them what it was all about.

Susie piped up as cool as a cucumber and said that she had been into the bank with Ed but had forgotten her check.

"How do you know Ed?" Bill asked.

"I met him when I spent time with Maria visiting her family in Rock Falls. We go back to high school days." She smiled innocently.

Maria marveled at her quick-witted answer and silently thanked her for helping her out of a mess.

The snow was really coming down and sticking to the windshield and road. As they drove along, Bill said that it wasn't slippery yet, but they probably shouldn't try to go out for dinner. "I'll give you a rain check."

Bill parked at the ticket office in Boone. Maria and Susie went to the ticket window while he looked at old photographs of famous train engines on the ancient walls.

A little old guy who looked like Santa Claus was sitting behind the window and evidently was the ticket master. "What can I do for you young ladies?"

"You first, Susie, you have less to do than me."

"Round trip to Oak Park, Illinois. You don't stop in La Grange, by any chance? There was some talk of it a while back."

"No," he said, "the railroad decided not to do it. You'll have to take a bus back to La Grange. What are your going and coming dates?"

"I'll be leaving on December 17 and returning to Boone on January 7."

Santa Claus handed her the tickets with a big smile. "By coming over two weeks early, I can give you seat reservations. If you waited until you got on the train last minute, like so many young people do nowadays, you'd have had to sit on your suitcase all the way there." He seemed very pleased that he could seat Susie.

Maria stepped up. "I need a one-way ticket and seat reservation with my friend to Chicago, and then a one-way from Chicago to Sterling, Illinois, on January 2, 1949."

"So you gals are riding to Illinois together and coming back separately. And you, young lady, are going to big, bad Chicago? Don't let any gangsters get you." Laughing at his little joke, he made out her tickets. "Is that all for you? What about you, young man. Where are you going? I recommend that you go with these pretty young ladies," and really chuckled.

Maria said, "I also need a ticket for Miami, Florida, leaving Chicago on December 17 and returning to Chicago on January 2, arriving in time to catch my train to Sterling. Can you work out the details for me?"

He looked at her almost indignantly. "I'll help you make your connections. That's my job." He gave her round-trip tickets to and from Miami, going over the times and dates with her. He was very thorough.

By the time they got out of there, the snow was coming down hard. Bill cleaned off the windshield and turned on the defroster. He drove slowly back to school. It took them twice as long to get back.

When they got to the dorm, the girls said in unison, "Don't get out, we are fine. Thanks so much for helping us." They grabbed the railings and pulled themselves up the stairs, carefully climbing through lots of snow.

After dinner, Bill called. "I'm happy we all got back safe and sound. Can you believe it out there? So why aren't you traveling back from Illinois with Susie?"

"I want to spend a few days with my family in Rock Falls."

"How are you going to get from Rock Falls to school? Don't tell me, Ed is going to bring you back again."

"Yes, me and four other girls, just like Thanksgiving. I call it Ed's Harem. He doesn't think it's very funny, but I do. So, handsome, are you jealous? Don't be, Ed's trying to impress my brother-in-law by taking care of his sister-in-law."

"The guy didn't seem like an old family friend that day in the Union."

"Bill, darling, you are my true love who loves me. Just remember our trip to Des Moines and the Berkmar, if you have any doubts." She paused. "Say, I like the ring of that. 'Remember the Berkmar.' It sounds like a battle cry." She laughed at her comment.

"I know. I guess I'm dreading saying goodbye to you for three weeks. I need your mom's phone number so I can call you in Florida and hear your voice."

"I'll give it to you tomorrow. Now to more pleasant thoughts; let's think about playing in the snow tomorrow."

"Great idea. Let's go sledding on the hills above Lake Laverne. I can get some trays from the kitchen to slide on, and I'm sure the guys will be game for anything. You bring some gals, if you can, and we'll have quite a party."

"Bill, you are such fun; let's do it. Call me early tomorrow morning so we can finalize our wild time. I love you, and remember what you told me when we first started dating: we are a matched team."

"Oh, Maria, I love you in so many ways. You make up my life."

"Good night, sweet prince."

When Maria got back to the room, Susie was out like a light. She hadn't had a nap like Maria had.

27. The Snowstorm Party

There is no next time. It's now or never.
—author unknown

On Saturday morning, it was still snowing. It looked like a fairyland, everything blanketed in snow.

Maria thought, *I'll get up and make lots of noise to wake Susie up so I can ask her about sliding this morning.* Maria began rattling around in her closet, looking for her heavy wool pants and high-topped snow boots.

After a few minutes, she heard Susie say, "What are you doing in there?"

"I'm getting ready to slide down some hills on my rump."

"Why? I can't think of anything that appeals to me less than that."

"Because it's fun. The last thing Bill said last night was to invite us to go sliding this morning down the hills around Lake Laverne."

"How do you propose we do this?"

"Bill is bringing metal trays from the kitchen—and a bunch of guys. He especially invited you to come."

"Ugh, I'm not the outdoor type."

"Susie, come on, it'll be fun. You might meet some nice guy over there."

"When are you going?"

"As soon as I hear from Bill. He said that he'd call me this morning."

Susie put her head under her pillow. "Go away."

Maria heard the phone ringing, and she knew it would be Bill. No other fellow dared to call so early. She ran to answer it. "Hi, handsome."

"How'd know it was me?" Bill laughed. "Are you ready?"

"Yes, I am, but I can't get Susie to get up and come."

"Tell her that Dick Bailey, our great president, wants to meet her. I was talking with him last night and told him that I had finally met my girl's roommate, Susie Dunnigan. He really sat up and took an interest in what I was saying. I'm sure he'll come if he knows she's going to be there."

"I'll give it another try. When shall we meet you?"

"In about another hour, don't you think? That will give us time for breakfast."

"Bill, as far as getting any other girls on this floor going, I think it's a lost cause."

"If you can bring Susie, Dick will think it's enough."

As she was walking back to their room, Maria wondered what Susie would say to her juicy tidbit about Dick. "Susie, wake up, I've got some interesting news for you."

Maria heard a muffled groan from under the pillow. "What news?"

"I'll tell you when you come out."

Susie peeked out at Maria. "All right, shoot." She threw the pillow at Maria.

"Dick Bailey wants to meet you."

"Who's he? I don't know anyone by that name."

"Well, he knows you from the meetings you go to."

"I go to lots of meetings."

"Bill said it has to do with sorority/fraternity council business."

"Oh, I remember him now. You mentioned that he asked about me when you talked to him at the house. I go to the meetings as a reporter for the school newspaper." Susie sat up in bed and seemed more interested. "I remember him vaguely. He is good looking."

"Not as handsome as Bill, but a close second. I've met him several times now." Susie was looking more happy than sleepy. She was obviously thinking about it. "Come on, girl," Maria pressed. "Get dressed in your warmest, oldest clothes. We've just enough time to eat and go."

Susie hopped up, rummaged around in her closet, and came out with some clothes that looked like they had seen better days. She said, "We're going to look like those creatures farmers put out in their fields to keep the birds away."

"You mean scarecrows? I know," Maria said, starting to laugh as they struggled into their pants, baggy sweaters, and heavy boots. They stuffed extra mittens in their coat pockets. By the time they had finished, they were hysterical, looking at themselves in their full-length mirror. "All we need are brooms," Maria said, which sent them off into gales of laughter again. "Let's go eat before anyone sees us."

"I can't stand wet hair outside in a snowstorm," Susie said. They wound their long hair up in knots and tucked the knots into their wool caps.

No one was in the dining hall. Good, no one around to laugh at them. They didn't want to get caught by any of the "smooth" girls who would have given them a critical once over. Maria thought, *Those gals miss out on the fun that goofy people like us have.* She had always been a tomboy, because she'd realized at an early age that boys were freer and had more fun. Following in their footsteps, she'd had some great adventures, even though the culture at the time didn't encourage young women to try things that were physically demanding and exciting.

After stuffing some toast and juice down, they decided they had had enough food. They scurried out the front door, looking like aliens from another planet, and literally slipped down the front steps that were piled high with snow. The sidewalk had been shoveled, but it was quickly covering up again because of the wind and the continually falling snow. There was an eerie silence when the wind died down and the snow kept softly falling. No cars were out on the highways, the snow muffled the normal noises, and silence prevailed.

They made the decision to leave the sidewalk and go overland, which made the trek much more difficult, but it was the only way to reach the hills behind Lake Laverne. They were soon puffing from exertion.

"I've had enough exercise just getting my clothes on and walking over these darned hills," Susie stated firmly. "I'm not sure this is fun anymore."

In the distance, they could hear the men yelling and having a wild time. When they got closer, they watched the guys sailing down the hills in various positions ranging from normal sitting up to lying on their stomachs to going down backward. One guy was even standing in a crouched position while flying down the hill.

"I wonder who that idiot is?" Susie asked.

"It's Bill," Maria admitted. "He must be practicing for the Olympic tray team competition." A loud cheer went up when he made it all the way down without falling. "It's pretty hard maneuvering a tray down that hill and staying upright," Maria said, defending him. She wondered what he would do with a pair of skis.

"Congratulations, tray-slide star," Maria said, panting, as they finally climbed to the top of the hill where he was standing.

"Who's in there?" he asked, peering into the fur and putting his face close to hers. "A visitor from Alaska or some other world? Identify yourself."

Susie and Maria laughed from sheer exhaustion after climbing through all the snow drifts and then up the hill. Maria fell backward into the snow and lay there, looking up at Bill who was laughing at their outfits and her antics. As she sat up, Maria saw Dick fast approaching with a bead on Susie, who was sitting in the snow and aimlessly making a few snow balls.

"Hi, gals," Dick said, looking very handsome, his hat in his hand.

Maria thought *he was willing to freeze his ears to impress Susie.* Bill sprang into action and introduced them to each other. Dick helped Susie to her feet and was smiling like the cat who ate the canary.

Maria could tell that Susie thought Dick was pretty cute from the way she was smiling back at him. *Put your hat back on, you silly guy, before your hair freezes from the snow and your sweat,* Maria scolded silently. Bill had his hat glued to his head and looked adorable and warm. Dick should do the same.

"Are you going to lie there in the snow until you freeze?" Bill asked Maria, leaning over her face, ready to give her a little nose kiss. "Now I know why the Eskimos don't kiss each other on the lips. They might freeze together." Bill pulled her up, acting like he was raising a sunken ship. "It must be all those heavy clothes full of snow that make you so heavy."

Once Maria was upright, she tried to whack him with her gloved hand, but he jumped back too fast. Bill had learned to watch his opponent on the wrestling mats in high school.

"Let's go and get some trays that are taped together, Dick, so we can take the girls down the first time. I'm sure Nanook will want to slide down on her own afterward. Right, my little Eskimo?"

As they settled themselves on the trays, side-by-side for Bill and Maria and one in front of the other for Susie and Dick, Bill said to Maria, "You look like you've done this before."

"Remember who raised me? We went sliding, sledding, and tobogganing from the time I was three. My dad said that he didn't want to raise his girls to be sissies." Looking down at frozen Lake Laverne, Maria thought, *We're higher than I'd realized. This should be fun.*

"Ready?" Bill asked.

Maria nodded and down they went after a push from one of the guys at the top of the hill. Maria laughed from the sheer excitement of it all. They ended up sliding partly across the lake on the ice, they were going so fast.

When they climbed back up, Maria saw Susie standing up, looking down the hill. Maria wondered if she had ever gone sliding or sledding. Susie looked really frightened. Dick was coaxing

Susie to sit back down on the tray. She gingerly sat down again and looked over at Maria. Susie made a slit-your-throat motion, wrapped her arms around Dick, and closed her eyes.

"Okay," she said, "I'm ready to die."

Maria watched them bounce down the hill, picking up so much speed that they flew across the ice even farther than she and Bill had. Maria watched Susie extricate herself from the tray, take Dick's hand, and trudge up the hill. When Susie got closer, Maria raised her arm in a salute; Susie gave Maria an ironic look and wiggled her nose at her.

Maria couldn't count the number of times they slid down those hills. They moved from one to another to get different rides. Bill was still practicing for the Olympic tray team by standing up and taking all kinds of chances: turning the tray one way and then another, going backward, trying to stand just on one leg, crouching down, holding his legs, and racing other guys down the hills. He looked so handsome with his cheeks getting pinker and pinker from the cold. He balanced so deftly on the trays, Maria didn't see him take a tumble all morning. As she stood watching him, she thought that he would make a great skier.

When Bill came back up the hill from a particularly good trip, Maria caught him before he went down again. "I'm getting tired. Why don't we take a break and go to the Union for something hot to drink."

"I'm sorry," Bill said. "I didn't realize how long we've been up here. Let's get Susie and Dick to come with us."

"They've already gone. Susie was all wet and wanted to dry out. They're probably there now. Just between you and me, I think we are seeing the beginning of a new friendship. Susie wouldn't stay around if she weren't interested." As they walked back, Maria said, "You're a natural at this stuff, you know. I watched you do things on those trays that were remarkable"

As always, Bill shrugged off her compliments, probably because he didn't consider sliding down a hill a remarkable feat. Maria figured that he was most likely only interested in things that took some real intelligence or made a difference. She knew that he liked the series of talks that he was doing because he was helping the farmers raise their productivity, but he wouldn't accept praise for that, either.

When they reached the Union, Bill looked around for Dick. He spotted Susie first, because of her red hair, and pointed them out to Maria. "Let's get something to drink and join them."

"Yum, yum. I could sure use some hot liquid running down my throat about now." Maria grinned with delight at being where it was warm and having her darling man beside her.

Bill put his arm around her. "You are so cute sometimes. I just want to kiss you for the pure joy of it."

Bill bought them some hot chocolate and took the tray over to Dick and Susie's table. "May we join you?" He set the mugs down on the table.

"It wouldn't do us any good if we didn't want you; you have already staked out your space," Dick said, grinning at them.

As Maria peeled off her wet gloves, undid her knot of hair, and opened her coat, she began to thaw out. Her boots were squishy and as she sat there, Maria could feel the water sloshing over her toes. She smiled and took a big sip of chocolate, scheming how she was going to get her mother to buy her some really good waterproof boots before she returned to Nanook Land after Christmas.

"You're very quiet, Maria," Dick said. "You usually are pretty bubbly, at least you are when you're at the house."

"Well you know how it is." She squished the water around in her boots. "I'm just tired, I guess." She was actually starving but didn't want to appear like a piggy, especially around Susie and Dick.

"What are your thoughts on sliding, Susie?" Dick asked, leaning across the table as if daring her to complain.

Susie has met her match with Dick, Maria thought. *She will be intrigued by him.*

"I may turn into an outdoor girl, yet, after today," Susie said. "It all depends on who plans on teaching me the ropes. I don't want any novice; I need the best." She leaned across the table right back at him with a smile on her face.

Maria poked Bill under the table at their interesting exchange. Bill looked at Maria and grinned.

Maria was wet and getting hungrier. "Let's go home, Susie. We need to change before lunch, although I doubt it will be much except sandwiches. I'll bet the cook can't make it in to the school the way the roads are."

"Speaking of food," Dick said, "what do you gals think about coming over to our house for a light dinner later today? We'll think of something to eat. I know our cook won't get to the campus. He lives twenty miles away."

"It's nice that we are privy to the decisions that the president can make just because he is the president," Susie said, with a wicked grin on her face.

"I try to treat my subjects with fairness and honesty. What say you? We might have another snow activity. I heard the guys talking about building a couple of snow forts and having a snowball 'fight to the finish.' Bill and I are going to decide the rules of war when we get home, right, vice president? Come over anytime after two and bring more young ladies with you if you can."

Maria was amazed to hear that Bill was the vice president of his house. When did that happen? He had never once mentioned anything about it to her. He was such a cool character. "We'll see what we can do as far as bringing some girls with us," Maria said.

"Maybe I can persuade some of the Chi O pledges and actives to stop by your house for an impromptu party. They're the best kind of parties," Susie said.

The snow was still coming down lightly when Maria and Susie trudged back to the dorm. "I'm so ready for a shower and some lunch. Aren't you, Susie?"

"Am I ever. It was fun in the Union with those two nuts, but I can't wait to strip off all my wet clothes. You know, today was more fun than I'd expected, and I kind of liked Dick, at least enough to go to his frat house and find out a little more about him. If he is going to be a farmer, though, I'm through. I love what farmers do for America, but I don't have a farming background, and I would be miserable as a farmer's wife.

"I'll call a few people at the Chi O House, and I'll try some of the pledges that live in Stevens Dorm. Chi Omega will have the best representation if I can convince them to come."

"I'll help you make calls after I have a shower and lunch. My brain doesn't work too well on an empty stomach. Bill told me that Dick just broke up with his girl. Maybe you were fated to be with him."

Susie said, "I don't know about fate, but I'm keeping an open mind."

By two, it was still snowing lightly. The housemother had told everyone at lunch that the Iowa state police had issued a warning that no one was to be on the roads unless it was an emergency. The girls had been successful in gathering a few gals from the dorm to go to the party, including their dorm mates across the hall who had a couple of dancing partners at the Farm House. Susie had called the Chi O House and invited everyone there to come. Several actives from the Chi O House sounded interested, simply because it would be something different for them to do on a snowy afternoon.

It was nice to have dry, warm clothing to wear over to the Farm House party. Maria felt good after getting cleaned up, having lunch, and relaxing a little. She had found it fun helping Susie make calls. Maria liked most people and enjoyed talking on the phone.

Trouping over in a group, the Stevens Dorm contingent arrived at the Farm House, eager to see what the fraternity men were like. They were greeted by loud shouts, much yelling, and wild activity outside the house. The men were having a snowball, take-no-prisoners war in the backyard. They had built two huge snow forts and were pelting each other with deadly, hard-packed snowballs. Thank goodness, the fight wasn't in the front yard. It would not have been worth their lives to walk up to the front door.

As the girls entered, a couple of fellows ran by, said "Hello," and ran out to join the fight again. Inside, the frat was a madhouse; guys were coming and going, getting dry gloves and hanging wet ones up by the fire on a rack. It looked like there were fifty pairs of gloves and mittens on that rack. Maria heard someone say to watch out for Bill Morgan, he had a rifle for an arm and deadly aim. Maria smiled when she heard that and imagined how much fun he must be having.

All the gals sat down on a long sofa in front of the large, beautiful fireplace in the front room and began toasting their bodies and feet. The fire was hypnotic. A couple of cute pledges came over and asked if they wanted anything to drink. Maria was sure their ulterior motive was to see if any of them were date material.

Full from lunch, most of the girls just wanted to sit and observe the sea of activity and energy all around them. More men started drifting over to the large group of gals sitting in their living room, like bees to honey. Soon, all kinds of conversations were springing up. The guys had pulled up chairs and were asking the girls where they lived, what they were studying, and anything else they could think of to engage the girls. Maria chuckled to herself, observing the interest and enjoyment that the afternoon snow party had engendered.

Susie nodded. "I like the feeling of this house. Everyone seems friendlier than at the Greek fraternities."

"I've never been to another frat house, so I have no comparisons. I just like it here," Maria replied.

Suddenly, it was quiet outside, and Maria could hear a lot of stomping. The doors burst open and lots of wet men came streaming into the house and wandering off to their rooms, no doubt to dry off and clean up.

"The war must be over, and either one side killed the other or a truce was signed," Susie observed. "Here come the knights themselves." Susie called out, "Over here, by the fire. Come see us."

Bill and Dick had walked in, soaked, happy, and laughing like fools. *They are very good friends*, Maria thought.

When Dick heard Susie's voice, he looked up and yelled back, "We're coming." Both men became more subdued as they walked across the room.

Maria asked, "Where are those wild men who were here a minute ago? Have you already shifted into dating gear?"

The guys turned their backs to the warmth of the fire and faced the girls. Water was dripping off their clothes. "Have you been here long?" Dick asked, gingerly pulling off his wet gloves and trying to look smooth with water pooling at his feet.

"Go get dried off before you freeze—and soak us," Susie said to Dick.

"Me too?" Bill asked, pulling his gloves off and flicking the water from them at Maria.

She got quite a face full, was surprised and laughed. Maria couldn't help it. She loved his spirit when he was provoked. "You're going to get in a lot of trouble," Maria said, trying to control her giggling and wiping off her face.

"If you are included in the deal, I hope so," Bill said. "I'll see you in a few minutes."

Off they went, shoving each other to see who could get through the door first.

"You're tough, Susie, but Dick seems to love it. I think he's very interested in you and your personality."

Sounding slightly upset, Susie said emphatically, "I don't care if I sound tough. I've decided to change my behavior pattern around guys. I have been operating in a high school sweetheart pattern, and it doesn't work. It's time I grew up. I'm looking for someone who is mature enough that he doesn't have to be idolized all the time to keep him happy. I spoiled Chuck, and what did it get me?"

Susie jolted Maria into questioning her own attitude around both Bill and Ed. With Bill, she felt that he was just as committed to her as she was to him, except for the fact he hadn't even mentioned a pinning party for her. He did encourage her to be herself and seemed to believe in some measure of equality between them. His parents had been good examples.

With Ed, she had been out of that high school crush stage ever since Thanksgiving and Thursday night. Her decision to stop playing around with him unless he had something more permanent to offer had put them on an even more adult footing.

The place was filling up with young women from the dorms and sororities. Susie recognized a couple of Chi O actives walking in. She got up and brought them over to Maria, making introductions all around. Ginny was a junior, blond, tall, skinny and had a great sense of humor, which was evidenced by the funny comments she was making about guys in the house. Rachel was her roommate and also a junior. She was very pretty and appeared to be Ginny's "straight man." Maria saw a few guys watching Rachel with interest.

Bill and Dick came bounding back into the room, looking and smelling good. They were all hopped up and ready for a party. *Those guys are filled with energy. They must have a tank of it in the back room that they tapped when they needed to,* Maria decided.

Dick, ever the president, said in a booming voice, "Welcome to Farm House," and waited. This was the same trick Bill used when he wanted other people to say something. Susie took the opportunity to introduce the Chi O gals. Dick looked at some of his men standing nearby and gave them a "come over here look," so they did. He asked them to rearrange the furniture so the girls would be comfortable. More chairs were brought in so that Ginny and Rachel could sit down and the guys could join them.

Maria heard chairs and tables being moved in the dining room area, then the music started up. The music altered the general mood, and thoughts of romance began to seep into everyone's minds. Maria was glad that even more gals were showing up and mixing with the guys. Everyone was looking at each other and the pairing began. Couples started dancing in the dining room. Bill looked at her, and she was a goner.

As he started to dance with her, Bill whispered in her hair, "God, it feels so good to hold you again." He had both arms around her, one at her shoulders and the other around her waist, holding her close.

"Is it possible to dance this way?" Maria asked, her eyes sparkling.

"Just watch." He leaned down and gave her a little kiss.

They danced for quite a while as close as possible, but Maria knew that she needed to save some energy for the dinner preparations later on. "Hey, handsome," she said, "let's sit the next one out."

Bill led her into the study, which was much more intimate than the big living room. There were several other couples in there, embracing and kissing gently. Maria and Bill sat down in a corner on a small sofa. Looking at her with those soulful eyes, he said, "Well, I don't think we'll be able to spend tonight together the way we had planned because of the storm."

"What's your talk schedule for next week? Maybe we can connect some way." She laughed at her intentional pun.

"No talks next week, but I've got a killer exam schedule. Then the following week, right before the end of term, if you can believe it, I've got to go to Mason City on Tuesday, so I'll need Monday evening to prepare for that, then on to Waterloo on Thursday. Also, my professor informed me on Friday that I need to bring everyone up to date on the success of the talks, so he scheduled a meeting with the dean and the Board of Regents for Wednesday evening. If they give me the go ahead, I need to submit a description of my talks to the school newspaper before the holiday. There isn't a free evening for us to get away because of my infernal schedule."

Maria said, "We may have to let our plans go until we come back after Christmas vacation."

Bill's face fell when she said that. "Yeah, but I hope I can spend at least a little time with you here before you leave. It's just that I'm really going to miss our motel rendezvous."

"Just remember the Berkmar when you feel lonely. We'll be together again that way in January," Maria said, looking at him with sad eyes.

She saw his face take on a determined look. Things were going around in that head of his. He seemed to come to some conclusion and looked at her with an adorable smile. He slipped his arms around her, put his face in her hair, and began to breathe a little faster than normal. His cheek rubbed against the side of her face, and he put his lips on hers and kissed her into next week. By the time they pulled apart, sex had reared its head again. Maria was sure that the whole room had been watching them, but when she looked around, no one had even noticed they were there. They were all very interested in their own dates.

Bill whispered that he loved her so much, and she could feel how fast he was breathing. Maria gave him a little kiss and put her hand up to his face, touching his soft, shaved skin. They hugged each other on the sofa until Maria said, "Should you go find Dick and decide about supper?" She took his hand. "Come on, I know you must be getting hungry because I am. Let's get this show on the road."

They went looking for Dick and Susie and found them curled up in front of the fire in the living room. They were having an animated conversation, waving their hands about. Susie must have said something very funny, because Dick was laughing hard.

Bill and Maria sat down on the sofa with them, and Maria asked if they were getting hungry. They paid no attention to her. Maria waited.

Dick finally looked at her and realized she had asked them a question. He said, "We may be on our own tonight. I'll go and investigate."

He went to the phone and called someone, probably the house's cook, and came back after a short conversation. "Could you gals help us out? I'll get the guys to do whatever you want. Our cook can't get here. The storm has paralyzed most of the state. Mother Nature is beginning to let everyone know who is boss."

Susie said, "I'll go find Ginny and Rachel to help out. Ginny is a cooking major. She's hoping to run her own restaurant someday and should be able to put this thing together."

When Susie brought Ginny and Rachel into the kitchen, Maria was just standing there, looking at the huge kitchen and wondering how to start the project.

Ginny, wailing a little, asked, "Where is my teacher when I need her."

The way she said it made everyone laugh and feel better. Someone was in charge—sort of.

In came Dick and Bill with a group of actives, all laughing and joking. "Okay, men, listen up," Dick said. "The gals are in charge, and you will need to follow directions. Do any of you know how to cook?" There was dead silence.

Bill went to the storeroom and returned with as many loaves of bread as he could carry. He said, "There are about fifty actives, ten pledges, and maybe twenty gals here. That's about eighty people we need to feed." He picked out a fellow standing near him. "John, go out and make an accurate head count. Let everyone know that we're going to feed this unruly mob and ask for help."

As Maria listened to him, she knew why he was the vice president.

"Now, gals, what do you want to tackle?" Bill asked and looked at Maria.

She shrugged and turned to Ginny, hoping she would save the day with some bright idea.

As quick as you please, Ginny offered, "Spaghetti and meatballs."

A big cheer went up from the guys, who were fearing it would just be sandwiches.

"Okay, Ginny, I admire your courage. Tell us what you need, and we'll supply the manpower," Dick said.

As Ginny was writing out a list of ingredients she needed from the storeroom and the huge refrigerators, Maria offered to make enough salad for everyone. Susie said that she knew how to make garlic bread, and Rachel offered to make chocolate cake for dessert. Bill and Dick organized the guys into groups to work with each of them. John came back and announced that there were eighty-five people for dinner.

Maria wondered if they could really feed that many people. She felt a little panicked.

Ginny put her fingers in her mouth and gave a piercing whistle. Everyone stopped dead in their tracks. She insisted, "Before anyone touches the food, wash your hands well. Salad makers, you must wash all the lettuce and fresh vegetables carefully. If you have questions, please submit them to your advisors."

Everyone looked at each other. Someone asked, "What advisors?"

Ginny said, "I'm only kidding. I wanted to see if you were listening to me."

Maria had five very willing guys ready to chop, mince, or grate anything she gave them. As the crews swung into action, Maria marveled at what a blanket of snow could produce from fun loving, young bodies. Because of the high energy levels of college kids, it was amazing how quickly and easily events took place in a college setting. All it took was a combination of brains, ingenuity, and ability.

Soon the sauce was bubbling, the meatballs were sizzling in a huge pan, and the salad veggies had been prepared. Maria had been delighted to find so many heads of lettuce tucked away in the refrigerators, plus carrots, cucumbers, and tomatoes. The house's cook was a good manager. The smell of Susie's garlic bread permeated the kitchen, and Rachel was ready to pour the contents of a huge mixing bowl into the sheet-cake pans. What an amazing team they all were.

Bill and Dick strolled in and out of the kitchen more than necessary. They seemed unable to wait for dinner. Their appetites were being stimulated by the delicious smell of spaghetti sauce drifting into the other rooms of the house. Other hungry men peeked in to check the progress of the dinner. Ginny shooed them out with comments about not being fed if they bothered the cooks, making them retreat quickly.

Someone put candles on the tables and set the places for eighty-five people. The romantic music was left playing, and everyone waited for word from the kitchen that the food was ready. About a half hour later, Ginny produced another piercing whistle. There was dead silence again.

"Put the food on the tables and let's eat," she ordered. She supervised the pasta, meatballs, and sauce being ladled on the plates for the volunteer waiters to serve. They also brought out the bread, putting two big baskets of it on every table. The salad crew carried out big bowls of salad, and dinner was ready. The cooks and their helpers were last to be seated. Everyone quieted down, waiting for their president to say something.

Dick looked at Bill. "Let's give a cheer for the kitchen crews, especially Ginny, Maria, Susie, and Rachel." The place exploded in loud cheers. Dick said, "Thank you, ladies, for your hard work and great talent." The place erupted again.

Ginny stood up and whistled her now famous whistle. Everyone was quiet. Maria thought she was going to say thank you or something like that, but she didn't. Ginny said, "Stop cheering and start eating, or it will get cold." Everyone laughed and ate like it was their last meal. All that energy that they expended today playing needed to be replenished.

Bill asked Maria if she was tired. She didn't want to give him a guilt trip. "Of course not," she lied, but really she was exhausted.

After dinner, Dick issued orders to the clean-up crew, turned to Susie, and said something to her. They got up and began getting ready to walk outside, probably to the dorm because it was getting near curfew time. Everyone was pulling on jackets, hats, and gloves.

Bill and Maria looked at each other. Maria said, "We had better go, too," and gave him a little smile. As they were walking back to the dorm, she said, "Who'd ever think a snowstorm would generate so much fun?"

"The whole day and evening were a little out of the ordinary. I think the guys were getting revved up for Christmas vacation. They were really more cooperative than usual. I know having all the girls come over made a huge difference in their behavior. They can act like animals, sometimes, but that's normal for guys."

"I loved having you there helping Dick keep things going in the kitchen. Susie was great, too. It's funny how things work out, almost like they were planned." Maria paused. "I know that I was supposed to meet you."

Bill said, "I don't know if it was planned, but I do know you have changed my life."

When they stopped at the bottom of the stairs, Bill said, "Well, Nanook, I'll have to add another name to your growing list of nicknames: Salad Chef. The one I like the most, though, is Passion Flower."

Maria loved the way he used nicknames for her. It made her feel so special, each nickname a different part of her.

"What's your plan for tomorrow?" Bill asked. "I'm sure you're studying for all the tests the professors are cramming into the last couple of weeks, but I was wondering . . ." He had his arms around her and was looking at her intently. Sex took preference over everything else when one was a young male.

Maria thought, *I'd climb Mt. Everest, if he asked me.* She smiled at him. "What do you have in mind?"

Those words triggered a big response. He swept her up close to him. "I'll figure that out, don't worry. I could pick you up around four tomorrow afternoon." He brushed his lips around her face and kissed her gently. "What do you think?""

She could tell that Bill had been thinking about this for a while. "I bet I know when you decided this—in the study today. You had a look that told me you would figure something out when it came to sex. Am I right?"

Bill grinned. "You're really getting to know me. Leave the details to me. What do you say?"

"I'm ready for another adventure with you tomorrow at four. I'll be waiting." She left him standing there, watching her climb the stairs. When she turned at the top, a funny feeling floated through her body as she blew him a kiss and he returned it.

Walking down the hall to her room, she shivered a little and took a deep breath. When Maria entered the room, she was ready to get an update on Susie's life as it pertained to Dick. Susie was gathering her shower essentials and stopped. Maria looked at her and grinned.

"What's the grin for?" Susie asked. "You look like you just ate the canary. Okay, I admit I think Dick is nice; in fact, he's very nice. Add to that: I'm interested."

"Go take your shower and think about this while you're in there: We'll have a lot of power in the fraternity world. We're dating the president and vice president of Farm House."

"I'll have to think about what we can do with our newfound influence," Susie said over her shoulder as she walked out of the room.

Maria sat down at her desk to think. With all this fun she had been having, her course work was piling up by the minute. It might fall over and suffocate her if she didn't settle down and get it under control. Her college work was ruining her social life. She was glad that her dad couldn't see her now.

She began an evening of earnest effort, and it was amazing how much one could do when one concentrated. It was so simple. She felt she could make it for a couple of hours more if she took a shower. When she finally fell into bed like a lump, she had skimmed everything. Before she closed her eyes, she looked at Susie, who had been asleep for an hour or so. *Gosh,* she thought, *I wish I had Susie's brains.*

Surprisingly, they didn't sleep late Sunday morning and were mostly awake by seven thirty. The sun was streaming in their windows, making everything look so clear. Maria decided on another shower. The water felt good and woke her up. She also washed her hair to get rid of all the dried sweat from yesterday's exertions. Yesterday was wild fun sliding down the hills, but today was different. She gave herself a pep talk in the shower. It was time to get going. She had lots to do before she would be ready for classes that week.

Susie was sitting up in bed, looking all fuzzy, when Maria got back. "Ready to eat," Susie croaked, trying to wake herself by sticking her feet in the air and doing leg bicycles.

Susie would be another half an hour before she was ready to eat, Maria decided. Maria dressed quickly, brushed her hair, and sat down at her desk. She skimmed over some more material while waiting for Susie. By the time Susie came back from the showers, Maria had covered over a hundred review pages for her history test. She only had another hundred to reread and remember.

"Okay, I'm ready," Maria said, as she snapped her book shut. She stood up, grabbed her coat, and waited.

"You must be very hungry this morning. You have a no-nonsense air about you. I feel like I need to salute you or something," Susie said and saluted.

"I'm all energized this morning. I think it was all the fun we had yesterday and last night."

"Last night was a nightmare, trying to feed all those people," Susie cried. "What do you mean 'fun'? If I ever see another piece of garlic bread, I may throw up."

"All right, it got a little tense trying to get everything done at the same time, but everyone helped, and they certainly appreciated our efforts. To change the subject, sometime today I want your appraisal of your new friend. Did you find out where he was from and what he plans to do with his life?"

"Yes to your prying questions, which I will endeavor to answer more fully after I've had some food. Come on, Miss Nosy, let's eat." With that, Susie left the room and started running down the hall.

Maria finally caught up to her at the dining hall. "What was that all about? Why did you run away?"

"I was tired of your questions and wanted to stop any more of them until I was properly nourished."

"I can just hear your conversations with Dick. He'll be saying 'Huh?' all the time when he can't decipher your language."

"Anybody who can't understand me doesn't deserve to date me," Susie said, picking up a sweet roll from the buffet.

Maria couldn't stop laughing. Susie was continually entertaining her with the words she used and the way she said them. She was such a comedian, but Maria bet that Susie would be surprised if she heard anyone call her that.

When they got back to the room, full and ready for the day, someone told Susie that she had a call. Maria thought, *That's Dick calling her to make some plans for the day or evening.* Maria was so happy for Susie. She had been watching Maria flit in and out of the dorm for weeks, while she despaired about Chuck and worked on her school projects. Now it was Susie's turn. Maria raised her eyebrows at Susie as she waltzed out the door to the phone.

Maria's work was waiting for her on her desk and she waded into a big lab report that counted heavily for her lab grade this semester. *It's amazing,* she said to herself, *how clear everything is in the morning and how difficult it is to understand in the evening.*

She had a eureka moment while looking over her math notes. Now she could finish that darn report and get onto a huge English paper that she had to write on Edgar Allen Poe. She was busily talking to herself about the report and how happy she was that it was falling into place when Susie walked back into the room looking very pleased with herself.

"Guess what? Dick and I are going to a special meeting of the fraternities on campus that was cancelled yesterday because of the storm. He has to help decide how to write the new bylaws that the school wants the fraternities to enact, and I am going to report on the meeting for our paper. Then we're going out for dinner. He won't tell me where. It's a big surprise. Anything we do after that is *my* business. And what are you and Bill hatching up, or did you already do it last night?"

"He's picking me up at four, and that's all I know. He's handling all the details. By the way, Bill won't be able to make my gyno appointment. He'll be out of town. Would you come with me?"

"I'm glad to come, but I won't be able to hold your hand. I'll be in the waiting room."

"Thanks, Susie. I really appreciate your support. Now back to my question of the day. What did you find out about Dick's background?"

Susie threw a pillow at Maria's head. "I won't get any peace until I answer your questions, so here goes. Dick lives in Omaha, Nebraska, and came to Iowa State to study coffee beans, among other things. His grandfather started a business importing coffee from Central and South America. His father runs the business now and wants Dick to join him after he gets out of school. They have traveled extensively to the countries that grow coffee beans."

"Why did he come to Iowa State and not go to a school in Nebraska?"

"I asked him that, and he said he believed that Iowa State had the best agricultural program in the Midwest and wanted to go where he could learn the most about beans."

"So are you happy you gave him a chance?" Maria asked, waiting for a another pillow to come sailing across the room.

"Yes, smarty, I am, and now I've got to do a little preliminary work for the meeting today and a little studying, although I resist the thought."

They both settled in for some serious work over the next several hours. Around twelve thirty, Maria threw her pillow at Susie and asked her if she wanted to eat something before the dining hall closed.

"Yes, let's get something, because it will be a long time until dinner, which will be good and a welcome change from Sunday-night sandwiches."

After lunch, Maria closed her eyes on her bed for a little while. All that physical activity on Saturday was catching up to her. When she woke up, it was after two. Maria couldn't believe it. She had stayed up too late last night, but she couldn't help it. She had been all hopped up from the excitement of the day and wasn't sleepy. She had gotten her second wind, so she had studied. Today she was paying the price.

Susie wasn't in the room. Maria went to the bathroom and splashed water on her face to wake herself up. When she came back to the room, Susie was getting ready for her big date. She looked nice and smelled good, too. "What perfume do you have on?" Maria asked.

"Yours. Don't you recognize it? Chuck didn't like perfume, but I think Dick does, because he mentioned how nice my hair smelled last night."

"So you were wearing my perfume last night, too? And he liked your nice-smelling hair, did he? Very interesting. Any other tidbits you want to tell me?"

"No, and anyway it's time for him to pick me up, so I'm going out to the front room to wait for him."

"Whose car is he driving?"

"He's driving his own. He has it stashed in the fraternity parking lot and is allowed to drive it on campus today because of the big meeting. During the week, he can't, unless he starts doing business for the school like Bill does."

"Have fun and enjoy. I'll see you tonight after curfew."

"Thanks, you too, and remember, don't get pregnant."

"Is your relationship ready for the same advice?"

Susie picked up her pillow and as she ran out the door, she heaved it at Maria.

A while later, Maria put the finishing touches on her lab report, smiled at it, and said to herself, *Magnificent.* She started reviewing her history assignment again, but was having trouble focusing on the text. Tired of studying, she shut her book. Besides, it was time to get ready for Bill. She changed into her favorite fuzzy, salmon-colored cashmere turtleneck sweater and black, lined wool pants. Pausing in front of the mirror, she surveyed her outfit and pronounced it perfect; the salmon color looked really good on her. *Hmm,* she thought, *maybe I can get my mother to buy me another cashmere sweater.* It all depended on how guilty her mother felt about their past life together.

28. One More Time

The only true gift is a portion of yourself.
—Ralph Waldo Emerson

It was almost four o'clock. Maria decided to get out of the room before the walls squeezed in on her. She put on her arctic gear and assessed how she looked in the mirror before she went out. She thought, *Maria Banks, you are as ready as you'll ever be for your last love interlude with Bill before Christmas vacation.* As she swung into the front room, she saw Bill waiting there, which delighted and surprised her. "Were you as sick of working as I was?" she asked, as she hooked her arm into his.

"Yes, I know the feeling. I also couldn't stop thinking about our destination," Bill said quietly, looking around the room. As they made their way down the steps, he said, "All afternoon, I kept checking the time. I was ready to pop about an hour ago and had to come over a little early to see if you were ready, too. I was just going to ask someone to go find you when you came through the door."

The car was nice and warm and felt good. Bill leaned over and gave her a nose kiss. He said, "I don't want to mess up your makeup."

Maria said, "I'll wipe it off before we get to the motel. I just wanted to look good coming through the doors, for a change."

"You always look good." He turned to look at her with those sexy, big blue eyes of his, and Maria knew the testosterone was pumping through his veins.

Maria felt herself start to get all goose bumpy. There was more than enough lust pulsing between them. "So what do you have in mind when we get to the motel?" she asked, her eyes big and wide. She loved teasing the heck out of him.

"You are a little dickens, and I love you in spite of it." He grinned at her and pulled her closer to him.

She turned on the radio and found some romantic music. Sitting next to Bill, she heard his breathing move up a notch. "Did you get lots done today?" she asked, trying to take her mind off their afternoon interlude.

"Actually, I have things all set for my talks next week, which is mainly what I wanted to do today." He didn't add anything more, but Maria surmised he was thinking about their very special date that afternoon.

"I'm all set for tomorrow and hopefully for Tuesday, too." As she was speaking, Bill pulled up to their agreed-upon motel.

It looked quite pretty with the snow piled up outside the building. There were little lights on, producing a glow over the snow. Bill got out, went in, and came back out holding their key and grinning at her. They drove around the corner to a set of rooms away from the main section. He grabbed a bag, ran around the car, and opened her door. "Your castle awaits you, my princess." Once they were inside, Bill locked the door with the safety bolt. "We don't want any surprises."

Maria quickly checked the cleanliness of the place. Bill was watching her, waiting for her nod of approval. She sidled up to him. "Good work, handsome."

Bill threw the coats on a chair, picked her up in his arms, and carried her over to the sofa. They sat down, Bill holding Maria in his lap. He put his face in her hair. "You smell so good, it's hard for me to concentrate on what I want to say to you."

So what was Bill up to with this different behavior? She had wiped off her lipstick in case he was going to kiss her, but he didn't. He looked at her with those blue, inviting eyes.

Maria said, "Listen, you'd better spit it out before I pop. Are you going to ask me to do something kinky? I'm not sure that I want you to do something too different from what we've been doing. I reserve the right to say no, okay?"

"Absolutely. You are my darling, and I wouldn't do anything that you didn't want. I love you too much and would never hurt you in any way."

"Come on, you big lug, let's use up some of that money you've invested in this evening."

They stood and he looked at her. "You have the most beautiful body. Every time I see you naked, I can't believe that you love me enough to let me make love to you."

"Listen, honey, this not just a one way street. Your body is very sexy to me, too. In case you haven't noticed, I get as much out of our lovemaking as you do. Your muscles, that strong physique of yours, turn me on." She couldn't resist caressing his back and butt. "I love everything about you."

"Okay, now for your surprise," Bill said.

"You're sure I'm going to like this? No unexpected sexual activities?"

"None, I promise. Come on, let's get naked and into bed. You lie on your stomach with your head flat on the bed, no pillows." He turned the heat up high so that they wouldn't get cold and took a bottle of oil out of his bag. He straddled her on his knees so that he wouldn't mash her, poured a few drops of oil on his hands, and began massaging her from the top of her back all the way down to the bottom of her feet—all the while, commenting on every area: her smooth skin, her cute butt, her strong legs, her little feet and even tinier toes.

"What kind of oil is that? I love the scent."

"The label says lavender oil. I can't get over how tiny your toes are."

"You make me feel so relaxed and also very sexy, but don't use up all your energy." Maria thought, *If a gal was nervous about making love with a guy, he should massage her like this first.* When Bill turned her over, she said, "We could open up a massage parlor, with services rendered afterward."

He grinned and whispered, "You take my breath way." He put a few more drops of oil on his hands and began rubbing her breasts, but that was suddenly the end of the massage. He got up, baby proofed himself, and was breathing pretty hard when he came back to bed.

She took his face in her hands kissed his lips. "You did a wonderful job. No more preliminaries. Let's go." She was sufficiently worked up from his exquisite massage, and Maria opened her arms to him.

They spent a frenzied few minutes connecting physically and emotionally. Bill began murmuring, "We're almost there," as he built the explosion of feeling between them. When at last those incredible few moments came, they felt the ecstasy and then the sought-after release. Bill stopped and rolled over on his side. They were breathing hard and hugging each other.

Maria whispered, "Oh my God, Bill. This was the best."

He didn't respond; he just held her tightly in his arms until they stopped trembling. He pulled the blankets over them, tucking them carefully around her, and lay there with her in his arms.

She began to wriggle around, and he asked, "What's the matter? Is anything hurting?"

"No, I'm thirsty. Let me up, and I'll get us some water, my big love machine." Maria jumped out of bed, looked at her wild hair in the mirror as she filled two glasses, and laughed. "Your wild woman from Borneo has brought you water, master." She gulped down a glassful. "Ah, that's better." Smacking her lips, she said, "I want to tell you about something. Today when I was studying for my big history test next week, I came upon a statement that Plato made about playing. He said that a person learns more about another person when playing with them for an hour than engaging them in conversation for a year. What do you think of that after our day in the snow yesterday and your massage for me today?"

Bill was quiet for a minute or two, then he said, "When I saw you coming up that hill, your cheeks red with the cold, your big brown eyes flashing, I said to myself, 'How could I have been so lucky to find a gal who loves to play like you do?' I loved you so much when I watched you flying down the hills, never complaining, just laughing and having so much fun. Plato was right. I must read more about him. He was a philosopher from Greece, right?"

"Yes, he was a famous philosopher. Now, to change the subject, I have a question for you." Maria sat up in bed and looked at Bill's face, smiling up at her. "I'm dying to know where you learned to do a massage like that. Who taught you? And did she help you with your lovemaking technique?" Maria paused and leaned close to his face. "You seem to know when I'm ready to go. How do you do that? You make me crazy for more."

By this time, Bill was actually laughing.

"I don't need to know names or dates," she said. "I just can't believe the techniques you use to bring me along so that I have such sexual satisfaction. Is there anything you can tell me without incriminating someone or divulging something that you want to keep private? When you massaged me tonight, I couldn't believe how wonderful it was. Even the lavender oil was delightful. Stop laughing and tell me!" She bounced him against the bed.

"Okay, okay. I've wanted to share my story with you for a long time. I had to wait until we knew each other better, sexually, to talk about this, because I was afraid that you might think badly of me. Don't judge me, you asked for it. Chalk it up to being a horny teenager.

"When I was just a kid, about seventeen, I was on a baseball team in a summer league near my home. One night, after a practice or a game, everyone had gone home. I was hungry, so I went to our local diner before I went home. I was driving my dad's old car, and thought I was really hot stuff, having my driver's license. Although I had been driving tractors on the farm for two or three years, this was the first time I could actually go out on the public roads.

"The cafe was pretty quiet. I sat at the counter and ordered something. The gal who was working there as a waitress was new to me. When she put the plate in front of me, she looked at me and said, 'Enjoy.' There was something in her voice that made my pulse rise. She was funny, too, as I remember. I was intrigued by this older woman who was flirting with me. Maybe she thought I was older than I was, but for whatever reason, she hung around me while I was eating, talking and laughing. I hoped that something might happen between us. I was your usual, horny farm boy, with all my hormones pumping. It didn't take much to set them off.

"When I finished, she said that it was time to close up and wondered if I could give her a ride home. I thought, 'Bill Morgan, you may have just walked into an opportunity.' I said that I would be happy to take her home, thinking I might be able to give her a few kisses if I were lucky. She hopped in my old clunker and off we went to her house, which was only about a block from the diner.

"She pointed out her little house, and when we stopped, she asked me if I would like to come in for a cold drink. I thought, 'Bill Morgan, you may really score tonight.' I didn't have any condoms with me because I'd never thought I would be so lucky in a million years. When I walked into her house with her, I was getting aroused. I couldn't help it. She took my hand, and we walked into her bedroom. She had a fragrance that permeated her bedroom. While she was in the bathroom, she told me through the door to take off my clothes, get into bed, and she'd be out in a minute. I didn't know how to ask her about protection, but she had read my mind, because she came out of the bathroom stark naked and said not to worry about a condom, she had her diaphragm in place. Then she gave me my first lesson on how to make love to a woman. Over the summer, I had many more lessons. I dreamed about her when I wasn't with her and couldn't get her out of my mind.

"I thought I loved her, but she said it was gratefulness, not love.

Over time, I realized that she was right. It was just horny lust. My friends never found out why I was so happy all summer, but they sure were suspicious."

"What happened to her?" Maria asked.

"She met a real nice guy whose wife had died from a heart attack. They got married the following year and started a family. He's a good farmer and has made a good marriage with her. I see them occasionally in town. We always smile at each other, keeping our little secret safe between us.

"So now you know where I learned all I know about making love and massaging with lavender oil. The bottle I used today is all I have that was hers. She was lonely, and I hope I filled a place in her life. She certainly taught me to grow up sexually. I remember one thing that she told me over and over that summer: If both partners aren't sexually satisfied, the relationship won't last. A women's arousal rate is much slower than a man's, and it is up to the man, if he wants her to have a satisfying experience with him, to help her become aroused. Needless to say, her lessons taught me about loving a woman properly. I thank her to this day for showing me how to be a good lover."

Maria felt tears welling up in her eyes. The story was so poignant and sweet, and she respected him more than she thought possible. His quality as a man and how he valued women really showed, and now she knew why. How she loved him at that moment.

He held her in his arms and nuzzled her neck. "So now you know a big secret about me."

"Bill Morgan, you are my kind of guy. I love you and your story. I think I'll keep you." She kissed his nose.

After a few moments, Bill asked, "Are you hungry? I am. Making love gives me an appetite."

Maria had been engrossed by his story and had lost track of time. "What time is it? I'm not too hungry, but I'm happy to go."

Bill looked at his watch. "It's six thirty. We've been here for a couple of hours. I can't believe it."

"When you're in the magical kingdom, time has a way of disappearing."

"Let's rinse off before we go. You go in first, and that way, I won't drown you."

Maria took a towel, stepped into the shower, cleaned up, and stepped out, all in a matter of minutes. She was careful not to wash off too much of the lavender oil. Rubbing herself dry, she watched Bill step into the shower and step out after a quick rinse. He was fast, and she loved looking at his beautiful muscles.

They struggled into all their warm clothes, looked around to make sure they hadn't left anything behind, and walked out to the car with their arms around each other, still not quite back in the land of reality.

Maria poked Bill when they were in the car, and he looked at her. She asked, "Can you drive, magical prince?"

He chuckled a little and said that he was sobering up, so to speak. He backed around the snow piles and pulled out on the highway back to Ames. "I know a little diner that has been there for years down the road a piece."

"'Down the road a piece,' huh? You sound like a down-home farmer."

"Yep, I knowed where it is." He grinned.

"You are such a tease, you know." She put her hand up to his face and rubbed his cheek with the tips of her fingers. Maria loved touching him.

In a few minutes, Bill said, "There's the Iowa Diner. Their name certainly is original, isn't it?"

After being so sure that she wasn't hungry, Maria was fast becoming a liar. Walking in there and smelling meatloaf made her mouth water. They sat down across from each other in a rather tired-looking booth. It was covered with crude artistic carvings made by many bored teenagers with pen knives. Coming down from the high generated by their successful sexual interlude, they just sat there, holding hands and smiling at each other.

"Do you feel like me, relaxed and hungry?" Bill asked.

"Absolutely, my amazing friend," Maria replied.

A cheery waitress of ample girth and a red face came over and gave them menus. With customers lacking because of the snow, Maria and Bill got all her attention.

"What's good?" Bill asked, flashing the waitress a quick smile.

"Either the pot roast or the meatloaf. We just took them out of the oven," she answered, returning his smile.

"How about it, Maria? I have plenty of money to spend, so order what you want."

"You get one, and I'll get the other, and we can each try some of the other's." She thought, *What I really want is Bill's fraternity pin before I leave for Christmas.* Today would be the perfect time for him to promise it to her.

When the waitress came back with their tray, she looked so proud of the food she was serving. Bill put a big piece of pot roast on Maria's plate, and she gave him some of her meatloaf. Laughing together and eating like it was their last supper, Maria knew that they wouldn't have another night like this until after the holidays. As she sat there, smiling at Bill, Maria felt that premonition of dread again, this time a bit stronger and lasting a little longer.

What was the matter with her? She hadn't felt that since they'd first met. Maria shivered, slid out of her side of the booth, and pushed in next to Bill as close as she could.

Bill smiled and smoothed her hair with his fingers. "What's wrong?"

"Nothing. I just want to soak you up because I won't be seeing you much after this."

He frowned. "That's true." Pushing back his plate, he kissed her lightly. "We'd better go."

"Are you as full as I am?" she asked as they stood at the counter waiting to pay the bill.

Bill stuck his stomach out and laughed. "Does this give you your answer?"

Bill drove to Iowa State slowly and carefully because of all the snow piled everywhere. He looked over at her. "Thank you for being the best thing that has ever happened to me."

She was touched by his sweet comment and waited for him to follow it with a promise to give her his pin. If he really meant what he just said, he'd do it. Giving her his pin would tell the whole world that he valued her above everything else.

Bill stopped outside the dorm, and they looked at each other, neither one of them speaking, just listening to the music. Finally, Maria said, "I guess I won't see you for a few days. Please call me every evening and let me know you're still alive."

"I can't believe the pileup of meetings, talks, and tests all hitting us during these last couple of weeks. I'll call you every night, maybe twice if I need to, because I'll miss the sound of your voice," he promised.

"I'll miss your voice, too. Remember the Berkmar: that will be our battle cry to help us get through the next five weeks."

"Oh my gosh," Bill said, "when you put it that way, it seems like an eternity."

"Well, it's not like I won't see you at all before we leave; it will just be a little less . . . um . . . personal."

"You little dickens. I love how you try to put a bright spin on everything. You're right, I'm sure we can get together for at least a little while next weekend."

"I just wanted to say before I go, wasn't it fun this afternoon? I loved our lovemaking and my massage, you rascal." Maria kissed him quickly and went into the dorm.

The next week passed by in a blur of studying and exams. Part of Maria was glad that the tests were spread out over the two final weeks of school, which at least left some time for extra review, but mostly she wanted to just get them finished and get out of there.

Bill, as promised, called every night. Their conversations were brief, but it was always so good to hear his voice. When the weekend arrived, Bill said that he couldn't stand it any longer; he just had to see her. Maria agreed, and they decided that Sunday afternoon would be the best time.

Although it was still quite cold, there wasn't any fresh snow. The sun was shining and it was beautiful out. They decided to take a walk, rather than stay cooped up in the frat house. Plus, they would be less inclined to do anything that would get their juices flowing too much and not be able to do anything about it.

Bill walked slowly with his arm around her. "I can't believe that this is the last time I'll see you until I pick you up for the train on Friday. I don't know if I can take a whole month of not being with you; last week was hard enough.

"Let's not talk about that," Maria said. "We're together right now, and that's what counts."

They had reached the shelter of some trees, and Bill pulled Maria into his arms. He kissed her with such passion that Maria could swear they were melting the snow around them. She returned his kiss and without even being conscious of it, she put her hands inside his coat and caressed his chest.

Bill let out a little moan and backed away. "Whoa, don't start something we can't finish." He was breathing hard. "You know, that's a change. Normally you're stopping me."

Maria smiled and apologized. "Sorry, but I told you what you do to me. Plus, I've got to store up your loving to last me through the next few weeks."

Reluctantly, they broke apart and continued their walk. They didn't speak; they were just content to be with each other. After about an hour, they were getting cold, even with the sun on them.

Bill said, "Well, Nanook, you nose looks like an icicle, so I'd better get you back."

"Couldn't we go for one more drive first? I'll warm up in the car."

Bill looked at her sternly. "Okay, but no funny stuff." He grinned.

He ran to fetch the car, and Maria tried not to feel too upset that this would be the last time they would be alone together for a long while. When he pulled up, she hopped right in. Maria turned on the radio. The music always had a soothing effect. They drove around aimlessly, not going anywhere in particular, just being together. Maria sat close to Bill.

When they finally returned to the dorm, Maria said, "I'll see you Friday around one. Our train leaves at two, so that will give us enough time in case there is more snow and the roads are a mess."

Bill promised to call often. "I should get back from Waterloo late Thursday evening, but I'll still call you."

"Okay, my handsome prince. No goodbyes. I hate them, and I don't want to drag this out any longer, so I'm going in. I'll keep our last evening in mind every time I feel lonesome. It'll have to hold us until 1949." She purposely lingered, hoping he might say something about a pinning ceremony. There was still time.

Bill took her in his arms, kissed her gently with so much tenderness that Maria felt the tears rimming her eyes. She didn't want him to see her cry, because she felt so silly about it. There was no good reason to cry.

Maria kissed him back as "Blue Moon" played softly on the radio. "I love you, Bill Morgan." She touched his face one final time, opened her car door before he could react, and ran up the stairs.

He opened his door and yelled, "I love you, Maria. Remember the Berkmar."

She waved at him and blew him a kiss.

29. An Unsettling Week

Either write something worth reading
or do something worth writing.
—Benjamin Franklin

Maria was really crying when she walked into her room. It was empty. Susie hadn't come back from yet another date with Dick. It wasn't fair; Susie had been able to see Dick all week. Maria ran to the bathroom and washed her face. She still had that strange feeling about Bill, and she couldn't put her finger on it. What was the matter with her?

By the time Susie appeared, Maria was in her pajamas waiting for the dorm phone to be free so that she could call her mother. Susie looked wonderful, and Maria knew without asking that Susie and Dick's relationship was going well. It was obvious. Maria was glad for her.

"You beat me in," Susie said. "What happened, did you two fight?"

"No, we're just sad that we are going to be separated for a month, and we didn't want any long goodbyes."

"I know the feeling. I just meet someone whom I enjoy and who enjoys me, and, bingo, we'll be put on hold for at least three weeks," Susie said.

Maria picked up her tickets and backed out of their room. "I've got to call my mother and let her know my arrival time in Florida, so she and Winston can pick me up." She turned and ran for the open phone before another dorm mate could grab it. Maria dialed the operator to place a collect call. The phone rang twice at the other end, then her mom answered. The miracles of modern technology had connected her to Florida and parent. With her mom agreeing to the operator's collect call request, Maria was free to speak.

"Hi, Mom, it's your long-lost daughter finally checking in. Thanks for my check and your phone numbers. How are you, by the way?"

"I'm fine, Maria. Where are you calling from? You sound like you're next door."

"I'm calling from my dorm phone at Iowa State University. You remember, that's where I go to school."

"Of course, I sent my check to your post office box in Stevens Hall."

Maria had hoped to get a rise out of her mother with the slight dig about where she went to school, but her mother was playing the ignoring game. She was very good at sweeping anything she didn't want to face under the rug. Maria wondered if her mother had been drinking.

"The post office box also holds letters, and this phone is always in the dorm too, Mom." Maria couldn't resist giving her mom another little pick about not writing or calling. Her family seemed to forget each other. Maria felt that she always had to make the effort to keep in touch with them. They rarely wrote, except to send money, and never called unless it was an emergency. She heard other kids talking to their families all the time, but no such luck for her.

"How's school?" her mom asked, again ignoring her daughter's remarks.

"It's fine," Maria said curtly. Maria thought that her mother wasn't really interested, and she'd not bore her with the details. "I'll be coming to see you at the end of this week. I'm taking the train to Chicago on Friday afternoon and will catch the Miami Limited later that night. I should arrive in Miami on Saturday evening around ten."

"That's wonderful, Maria. Winston and I will be waiting for you at the station when you get here. I know you're going to like him. Now, I must ring off because we are going out to a dinner party in a few minutes. I hear Winston calling me. Bye, Maria, thanks for calling."

Maria thought, *That's so typical of my mother. She could have spent two more minutes on the phone, but she'd rather run away.* She had never let Maria into her life, and mostly only showed the surface. She kept her dark side hidden most of the time. Maria had wanted to tell her about Bill, but a snowball had a better chance in hell than her mother being interested in her life, she thought angrily.

When Maria came back to her room, Susie asked, "So how's Mom and her new husband?"

"I hope fine, forever," Maria said, grinding her teeth. "Mom was a mess during her divorce from my dad, and that was a scary thing for me to deal with."

"Perhaps when you see her during Christmas, she will have changed. I hope so, for your sake. Excuse me, but I should call my mom, too, and tell her my plans." Susie picked up her ticket and headed to the phone.

The phone was actually pretty quiet tonight, Maria noticed. Everyone must be hitting the books.

After fifteen minutes of looking at the same page in her history book, Maria cursed silently and shut the book with a resounding snap. She crawled into bed and passed out.

Monday morning stole in and was waiting for Maria when she opened her eyes. She rolled out of bed a few minutes before her alarm went off and went through the motions of getting ready for breakfast and classes with little enthusiasm. Susie was stumbling around, mumbling to herself.

"Wake up, Susie, before you walk into a door or your desk and hurt yourself. You've got to stay in shape for the week."

Sitting quietly together at breakfast, Susie and Maria put food in their mouths hardly tasting it. It was too early in the morning to care. After breakfast, they headed out to class, again braving the Iowa winter morning.

"See you for lunch, unless we freeze solid," Susie said. Off they went in opposite directions, picking up their pace to get back indoors as soon as possible.

At lunch, things were very quiet. All the gals were subdued because of the work facing them that week: more tests, lab reports, and term papers. Susie and Maria were filling their trays from the buffet line when they saw Maude's little band of followers come in. Maria watched them go to a table and sit down. They looked at her and Susie and immediately huddled together, talking and furtively looking in Maria's direction.

Susie said quietly, "That's trouble over there. I had the misfortune of being in a couple of classes with Maude. After her suicide attempt, I wouldn't bet on her being here next semester, especially if she operated in her other classes the way she did in the ones with me. I heard the English teacher talking to her about available tutors. My guess, she came here, getting in by the skin of her teeth, to be with Bill. She's not college material.

"You remember how she cornered you in the dorm and let you know, in no uncertain terms, that Bill was hers? That was an ugly interlude with 'ole Maudie,' wouldn't you say? She's still a real threat to your relationship with Bill."

In response to Susie's cautionary comments about Maude, Maria said, "If you have time tonight, I'll tell you what she did to Bill this fall. I don't want to talk about it in here."

After dinner, when they were in their cozy, warm room with the radiators pumping out the heat, Susie said, "So tell me about our friend Maude."

Maria explained that because Maude decided in high school that she and Bill were going to get married, her family had sweetened the pot and promised them two hundred acres of their farmland when they married. "The kicker is that they expected Bill's family to do the same. Bill's father and sons have been improving their farmland every year since they've owned it, and it is in far better shape than Maude's family's farm. The Jenkinses have been pressuring the Morgans to promise their land, clinging to the ridiculous belief that somehow Maude was going to get Bill to marry her. It didn't help that in the back of Bill's old man's mind, he wanted it, too." Maria stopped for a moment. "You know what my dad always says in situations like this; follow the money."

Susie was transfixed by Maria's story. "I knew it, I knew it, I knew it. I think things are really going to come to a head over Christmas. Maude knows that Bill is slipping away, and I'll bet she is planning something with her family. I agree with your dad, people will do bad things if they think they stand to gain a small fortune."

"More like a large fortune, with two hundred acres of prime Iowa land coming from Bill's family. I hope you are wrong on this one, Susie, and Maude just gives up. To change the subject to a more pleasant topic, how are you and Dick doing?"

Susie's face took on a dreamy look. "Were having a lot of fun together. I'm so glad that I met him."

"Well, you know how happy that makes me. I've watched you suffer all fall with Chuck and couldn't do a thing about it. I hated feeling so helpless."

"You were in my corner, and I knew it. That was important. I feel so relieved that Chuck is on his way to Iowa University to play football. Iowa State lost out with him. He is a good football player. Iowa University thinks so. and they are in a tougher league than Iowa State."

"Well, it's not your problem anymore. Now, my friend, I must study, although I realize that there is only one person in this room who has to do that. Next semester, when I have to take Physics 101, I hope you can tutor me. I'll do all of your flat-pattern sewing for you in exchange."

"How did you know I can't sew a straight line on the sewing machine? I think the course structure is antiquated, expecting college women to take sewing," Susie complained.

"I agree. I guess that is a holdover from an earlier time. Is the deal on?"

"You bet! I'll save your bacon and you can save mine."

Maria turned to her history book and opened it. A lot was riding on that grade. It would help her get a 3.0 for the semester and ensure her pledge status with Chi Omega.

The floor was unusually quiet: no continually ringing phones, girls laughing, or doors opening and closing. Everyone knew that this final week could make or break them as far as staying at Iowa State. The college gave their students one semester on probation. If their grade point average was below 2.0, they had the following semester to improve or it was goodbye. The phone did ring just once. Dick and Bill broke the silence of the dorm and called to talk to Susie and Maria, respectively.

When the phone rang, Maria was trying to commit to memory some important events in history that were sure to be essay questions on the final. She came out of her concentration pattern and breathed a sigh of relief. It would be good to have a break and talk to her sweetie. Maria ran down the hall to pick up the phone quickly so as not to disturb the whole floor. It was Dick calling for Susie. Maria couldn't resist asking Dick if he and Bill had tossed a coin to see who called first. He laughed and said that he had muscled Bill out of position and claimed the phone.

Susie came back to the room, grinning about something, and said that Bill was waiting on the phone.

Maria ran down the hall again, happy to have a proper break. "Hi, handsome, what's up?" She waited to hear his voice; it was so sexy, especially late at night.

"You cute little dickens, are you in your fuzzy caterpillar robe? I can just picture you. I miss you, and wish I could see you, but I'm up to my armpits in work over here. How about you?"

"Same. I think I have my final in history knocked, however, for tomorrow. What time do you go to Mason City tomorrow?"

"It's north of Ames, so to get there by six, I'm leaving early. I want some time for dinner first and to go over my notes for the meeting. I wish you could have dinner with me, but I will be far away by then."

As they were talking, Maria felt that both of them were preoccupied with all the work that was facing them this week and that they were a little removed from each other. She didn't like it but couldn't seem to change it. It was do or die that week with exams.

"I'll call you tomorrow night after I get back and talk more," Bill said. "I keep thinking about us being separated for three weeks, and I shouldn't do that."

Maria said, "Please call me when I get to Florida. Give me your folk's phone number now. I have a slip of paper and pencil with me; I'm finally prepared." Maria wrote down the number carefully and repeated it back to him. Then she tucked it away in her pocket, feeling better that she would be able to easily reach him. "Think of this, Bill. When we see each other again, we will have been going together almost since the beginning of school. We can really begin to make some long-range plans." She wanted assurance that Bill was maintaining his commitment, especially since he hadn't pinned her.

"That's the only thing that keeps me going. I think about our times together, and I can hardly stand not being with you. Maria, I love you with all of my heart, and I want to take care of you forever."

"Forever is a long time. Be sure you mean it." She could feel her emotions starting to race when he said the things like that in his soft, sexy voice. But then she thought, *Talk is cheap.* She would have liked to have his pin before they went their separate ways. He had never once brought that up.

"I'm sorry I can't take you to the clinic on Thursday. I want to be there for you, but I can't. Thank Susie for me."

Again, he said all the right things, but somehow he wasn't backing them up. She wanted him to be with her at the clinic. It was important to her.

"Maria, are you all right? What's the matter?"

She lowered her voice. "I love you, but I guess I feel sort of vulnerable about this clinic thing."

"I know, and I would change it if I could. I'm trying to get a toehold into this world so I can have a way of taking care of you in the future. I love you, Maria. That's all I can offer you right now."

"You have enchanted me again. Good night, my love." When she hung up the phone, she stood there for a minute wondering why she had said that. She realized that she was guilty of not saying what she really felt. That last statement was ridiculous. She didn't feel enchanted; she felt let down. Was she afraid that if she really spoke her mind, he'd leave?

She slowly walked back to the room. Susie looked up at her and said that they were a pair of idiots, looking and acting so goofy after talking to their men.

"You are so right, Susie. I'm beginning to feel a bit like an idiot around Bill. There's a part of me that's so confused. Bill talks a good game, saying he'll take care of me always, but he hasn't offered me his pin—such a simple thing to show his commitment. He seems perfectly content to go on the way we are, especially now that we're having a sexual relationship. Maybe that was a mistake, but I don't think I could have kept him without it."

"I think you should take it easy about wanting a pin. If you and he don't work out, it gets awfully sticky running into a guy on campus after you have given his pin back to him."

Maria looked at Susie and just shook her head. She was done talking for the night. After setting her alarm, she went to bed. She was tired; maybe that was why she felt so needy and childish.

It was gray and overcast the rest of the week, and there was a hint of snow in the air. With the winter sun hidden, getting started every day was harder than ever, but they braved the weather and made their way to classes all week.

Bill called faithfully every night after his big days and evenings of traveling to the Grange meetings and everything else. He had so much stamina. Maria was amazed by his strength. He was doing something that was challenging, making him money, taking him to new places, and giving him a sense of freedom. Perhaps that was why he had so much energy.

On Thursday afternoon, Susie met Maria at the Union in plenty of time to walk to the clinic for her appointment. Maria didn't know which of the two doctors she would get, but she was hoping it would be the woman. She would feel better having a woman looking at and working on her reproductive parts. As luck would have it, Maria did get the female Dr. Summers and was relieved.

The doctor was nice and so expert at fitting Maria that Maria was hardly bothered by the procedure at all. Dr. Summers gave her a prescription for another diaphragm, plus the one she had used to fit Maria. Maria tucked the precious little piece of paper away in her wallet, along with Bill's phone number, and thanked the doctor.

Susie was sitting in the waiting room and looked pleased to see Maria's smiling face. Maria gave her the thumbs-up signal. Susie smiled, got up, and hooked her arm in her roommate's arm. As they left the clinic, Maria was very relieved.

"I'll buy at the Union," Maria said, trying to think of something nice to do for Susie.

"I accept. In this kind of weather, I'm going to have hot chocolate or coffee."

"What freedom this thing gives me. Thanks, Susie, my sexual mentor." They shifted into high speed to get out of the cold as quickly as possible, and made it to the Union in record time.

"We have a lot to celebrate, Maria. Your sexual freedom, the end of our exams, my new boyfriend, your old boyfriends, seeing our families and friends for Christmas, and the fact we have survived the first semester so well out here in the boonies."

After Maria bought a couple of hot chocolates, they found a table and sat down with great satisfaction. Susie said, "I almost forgot to tell you that Dick wants to take me to the train station tomorrow. If something happens and Bill can't get back from Waterloo in time, you can ride with us. In fact, Dick said that Bill asked him, specifically, to be sure to include you.

"Your friend is very high on my list now, I want you to know. He's been rising all fall. I hadn't known that he was the vice president of Farm House. Bill's very quiet about his accomplishments. Dick really respects him and so does everyone else in the house," Susie proclaimed.

"We'd better get back to the dorm soon for dinner, Susie." Maria was feeling agitated by the picture Bill presented to everyone. Why did what Susie said bother her? Susie probably thought she was making her feel good, complimenting her boyfriend. As they walked out, Maria looked at Susie and said that she was happy that Bill was so well liked and thanked Susie for sharing her feelings about Bill. But she was beginning to ask herself, *How much of what Bill says is real and how much is phony?* That subject was too sensitive to talk to Susie about, however.

After dinner, Maria started packing. That way she could see what she needed to wash and what was ready to go. She was jubilant at being finished with her tests; she just had to hand in her English term paper tomorrow morning. She felt that the exams had gone well and knowing that put her in a party mood. "I wish there was a way to celebrate the end of term."

Susie said, "Dick is picking me up, and we might go to Ames. We could get a six pack of beer at the state liquor store. Shall I bring you one?"

"Thanks, but no thanks. It's too cold to drink a chilled beer. It would be nice if you two could be in front of the fire when you down one. Thinking about drinking them in the car gives me the shivers."

"That would be great, but it wouldn't be good idea to break the university's rules against drinking in fraternities and sororities."

Maria said, "Don't worry about me. Relax and have fun tonight, whatever you do. I'm going to try to stay up late tonight so that I can talk to Bill. I'll see you later." After Susie left, Maria gathered up her dirty clothes, stuffed them into an old pillowcase, and went to the basement to use the washers provided by the dorm.

Gad, she thought, *my laundry has piled up over the last couple of weeks.* Everything had taken a backseat to her love life and finishing up the semester. After running back and forth to the basement, washing and drying several loads of clothes, Maria was glad to be done and back in her room for the remainder of the night. Her packing was finished and she was comfy in her pajamas and fuzzy robe.

It felt funny not to have to do anything. The room seemed so quiet. What was missing? *Music,* Maria thought. She liked music so much, why didn't she have a radio? What had she been thinking about? She would ask her mother for a radio. Maria wondered if Winston was well enough off to be able to afford a radio for her. She decided to wait and see when she got to her mother's home before asking.

Maria was brought back to reality when she heard the Campanile striking the witching hour: nine o'clock, curfew time. Susie would be coming back soon. What a turnaround. Maria used to be the one coming in all dewy eyed; tonight it would be Susie. Sure enough, Maria heard her talking in the corridor.

Susie stuck her head in the door. "I'm slightly tipsy. Dick and I had a couple of beers, and one should have been my limit. You're still up. You must have gotten your second wind. Are you all packed?" Susie fell onto her bed. "I think I love Dick." She looked at Maria and raised her eyebrows, waiting for Maria to comment.

"He's a great guy, Susie. I think you two are made for each other. He's as smart as you—well almost—is handsome as the devil, and sounds like he has a nice family background. What's not to love?"

"I knew you'd see it my way." Susie smile widely.

"Are you going to pack, or are you too besotted by Dick and beer to do anything more than lie on your bed?"

"I'm going, I'm going," Susie said, moving slowly. She gathered her clothes and ambled out the door with an armload.

An hour or so later, Maria heard the phone ringing. She thought it might be Bill checking in before he left Waterloo. She ran to answer it, and he asked for her. "It's me," she said. Maria loved listening to him talk. He had such a rich voice, and he sounded so happy tonight.

"I'm done for two weeks. No more Grange meetings until after the first of the year. The talk finished earlier than I'd expected, so I'm back already. I wish I could have seen you tonight. I'll pick you up whenever you want tomorrow morning. Let's go out for breakfast and talk. I have a couple of things to tell you, and I want to catch up on your life this past week."

"I need to go to my English professor's office around ten or so. He said there would be no class tomorrow, just the term papers due in his office. Then we can go out for breakfast and be together until my train comes. Dick is taking Susie to the train station, so she is all set. Bill, honey, thanks for helping link them up."

"Dick's walking around in a trance most of the time now. They seem good for each other."

"Are you all packed? I spent the evening figuring out what to take and packing it so I wouldn't have to do it tomorrow," Maria bragged.

"I'm glad somebody's organized. I just got in before I called you. I'm going to throw everything in the trunk of my car and see if Mom will wash my stuff when I get home. I'd much rather talk to you than do anything else."

"I'll bet I know one thing you'd rather do with me than talk."

He laughed. "You caught me with my guard down, you little dickens. I love you so much. Sweet dreams of me making love to you. Good night; see you tomorrow."

"You sleep well, too, and I will follow your suggestion." Maria walked back to her room reassessing her feelings toward Bill. He always excited her when they talked. His enthusiasm was catching. When they were apart, she could be rational and cautious about her feelings for him, but when he called or took her in his arms,

416

she would change and act so differently. All she wanted to do was to be loved when they were together. It was like she was two different people. As she lay down to think about it, Susie came back with her last load and started packing. Maria said, "I'm going to sleep, so be quiet please, Susie." For once, she was in bed before her roommate. It was a nice feeling.

It was morning, and Maria was lying in bed, stretching and yawning. She realized that she had slept great. No tests or lab reports were due today, just her English paper, and it was all done. She smiled with delight. Today would be a long day but an exciting one. She looked at Minnie Mouse, who said it was nine o'clock. Neither of them set an alarm because they were done with classes for the semester; good or bad, it was over. How wonderful and luxurious to sleep that late on a weekday. Maria put her arms over her head and stretched for the last time in that bed for three weeks and got up.

After a leisurely shower, Maria dressed slowly, taking particular care with her hair and a tiny bit of makeup. When she returned to the room, she saw that Susie was still inert under the covers. Maria realized that she had forgotten to tell Susie that she was going to meet Bill and have breakfast with him. Maria was composing a note to Susie when she heard a little groan from under the blanket. Susie was coming to.

"Maria, are you still here?" Susie's voice came from somewhere in the bed.

"Yes, I was just writing you a note, but now I can tell you. I'm meeting Bill in a few minutes for breakfast. I'll see you later at the train station, okay?"

Susie sat up, her red hair sticking out in every direction. She smiled. "That's fine, I'm going to meet Dick, too. What time is it?"

"It's quarter to ten."

Susie bolted upright, then jumped out of bed. "I'm meeting Dick in fifteen minutes. Have fun. I'll see you later," she yelled over her shoulder, running with her towel to the shower.

From the window, Maria saw Bill pulling up in front, and her pulse started to race just looking at him. He was so gorgeous. She would never say anything like that to him, but she could think it; she was sure other women thought the same thing. Maria picked up her big suitcase, slung her duffle bag over her shoulder, grabbed her purse, and waved goodbye to her room.

He was standing in the front room looking at her when she struggled into the room with her stuff. Quick as a flash, he took her heavy suitcase, leaned over, and gave her a kiss, right there in the room. No one was around, which was good. There was a rule that all personal activities of any kind were to take place outside the dorm.

Bill said, "Hi, sweetheart," in his deep, sexy voice. "I've missed you so much."

No wonder she forgot about mundane things like radios when she was around him. Maria's voice caught in her throat, even though she struggled to sound perky. "Handsome, it's so good to see you. I feel like we haven't seen each other for a month, instead of a few days."

Bill took her duffle off her shoulder and slung it over his own. He had the suitcase in the same hand, which left his other hand free to hold hers. They walked down the stairs. He opened her door, put her suitcase and duffle in the back seat instead of the trunk, because, he said, he didn't want her to see the mess he had back there.

Maria purposely hadn't put on any lipstick so it wouldn't get all over him. He looked at her in the seat beside him, leaned over with his eyes closed, and began to kiss her, gently at first but then with such passion that Maria had to give him a little push. "No funny stuff," she scolded. "We've got to breathe, relax, and get going."

Bill stopped. "I'm sorry. I let my feelings get away from me." He gave her a quick one-armed squeeze, started the car, and drove her to her English professor's office.

After she had successfully delivered her term paper, got a check by her name, and a smile from the assistant, she ran back to the car. "Honey, where are we going to go for breakfast, or don't you know?"

Bill looked at her with those big blue eyes sparkling. "Trust me."

"That may get me into trouble, especially if you offer me candy, too."

Maria cuddled up next to him as he pulled out onto the highway heading toward Des Moines. She was happy to be tucked in close to him.

Bill said, "My folks took me to this restaurant many times when I was growing up, usually when we were on our way somewhere, and Mom didn't want to make breakfast before we left. It was a big treat to go out for breakfast." In Des Moines, he wound his way around several streets until he pulled up in front of a big and very busy restaurant. It looked very inviting and had lots of cars parked outside.

As Maria was gathering her purse and zipping up her coat, Bill had run around to open her door. "You are so quick, my sweet," Maria said.

He reached in and took her hands in his. "Come with me, little girl, you're going to like this place."

When they walked in, a hostess came over to seat them. Bill said, "Please seat us in the back in a booth." He gave her a great big smile.

She said, "Yes, sir, follow me."

"This is a really nice place for breakfast; it's clean, light, and pretty. You are very smooth about where you take me," Maria said.

"Nothing but the best for you." After they had ordered, he looked at her with a serious expression. "I don't know how to start this conversation."

"Take a chance; I'll help you." Maria held his hands from across the table.

"My folks called me a couple of days ago and said that Maude and her folks have been making up all kinds of new things about me—and about you, too."

"Me? What could she say about me?"

"She said that her friends have seen you leaving and coming back with an older man who has a car. She said that it was obvious that he was another man that you were seeing on the side. He came at odd times, and you returned late at night, just before curfew."

Maria felt a shock go up her arms and legs, and her hands got cold all of a sudden. She thought, *I've got to make this good.* She gulped. "I guess they must have seen Ed picking me up for Thanksgiving vacation and returning me. He had a car full of gals. I got in the back with two other friends of his. Coming back, he dropped them all off first. I was the last to get out. There was no way Maude's friends could have seen who was in the car because it was dusk."

Bill looked so relieved at her story that he said, "I'm so sorry to even bring this up on our last day together, but I needed to hear what you thought of the accusations. She's grabbing at straws. I can't figure out what she thinks she will gain from these attacks. It just drives me further away, if that is possible. I used to feel sort of sorry for Maude because I guess I felt guilty about leaving her, but now I'm really losing any positive feelings toward her."

Maria thought about her afternoon trip to Ames with Ed. Evidently, Maude's friends weren't around when Ed picked her up. What a relief. By the time their food came, Maria's appetite was returning. The delicious aroma of the coffee and bacon drove the concern out of her. She smiled at Bill and picked up her fork. "Dig in, it looks delicious."

They ordered a second cup of coffee after breakfast to finish off their meal. Maria reached across the table and touched his hands. "Oh, Bill, I wanted to tell you about how well my appointment went with the woman doctor at the clinic. She was so quick and efficient, and gave me a prescription I can fill anywhere for up to six times. If a diaphragm lasts for two or three years, think how long I have with six refills! Isn't that great? All that worry I had was so ridiculous." Maria had wanted to make Bill laugh, which he did. "When we get back from vacation, I'll show you what it looks like. It's packed away now. I can't wait to shock my mother and sister with it. I'm going to tell them that I use it all the time."

"You are so feisty, even though you are a little liar, but I just love that about you. You remind me of our Banty hens. They are small, but great little mothers and fighters. They fight any wild animals that break into their roost. They don't just stand there and let the animals kill them; they make such a racket, we hear them and usually can get out there and save them from a fox or skunk.

"I have some good news to tell you, too. Mr. Addison called. He wants me to stop by on my way home today and set up a schedule with him regarding working over Christmas vacation. He wants me to get acquainted with the newspaper and make a start on my column. The best part is, now I don't have to ask Mr. Gunderson for a job in our little town. I have you to thank for this whole new opportunity. You are my lucky star." Bill sat back with a big smile on his face and waited for her reaction to this wonderful news.

"I will shine my star-like qualities upon you anytime. We're a team, aren't we? Call and tell me everything about your meeting and what you are doing at the paper. Promise? I'm so proud of you and happy for you."

"Maria, I just don't know how I'm going to stand being away from you for three weeks."

"We'll make it; we're made of sturdy stuff. We'll appreciate each other more, if that's possible." She didn't want to mention the strange premonitions she'd been having because she really didn't trust them, and she didn't want to worry Bill.

"Mr. Addison asked about you and said that you were part of the bargain. His ultimatum to me was that if I can't keep you happy, he'd have to reconsider my contract." Bill laughed.

"I like Mr. Addison. He's my kind of guy."

"Isn't he a little old for you?"

"I will have to find out how much money he makes."

"I'm not worried." Bill chuckled, reached over, and kissed her.

Maria looked at her Minnie Mouse watch. "We'd better think about getting going. It's twelve noon. Can you believe that?"

Bill took her hand and looked at the watch. "This is cute. Where did you get it? I haven't seen it before."

Gad, another lie, she thought. "Do you like it?" Lying as smoothly as she could, she said, "I got it at Thanksgiving at the same time I bought my coat."

"It's very nice and fits you to a tee, my little Minnie Mouse. Come on Minnie Mouse, we had better get the check and get on our way. As much as I don't want to let you go, I know you will enjoy seeing your mom and her husband. I'm jealous about the weather you will be having, but I hope you have a really nice time. It's important for you to reconnect with your mom. Someday, we'll go down there together."

"Promise? I will hold you to that." Maria slid out of the booth.

Bill helped her with her Nanook coat, paid the bill, and away they went to Boone and her train. When they pulled into the station parking lot, students were standing around, their coats buttoned up against the cold. Boxes, bags, and suitcases were everywhere.

Maria felt so fortunate to be sitting in a warm car with her darling man. She looked around for Susie and Dick, but didn't see them. She hoped they wouldn't be late. She was trying to put up a brave front, so Bill wouldn't feel any worse than he did. "So my darling friend, I guess this is goodbye for a little while. I have your number, and you have mine, so we are all set to keep in touch."

"Maria, just remember that you are the most important person in my life, and I love you. I'll be counting the days until we see each other in the new year."

As he was talking, Maria could hear the train coming in the distance. she turned to him and he took her in his arms. He put his face in her hair and stayed like that for a minute or two. Then he took a deep breath, found her lips, and kissed her so gently it almost made her cry. Maria kissed him back with more intensity. That released him, and he kissed her so long and hard, she finally had to stop him. They were still hugging as the train pulled into the station.

Bill said in a quiet voice, "I'll help you onto the train and get you settled." Out he popped, opened her door, and took her luggage. They walked to the train hand in hand.

Maria had her ticket out for the conductor, who smiled and said, "I'll collect it when we're underway."

Bill climbed aboard first, took her bags, and waited for her to come up the steps. He quickly found her reserved seat and put her suitcase in the overhead bin. "You're all set now."

Maria was getting that strange premonition again. She felt panicky about it. It was as if she weren't going to see him again or something equally bad. She grabbed him and gave him a kiss, trying to dispel the feeling.

He put his mouth close to her ear, not quite understanding her frantic kiss. "I love you, my darling."

Maria said, "I love you, too, so much." She hated to see him go. He might be gone forever.

Bill walked to the door, turned and nodded to her, and hopped off the train. As she watched him, Maria saw Susie running to the train with Dick right behind her, carrying her bag. When they leaped on the train, she waved at them. Susie grabbed her bag, gave Dick a little kiss, and he jumped off as the train started to move.

"That was close," Susie said and grinned.

Maria helped her get her bag into the overhead bin and watched as they pulled out of the train station. Maria saw Bill waving, standing next to Dick, who was waving, too. They looked so cute together. Maria shivered when they disappeared from view. She mouthed a silent prayer to take care of him until she returned. At least the men were together and good friends. That was a blessing.

About the Author

ELLA MURPHY was born and raised in Chicago, Illinois. Her Midwestern roots are reflected in the settings of her books.

After Murphy and her husband had raised a son and daughter, Murphy returned to school, earning a BS degree from Northeastern and two MS degrees in education, school psychology, and special education from Fitchburg State in Massachusetts. She then taught special education in Massachusetts.

Now retired, she resides near her daughter and grandchildren in Virginia, where she enjoys gardening, writing, church, social activities, and sports such as tennis and golf. Her lifetime of experiences—marriage, children, traveling, and teaching—serves as inspiration for her work.

Follow the saga of Maria in the next book in the series:

A Matter of Choice

Ella Rea Murphy

Available Fall 2012

Maria's Awakening is available from amazon.com and Barnes & Noble. A direct link to these sites is available on the author's website:

www.ellareamurphy.com

Or you may use the form below to order books directly from the author.

Order *Maria's Awakening*

Please send _____ copies of *Maria's Awakening* at $17.00 each, plus $5.00 per book for shipping, to:

Name_____

Address_____

City, State, and Zip_____

Make checks payable to Ella Murphy and mail your order to:

Ella Murphy
PO Box 581
Earlysvllle, VA 22936-9998